PRAISE FOR

OUR AMERICAN FRIEND

"Pitoniak braids timelines to create a portrait of a woman torn between two countries, two belief systems, two selves. . . . Elegant and well-paced . . . Like *Emily in Paris* meets *Scandal*—fantastic fun."

—*The New York Times* (editor's choice)

"A gripping tale of the Cold War and its legacy."

—*People*

"Wholly original . . . [The book] follows journalist Sofie Morse as she begins work on what she's told is the First Lady's authorized biography but, like the dolls from Mother Russia herself, the assignment reveals itself to be nothing like what it seemed."

—*Entertainment Weekly*

"Riveting . . . *Our American Friend* interweaves the increasingly suspenseful story of Lara's youth with the present-day partnership between Lara and Sofie. The back-and-forth gives the novel a propulsive energy, especially as the truth behind Lara's clandestine activities in Paris—and their role in her present political position—come to light."

—*The Christian Science Monitor*

"A smart, timely take on American politics, Soviet spy craft, and the lengths we'll go to for love and revenge."

—*Town & Country*

"Spectacular—a global thriller with pace, tension, and ever-higher stakes, born of an intimate and unlikely friendship between two very different women . . . the story succeeds on every level."

—Lee Child, #1 *New York Times* bestselling author

"Though their settings have varied, Anna Pitoniak's three novels have all been about peering behind the curtain at those who hold power, and about the moral complexity privilege can engender. . . . Pitoniak is a fluid writer who knows her strengths."

—*The Globe and Mail*

"A Cold War spy thriller and a fictional tale of a mysterious First Lady is the unusual but compelling combo at the heart of this decades-spanning story. . . . A dangerous cat-and-mouse game."

—*E! News*

"An intriguing Russian nesting doll of modern Washington politics, Cold War spy games, and above all women with secrets . . . Just what is the president's wife hiding? Anna Pitoniak's masterful puzzle of espionage, love, and betrayal keeps us flipping the pages to find out!"

—Kate Quinn, *New York Times* bestselling author of *The Alice Network*

"Perhaps [Pitoniak's] best yet . . . a propelling Cold War spy thriller crossed with the fictional biography of First Lady Lara Caine . . . *Our American Friend* is a fast-paced page-turning thriller that will have readers invested from the very first page."

—*Daily Hive*

"An exhilarating ride through recent Cold War highlights, framed cleverly with the story of a disenchanted journalist hired to ghost write the First Lady's memoir; in this case, the First Lady comes from the Soviet orbit, is a former model, and has shadowy ties to the KGB. So why is she revealing her secrets now? That's the question that will keep you reading."

—*Crime Reads*

"Fast-paced . . . Smart, twisty . . . With sharp observations on everything from DC insider politics to the mundane details of family life, *Our American Friend* is both an engaging feminist thriller and a meditation on the ways history often surprises even the people who make it."

—*Shelf Awareness*

"A journalist gets sucked into the orbit of an enigmatic first lady—and her life will never be the same. . . . This lively political thriller mulls love, loyalty, and the rewards of playing the long game."

—*Kirkus Reviews*

"Viewers who followed the TV series *The Americans* will recognize and enjoy its thrilling hallmarks in this exciting novel about the erstwhile first couple."

—*Library Journal*

"An enthralling journey into the life of one of the most powerful women in the world . . . Exploring interpersonal loyalties and the difference between cowardice and patience, the well-researched and twist-filled *Our American Friend* is a natural next-read for fans of Curtis Sittenfeld, A. Natasha Joukovsky, and Stacey Swann."

—*Booklist* (starred review)

"Packed with Cold War spy intrigue, complex women characters, and rich historical details. I read this novel in one sitting, pouring over the pages, wanting to know what secrets the unforgettable character of First Lady Lara Caine held. *Our American Friend* does what good fiction does best—it reaches across time to speak to the present moment."

—Lara Prescott, *New York Times* bestselling author of *The Secrets We Kept*

"An irresistible political thriller with wit and heart, *Our American Friend* is a fascinating take on a mysterious fictional First Lady and a moving, rueful exploration of love, loyalty, and the presence of the past."

—Amy Bloom, *New York Times* bestselling author of *White Houses*

"I was immediately hooked on this novel about Sofie, a burned-out political reporter, who develops a friendship with the mysterious and elegant First Lady. Pitoniak blends a sharp look at present-day Washington, DC, with an exploration of power, love, and politics, and the result is this smart, addictive page-turner. *Our American Friend* is a delicious political thriller and I couldn't put it down."

—Jennifer Close, bestselling author of *Girls in White Dresses*

"This should be catnip to political thriller fans—a smart, witty take on a fictional, foreign-born First Lady with a secret tied to Cold War espionage who tests the boundaries of friendship with her would-be biographer. This fast-paced novel about love, loyalty, and the secrets we should or should not keep will keep you gobbling up each page."

—Melanie Benjamin, *New York Times* bestselling author of *The Aviator's Wife* and *The Children's Blizzard*

"A smart political thriller, sharply observed and well-written."

—Alan Furst, *New York Times* bestselling author of *A Hero of France*, *Midnight in Europe*, and *Mission to Paris*

OUR AMERICAN FRIEND

A NOVEL

Anna Pitoniak

SIMON & SCHUSTER PAPERBACKS
New York London Toronto Sydney New Delhi

Simon & Schuster Paperbacks
An Imprint of Simon & Schuster, Inc.
1230 Avenue of the Americas
New York, NY 10020

This book is a work of fiction. Any references to historical events, real people, or real places are used fictitiously. Other names, characters, places, and events are products of the author's imagination, and any resemblance to actual events or places or persons, living or dead, is entirely coincidental.

First Simon & Schuster trade paperback edition February 2023

Interior design by Carly Loman

Manufactured in the United States of America

10 9 8 7 6 5 4 3 2 1

Library of Congress Cataloging-in-Publication Data has been applied for.

ISBN 978-1-9821-5880-4
ISBN 978-1-9821-5896-5 (pbk)
ISBN 978-1-9821-5881-1 (ebook)

For Angela,
who changed my life

The old disease, thought Rubashov. Revolutionaries should not think through other people's minds.

Or, perhaps they should? Or even ought to?

How can one change the world if one identifies oneself with everybody?

How else can one change it?

—**Arthur Koestler, *Darkness at Noon***

CHAPTER ONE

The Mediterranean was a deep winter blue, cold and dimpled like hammered steel, on the morning that I began wondering if I had made the worst mistake of my life.

The night before, I'd been walking home through our quiet corner of the city, no more or less nervous than usual. Light flickered from the dying bulb in the streetlight. Cars were parked tight up against the white stucco buildings. We lived on a narrow street where no one knew our name, in a home that was meant to remain anonymous. But in the doorway—our doorway—there was a strange figure, standing and waiting.

A young woman, blond hair peeking from beneath her knit hat, wearing a plush parka, bent over her phone, her face illuminated in an eerie glow. Hearing my footsteps, she suddenly looked up. "You're Sofie, aren't you?" she said. "Sofie Morse?"

She held out a business card and I glanced down. I recognized her name. My heart began thudding against my rib cage. With a patient smile, she explained how much effort it had taken for her to track me down, given that I hadn't returned any of her emails or phone calls, and she didn't mean to startle me but she really *did* have some important questions to ask.

I took the card from her and looked away, mumbling, "Right,

right, thanks. Uh, sorry, got to get these groceries inside." I could sense her continuing to stare at me. She stood in front of the door, blocking the way. "Sorry," I repeated. "Do you mind?"

As she stepped aside, she placed her hand on my arm and said: "So you'll call me?"

Though I had no intention of seeing this woman again, I needed to get away from her. I nodded, and said I'd call her, because every second we stood here was another second in which she might see through me.

Upstairs, I unlocked our apartment door with shaking hands. I dropped the grocery bags to the floor, forgetting the carton of eggs, which now seeped from their cracked shells. I took deep breaths, trying not to panic. *Stop freaking out*, I told myself. *You're okay.*

Except that a stranger had tracked me down, flown across the Atlantic, and waited on my doorstep for who-knew-how-long in the cold January night, because that's how badly she wanted to know the truth; the truth, which, if revealed, could cause the entire operation to collapse. It wasn't just my safety, or Ben's safety. I'd been reminded, time and again, that the stakes were much bigger than that. No, I wasn't okay. I was definitely *not* okay.

"It's unlikely that you'll need it," the man had said, last year, back in New York. He had the seen-it-all sangfroid of a person familiar with the furthest edges of life. "But if you're in real trouble, and you need to signal for a meeting, here's what you do."

I hurried into the bedroom and took the red towel from the shelf in the closet. I grabbed a few stray items from the laundry hamper—a T-shirt, a sweatshirt—and soaked everything in the kitchen sink. The towel was brand-new, never washed before. The red dye bled and stained the water. The wet bundle left a trail along the floor as I carried it to our small balcony, where we kept a collapsible laundry rack. On the outermost edge, clearly visible to anyone passing, the red towel dripped and dripped.

When Ben got home an hour later, his eyes were wide. He had seen the towel. Silently, he nodded toward the balcony. *Why the towel? What happened?*

I slid the business card across the counter. His eyebrows arched in recognition. The woman was a journalist from a TV network back in New York. She told me she would love the chance to talk about my relationship with Lara Caine, the First Lady of the United States. *Would love*, that's how she phrased it. *Would sell a kidney for* is a better way to put it.

That night I lay wide awake, unable to sleep. The fear had ebbed and flowed since we arrived in Croatia four months before, but this was the worst yet. Ben breathed steadily in the darkness. *Okay*, I thought, engaging in my usual practice. *Ask yourself this*. What was I scared of? Was I scared of her? I was familiar with the hunger she felt, the relentless drive to uncover the truth. Wasn't she just a journalist, not so different from me? Anyway, it wasn't like she was interested in *me* specifically. She was only doing her job. As the gray light of dawn softened the edges of the bedroom curtains, I convinced myself that I had overreacted.

"What are you doing?" Ben said drowsily, as I climbed out of bed.

"Nothing," I said. "Go back to sleep."

No harm, I thought, bringing the laundry back inside. It had been an unusually cold night, and the towel had frozen stiff. Maybe no one had seen it and I would be spared from embarrassment. I ran a hot shower. I got dressed, brushed my teeth, and put away last night's dishes. *You're fine, Sofie*. I would live my life like it was any ordinary day, because that's what I wanted it to be.

And I began every day with a long walk through town and along the corniche, where the towering procession of palm trees shivered in the wind. Or, more accurately, shivered in the bora: the name of the winter wind that swept along the undulating Adriatic coastline. Ben had defined the word *bora* for me. He read constantly, to keep his mind busy. He'd recently read Ernest Shackleton's memoir, which inspired his suggestion that we each establish our own daily routines to maintain our sanity during this strange exile.

We'd arrived in Split the previous September. I thought we'd be in Croatia for a month, two months tops. We'd left behind our life in New York in a hurry, figuring we'd be back soon enough. Then two months turned into three, and then it was Christmas, and then it was a new year, and still there was no end in sight. Whenever I expressed guilt about the mess I'd gotten us into, Ben shook his head.

"Stop," he'd say. "We did this together, Sofe."

Except that my decisions—mine, not his—had brought us to this point. And no matter how many times Ben told me that it was okay, I couldn't quite bring myself to believe him.

That morning, walking along the corniche, as the cold wind whipped my hair into a frenzy, I scanned the faces of everyone I passed. I didn't know exactly what I was looking for—a returned gaze? surreptitious sign language?—but whatever it was, it didn't materialize.

"We'll have people on the ground," the man had said to us, before we left. "They'll be watching, just in case."

I remembered nodding. I remembered feeling relieved by his reassurances. I remembered thinking: *This man is a stranger, and yet we're trusting him with our lives.*

The bell on the café door jangled, and the waiters waved at me as I headed to my regular table. I liked this place. The café was too haphazard to be elegant, but it was cozy and generously heated in the wintertime. The room was tall and narrow, like a shoebox stood on its end. The tables were covered in red damask, with squares of white paper to shield the fabric, and the warm light of the sconces were reflected in the wall-hung mirrors.

They made a decent cappuccino, and the pastries were passable, but mostly I liked this café because the waitstaff remembered me, and that kindness made a tiny dent in our anonymity. The waiters—teenagers for the most part—were as bored and affable as high school students sitting through last period. The café was cramped, so they were constantly colliding with one another, spilling coffee and yelping in indignation, but they also never had quite enough work to keep themselves busy, and they bickered to pass the time.

My waiter that day, Mirko, was my favorite. He was gangly and gregarious, and saving money toward the goal of achieving his greatest desire, which was to travel to America—specifically to Chicago.

(He was obsessed with Michael Jordan and could recite the entire roster of the 1996 Bulls.) That morning, as he placed my cappuccino and cornet pastry on the table—I hadn't even needed to order it—Mirko said, "There is a big story about your president."

"Oh?" I said. Even though a lot of Americans had long since wearied of the conversation, the foreigners I'd met remained intensely curious about President Caine.

"Yes," Mirko said, standing up straight, looking slightly indignant. "It is very bad news. He says he is planning to visit Serbia next month for an important meeting."

"Why is that bad news?" I asked.

"Bad for Croatia!" he exclaimed. "We are much more beautiful than Serbia. Why would he go there instead of here? He is choosing our greatest rival instead of choosing us, even though we are so much better. It is very bad." Mirko's eyes were wide. "Why do you think he did this, Sofie?"

"Who knows?" I said. "No one understands him, Mirko."

After Mirko left, I scrolled through the news on my phone, just like every morning. I glanced up whenever the bell on the door jangled—a pair of tourists chattering in German; a mother with a baby swaddled against her chest—but none of the new arrivals met my eye. There was a story that day about Caine's recent phone call with Russian president Nikolai Gruzdev. The White House released little detail about the conversation, except to emphasize that Gruzdev was fully supportive of Caine's recent decision to withdraw American troops from Mozambique.

"Great conversation with President Gruzdev, or as I call him, NICKY!" Caine tweeted. "We are making progress!"

I kept scrolling, but stopped abruptly when I saw a story about the construction of Nord Stream 2. Nord Stream 2 was Russia's new natural gas pipeline, which would begin at the country's western edge, snake through the Baltic Sea, and end in Germany. Officially, America was opposed to the pipeline for geopolitical reasons. Unofficially, President Gruzdev knew that his American friend Henry Caine wouldn't do anything about it. The article described how worried the state department and foreign policy wonks in Washington were about the rapid progress of the pipeline. But no amount of saber rattling could change reality, which was that Caine wasn't going to stand in Nicky's way.

For a long time now, the world had suspected there was an understanding between the American president and the Russian president. Almost two years earlier, at the conclusion of a lengthy investigation, the Special Counsel released his report, which contained certain clear facts. Yes, the Russians used disinformation and propaganda to help Caine win his first election. Yes, Caine treated Gruzdev with special favoritism once elected. Yes, there was an increasingly worrisome pattern of their agendas aligning. But there was no smoking gun. No secretive backroom deal. If there was something distasteful, something *ugly*, about the relationship—well, Caine never let himself become troubled by mere ugliness.

My coffee and pastry long since finished, I was standing up and leaving a tip for Mirko when I noticed a gray-haired woman across the room. She stood at the bar, talking with the waiter. Another regular, it seemed. (But why had I never seen her before?) She turned away from the bar, carrying a brimming cup of coffee, but kept looking back at the waiter. As she walked blindly across the room, right toward me, the collision seemed to happen in slow motion. Scalding coffee, up and down my sweater.

"Oh my God! Oh my God, I am so sorry!" she exclaimed. She launched into a multilingual apology: "*Je suis désolée! Mi scusi! Es tut mir Leid!*"

I shook my head. "It's fine," I said, reaching for a napkin.

"No, no, I am *so* embarrassed. Please let me help you." She seized the napkin and began dabbing. "Oh, your poor sweater. I ruined it. I am so sorry. Here, please. Come with me. I'll help you."

She grabbed my hand and, before I could object, dragged me toward the bathroom. She ran the faucet, and then turned around to lock the door.

"Well, Sofie," she said in a brusque tone. "I'm sorry about the sweater, but it was the only way."

I swallowed hard, performing rapid calculations. "You're . . . ? So you saw . . . ?"

"My name is Greta," she said. In the claustrophobic bathroom, with the harsh light and the scent of chemical cleaner, this woman had undergone a chameleon-like transformation. Her mouth set in a grim line, her eyes hard and unblinking, she looked nothing like the carefree woman of a few minutes ago. "I am a friend of your friend. Are you and Ben okay? You have something you need to tell us?"

I felt vaguely terrified of Greta, and inclined to do whatever she told me. But as I was starting to sputter out an explanation, it came back to me: another instruction from that distant day.

"No, wait. Wait a second," I said, shaking my head. "How is . . . How is my neighbor Maurice doing?"

She gave a brisk nod. "The soil is healthy. The tulips will have a good spring."

"Okay," I said, mirroring her movement, nodding to myself. *Okay.*

I described what had happened the night before, how the producer, who had been calling and emailing for weeks, had actually shown up *in person*. "On my *doorstep*," I said, my voice straining. Saying it out loud made me understand just how real it was. "Where we live. Where we're supposed to be *safe*."

"Yes," she said. "I thought it might be that. We saw her, too."

"Then you need to help me!" I exclaimed. "Get her to leave me alone."

"No, Sofie. Think about how it would look if we interfered."

"I don't care how it looks!" I said, the heat rising in my cheeks.

"Certainly you care." Her tone was cold, as if the concept of *caring* was mere abstraction. "Think, Sofie. Why would she come all the way to Croatia? She suspects something. Likely, that you haven't told the full truth about your relationship with Lara Caine. You're a journalist. If someone tried to stop you, what would it make you do?" She stared at me bloodlessly. "You'd just work ten times harder, wouldn't you?"

A knock on the bathroom door.

"One minute!" Greta shouted. Then she continued: "Here's what we want you to do. Take the meeting. Show her that you have nothing to hide. You might even learn something useful in the process. The nature of her suspicions. The reason for her persistence. Really." She arched an eyebrow. "You have nothing to fear from her. She's exactly who she says she is. She's just looking for a good story."

"I can't do it," I insisted. "I'm not a good enough liar."

"She wants a good story," Greta repeated, like a teacher instructing a slow-witted student. "Isn't this the nature of your work? Certainly you have experience coming up with a good story."

She grabbed a handful of paper towels and held them out to me. "Here," she said. "You ought to clean yourself up before you go back outside."

•

As I walked home through the cobblestoned streets, I pulled out my phone. Maurice was our upstairs neighbor in New York. It gave a pretext for my regular calls: he was checking our mail, watering the plants, keeping an eye on things. His landline rang, and there was his familiar voice, his Russian accent still strong even after decades in America: "Good morning, Sonechka."

"How did you know it was me?"

"You're the only person who calls this early," he said. It would be dawn in New York, darkness out the window. Maurice was an early riser, brewing tea to the soft strains of Mozart on WQXR while the rest of the building slept. "But I'm glad you did. I have some news."

"News?" I said, pricking to attention.

"I spoke to our friend yesterday," he said. "Our friend was in good spirits."

"That's good," I said, my heart suddenly thumping. "Isn't it?"

"I said you were very happy with your new routine."

"Oh," I said. "Uh, yeah. Of course we're happy. But there was nothing about"—I searched for the right words, the right disguise for the question I was asking—"about, you know. How the work is going?"

"I'm sorry, Sonechka," he said. "We spoke for only a minute or two."

"Ah," I said. (Why did I bother? Why did I search for reassurance when I knew, I *knew*, there was none to be found?) "Okay. Well, the reason I called is that, actually, something weird happened last night."

"Oh?"

"This TV producer from New York," I said. "She wants to interview me for a feature about Lara Caine. She showed up on my doorstep. I don't know how she found me."

"Interesting," Maurice said quietly. "Do you think you'll say yes?"

"I think"—I coughed, my mouth gone dry—"I think I *have* to."

A brief silence on the other end. I could picture it so vividly: Maurice walking to the window, pulling back the curtain, checking to see if anyone else on the block was awake. Keeping an eye on things, like always. I heard the clink of his china cup in its saucer.

"Yes, that sounds sensible. Curiosity is to be expected," he said. "What you had with Lara Caine was very unusual. Of course this person wants to know more."

•

Looking back, it's strange to think how quickly everything happened. Lara Caine was the third wife of President Caine, the only First Lady since Louisa Adams to be born outside the United States, the most enigmatic occupant of the East Wing in decades, the silent companion of the most toxic leader in American history, the couture-clad Rorschach test for the nation at large—and the subject of my next book.

That was the plan, at least. After her husband was, horrifyingly, reelected to a second term, Mrs. Caine had approached me to write her biography. The access she granted was irresistible, giving me free rein with memories, diaries, photographs, and family members. She had no desire to write her own book. Like any wealthy woman, Mrs. Caine was comfortable with delegation: she relied on professionals to cook her meals, style her hair, tailor her clothes. So why not have a professional tell her story? The First Lady demanded no control over the final product. As far as I could tell, there were no strings attached.

I hesitated at first. I wondered whether it was selling out; whether devoting so much time to this project would be amoral, or immoral. Wasn't it cynical to say yes? But Lara Caine had made it impossible for the public to get to know her. Like the rest of America, I'd assumed things about her without really *knowing* anything about her. So was it cynical to say no? I spun in circles for a while, but in the end, my curiosity decided for me.

And her life, I soon discovered, had been unusual and eventful. The material was rich. Mrs. Caine and I settled into a comfortable routine. Trust blossomed. We grew closer. I expected the arrangement to last awhile. There would be a lot to cover.

Before we began, I hadn't been planning on doing anything like this. I'd written a book years earlier, but that was an accident more than anything else; after graduate school in England, I was able to turn my history dissertation into a book that sold modestly but respectably. After that, at the tail end of my twenties, I'd moved to New York. I began working as a journalist just as the brash oil tycoon Henry Caine was casting his eye toward Washington, DC.

Calling myself a journalist was charitable, at first. I had no training in cultivating sources, or digging up scoops, or writing on deadline. But I could reach into the past and unwind dusty skeins of context for readers, and my new boss, the managing editor of the newspaper, thought that was useful for the times we were living in. The day after Caine won his first election, she reassigned me to the White House beat.

"We need someone like you in that chair right now," Vicky said. "And you wanted to learn, right? Well, you're going to learn a lot on the fly."

The newspaper was a lean operation, a few steps above the local city tabloids but nowhere near the *New York Times* and *Wall Street Journal*s of the world. It was mostly propped up by analog subscribers who were too loyal or apathetic to cut bait, and while it had no national presence to speak of, it *had* been chronicling Henry Caine, a born-and-bred New Yorker, for decades. These were stories that the wider world suddenly cared about, and it led to a resurgence of readership, and profit. For the first time in years, the budget steadied. For those of us at the newspaper, it was nice to get a raise and a 401(k) match, but it was also unsettling to realize the source of this newfound prosperity.

Four years, which seemed like a life sentence at the outset, went by quickly. Despite his constant sabotage, both of himself and of the country, Caine had enjoyed an unbroken streak of luck. The corruption investigations resulted in a collective shrug; the impeachment proceedings failed to pass; and the economy remained white-hot, which apparently was all that mattered, because there we were, gathered in the newsroom on a Tuesday night in November, a little after 9:00 p.m., and the networks had just called Pennsylvania for President Caine.

Vicky Wethers crossed her arms as she stared at the TV. The electoral map disappeared from the screen, replaced by a panel of pundits, arguing about what to expect from his second term. Vicky said to no one in particular: "Well, of course. Who's going to vote against three percent unemployment?"

"Someone with a conscience," Eli chimed in. "Someone who gives a rat's ass about more than their bank account." Eli was old-school, coming up during the New York tabloid wars. He had the habit of cracking open hundreds of pistachios a day, which he started doing after he quit smoking because he had to do *something* with his hands.

Vicky sighed. "This is so depressing."

"It's like he's made out of Teflon," I said. "The normal rules just don't apply to him."

Eli craned his neck toward me, popping in a handful of pistachios. "When'd you get to be so jaded, Morse? Nah, the rules apply to everyone. Sometimes they just take longer to catch up."

"How long is longer?" I said. "At this rate, he'll be dead before they catch up to him."

He shook his head. "Eventually something's gonna stick. I've got this guy at Langley, he's convinced there's something weird about that Dresden meeting."

"Dresden?" I echoed, half listening while texting with a White

House source (on background, she said, most of them were miserable that night; his aides wanted nothing more than for Caine to lose, and for their lives to get back to normal). I didn't give much attention to what Eli was saying. Eli had a lot of guys, and those guys tended to have a lot of theories.

"Yeah. That summit he had with Gruzdev, a few years back? Where the two of them snuck off and Caine wouldn't let anyone else inside the room? Not even our side's translator? My guy thinks that—"

"Hold up," Vicky said, waving at Eli to be quiet. "We're getting something out of Ohio."

In unison, we swiveled toward the TV screen. Nights like this were when the office was most alive. Some moments in history arrive quietly. In graduate school, we talked about the hidden turning points, which are only revealed with plenty of retrospect. Who could imagine the ripple effects of these contingencies—the heir born with hemophilia; the Austrian boy rejected from art school; the invisible mutation of a spike protein structure? But other moments in history arrive like a screaming meteorite. You can't help but know that you're living through something. When that happened, we sprang into action.

That night, while Vicky paced the floor and asked for updates, I thought about Ben and our group of friends. They would be watching the returns at someone's apartment on the Upper West Side, frantically changing channels, sifting for nuggets of hope as the night unfolded. I could imagine the empty bottles of wine on the sideboard, the remnants of cheese rind drying out, the shattered fragments of tortilla chip at the bottom of the bowl. I was glad not to be there; I was glad, at least, to have this task to keep myself busy. And yet that gladness left a sour taste in my mouth. It was an awful, ironic privilege of this job—to always be distracted, to always have more work to do. Chronicling the nonstop drama had created a strange set of blinders, numbing me to the pain. I hated that I felt this way. Four years of this had left their mark. *What*, I asked myself, *will another four years do?*

Vicky stepped behind me, leaning forward to look at my screen. "How's it coming?"

"Almost done," I said. "It'll be ready to go as soon as the networks call it."

Vicky once said it was my job to tell readers how bad it really was. Taking the long view, and considering everything we've been through before, tell us: Are we at DEFCON 3, or DEFCON 2, or, God forbid, DEFCON 1? I told her it wasn't possible for any one person to know such a thing, and certainly not within the moment itself.

She said, "I'm not asking for perfect empiricism, honey. I'm asking for a smart person's educated guess."

It had taken me a while to really understand her request, and figure out how to answer it. Vicky wanted an assessment that wasn't drawn solely from the brain. On a night like this, the screaming meteorite provoked a specific kind of physiological response: the adrenaline, the rapid heartbeat, the deepened breathing. Sometimes history announces itself within the bloodstream.

HENRY PHILIP CAINE, MORE THAN ANY CHIEF EXECUTIVE IN AMERICAN HISTORY, SPENT HIS FIRST TERM MIRED IN UNPRECEDENTED SCANDAL. AFTER DEVASTATING INVESTIGATIONS, REPEATED CALLS FOR HIS IMPEACHMENT, AND HISTORICALLY LOW APPROVAL RATINGS, PRESIDENT CAINE APPEARED TO BE A FATALLY WOUNDED CANDIDATE. BUT ON TUESDAY, AMERICA CHOSE TO RETURN HIM TO THE WHITE HOUSE FOR ANOTHER FOUR YEARS.

•

The next morning, I walked to a coffee shop on Eighth Avenue, a popular spot around the corner from the office. The sleek white walls and black concrete floors were a trendy picture of elegant restraint. There were only a few drinks on the menu (cappuccino, latte, drip coffee), and even fewer pastries available within the small glass case. Fewer options meant fewer chances to choose the wrong thing, and lately people seemed to crave that certainty.

A long line of customers snaked through the front door into the November sunshine, smartly employed men and women within that substantial bracket of thirty- to fiftysomethings who had enough money to splurge on high-end coffee but not enough power to send an assistant to get it for them. As the line crept forward, people were mostly staring at their phones, insulated by white earbuds. Despite the morning rush, the tables inside were nearly empty. Except for a table in the back, where Vicky sat, two coffees already procured.

"I thought I was on time for once," I said, unzipping my coat, which was too heavy for the mild weather. My neck was sticky, and sweat pricked my forehead. I felt vaguely, irrationally annoyed with myself. This was an important moment, and I felt like I was botching it.

"You are on time," Vicky said, removing her reading glasses and setting aside her phone. "But you know me. Always early. My congenital defect. Did you manage to sleep?"

"A little. Poorly. Did you?" I said, as she handed me the coffee.

"Four hours, like a rock." Vicky smiled. She somehow looked the same every single day, regardless of sleep or weather or season. Neatly cut gray hair, colorful blazer, her blue eyes radiating tiny deltas of wrinkles. "So this is it, huh? I'm guessing that if you'd changed your mind, you wouldn't be looking so forlorn right now."

I smiled weakly. "Do I really look that bad?"

"Well, you look ready for a change."

"Vicky, I wanted to say thank you." A lump was swelling in my throat. "For everything. I'm going to miss you. I'm going to miss *this*. And I wish I could keep going, but I just—"

"Oh, Sofie," she said, waving a hand. "Sweetheart. Don't say another word."

Quitting had been contingent on the election. If Caine lost, I'd stick it out for at least a few more months and cover the transition, and then decide. But Caine winning only meant more of the same: more stress, more sleepless nights, more exhaustion. Other people, like Vicky, seemed to stay centered in the chaos. But I hadn't figured out how to do that.

Vicky understood. And life was long, she said; maybe I'd come back someday. In the office, it took me only an hour to pack up my desk. I said my goodbyes, handed out my personal email, promised to keep in touch. As I stood at the elevator, pressing the Down button and surveying the newsroom one last time, Eli appeared, carrying a cup of coffee from the kitchen. "Jesus, Morse," he said, eyes widening. "I almost forgot. You're really quitting?"

"Don't miss me too much," I said, with a tremor of slightly false cheer.

"But you'll be back," he said, wrapping me in a bone-crushing hug. "I know you will."

•

Many months after that, when I was in the thick of working on the First Lady's biography—at times feeling almost cocky at how everything had worked out—I had lunch with Vicky at her favorite spot in Midtown. She said, "Level with me, Sofie. This whole Lara Caine thing. Did you always know this would be your exit ramp?"

In that moment, I was tempted to say yes. Fudge the timeline a little, make the narrative work in my favor. Sure, of *course*, this had been my plan all along.

But it wasn't even the tiniest bit true, and the lie never felt worth it. Lara Caine had a meticulous memory. She hated half-truths and untruths muddying up the public record. If rumor reached her that her biographer was claiming to be the mastermind—well. A mistake like that would just make both of us look stupid.

The biography was entirely her idea. We were clear on that. Later, the sharpness of this delineation proved exculpatory: it was a relief, more than anything, to let her take the credit, to back away from what it had wrought. The same words, the same truth, took on a new valence: *It wasn't my idea*, said quietly with shrugged deflection, became *It wasn't my idea!*, shouted in defiance.

On that day in November, as I left the office with my box and tote bags, I *did* have vague ideas of writing another book—that much was true. Ben and I had repeatedly calculated how to pull this off.

Our rent was this much. Ben's law school debt was that much. His twice-monthly paychecks, my twice-yearly royalty statements from a book that continued to sell modestly, and a small mutual fund that could be liquidated if needed. All of this could keep us going for a while, as long as we kept our costs low.

After that last morning at the office, I came out of the subway at Sixty-Eighth and Lexington, emerging into a scrum of Hunter College students who were perched on stone ledges, shrieking energetically on their lunch break. The halal cart on the corner was doing brisk business, sending up savory billows of smoke and the mouthwatering scent of lamb gyro. The intersection had an almost summery mood. Virtually no one in New York City was happy about last night's results, and yet life was carrying on, in the usual way.

I walked north on Lex and turned down Seventy-First Street, where Ben and I had lived for the past five years. We'd met on a dating app when I was thirty and Ben was thirty-one. Love was instant, borne both of chemistry and sheer relief. Neither of us felt like wasting time. Three months after our first date, we moved in together. Six months after that, we got married. Most people assumed the accelerated timeline was because we wanted a baby, or that one was already en route. They never imagined the opposite to be true: that part of our certainty sprung from a shared *lack* of that desire. Our apartment on East Seventy-First Street was charming and tiny. "Just right for two," the broker said, when she showed us the space, five years earlier. She had given me a meaningful look, one that lingered on my midsection, one that any woman in her thirties quickly learns to decipher.

I loved our little apartment. We lived in the garden level of a narrow town house. The house had been divided into four apartments, one on each floor, and if you were lucky enough to land in one of them, you tended to stick. That day, in the small front courtyard outside the building, our neighbor Maurice Adler was watering his trough of bright yellow goldenrod and his hardy witch hazel shrub. Maurice was an elegant man, probably in his seventies, though I was never sure of his exact age. He was originally from Saint Petersburg

("Peter," as he always called it), and had lived in the parlor level of the town house since moving to New York in the 1990s. He knew everything and everyone in the neighborhood. He liked to stroll around the block on summer evenings, and to linger at the coffee shop on Lexington. The moment he moved here, he said, he knew that his years of wandering were finished for good.

"Sonechka," he said. The arcing spray from the hose caught in the sunlight, glittering like a chandelier. "Was today the day?"

"It was," I said, stepping down into the courtyard, which wasn't much bigger than a parking space and just deep enough for a few stone planters. "And I survived."

"Bravo," he said. "I had a good feeling about it. The sunshine is an omen."

The faucet squeaked in rusty protest as Maurice bent to turn off the water. He'd retired a few years ago but still dressed as he did when he was a professor at Hunter. Pleated khakis, checked Turnbull & Asser shirt, softened penny loafers, trimmed gray mustache. As he wound the garden hose into a neat coil, he said, "Are you hungry? I was just about to have some lunch."

I followed Maurice through the main door, to the right. Because Ben and I lived on the garden level, we used the old service entrance over to the left. This was one of my favorite details of the apartment. To live in Manhattan, and to have a proper front door? During our first winter in the apartment, when I bought an overpriced wreath from the Christmas tree stand on Third Avenue and hung it on that door, I felt anchored in a way that I hadn't felt in years.

Maurice opened his door and ushered me into his bright, high-ceilinged living room. When he instructed me to sit, I sat, because I knew better than to offer my help in the kitchen. Even for a spur-of-the-moment lunch, Maurice took hosting seriously.

Several minutes later, he carried in a tray with two steaming bowls of chicken soup, shimmering gold studded with fragrant dill. On the side were slices of dark rye bread and a pot of sour cream. Maurice was a good cook, although his repertoire was mostly limited to the food that reminded him of home. When he was in the mood for

French or Italian, he said, he would rather it be cooked by someone who knew what they were doing.

"I read your story in the paper this morning," he said, spreading sour cream on his rye bread. "I liked it. It was quite good."

I smiled. From Maurice, "quite good" was the highest compliment you could hope for.

"Thank you," I said. "It's funny, it felt hard to get that one right. Even though everyone knew Caine was going to win."

Maurice nodded. "There's a difference between knowing a thing and articulating a thing."

"And a difference between articulating a thing and understanding a thing." I blew on a spoonful of soup, waiting for it to cool. "Which, I think, we're a long way from. No one knows what to do with a man like Henry Caine."

Maurice frowned. "If only that were true."

"What do you mean?"

"Well, I fear that *some* people know what to do with him."

Before I could ask him to elaborate (*Some* people? Was he thinking of anyone specific?), we were interrupted by a shrill ring.

"Pardon me, Sonechka," he said, standing to answer the phone. "My doctor is supposed to call about a prescription."

Maurice spoke quietly for a few minutes, occasionally saying, "Could you repeat that, Doctor?" while he took notes on a pad on a small end table. The rotary telephone, like Maurice, was old-fashioned and worked perfectly well. Maurice's health was sturdy, his mind sharp, his energy unflagging. He was one of those people who managed to locate the fountain of youth in the New York City water supply.

Once, in the early days of our friendship, I'd asked him if he would ever go home.

"To Russia?" he said. "No, never. There's nothing for me in Russia." A funny answer, it seemed, for a man whose apartment was bursting with nostalgic reminders of that past life. The old samovar on the sideboard; the sepia photographs of long-departed family members; even the too-warm temperature of the air and the lingering smell of woodsmoke spoke of his traditional Russian fear of the cold (from October to April, Maurice lit a fire in the fireplace every night, no matter how mild the weather).

"Did I tell you that I have a new internist?" Maurice said, as he returned to the brocade sofa. "She is very young. Younger than you, I think."

"What happened to Dr. Feltner?"

Maurice drew his hand across his throat and then shrugged grimly.

I burst out laughing. "Sorry," I said. "That isn't funny."

"Well, it comes for all of us, doesn't it? So tell me. You're still planning to write another book? Have you decided on a subject?"

I shook my head. "Not yet. I guess I could write about Caine. The gold rush is still going, you know? Those books do really well."

"Yes, the appetite is endless," he said. "But do you *want* to keep writing about him?"

"No. Not really. Actually, I want to get as far away from that as possible."

"It doesn't interest you anymore?"

"I just don't think my writing about it—I mean writing about him, that whole world—will do anyone any good." I paused, hesitating, but if Maurice wouldn't understand these things, who would? I said, "Is it stupid to say that whatever I do next, I want it to . . . I don't know, I want it to *mean* something?"

"My dear," he said, "that is the opposite of stupid."

We were quiet for a while, concentrating on our food. The old brass carriage clock on the mantelpiece ticked sedately. Maurice must have sensed what I was wrestling with, because he prompted: "Tell me again, Sofie, how you came to write your last book."

"It's not a very interesting story," I said. "My tutor at Oxford, he thought Raisa Gorbacheva was never correctly assessed or understood, from a historical perspective. It bothered him that Westerners didn't really know who she was. So that's what I wound up writing about. Anyways, that's my problem! It wasn't *my* idea."

"But you're the one who actually wrote it," Maurice said. "What I'm wondering is, why did you *pursue* that idea?"

"I was curious about her, I guess."

"Well, then, that's all you have to do." He sat back on the couch, crossing one leg over the other. "Just follow that curiosity, Sonechka. It will lead you in the right direction. And then you will write a wonderful book."

This was signature Maurice: he made it sound so simple. He'd adopted certain American habits over the decades—rooting for the Yankees, a weakness for Snickers—but he remained a Russian fatalist to his core. Things would unfold that way because they *had* to unfold that way. I wanted to believe him. But I also knew that wasn't how the world worked.

•

Maurice Adler, my upstairs neighbor. What can I tell you about him? He was born in Leningrad in the wake of the Great Patriotic War. He was a brilliant and promising student. In the 1960s, he enrolled at the newly opened Novosibirsk State University to study physics, but he came to loathe the violent application of that science in a nuclear-obsessed Cold War world. He wanted to switch disciplines and study philosophy instead, but the Soviet Union in the era of general secretary Leonid Brezhnev was not a place in which personal opinion mattered very much. So Maurice left. He went to Heidelberg for a new course of study and patched together an itinerant career from temporary teaching positions across Europe. Finally, he came to America in 1991, settling into a post at Hunter College, where, for over twenty-five years, he was busy, productive, and beloved. When he retired, Hunter students past and present crowded into the back room of a nearby restaurant to toast him.

What else could I tell you about Maurice? The names of his doctors, and how he took his coffee at the coffee shop on Lexington, and what time he went grocery shopping. His smile when talking about a book he loved. The way he arched one eyebrow and leaned back slightly while preparing to engage himself in argument. The creaking sound of his footsteps across his living room floorboards, announcing his retreat to bed every night at ten. His unfailingly direct way of speaking.

It was easy to trust in the wisdom of everything he said. But he had lived an entire lifetime before ever setting foot in New York City, and I only ever knew the broadest strokes about his past. Well, what did that matter? He didn't seem inclined to dwell on it. I never suspected what he was leaving out.

•

I thought it would come as a relief, having these acres of unbounded time, this chance for leisurely lunches and afternoon naps and unread novels. But that first week after leaving the newspaper, I only felt restless. I walked around the apartment, picking things up and putting them down, my attention span in tatters. Four years of President Caine had done something bad to my brain. I had to relearn how to live in the real world.

There was a diner around the corner from our apartment, with counter seating and vinyl booths and faded posters of Greek islands behind the cash register. That first week of freedom, I went for an omelet during the lull between breakfast and lunch, sitting in a booth and staring at the pages of a novel while the waiter refilled my coffee. I couldn't concentrate, but passing time felt like a more meaningful act when performed in public.

A woman slid into the next booth over. "Coffee, please," she said to the waiter. "And a blueberry muffin, toasted with butter." She pushed her black sunglasses into her blond hair and squinted at her phone. Cashmere cardigan, Chanel flats, Goyard tote bag. Midthirties, around my age. She was a neighborhood type, but which? Mother of young children? Overworked professional? Both, it became clear, as she answered her buzzing phone.

"Tell them I need to call in to the eleven thirty," she said. "Theo has some kind of stomach bug. That preschool is a hot zone. Anyway, listen, I looked at the board deck. The third slide is all wrong. You have to—"

Could I help feeling a slight envy? That life wasn't the life I wanted, but still—that woman was so busy, so certain, so *needed*. I was having trouble breaking the habit of constantly looking at my phone, so I'd left it at the apartment when I went to the diner, hoping an hour of forced separation might help. It was mostly silent these days, anyway.

But when I got home, there was a missed call, and a voice mail.

"Sofie," the vaguely familiar voice on the message said. "This is Gabi Carvalho, the First Lady's chief of staff. We met a few years ago, as you probably remember. Could you call me back as soon as you get this? It's important."

CHAPTER TWO

In my time as a correspondent, I only ever saw a small sliver of the White House. There was the press briefing room, which grew neglected and dusty because the president preferred to handle his own communications. There was the elbow-to-elbow warren of cubicles, crammed with journalists from the *Times*, the *Post*, the wires, the networks, the cablers. White House correspondent was a job that sounded more glamorous than it actually was. I worked in the White House in the same way that a mid-rise apartment on Second Avenue in Manhattan boasts of river views. Technically true, fundamentally misleading.

When I left the newspaper and turned in my hard pass to the press office, I expected it would be a very long time before I returned, if ever. But in mid-November, only two weeks after the election, I was back again.

Gabi Carvalho, the First Lady's chief of staff, was waiting for me inside the visitors' entrance. She shook my hand and said, "Nice to see you, Sofie. Thank you for coming on such short notice. Although I'm guessing your schedule is more flexible these days. Congratulations, by the way."

I had to hurry to keep up with her as she moved through the East Wing. Her speed was impressive, given her stilettos and pencil skirt.

Like a lot of women in the Caine administration, Gabi wasn't really the Washington type: her clothing was too stylish, her makeup was too perfect. She was one of the Manhattan loyalists whom the Caines had imported to the capital.

"Congratulations?" I said. "For quitting my job, you mean?"

"For being smart enough to leave the party early. Here, this way."

We stopped in front of the elevator, where Gabi pressed the Up button. I'd never been to the East Wing, but I knew that the most important office was housed on the second floor. My palms were sweaty; I tried to wipe them surreptitiously against my skirt. I still didn't know why I was there. I'd returned Gabi's call immediately, but she didn't give a reason for the summons.

"Mrs. Caine will want to explain it herself," she'd said.

We rode the elevator in silence. The doors opened with a ding. When we stepped out into the hallway, Gabi said, "A reminder that this is going to be strictly off-the-record. This isn't an interview. This is just a private chat."

I nodded. "I understand."

"Follow me," she said, guiding me down the unfamiliar hallway. The decor in this part of the White House was strikingly different. There was none of the stodgy red-and-gold traditionalism of the West Wing. Here in the East Wing it was pale carpets, cream-colored walls, bright pops of modern art (was that an Ellsworth Kelly?). I remembered an article that had appeared in the early days of the Caine administration, about the decor in the East Wing, how Lara Caine had worked hard to carve out her own distinctive portion of the White House.

"You know," Gabi said, as we reached the end of the hallway and she turned to face me. She was petite, but her high heels raised her to my eye level. Her shiny hair smelled expensive and tropical. "Mrs. Caine never remembers who journalists are. She really doesn't care. But she remembered you."

Gabi squinted at me. For just a moment, her professional veneer receded, exposing a hungry curiosity.

Oh, I thought, surprised. *So she's just as ignorant as me.* So the two of us were equally baffled as to why the woman on the other side of that closed door—the woman married to the most powerful man in the world—had such an urgent desire to talk to me, of all people.

•

Two years earlier, partway through her husband's first term, Lara Caine embarked on her first major international trip as First Lady. At the newspaper, the reporter who usually covered Mrs. Caine was on maternity leave, so the work fell to me.

"This is an opportunity, Sofie," Vicky said, holding up a finger when I blanched at the prospect of this fluffy, flimsy assignment. "Our understanding of Lara Caine is so ahistorical. No one looks at the bigger picture. For God's sakes, she was born in Russia, right in the middle of the Cold War. She was raised to see America as the enemy. And now she's in the White House! Why don't we spend any time thinking about that? About what it means?"

And so, before the trip, I grumblingly consumed whatever I could find about Lara Caine. There wasn't much: a few slapdash unauthorized biographies, a handful of thinly sourced magazine profiles, a series of soft-focus TV interviews. Even her Wikipedia page was half-baked, with no more than a few sentences about her life before Henry Caine. The First Lady was born in Moscow in 1970 as Larissa Fyodorovna Orlova. When she was a girl, her family moved to Paris, where her father served as a military attaché at the Soviet embassy for an unusually long stretch, throughout the 1970s and 1980s. At some unspecified point, her family returned to Russia. That was it. That was all I could find.

She only really entered the public record after the collapse of the Soviet Union, when she began working as a model in the 1990s, a career that eventually took her to New York. The public portrait was drawn almost entirely from the years she had been with Henry Caine: tabloid coverage of their romance, photos of her wedding dress in *Vogue*, a glossy feature about their Park Avenue penthouse, charity galas chronicled in the Sunday Styles.

The dearth of information struck me as strange. What about her childhood? What about those years in Moscow and Paris? Why did she never talk about them? Lara Caine had proved canny at cultivating a certain image of herself, both in her New York and Washington years. She was perfectly poised in front of the camera. Gut instinct told me that this lacuna didn't come from shyness.

The day before the trip, Vicky stopped by. "Find out anything interesting?"

"Yeah, actually," I said. "One of the few things I could find about her online—her father was a military attaché at the Soviet embassy in Paris."

Vicky tilted her head: *And?*

"And, well, military attaché? That's one of those jobs that only exists as a cover for another kind of job. What did he really do?"

"I've heard theories," Vicky said. "But no one has ever managed to get confirmation. FLOTUS certainly won't say a word about it. What do you think?"

"Military attaché means he was a spy," I said. "For the KGB. It seems pretty obvious."

Vicky smiled. "And if we could print that, we'd have a hell of a story."

The ten-day tour through Europe began in Germany, where Mrs. Caine visited the site of the Berlin Wall and the old Checkpoint Charlie. From Berlin we went to Warsaw, and then to Prague. The itinerary, skywriting the route of the old Iron Curtain, was strategic. Her husband was constantly threatening to abandon NATO. It was widely understood that Mrs. Caine was visiting these countries in order to reassure them of America's commitment.

Gray autumnal gloom, old European cities. The last stop on the ten-day tour was Paris. Mrs. Caine's schedule for those final two days was relatively light: she attended the ballet with the president's wife, visited a traveling exhibition of American artists at the Musée d'Orsay, met with female immigrants from the Côte d'Ivoire who ran a clothing company in the Eighteenth Arrondissement. At no point did Mrs. Caine or her staff remark on the fact that she had spent most of her childhood in this city. When the press pool asked questions along those lines, she glossed over them. The impersonality of the schedule struck me as bizarre, and a wasted opportunity.

As the press pool shuttled back to the hotel after the Orsay visit, I asked Gabi Carvalho if I could have thirty minutes of the First Lady's time. At that point, Gabi had just recently joined the administration and had zero political experience. She was a rich Upper East Side girl, the stylish daughter of an American socialite and a Brazilian sugar magnate, and had swerved into the low-rent world of politics for God knew what reason.

In response to my question, Gabi stared at me and said, "What's your name again?"

"Sofie Morse," I said.

"Right. Sofie. You're filling in for your colleague. And when we get home, you'll be waltzing right back over to the West Wing." She arched an eyebrow. "There are reporters who have been on this beat for *years*, and Mrs. Caine has never given them a sit-down. Why should you get to skip the line?"

"It's my job to ask," I said.

"And it's my job to say no," she said abruptly.

The hard authority in her tone surprised me. "Gabi," I called out, hurrying after her, across the hotel lobby. "Okay, okay, I get it. But will you pass along a question, at least? And the First Lady can decide whether to respond or not."

Gabi stopped. After a beat, she gestured impatiently. "I'm standing here, aren't I?"

"I want to ask her about her childhood, here in Paris." Mrs. Caine's avoidance of the subject had to be deliberate. But why? I took a deep breath. "Specifically, I'd like to ask her about her father's work. What it was like, growing up here during the Cold War, with a father who worked as a military attaché at the Soviet embassy."

Gabi rolled her eyes. "That's not really a question," she said.

"Please. Will you just pass it along?"

And then, nothing happened. What did I expect? Did I think that Lara Caine, when she heard my question, would be impressed by the fact that I'd done my homework and knew about her father's job and would happily invite me up to her suite in the Ritz for a chat? It was silly to entertain such ideas. In fact, I wasn't even confident that Gabi had passed along the message.

The ten-day trip was perfectly smooth. Perfectly smooth and perfectly dull, just as I had feared. During the tour, I'd filed a series of brief articles about Mrs. Caine's various stops and speeches. But what, if anything, did it add up to? Vicky wanted me to write a longer, in-depth analysis of the trip. What, during all this time spent watching Lara Caine, had I learned? But the First Lady had given us nothing to work with. The story I eventually wrote, after staring at a blinking cursor for many hours, was full of superficial cliché. *Just like her*, I thought irritably. No wonder there was never anything interesting written about Lara Caine.

But even after plunging back into the chaos of the White House beat, I found myself wondering, from time to time. The First Lady was avoiding something about her past. What was it?

•

The secretary nodded for Gabi to go ahead. Gabi eased the door open and said, "Mrs. Caine? Sofie Morse is here."

As Lara Caine rose from her chair, several things about her struck me in succession. First was her height. In her high heels, she towered over me. Second was her handshake, which was very firm. Third was the quality of her voice. In interviews, she sounded delicate and exaggeratedly feminine, with that thin Pan-European accent. But in person, her voice was almost an octave lower: contralto rather than soprano, comfortable and relaxed.

"Sofie," she said. "Thank you for coming today. I hope it wasn't too much trouble."

She gestured for me to step inside. Her office felt modern and cool. The walls were painted a faint shade of gray, and the floor was covered in a softly iridescent carpet, with blue tones echoed in the vases of hydrangea. I glanced from detail to detail, trying to take everything in. Mrs. Caine was known to have been intimately involved in these decorating decisions. Because she never spoke to the press, her aesthetic choices were the tea leaves that the public tried to decipher. What did the Burberry blouse mean, on the day she met the queen of England? What about the Navajo patterned coat she wore, shortly after her husband insulted Native American leaders?

"Please, sit," she said, indicating a tufted velvet sofa with a mid-century silhouette. We took our seats on a pair of these sofas, in a dusty shade of lilac, arranged in an L. Mrs. Caine wore a white crewneck sweater with bracelet-length sleeves, tucked into the high waistband of her cigarette-slim pants. The pants were bright red (*Soviet red*, I found myself thinking) and stopped just shy of the ankle. Stiletto pumps in crocodile leather, neutral manicure, no jewelry except for the massive diamond ring on her left hand. Most women like her—married, well-off uptown Manhattanites—stopped wearing their engagement rings at a certain point, trading them in for a meaty stack of pavé diamond bands. The red pants, the solitaire diamond: even within the moment I felt it happening, the assignment of meaning to the blank canvas of Lara Caine.

"You must be curious why I asked you here today," she said.

"I am," I said. "I'm surprised you remembered me."

"Gabi was surprised, too. But I have a good memory for these things. It was the question you asked. About my father, and his work."

I cocked my head. "I got the sense you weren't interested in that question."

"But you respected that I didn't want to answer it." She spoke so deliberately, so carefully, that I almost wondered if these lines had been rehearsed. "You didn't write your own imaginary story about it."

"Well, that's not what we do," I said. "Journalists don't write imaginary stories." *As much as your husband might claim otherwise*, I thought.

Mrs. Caine smiled slightly. "I'm a very private person," she said. "I never talk about my private life. Unfortunately, *other* people decide to talk about it anyway. They make things up. They have their own ideas and they call them facts."

It was a subtle kind of comment, a thorn also designed to seduce. She'd probably perfected this technique over countless white-tablecloth lunches on Madison Avenue. *They're barbarians*, she implied. *But thank goodness you're nothing like them.*

"I read your book," she continued, uncrossing and recrossing her long legs. "After that trip to Paris. I wanted to see who this woman was, this Sofie Morse."

"You read my book?" I said, genuinely surprised.

"It was very good. And then it made sense to me. You have an interest in that era."

"In the Cold War? I think a lot of people do."

"A lot of people, yes. But I'm talking to you specifically."

There was a long pause. She looked into my eyes with calm expectation—wanting something, but I had no idea what.

Mrs. Caine nodded, as if attributing my silence to wisdom rather than confusion. "There is so much more you can say in a book. More—what is the phrase?" She drew her hands apart, indicating length. "More room to breathe. Often people have said I should write my own book. Write my memoirs. 'You've lived such an interesting life, Lara.' 'You've seen so much, Lara.' But why should I pretend to be something I'm not? I've known writers, and I'm not a writer." She laughed; a startling break from her polished composure. "I never had any talent for it."

"Oh," I said blandly. "I'm sure that's not true."

"Some people say, why not use a ghostwriter? This is what my husband did, of course. It's what everyone does. But I don't like this idea." She leaned forward to emphasize her point. "It isn't *honest*. I won't pretend to be capable of something I am not. But if I keep my private life to myself, the media continues to print lies. So these are my options, and they are both bad. But then, recently, I thought: *There is another way*."

In this moment, did I have even the faintest intuition of what the First Lady was about to ask? But I'd be giving myself too much credit to pretend I was anything but baffled.

"A biography," she said.

I blinked at her. Shook my head. "A—what?"

"This is the solution. A biography." She leaned back, her posture relaxing slightly. "I have no desire to write my own story. And even if I did, half the people would say, 'Lara is a liar; she is corrupt; she is not telling us the truth.' I am not a stupid woman, Sofie. What good is it to try to convince people who have already decided to hate you? If I try to say something true, who will believe me? I would like my story to be told objectively. That is the only way. A biography."

Behind Mrs. Caine, the glass windowpanes filled with movement. Her office overlooked the Kennedy Garden, where the last leaves of autumn swayed in the breeze, their fading color clinging to the branches. The dappled tree shadows stretched and retracted across the pale walls and carpet. The iridescent silk threads caught the light, and the whole room shimmered.

"A biography," I repeated dumbly. "And—and you want me to write it?"

There was a knock, the secretary peeking in. "I have your four o'clock, ma'am."

As Lara Caine walked me to the door, fixing me with her feline gaze, she said, "Please think about it, Sofie. I'd like to talk more. Will you come back tomorrow for lunch?"

•

My sister, Jenna, lived with her husband, Sam, and their twin boys in a small row home in Northeast. They had an office with a pullout couch that doubled as a guest room, which was where I'd always stayed when I was in DC for work. Jenna was seven years older than me and an emergency room doctor at George Washington University Hospital. I'd idolized her as a kid, and still did, although less overtly, because I knew it embarrassed her.

"Oh, come on," she'd say, rolling her eyes, when I pointed out that, for instance, one of the differences between us was that she was *literally* saving lives on a daily basis. "It's a job, Sofe. I'm just doing my job."

She was always so practical. Even as a teenager, she was like that. We grew up in the New Jersey suburbs, where the Manhattan skyline was visible from the highest part of town. Fifteen miles as the crow flies, an hour in traffic, a different world altogether. A suburban utopia of falling leaves, slammed lockers, squeaky linoleum floors, endless repetition. "You don't like it here," Jenna once said, with blunt clarity, when I was a lonely ten-year-old and she was an impossibly mature seventeen-year-old. "Don't worry. You can leave someday."

I liked bookending my Washington days at the Morse-Chung household, leaving behind the nauseating fight of politics for the firm grounding of reality. Two overworked parents, two six-year-old boys, one tagalong aunt, but in this crowded house, I learned that certain kinds of chaos could actually be bliss. In their family's endless river of daily living—art projects, grocery runs, soccer games, birthday parties, sick days, temper tantrums, cartoons, LEGO bricks—the permanent foundational pillars made themselves visible. Here were the things that hadn't changed in the four years Henry Caine had been president. The schools were decent, not great but not terrible. The mail was delivered on time. The families on their block were friendly. For all the rhetoric and bombast, some parts of American life weren't so different from four years earlier.

Some parts. Not all. It was dangerously easy for people like me—relatively affluent, educated, easily employable—to grow numb to the finer-grained changes taking effect. But at the hospital, Jenna and Sam saw it happening. The supply chain for crucial medical devices, like IV bags and syringes, was screwed up thanks to the trade wars. The visa paperwork, to accommodate a visiting surgeon from Nigeria, was proving nightmarish. The nurse who had fled from Iran with her parents when she was a little girl was now unable to visit Tehran to see her dying grandmother. The beloved cook in the cafeteria had been deported. At work, I mostly digested these things as bullet points; each policy was just part of the ongoing political chess match. My sister helped remind me that it added up to so much more.

"I thought you were sick of us," Jenna called from the back of the house, as I dropped my bags in the front hall. When I'd started spending a few nights a week in DC after my assignment to the White House beat, she'd given me my own key. I followed her voice toward the kitchen. Sam had his hands in the sudsy sink, washing up the dinner dishes. Jenna said, "I told Sam that was the real reason you quit. To get away from us."

"That was the only reason I *didn't* want to quit," I said. When she hugged me, her body felt solid and warm. Faint shampoo, citrusy clean. "Did I miss the boys?"

"They were being bratty," Jenna said. "I sent them to bed early. No dessert."

"Their real punishment is missing you." Sam smiled, drying his hands on a dish towel. "They were asking about you all day."

I'd taken the train down from New York that morning, going straight from Union Station to the White House, and straight from the White House to drinks with a friend from college. Even though I'd been in DC almost every week for the last four years, I'd done a bad job of keeping up with my friends in the capitol. Work always got in the way. And on the rare occasions it didn't, I just wanted to be here: hanging out with Jenna and Sam, helping myself to leftovers, pouring a glass of wine, collapsing at their kitchen table. Here, nothing was demanded of me. Here, I didn't have to be interesting or charming or smart. I only had to applaud, every now and then, when Derek and Luke showed me their latest dance moves.

The three of us chatted for a while, Jenna emptying the last of the pinot noir into my glass. Eventually Sam went up to bed; he had an early shift the next day. He was a doctor, too. Sam and Jenna had been together forever, since college, when I was an awkward teenager and regarded him as a demigod, when it seemed impossible that the boys around me might grow up to look like him. (Most of them didn't, of course; he was exceptionally handsome.) Sam was tall, suave, Korean American. Captain of the soccer team, premed, besotted with my sister. He was the nicest guy, but his self-assurance could be intimidating if you didn't know him. When I brought Ben to DC for the first time, he'd been unusually nervous. ("I feel like I need to impress him," Ben had said, jiggling his knee. "Like I need to win his approval.")

"So how did it go?" Jenna said. "Tell me everything."

"Huh." I tilted my head. "You're never this interested in my work."

"Don't pretend like it's the same thing," she said, pulling a face. We both found Henry Caine repulsive, but she voiced it more strongly than I did. Because my old job had required a measure of objectivity, and because that job had occupied so much of my life, the muscle had gone flabby: the ability to just *say it*, to call a thing what it was. Jenna, being a sane person, had no such issues. "That's when you were writing about him. This is *her*. What was she wearing?"

I smiled. "I was gonna take a picture for you, but I didn't want to be a total creep."

"Wait a second!" she said, jumping to her feet. She rummaged through a cabinet next to the fridge, and then pulled out a bar of dark chocolate, wagging it like a mafioso with a wad of cash. "This is what we need. Spill. Her clothes! Start with her clothes."

DC real estate, med school debt, two kids: all of this meant that Jenna and Sam lived modestly. But in her imagination, Jenna spent money like a millionaire. She read *Vogue* religiously; she watched real-estate porn on HGTV; she coveted all manner of beautiful things. At times, I'd been judgmental about this. It seemed so unserious, so *unpractical*, so unlike my sister. I'd asked her about it once. With everything she witnessed in her work, with the poverty and suffering so evident in her emergency room, how could she fantasize about things like Birkin bags and Viking ranges?

Jenna responded by shaking her head and laughing. "Sofe," she said. "I think about this sad stuff all day long. I need to come home to something *easy*. And, you know, I can be more than one thing at once."

She was right, of course. And eventually, she rubbed off on me. I became more attentive to the visual details, to the intricacies of fashion and decor, to the pleasure of beauty for beauty's sake. "God,

I love it," she said, sighing contentedly when I described Lara Caine's office. "It sounds kind of gorgeous."

"It kind of was."

"So you're going back tomorrow, right?"

I snapped off a square of chocolate. "I don't know. My plan was to get a million miles away from politics."

"It's just lunch. You're not committing to anything."

"But this biography is obviously a bad idea."

But Jenna saw the lift in my eyebrows; she heard the silent question mark at the end of that sentence. "Is it?" she said. "You don't know that yet. Come on, Sofie. Lunch with the First Lady? In the White House? When else are you going to get to do this?"

•

In hindsight, I can see how much that conversation was a turning point. How a decision, which at first seemed both stupid and craven, started spreading delicate roots.

For me, there were two people in the world whose opinions trumped everything: Ben and Jenna. It mattered to me whether Jenna thought a thing good or bad. And in her mind, there was a difference between the two Caines. On a subconscious level, Jenna's curiosity about Lara Caine began opening a door in my mind that seemed firmly shut.

"When else are you going to get to do this?" she'd said, and that was the other imperative that began to seduce me.

I soon surrendered myself to the constant pull of novelty: a one-on-one meeting with the First Lady. Lunch with the First Lady. Long conversations with the First Lady. And later, visits to the residence upstairs. Meals with her mother and sister. Meals with her daughters. Meals with all of them, together: three generations of women around the table, one happy Russian American family. With every week, the boundaries grew blurrier, and my curiosity only grew stronger. I was intoxicated by the newness of these experiences.

The world we live in has been mapped and conquered. The frontiers of the twenty-first century aren't continents and coastlines. Instead, they're the invisible mysteries, the abstract unknowns, the realms of math and science and beyond: things too tiny or too vast to behold. Among those invisible mysteries, I would argue, are the intricacies of an individual human life. That's a kind of exploration, too. To write your way into another person's life, to lay your hands on the moments that altered them, to gaze out through their eyes, to make that invisible mystery visible: it's like a plunge into an unknown world.

I was proud of my first book, but it never quite went the whole way. Raisa Gorbacheva had been dead for over a decade when I started writing. As hard as I tried, I could never manage to summon the living woman. This was different. This was the woman who shared the bed of the most powerful man in the world: and she was inviting me across the threshold. To share meals with her, to ask her endless questions, to watch her past come alive. Inviting me to understand her in a way that no one else in the world did. My curiosity was a factor, but so was my ego. How could I resist what Lara Caine was offering?

•

Lunch was served in the Family Dining Room, on the first floor of the residence. Despite the friendly-sounding name, the room was large and formal, with a footprint that could have easily swallowed my entire apartment.

A sparkling chandelier hung overhead, the light reflected in the glossy surface of the dining table. A gilt-framed mirror above the fireplace made the room look even bigger. Mrs. Caine sat at the head of the table, and I sat kitty-corner to her right, the two of us alone except for the occasional appearance of a White House butler, a gracious older man in a tuxedo. The weather had shifted overnight, a cold gray squall sweeping in. Rain spattered against the windowpanes, but the room remained immaculately silent, insulated by layers of glass.

Blini with smoked salmon and crème fraîche, followed by a green salad with sherry vinaigrette. China plates with red and gold borders, the presidential seal at the outer rim turned to twelve o'clock. When I left the house that morning, Jenna had told me to relax, to just *enjoy* myself, if nothing else. That was easier said than done. As we began to eat, we were equally ill at ease, both Mrs. Caine and I. The First Lady was rarely in the position of wanting a thing without guarantee of getting it. The power was momentarily in my hands, but this was an unpleasant feeling, because I didn't want to *do* anything with that power. We ate, and made small talk, and the butler slipped in and out to refill our water glasses.

Finally, Mrs. Caine cleared her throat and said, "Sofie, I'd like to be clear about a few things. I promise that I won't ask for approval or authorization over what you write. I know you won't agree to that."

I noticed that she said *won't*, rather than *wouldn't*. "Mrs. Caine," I said. "I'd like to be clear, too. I haven't agreed to *anything*. I'm not sure this is a very good idea."

"And why is that?"

"Because I've never worked like this before. And I might not enjoy the feeling of the subject watching over my shoulder." *And because trusting the word of a woman married to Henry Caine seems stupid*, I added silently.

She smiled. "Then I'll ask you to listen for a moment. Let me tell you how I would envision this working, and then you offer your protests, if you like. Okay?"

The First Lady told me what she could provide: access to her, of course, but also access to her mother and sister, both of whom frequently stayed in the White House residence. Her mother had kept journals during the Paris years; I could use those, too. There were old photo albums. And, if I decided it was necessary, she would encourage the president to cooperate with an interview.

"But I will insist on something," she said. "That we approach this chronologically. For so long I have been Mrs. Henry Caine. This is the only way the world knows me. But I'd like to tell the whole story, from the beginning. I wasn't always Mrs. Caine. I am more than just *this*." She gestured widely, pointing at the antique furniture, the red-and-gold Reagan china, or maybe the entire executive branch. "I don't care to spend our time talking about what my husband did or said yesterday. That's *him*. That's not my story. We're different people. Completely different. I would like the world to understand this."

I was surprised to see her cheeks turn pink and her breath grow rapid. Far from her usual hauteur, she suddenly looked so raw and needful, asking for something apparently only I could give her. It was uncomfortable to behold this expression and not say anything, but at that point, I still hadn't made up my mind.

So I changed the subject.

"Well, Mrs. Caine, one thing I've wondered is—why now? You could have told your story before the election, when it might have mattered more. Or you could wait until you leave Washington, when you'll be free to say whatever you want."

She nodded. "Because," she said. "I simply haven't been ready. But now I've realized a certain urgency. I'm getting older. My mother is getting older. How long will she be around? I want to have a record of what happened. I want my daughters to have that record, too. Wouldn't you want the same? To know what happened in your parents' lives?"

Without thinking, I blurted, "My parents have been dead for a long time."

"I'm sorry," she said, gazing steadily at me. "You know, my father died when I was eighteen. I don't think a person ever really gets over that loss."

The butler came in, placing a silver tray with tea service onto the table. Delicate cups and saucers in that same red-and-gold china and fingers of shortbread. Mrs. Caine poured the tea, dark as mahogany, into her cup and mine.

After a moment, she continued. "Sofie, I can see that you're hesitant. So what can I do? How can I show you that I plan to be candid?" She lifted an eyebrow. "You once asked about my father. The work he did in Paris. What if I answer that question right now?"

"With respect, Mrs. Caine," I countered, "you and I both know that's not such a big mystery. Your father was KGB." (She didn't even flinch—that was a yes! Inwardly, I did a little fist pump.)

"All right," she said. She lifted her tea, blowing away the ghostly steam, taking a small sip. "Leaving aside my father, then. Let me tell you about another person I lost. Alexander Kurlansky. Look for his name in the archives of *Le Monde*, or any other Parisian newspaper, around December 1985. You'll find a story about him. A young man who died a tragic death. They said it was suicide, but it wasn't suicide."

"Alexander Kurlansky," I said. "Who was he?"

She smiled sadly. "He was the great love of my life."

CHAPTER THREE

Ben and I had arrived in Split at the end of the tourist season, when the city was in full swing: warm nights, loud music, hectic happy hours. During one of those September evenings, when we were still adjusting from New York jet lag, sipping Aperol spritzes that matched the color of the Mediterranean sunset, I'd asked him, "Do you think this is going to work?"

He wrinkled his brow, gazing out at the sea. "Honestly?" he'd said. "Fifty-fifty."

"Did we just throw our lives away for fifty-fifty odds?"

Ben shook his head. "Could we have lived with ourselves if we didn't try?"

If we'd had our pick, we might have spent these months of exile in another country. Maybe a small town in Sicily, or the Costa del Sol in Spain. Somewhere with milder weather and better food, and languages with familiar rhythms. "But why Croatia?" our friends asked, to which we gave fuzzy answers. The truth was that Croatia didn't have a history of extraditing American citizens. If our government wanted to bring us home, they'd have a hard time doing it from here.

Until this was over, our lives didn't really belong to us. So much of this felt like we were just passing time. On a bright January morning, shortly after the visit from the TV producer, Ben and I sat on a bench on the corniche, overlooking the water. It was smart, we were told, to assume our apartment was bugged. The safest place to have a private conversation was in public.

My lunch with the TV producer was a few days away. Greta said that it was going to be fine—that *I* was going to be fine—but how much did Greta know about me? How could I trust her judgment of my capabilities?

Ben offered to practice with me. "I did this all the time, Sofe," he said. "Come on. You be you, and I'll be the producer. It's just like prepping a witness for cross-examination."

I blushed slightly. "You don't have to do this."

"I know I don't have to," he said. "I *want* to."

Ben sat up straighter. Mimed retrieving a pad and paper from his pocket, and frowned intently. "How do I look?" he asked. "Appropriately intimidating?"

"Close enough."

"Okay," he said. "So. Sofie Morse. Tell me about your work with the First Lady."

"We worked together for about nine months," I said. "She approached me in November, just after the election. She wanted me to write her biography."

"Nine months," Ben said. "You must have developed a good relationship in that time."

I nodded. "We did."

"So what changed?" he prompted. "Why did you decide to publish your story, instead of continuing with the biography?"

"Well," I said, "she shared certain information with me, and it was . . . important. Important enough that I couldn't justify keeping it to myself. The public deserved to know it. I knew it could damage the relationship. But I thought it was worth the risk."

Ben remained in character, solicitous sympathy creasing his forehead. "That must have been a difficult decision," he said. "I imagine the two of you had grown close."

"Yes." My heart thumped. "We had."

"And what happened after the story was published?" He leaned forward. "Did you ever talk to her again?"

Keep it simple, I reminded myself. *Find the kernel of truth and stick to it.*

"We did have a conversation," I said. Looking straight at him. Ignoring the sweat coating my palms, the heat flushing my neck. "It was complicated, of course. But we had our chance to clear the air."

"Was she angry? Did she see it as a betrayal?"

"It was an emotional conversation," I said, trying to keep my voice even-keeled. "But in the end, she understood that I had a job to do."

Ben kept jabbing with a few more questions, but I managed to parry them. Finally, he broke into a wide grin. "Look at you," he said.

The sun was high overhead. Workers on their lunch breaks bee-lined for the cafés. Though this place remained strange and foreign, there were fleeting moments when it felt like it was all going to be okay.

Ben took my hand and said, "You're a natural, Sofe."

•

During that first lunch at the White House, Mrs. Caine had told me to look up Alexander Kurlansky. The Wi-Fi on the train from Washington back to New York had been too shoddy to work with, so when I got home, I immediately took out my laptop and navigated to the *Le Monde* archive. A few minutes later, there was the article she had mentioned, which I translated from French into English:

> DECEMBER 26, 1985—PARIS: On Tuesday night, police discovered the body of 20-year-old Alexander Kurlansky in his apartment on rue Saint-Bernard. They responded to a call from his concerned roommates, who were unable to enter his locked bedroom. The cause of death has been ruled suicide by an overdose of sleeping pills. The police have said they suspect no foul play.
>
> Kurlansky worked at a small literary magazine called *Iskra*,

or *The Spark*, which publishes work by Soviet émigrés and dissidents. He was also a university student in Paris.

Alexander Kurlansky: "The great love of my life," Mrs. Caine had said. I tried searching for his name along with her name, in all various combinations, on the *Le Monde* archive, and then other French newspapers, and then the Internet as a whole. There was no trace of a relationship to be found. No public link existed between Lara Caine and Alexander Kurlansky. She had never spoken about him to anyone in the press.

Above, I heard footsteps in Maurice's apartment. I checked my watch: 10:00 p.m. on the dot. He would be turning off the lights in the living room, getting ready for bed. This town house showed its age, with creaky floorboards and drafty windows and warbling radiator pipes, but it was the first apartment I'd lived in where the flaws were a plus rather than a minus. I liked how the old quirks reminded me that this had once been a house designed for a single family, a building to bring people together rather than keep them apart.

Alexander Kurlansky, the Soviet dissident, employee of a magazine called *Iskra,* or *The Spark*. (A clever, ironic nod: *Iskra* was also the name of the magazine Lenin founded during his years of European exile, before the 1917 revolution.) I drummed my fingers on the keyboard. What to make of it? It was interesting, for sure. In the span of several hours, I'd learned two important facts about the First Lady. One was that her father had indeed been a KGB officer, and therefore a Communist Party loyalist. Two was that she had been in love with a young man who openly critiqued those KGB and Communist systems. Larissa Fyodorovna Orlova, the teenage girl in Paris, had been torn between starkly opposite loyalties.

Her boyfriend died in 1985. *They said it was suicide, but it wasn't suicide.*

And then her father died four years later, in 1989.

Were they linked? Were their deaths a coincidence? But this didn't feel like a coincidence.

I stared at the computer screen, my mind stuck in a cul-de-sac of speculation. It was nearly midnight by now. Ben had texted to say he was still at the office and would be for a while. In our bedroom, which faced the town house's small backyard, a thin whistle of winter air snuck under the window frame. The sheets felt cool and smooth, the comforter pleasantly heavy. I curled into a tight ball and dropped into a dreamless sleep.

•

Four years earlier, when Vicky assigned me to the White House beat, I had one requirement: that I could keep living in New York. Ben and I had only been married for a few months. I didn't want to live apart from him. I couldn't.

"Huh," Jenna had commented, when I told her about the arrangement. That I would remain based in New York and travel to Washington as needed. "So, basically, the exact opposite of what Mom and Dad did."

Too much ambition can make you brittle. My parents were competitive people—with the world, with each other—and it made them miserable. When I was little, my father took a job teaching at a college in Pennsylvania, a seven-hour drive from our town in New Jersey. Tenure, a named professorship, funding for his lab: How could he pass that up? But my mother's career was in New York, and there was no question of her leaving it. So he came home on Saturdays and Sundays, and she took care of us alone during the week. In retaliation for his leaving, she doubled down on her own work. Most of the time, the house was empty and quiet. My parents were like stars in the night sky: sparkling, coldly brilliant, the source of an impossible loneliness.

Ben was next to me when I woke up. The window in our bedroom faced north, the backyard visible through the window: the rosebushes, shrouded in burlap for the winter; the empty trellis rising from the vegetable bed. When we moved in, once we befriended Maurice, he asked if he could do some gardening in the backyard, which technically belonged to our ground-floor apartment. We said yes, of course, and it turned out that Maurice had a miraculous green thumb. There was an internal staircase that connected our two apartments, with locking doors at the top and the bottom. Eventually we gave Maurice a key to let himself in and out. It was a small price to pay for the bounty he shared with us: bouquets of roses in the spring, strawberries in June, tomatoes in August.

The coffee had just finished brewing when Ben emerged from the bedroom, wearing an old T-shirt and boxers, his eyes squinted behind his glasses.

"Did I wake you up?" I said, wincing. "Sorry. You should stay in bed."

"No, I was up." He yawned. "Coffee smells good."

We didn't cook much during the week, but on Saturdays and Sundays, Ben liked to make a real breakfast: a little bit of indulgence to offset the usual Greek yogurt and whole wheat toast. I'd texted him to tell him about my lunch with Lara Caine, but we hadn't yet talked in-depth about the idea. While the bacon sizzled in the skillet, and Ben whisked together batter for pancakes, he said, "So. This biography. What are you thinking?"

"I don't know," I said. "It seems risky."

"Risky how?"

"For starters, what if she tries to control it? What if she hates what I write and comes after me and makes our life hell?"

"Well, if you don't sign anything that you shouldn't—and you won't, because you're married to a lawyer—then she'll have a hard time making anything stick. She's a public figure. It would be almost impossible for her to claim libel. Can you grab the butter?"

I passed it to him, and Ben lopped a tablespoon into the hot frying pan and ladled out two circles of pancake batter. I told him about what I'd learned, the details about her father and Alexander Kurlansky, the question of her competing loyalties. The image was now engraved in my mind: the First Lady, passionately insisting that she wanted to tell her story, the *whole* story.

"I feel bad for her," Ben said. "It must be miserable, to be swallowed up by that man."

"But she has free will," I said. "If she hates it so much, she could just leave."

"And what would happen to her daughters? Can you imagine how ugly Caine would get during a custody battle? And what about her mother and her sister? I read that they're still waiting to get their citizenship. I'm not necessarily disagreeing with you," he said, sliding the pancakes onto two plates and drizzling them with maple syrup. "I'm just playing devil's advocate."

It was the week of Thanksgiving, and the neighborhood was beginning to transform. Christmas tree stands appeared along Third Avenue. Store windows on Lexington were decked in cotton snow and sequined ornaments. Workers strung delicate bulbs on the trees along Park Avenue, preparing for their lighting the following week.

Later that afternoon, as Ben and I walked back from the grocery store, he said, "It's a pretty big opportunity, Sofe."

"I know," I said. "I can't really imagine turning it down."

"So don't turn it down."

"But the whole reason I quit . . ." I shook my head. "I was getting to be so cynical."

"If she's telling you the truth, doing this won't be cynical."

We stopped outside our building. Ben dug in his pocket for his key. Above us, Maurice's windows glowed in the dusk. The sight of home, our sweet little home, invited retreat from the world. What if I just did nothing for a while? A couch, a soft blanket, a glass of wine, the coziness of the holidays. In theory, it sounded wonderful. In reality, I knew I'd hate it.

It came down to this: How could I know if Lara Caine was telling the truth? How could I *know*? As I stepped through the front door, strangely, it was Vicky's voice that popped into my head. *I'm not asking for perfect empiricism, honey.* An educated guess would have to be enough.

•

"Sofie," she said, when I called the next day. "I'm hoping you have good news for me."

But there was one more question I had to ask. "Mrs. Caine," I said. "You really aren't going to ask for approval? You really don't want to read what I write before it's published?"

"Certainly I would *like* to," she said. "And perhaps you'll choose to give me that courtesy. But I won't insist on it. You would never agree to a restriction like that, would you?"

"No," I said. "I wouldn't."

"So, there it is. It's a risk, but I must take that risk. And besides, you've already showed that I can trust you."

I frowned. "I have?"

"What I told you a few days ago, about my father," she said. "I imagine you're still on good terms with your old employer. You could have easily shared that with them. That revelation would be quite a story, wouldn't it? Lara Caine, daughter of the KGB? But you didn't. You kept it to yourself. I trust you, Sofie. Is that enough to convince you?"

I paused for a moment. *This might be a mistake*, an inner voice said. *But so what? Not doing it would be a mistake, too.*

"Okay," I said. "When do we begin?"

Most people, Irina Mikhailovna Orlova believed, reveal their essences from the very beginning. Such was the case with her second daughter, Larissa Fyodorovna. From the moment when the baby took her first breath on that April morning in 1970, it was clear to Irina that this was a good girl—a sweet and obedient girl who would never cause any trouble.

The swaddled baby was placed upon Irina's chest while she lay in bed at Grauerman Maternity Hospital in Moscow.

"Look at her eyes," Irina murmured. "She has her father's eyes. And see how calm she is. She barely makes a sound! You know how tired your mother is, don't you? And now you are letting her rest. Larissa. Lara. My good, sweet Lara."

The nurse, leaning over Irina's bed, smiled. "She's beautiful, Irina Mikhailovna."

Irina returned her smile. She was grateful for the nurse's kindness. She was grateful, too, for her private room, which insulated her from the harshest aspects of this Moscow hospital. The Soviet Union in the 1970s wasn't the most comfortable place for a woman to give birth; from down the hospital hallway came the cries of other women in labor, crammed three or four to a room. Sometimes they were kept alongside women undergoing abortions. But Irina didn't pay much heed to those ugly realities. She was exhausted, and drenched with new love. Her baby had a rosebud mouth that puckered in soft pulses as she slept.

"A second girl!" Irina said, touching her finger to Lara's eyebrow, the tiny hairs nearly invisible and utterly miraculous. The nurse had left the room. Now it was just Irina, whispering to her baby. "Your father will be so happy. Your sister, too."

Irina might have said that her prayers had been answered. She might have lit a candle before a glimmering gold icon, thanking Saint Anna of Kashin for delivering her a second child and for sparing Natasha, her older daughter, from the burden of having no siblings. An icon, a candle, a prayer: in a different decade, Irina might very well have done these things. But this was the Soviet Union, where the old religion was strictly forbidden.

In her superstition, Irina felt it was foolish not to give thanks for a blessing such as this. She and Fyodor had been trying for so many years; had endured so many cycles of disappointment and sadness. And now they had a second baby, peaceful and healthy, their tender deliverance. But Irina was a loyal citizen of the Soviet Union, a woman who would never dream of uttering a clandestine prayer or thinking untoward thoughts about Saint Anna of Kashin. So, to whom ought she give thanks? How to stave off the dark demon of superstition?

"You're perfect, aren't you?" Irina said to Lara. "Yes, that's it. You *are* my perfect girl. I can see how proud you will make us. I can see it already. You'll make your family so proud. You'll make your country so proud. I will help you in this, my darling."

That, Irina decided, would be her project. During those grim Soviet decades, the years of Stalin and Khrushchev and Brezhnev, Irina Mikhailovna was one of the few who had managed to improve her station. To prosper, even. This prosperity had cemented her love of her country. She would return her good fortune by raising a girl, and then a young woman, of whom the Soviet Union could be proud. Yes, she was certain of it, even from that first day in the Moscow hospital room: Lara would make her country proud.

◆

Irina Mikhailovna's own life had begun in very different circumstances. She was born in Leningrad in 1943, during World War II, while the city was suffering the long Nazi siege. Irina's parents died soon after she was born. They clung to life for as long as they could, reduced to eating rats and sawdust, but in the end starved to death, like so many others in Leningrad. The fact that baby Irina survived was a miracle.

Irina grew up in a crowded communal flat, raised by indifferent relatives, aunts and uncles to whom she was just another mouth to feed. But she was smart, and she studied hard, and when she was seventeen years old, she left Leningrad and enrolled at Moscow Pedagogical State Institute, where she trained to be a teacher. No matter the criticisms leveled against the Soviet Union—and Irina wasn't stupid, she knew there were many—she was always fiercely proud of the free, rigorous, excellent education she had received. Education was one of two things that changed her life. The other was marrying Fyodor Maximovich Orlov.

To be born into one kind of life, to die in a better kind of life: that takes a great deal of luck. Most citizens of the Soviet Union experienced none of this luck. There were only empty shelves. Hungry mouths. Stores with nothing for sale. By 1970, when Lara was born, the country was six years into Leonid Ilich Brezhnev's term as general secretary. It was a time of brutal corruption and repression. There was no such thing as privacy. The KGB had its tentacles in every apartment and every workplace.

This was the reality for everyone—even for a happy, attractive, well-connected young couple like Irina and Fyodor. The Orlovs loved to entertain and often had friends over for dinner. At the beginning of every meal, the first toast was drunk to the health of the general secretary.

"To Comrade Brezhnev!" Fyodor would say, lifting his vodka.

The guests would echo him loudly, to ensure that anyone who might be listening heard their vigorous agreement. Then, and only then, could they safely move on to toasting other subjects.

Power demanded deference. Well, Irina often thought, that was a small price to pay for this life. The Orlov family never went hungry. They always had what they needed. Besides, she could tell that Brezhnev was a kind man at heart. He loved cats and children and fast cars. She knew these things for a fact because the Orlov family lived at 26 Kutuzovsky Prospekt, in the same building as General Secretary Brezhnev. In fact, on the day that Irina brought Lara home from the hospital, she encountered Leonid Ilich Brezhnev in the courtyard: a rare but not unheard-of occurrence. He leaned over the pram and waggled his fingers at the baby.

"Congratulations," he said, straightening up, smiling at Irina, who was glowing with maternal pride. "She is a beautiful child."

◆

From the outside, the apartment building at 26 Kutuzovsky Prospekt looked like a massive ship. It had an ornate stone facade that stretched an entire city block, with columns and pediments and balconies. The overall effect was heavy and drab, but for the time and place, it passed for elegance. It was a privilege to live there, to enjoy the spacious apartments and the courtyard full of linden trees and grassy lawns. The building was stocked with families like the Orlovs, the high-ranking and well-connected members of the Communist Party.

"You'll spoil them," Irina chided, when her father-in-law, Maxim Ivanovich Orlov, came to visit the girls, bringing a new outfit for Natasha's doll and a silver rattle for baby Lara. Fyodor's parents lived in the same building. They visited often, and always brought gifts.

"Nonsense," Maxim said, as he knelt down on the plush oriental rug. Natasha was happily examining the doll-size velvet dress he had brought for her. "It would be impossible to spoil these girls. Now, Nataschenka. Your doll's name is Masha, yes? Tell me all about what Masha has been doing lately."

Irina smiled and shook her head as Maxim—a tall man with an impeccably groomed mustache, a major general in the GRU, an old war hero—indulged Natasha with sincere questions about the imaginary inner life of Masha. He loved his granddaughters. He would have done anything for them. They were one of the great joys of his life.

It all comes from him, Irina sometimes thought. *We owe everything to this man.*

Fyodor, unlike his wife, had been born into this comfortable world. The Orlovs were long-standing members of the *nomenklatura,* the Soviet elite. As a boy, Fyodor had gone to superior schools, and always wore good clothing, and always had enough to eat, and took vacations at plush resorts on the Black Sea. Now, as a grown man, Fyodor had a cushy career as a KGB colonel. The family lived in comfort that was unimaginable to ordinary citizens of the Soviet Union.

Such comfort, in fact, that Irina had recently decided that she wouldn't be returning to her job as a teacher. She had her hands full with the two girls. The family didn't need her income. Anyway, money didn't take a person far in the Soviet Union, where theoretically everything was free: the housing, the education, the food, all of it handed out by the state. Fyodor's salary had nothing to do with this nice life. His connections were what made the difference.

◆

Lara has no memory of those early years. She was only four when the family left the Soviet Union. She grew up hearing stories from her family about Moscow, stories tinged with a rosy nostalgia. For a long time, this made Lara sad. She was the only one who didn't remember the yellow birch trees, or the countryside dacha, or the snow falling on Red Square. It would take Lara many years to understand the manufactured quality of that rosiness. That the rest of her family, like her, would actually prefer to never go back.

When the Orlovs left the Soviet Union, Natasha was old enough to bring her memories with her. One of Natasha's earliest memories is from the autumn of 1970, when Lara was still a baby. The family was at the dacha outside of Moscow, where they often went on the weekends. It was nighttime, and Natasha was supposed to be asleep, but she was restless. She decided to get out of bed and snoop around. She crept into the room where her parents slept, which also held Lara's crib.

Baby Lara was awake, her eyes wide open. In the dim darkness, Natasha waved a hand above the baby's face. Lara's eyes tracked the hand back and forth. Natasha stopped waving. Lara's eyes stopped moving. Natasha's heart began to pound. The perfect synchronization was disturbing. Here was this baby, who didn't say or do anything, who was proving a very boring addition to the family, and yet—she was *watching.* She seemed to see *everything.* Natasha fled the room, jumped into bed, and pulled the quilt above her head. But even with a wall between them, she had the creepy, unshakable sense that her little sister was still spying on her.

CHAPTER FOUR

We began meeting once a week. Afternoons spent chatting over tea in her East Wing office, lunches in the White House dining room. Despite her formality, and despite her husband's politics, I found Mrs. Caine remarkably easy to spend time with. It was like she assumed a certain blankness in everyone she met, symmetrical to the blankness she often exhibited.

Gabi always met me at the visitors' entrance and escorted me into the White House. The aides and assistants in the East Wing always smiled politely, and Mrs. Caine's secretary always asked how the trip from New York had been.

"Do they know why I'm here?" I asked Gabi, on the third visit.

"They don't *not* know," she responded, talking over her shoulder as she speed-walked ahead of me. "It's not really a topic of conversation. FLOTUS hates gossip, and everyone has plenty on their plate. No offense, Sofie, but you're not the most exciting thing happening in the White House on any given day."

Our first official working lunch was in early December. We were again in the Family Dining Room, where the table had been laid with three places. I looked at Mrs. Caine, quizzical. "I've asked my mother to join us," she explained.

A moment later, the door opened, and Irina Mikhailovna Orlova entered the room. She looked so much like her daughter—strong cheekbones, wide blue eyes—but right away, the difference was clear. Irina had an outspoken bluntness that her daughter lacked. She kissed me on both cheeks, lowered herself smoothly into her chair, shook out her napkin with a matador-like wrist snap, and began talking.

"So let me tell you about my life," Irina said, in an accent considerably thicker than her daughter's. "Oh, I don't like to talk about it, but for the sake of my Larochka, yes, yes, I will tell you everything."

What had she seen? Well, what *hadn't* she seen? Irina was born in besieged Leningrad during World War II; she had been a teenager when Sputnik was launched and the Berlin Wall was built; a young mother during the Brezhnev years; a loyal wife abroad during glasnost and perestroika; and a widow as the Soviet Union began to crumble. That last was the point she wanted to emphasize.

"My beloved Fedya," she said in a gravelly voice (I would later learn she was a lifelong smoker). "He would be so proud to see his Larochka like this. Like a queen, no? He knew that she was special, ever since she was a girl. I knew it, too, but a father's love for his daughter is a particular thing. No, it cannot be replaced, not by anything. This is why it was such a tragedy, a *tragedy*"—she smacked her palm against the table, causing the silverware to jump—"that Fedya was taken from his daughters when they needed him most. I was helpless. What did I know? The world was falling apart around us. What a tragedy. What an injustice. Larissa's father was a great man. Why are you not writing this down?"

"Mama," Mrs. Caine murmured. She touched Irina's hand and gestured at my digital recorder.

Irina lifted her eyebrows. "Ah," she said. "I see. Good idea. As I was saying. I became a widow on February 9, 1989. It was the worst day of my life. The very worst. Of course, it might have been February 6, or 7, or 8 when Fedya died. Or even earlier than that. Who knows? They tell you what they want to tell you. They said he died of pneumonia while being held in Lubyanka. Ha! They must have thought I was an idiot, to believe this story. Pneumonia! I will tell you this much, Fedya died from a bullet in the head. My husband was executed for treason. *So-called* treason."

"Wow" was all I managed to say.

"*Mamochka*," Mrs. Caine said, more firmly this time. "This is like gibberish to Sofie. We have to begin the story from the beginning. Yes? As we discussed."

Irina pursed her lips. After a beat, she nodded. From there the lunch proceeded in more orderly fashion. Mrs. Caine would prompt Irina ("Mama, tell Sofie about the time that . . ."), and Irina would smile in recognition.

"Ah, yes, of course," Irina would begin. Her smile was wide and slightly wicked. She had a tendency to interrupt her own stories with harsh barks of laughter, a bleak "Ha!"

I liked her immediately. From those very first moments, it was obvious that Irina was going to be a godsend. She had an excellent memory (a feature shared by mother and daughter), which she unspooled with off-the-cuff lightness. As we ate our poached salmon and cold vegetable terrine, and drank our black tea, Irina recalled the week Lara was born. My eyes widened at the intricate details. I wondered how she could possibly remember so much, from the tinge of jaundice in Lara's skin to the nubbly pink blanket in the crib. When she noticed my expression, she barked that "Ha!" again.

"Why are you so surprised by this, Sofie?" she said. (How easy to imagine Irina as a teacher, once upon a time. Commanding and capable, with her hair swept back into a no-nonsense bun.) "These are my memories. My most treasured possessions. I kept journals, too. I will look for them next time I'm in New York."

Lunch was cleared, and an aide appeared to summon the First Lady to her next meeting. Irina stood up and kissed me on both cheeks in departure, declaring that she was very glad to know me. After Irina left, Mrs. Caine gestured for me to remain for a moment.

"Sofie," she said. "We're clear about what this is, yes? Everything I am telling you, everything my mother is telling you—this is meant for the biography only."

I nodded. "Right."

She stared at me. It had a chilling quality. "I am not going to interfere with the way you work," she said. "But this is my condition. I don't want these details appearing in a story here, a story there. Everything is for the book only. Perhaps we will draw up paperwork, to make it official. But we understand the same thing, yes?"

•

Did we understand the same thing?

It felt foolish to trust in that, without any formal agreement to codify it. I was used to having rules. I *liked* having rules. The inherent combativeness of the White House beat—I had one job to do; my sources had another—was made easier by the fact that they always had other reporters to talk to, and I always had other sources. This biography was different. At the end of the day it was just the two of us, embarking on this project based on trust alone.

In the months that followed, I kept waiting for the paperwork Mrs. Caine had mentioned, but it never came. Part of me wondered whether I ought to follow up, but a larger part of me decided not to mess with what appeared to be working. Maybe it wasn't such a big deal. Even without any official agreement, other factors would keep the project in balance.

Like the promise of mutually assured destruction. We both had leverage. If I published a story with the details Mrs. Caine shared with me, she could immediately turn off the tap and stop cooperating. So I had to respect that privacy. But if I found out she had lied to me, any future information would be worthless, and I could go ahead and publish whatever I wanted. So she had to respect the truth. It wasn't a perfect solution, to be sure. But it seemed workable.

Dismiss one concern. Dismiss another. I can see, from here, how easily I was carried away. That what I had with Lara Caine was solid; that it was good. When we want to believe a story, we'll do everything we can to maintain that belief. Often a story is all you have. When life gets complicated, when every easy comfort has been taken away: the story is what you cling to.

Some might call it a crutch, but I've always thought: What's so bad about a crutch? It bears some of the weight you can't bear yourself. It allows the injured part of you to heal.

•

At breakfast one morning in January, in the Morse-Chung kitchen, Luke looked up at me with a curious expression. "Auntie Sofie," he said. "Are you back at your job?"

"Well," I said, wrapping my hands around my coffee mug. "Not really."

"Five minutes!" Jenna called out, as she sliced two PB&J sandwiches into triangular halves. "Luke, will you please finish your cereal?"

"What does 'not really' mean?" Luke said. He lifted one solitary Cheerio from his bowl, floating alone in a spoonful of milk, and slurped it delicately.

"Yeah, Auntie Sofie. You're here *all* the *time*," Derek said, pulling a dramatic face. His bowl was empty, only a film of milk in the bottom. The twins were sitting side-by-side at the counter. Derek started kicking his feet against the cabinet. Metronomic thumps: kick, *kick*, kick, *kick*.

"Cut that out," Sam called from across the kitchen.

Luke gazed at me, another Cheerio trembling in his milk-filled spoon. He was so sweetly serious about everything. "I'm not writing for the newspaper anymore," I explained. "A long time ago, before you were even born, I wrote a book. Now I'm writing another book. And to do research for it, I have to be here in Washington. So I'm going to be staying with you guys a lot. Is that okay?"

"You should really ask our parents," he said solemnly. Then he ate the Cheerio.

"Okay!" Jenna said, clapping her hands. She held up two matching parkas, green for Luke and blue for Derek. In unison, the boys slid off the kitchen stools and shouldered themselves into the jackets. "Say goodbye to Auntie Sofie," she said.

"I'll be back next week," I said, ruffling the tops of their heads. Luckily, the twins had inherited Sam's dark and beautiful hair; nothing like our mouse-brown Morse family genes. "I love you guys."

"Love you, too," they chorused, as Jenna hustled them out the back door and toward the driveway, where the car was already idling. She had slipped out a few minutes earlier to warm up the RAV4 in the winter chill. It baffled me, how my sister did everything that she did. She was like some genius quarterback of motherhood, scanning the field and anticipating her family's needs, seizing her openings in a way that looked fluid and effortless in the moment but that, I knew, left her utterly drained at the end of the day.

After the back door slammed shut, Sam and I were alone in the suddenly quiet kitchen. His shift at the hospital started later that morning, so he'd take the Metro to work. He began to clear the dishes from the counter, but I said, "Oh, don't do that. I'll clean up."

He shrugged. We'd done this dance many times.

"Thanks, Sofe," he said. "I feel bad, though. You're always cleaning up after us."

"It's the least I can do. Besides, Ben does all the dishes at home."

"How is he?" Sam said, leaning against the counter, sipping his coffee. Sam was wearing a faded GEORGETOWN SOCCER shirt from college, which still fit him perfectly. "Is he stuck on that awful deal?"

"The pharma acquisition?" I shook my head. "That's over. On to greener pastures. Bankruptcy restructuring for a German grocery chain."

Sam laughed. "Thrilling."

I smiled. "He misses you guys. It's been, what? Since Fourth of July?"

"Way too long," Sam said. "Get him to come down with you next time."

The month before, Ben and I had spent Christmas with his family in Connecticut, just as we did Thanksgiving, just as we did every holiday. When we began dating, I think Ben's mother had been secretly pleased to find out I was parentless. Not in a malicious way, just in a practical way. I came with no strings attached, no compromises required. Jenna and Sam always spent the holidays with Sam's family in Los Angeles, or now that the boys were getting older, here in Washington. It was strange, sometimes, to think how little these parts of my life overlapped, the Ben part and the Jenna/Sam part. They loved one another, but they could go for months at a time without seeing one another, and this was perfectly natural, but it always made me a bit sad.

We chatted idly while I did the dishes and Sam finished his coffee. Later he went out for a run, and I had time to kill before my midday train back to New York, so I set up with my laptop at the kitchen table, planning to transcribe my interview recordings from earlier that week. The kitchen was silent, interrupted only by the gentle hum of the refrigerator and the occasional car driving past.

It had taken me until now, until mid-January, to figure out a basic strategy for tackling the interview recordings. There were software programs that produced automatic transcriptions, but none of them were entirely perfect, especially with the Russian names and phrases sprinkled through the conversation. I couldn't rely on the software to capture everything, so I went through the transcriptions manually to be sure: reading the text while listening to the recordings, pausing when I had to correct something, to smooth out a phrase that the software had misheard.

But often, when the audio was paused, I found myself lingering in the transcript. It wasn't just what the Orlov women said; it was the *way* they said it. The dreaminess in Irina's eyes when she remembered the lilacs and linden trees at the family's dacha. The bemused curl to Mrs. Caine's smile when she recalled her older sister's antics. Their stories were so *real*, and for some reason, the transcript failed to reflect that vividness. I wanted to capture that shimmering sense of reality, of the dimensions and places hovering just behind the written word, the people and places who were already—I was more than a little frightened to realize—grabbing hold of my imagination.

The transcript was cluttered with my augmentations, which began small, and then grew into something else entirely. I didn't really want to admit it, because it made absolutely no sense. What self-respecting biographer begins writing the biography when the research is still underway? When the research has, in fact, barely begun? When she has no idea of where the story is going?

There were ways of justifying this: immersing myself in the material while it was fresh, getting a jump-start on things. But the truest explanation was also the simplest one. I was doing this because I wanted to be doing this. Because, for reasons I didn't understand, it felt completely right.

It was a May day in 1974. Natasha had just gotten home from school. She sat at the table, her legs dangling from the edge of the chair, and babbled while Irina bustled about the kitchen in their apartment on Kutuzovsky Prospekt.

"And *then* it was my turn, and I leaned very close to the glass. He was so small, Mama! Anya's sister went to see him last year, and Anya said her sister saw him *move*. He moved his hands! But I looked very hard, and he didn't move, not one bit." Natasha shook her head gravely. "I wasn't scared at all. He looked just like a little doll."

"Good girl," Irina said. "You shouldn't be frightened. Lenin was a great man."

"My teacher gave each of us a flower. I wanted to keep it. I asked her, why does he need the flower? He's dead. But she scolded me and told me I had to leave it there, that it was selfish to keep the flower for myself. But I'm *not* selfish." Natasha pouted. "I just thought it was pretty. That's all."

"Well, Nataschenka," Irina said. "You should always listen to your teacher."

"Why?"

"Because she's your teacher. She knows best."

This was an annual pilgrimage for schoolchildren in Moscow: a visit to Vladimir Ilich Lenin's tomb in Red Square. For the formation of young Soviet minds, his embalmed body was a useful metaphor. Look upon the greatness of Lenin—brave leader of the October Revolution, almighty father of the Soviet Union—and see how it is unaffected by death! The past was glorious and perfect. It was immune to rot and decomposition. In fact, it was immune to change entirely.

Natasha had enjoyed the field trip, mostly because it meant a break from the usual classroom routine. It had been fun to visit Red Square, to step inside the sleek black tomb, to experience the reverent hush, all of which made her feel very grown-up. It was also fun to come home and brag to her mother about her adventures. This was Natasha's favorite time of day, when afternoon shaded into evening, when her mother made her a teatime snack (cottage cheese pancakes called *sirniki*, served with sour cream), when her father would soon return from work, and their family unit would once again be cozy and complete.

Across the table, her four-year-old sister gazed at her with wide and rapturous eyes. Recently, Natasha had realized that Lara's admiration came with advantages. Natasha noticed the uneaten sirniki on her little sister's plate. Her stomach grumbled; the older girl was still hungry. When Irina's back was turned, Natasha reached across the table and swiped the sirniki for herself. Lara glanced down at the plate and then up at her sister. Natasha held a finger to her lips.

Lara smiled. She didn't mind. She was good at keeping other people's secrets.

◆

That evening, when Fyodor got home, he had a stricken look on his face.

"I've just been told," he said to Irina. "They're stationing me in Paris."

"Paris!" Irina exclaimed. Though they had been expecting news like this, Paris was better than she could have imagined. "But this is wonderful, Fedya! Why the long face?"

"Because," he said, frowning with worry, "it ought to have gone to my colleague. You remember Daniil? He has fluent French, and they promised him this post, and he has been preparing for months. And now this! I don't understand it. I don't speak a word of French!"

Fyodor Maximovich was an officer in the First Directorate of the KGB. The KGB was a sprawling organization (a state within a state, it was often called), and the First Directorate was one of its most elite units. The officers in this division were responsible for gathering foreign intelligence about other countries, work that necessarily took them abroad. First Directorate officers like Fyodor were stationed in embassies throughout the world, working under diplomatic cover as they spied on foreign governments and enemies of the Soviet Union.

Fyodor and Irina knew that the posting would come soon. They imagined where it might take them: Warsaw? Berlin? Oslo? What would it be like when they got there? This was their greatest privilege yet: to daydream about experiencing life beyond the Soviet Union. In a country that was a so-called worker's paradise, the best hope for a KGB officer was the chance to raise his family in a capitalist society. The irony was deadly, and therefore unspoken.

Even the training that Fyodor received as a First Directorate officer brought with it certain perks. To prepare the officers for the decadent ways of Western capitalism—rather like using a live vaccine to inoculate against a virus—Fyodor and his colleagues were permitted to read *Time* and *Le Monde* and to watch American movies, which were prohibited among ordinary Soviet citizens. At the Red Banner Institute, the elite KGB training facility outside Moscow, Fyodor spent happy afternoons watching Gary Cooper stare down a posse of outlaws. After all, one had to know one's enemy.

Fyodor paced across the kitchen. He seemed genuinely agitated about his lack of qualifications for this post. Irina thought her husband was being too modest. Perhaps he didn't speak French; perhaps he lacked experience in cultivating agents, which, yes, was a crucial skill at such an important station as Paris. But Fyodor was a well-liked man, and that counted for a lot. For more, perhaps, than he cared to admit.

"Tell me, Fedya," Irina urged. "Tell me exactly what he said."

His superior at the center explained how it would go. Fyodor would become the military attaché at the Soviet embassy in Paris. Operating under that diplomatic cover, but in truth working for the KGB, he would build a network of agents and informants. Typically, an officer could expect a foreign posting to last five years or less. But Fyodor's superior told him that his posting could very well be longer than that.

Why? Well, the KGB had suffered a major intelligence breach in 1964. Most of the officers stationed in Paris had their covers blown and were hurriedly forced to return to the Soviet Union. Even a decade later, the KGB network in Paris remained anemic. The KGB desperately needed to rebuild, and for that, they needed a new approach. It took a long time for an officer to seduce an agent, to build trust and rapport—months, even years. It was an extraordinarily personal relationship, that between officer and agent, involving the riskiest intimacies. All too frequently, the officer was summoned home at the worst time, just when his agent was beginning to provide useful intelligence. So why the rush? Why rotate men like Fyodor through these postings faster than was necessary?

The superior shrugged as he offered this explanation. "We are screwing ourselves, Fyodor Maximovich, when we ask our officers to move around so often. And for what reason? So we will keep you there longer. You'll see. It will be better all around."

Fyodor considered his wife to be the sharpest person he had ever known. That day, recounting the exchange, he was anxious for Irina's assessment. "It doesn't make sense, Ira," he insisted. "They've never done such a thing before."

"But, Fedya," Irina said reasonably. "It's not for you to question why this is happening. What would be the point? You do what you are told. Anything except that, you're asking for trouble. Besides, this is good news. Why should we bite the hand that feeds us?"

Not for him to question why—but this was almost impossible

for Fyodor. He liked to understand how things worked, how they fitted together, how this part connected with that part. This inherent curiosity could be useful in his work. The best way to seduce a potential agent was to simply *listen*, and Fyodor was an excellent listener, always fully engaged with what a person was saying. Always wanting to know more, and more, and more.

But this curiosity collided dangerously with the second imperative of his work: to be a good cog in the KGB machine. What Fyodor lacked was the ability to keep his curiosity to himself; to hold it close and private, so that it didn't cause trouble.

Eventually, Irina succeeded in calming him down. He couldn't always have the answer. Life was full of mystery. In this case, he would simply have to trust in the system that had raised him.

◆

Of course, Irina saw what her husband saw. There was something strange afoot. A longer-than-usual tenure in Paris? Things like this didn't simply *happen* for no good reason. But she meant it when she said that it wasn't smart to ask questions. In the KGB, a person always did as they were told. Dissension carried too high a price.

Besides, Paris would be a wonderful adventure. After the initial shock, Fyodor became excited, too. He drew his daughters to his lap, one on each knee. "We're going abroad, my sweethearts," he said. He bounced his knees, and Natasha shrieked with delight. "Can you believe it, Nataschenka! We're going to live in another country!"

It happened that Fyodor's father was over for dinner that night. Irina had made beef stroganoff, which was his favorite. "This is excellent, Irochka," Maxim said. "My compliments, as always."

Fyodor was joking and teasing the girls, giving fantastical answers to Natasha's questions. ("Oh, yes, darling, they have cars in Paris. Cars bigger than you've ever seen. Cars bigger than this kitchen!") Maxim suggested they toast to the good news. As they raised their vodka, Irina looked across the table and met her father-in-law's eye. He stared right at Irina as he spoke, a slight lift to his eyebrows: "To your new life." In that moment, she felt the realization like the loud *clang* of a bell. A bone-deep vibration, impossible to ignore.

Not for another fifteen years would Irina receive a definitive answer to her question. But she didn't need Maxim to say the words in order to know that they were true. Maxim loved his son very much. He wanted him to thrive and succeed. But his main desire—the desire he shared with every parent—was that his child be safe. As comfortable as he made their life in Moscow, as well-connected as he was, Maxim could still not change the air his son breathed.

To possess a cushy job, a nice apartment, luxuries like Swiss chocolate and English tea—this was more than any ordinary Soviet citizen could dream of. Maxim recognized this; he also recognized that Fyodor hadn't asked for it, nor was he asking for anything more. But when the father looked at the son with a dispassionate clarity, he saw that the son was fundamentally ill-suited to this life. Sooner or later, if they stayed in Moscow, Fyodor would ask too many questions. He would let his curiosity get the better of him. He would irritate someone powerful. He would get himself into real trouble. So Maxim pulled the highest party strings he could. Maxim arranged to send his son away, for him to receive the safest posting possible, and for that posting to last indefinitely.

Eventually, years later, Maxim confided all of this in Irina. He was, he told her, rather proud of himself for pulling it off. And why shouldn't he be? For a long time, it seemed like Paris was the perfect solution. It seemed like he had rescued his son—and by extension, the entire Orlov family—from the worst possibilities.

CHAPTER FIVE

There were occasional last-minute change of plans. One day in February, when her daughters were home sick from school, Mrs. Caine decided to work from the White House residence. Our lunch was moved to the private family dining room on the second floor. It would be my first time setting foot in the residence.

Gabi led me upstairs and knocked on the door to the dining room. Mrs. Caine looked up, glancing over the edge of her reading glasses. She was wearing a simple white turtleneck, and her hair was pulled into a bun. She looked tired, maybe fighting the same cold as her girls. Her face was bare of her usual makeup.

"Sit anywhere you like, Sofie," she said. "Just one moment. I don't want to lose my place."

The dining room table was covered with papers, and a notepad at her elbow was filled with meticulous handwriting. I busied myself with setting up my recorder, but mostly I just watched her. She shuffled through an array of lists and charts, stopping frequently to make notes. Nearby were a tufted box of Kleenex and a torn-open bag of Ricola cough drops. There was a smudge of blue on the side of Mrs. Caine's right hand, where it had rubbed against the ink. Several minutes passed. She made a series of ticks, cross-referencing the list with another document; she was so absorbed by the work that I felt invisible.

"There," Mrs. Caine said, finally setting aside her papers and removing her reading glasses. "Enough for now, I think."

"Is this for the state dinner?" I asked, tilting my head to get a better look.

She nodded. "After our wedding, I was so relieved that I would never have to make another seating chart again. But this? This is like ten weddings at the same time."

"You can't delegate this kind of thing to your staff?"

"I could, but they will get something wrong. It's very difficult, satisfying so many people at once. Very difficult, but not impossible."

She was quiet for a moment, gazing at me. She seemed to enjoy these little pauses. In the early days, the silence seemed like a test, but now I understood that these pauses were more benign. They gave her time to process her thoughts; to prepare what she wanted to say next. I cleared my throat and said, "This is a lovely room. The wallpaper is beautiful."

She smiled, her eyes narrowing. "Funny. I'm beginning to forget what you have and haven't seen, Sofie. You've never been in this room?"

I shook my head. "I've never been up to this floor."

Mrs. Caine glanced over her shoulder, toward a doorway in the wall. From that direction came the sound of water running and dishes clinking. "There is a small kitchen through there," she said. "The chefs are exceptional, of course, but my mother also likes to cook. This room is where we eat most of our meals. When we moved in, I wanted everything in this room restored to Mrs. Kennedy's original decoration. The table is the only thing that isn't antique. The girls usually do their homework here. Their markers and pencils get everywhere." Mrs. Caine spread her arms wide. "And now it's where I feel most comfortable making a mess, too."

I could see why she liked this room: it was elegant, but less formal than the rest of the White House. My eye kept catching on the wallpaper. "Do you mind?" I asked, standing up from the table and moving closer to the wall. "It's very pretty. Very unusual."

"Those are battle scenes from the American Revolution," Mrs. Caine said.

The wallpaper displayed an intricately painted landscape. It was like stepping inside a diorama. There were pale blue skies, shading into gold along the horizon. Rich greenery, lush and almost junglelike. Stone cliffs and bouldered outcroppings, flat clearings and distant waterways, and red-coated figures dotted throughout the landscape. The fact that these were battle scenes was only apparent when you got up close. With a step back, the bloodshed and conflict were transmuted into beauty. Strange to think that the Kennedys had eaten their meals in this same room, surrounded by these same images.

"She knew how to make a statement," Mrs. Caine said.

"That she did," I said, squinting at what might have been the battle of Yorktown.

"It's unfortunate," she said. "What a confusion this house has become. Every First Lady wanting to leave her own mark on the decoration, when Mrs. Kennedy did it best. It's insulting for other people to come along and change it."

As I sat back down at the table, I noticed the scrapes and dings pockmarking the wooden surface. The mundane evidence of her girls doing their math and science homework, while literally surrounded by history.

"Well," I said. "Maybe those First Ladies just wanted to keep up with the times. And everyone has their own taste."

"Everyone has their own taste," Mrs. Caine said. "But not everyone has *good* taste."

(Later, when I recounted this exchange to Jenna, she laughed. "Oh God, that's perfect," she said. "Absolutely perfect. I mean, this can't surprise you, right? The woman wouldn't be caught dead in anything less than Valentino.")

My recorder had been running for only a few minutes when our conversation ("Now where were we?" Mrs. Caine said. "The summer we moved to Paris, yes?") was interrupted by a loud clatter from the kitchen next door, like something being dropped. There was a muffled curse.

"Mama?" Mrs. Caine called, rising from her seat.

She gestured for me to follow. We found Irina in the kitchen, wearing an apron, her hands planted on her hips. She was glaring down at the offending saucepan.

"Mamochka, why don't you ask for help with these things?" Mrs. Caine said, bending down to retrieve the pan from the floor.

"Help," Irina said, waving an exasperated hand. "If I ask for help, that makes me a helpless old woman. And then you will get rid of me. You will put me out to pasture and wait for me to die, like an old cow that won't give any milk."

Irina glanced over. She caught my amused expression and smiled in return. Often, I think, Irina hammed up the doomy-gloomy-Russian bit for my benefit.

"Sonechka," she said, crooking a finger. "Come try this. Tell me what you think."

A pot of borscht, deep red and fragrant, was simmering on the stove. Irina lifted a spoonful and passed it to me. I blew on it until it was cool enough to try. The soup was delicious: salty, savory, fatty, with an acidic punch of jammy sweetness from the beets.

"You made this?" I said.

"Of course I made this," Irina said. "You think I would let one of these American chefs make borscht for me? Come, sit down, Sonechka. You need to eat."

The two women bustled around, setting the kitchen table for our lunch. The rectangular room was surprisingly modest, with white wooden cabinets and Formica counters and an island in the middle. Mrs. Caine assembled a tray with bowls of borscht and slices of bread to bring to her daughters. "Emily and Marina love my mother's cooking," she said. "Especially when they're not feeling well. This is a treat for them. I'll be back in a minute."

As the First Lady disappeared through the doorway, Irina said, "They're good girls, you know. Even growing up in the White

House, they are good and ordinary girls. Larissa has made sure of that."

•

That day in February was a turning point, a breaking of the seal. Going forward, we mostly met in the residence. Lara and I often shared meals in the family kitchen or talked in the West Sitting Hall, with its graceful half-moon window.

Parallel to my conversations with the First Lady, I also began interviewing her mother. Irina spent most of her time in the sunny Solarium on the third floor of the residence, surrounded by books and half-completed knitting projects. Our weekly conversations were long and meandering, filled with detail and digression, in which she frequently grabbed my hand and said things like, "Oh, Sonechka, it feels so good to talk about this, I can't tell you how good it feels." Conversations in which Irina professed that she trusted me absolutely and was coming to adore me like a friend—and yet, in which she managed to avoid answering any questions she didn't want to answer.

For instance: Was she living in the White House? (It sure seemed like she was.) Was that her bedroom, just across the hall from the Solarium? And, for that matter, was Natasha living here, too? I never got a straight answer from her. She was also cagey on more substantive matters. I often thought back to our very first conversation, when Irina had burst into the room and talked about Fyodor being executed: *Treason. So-called treason.*

"Irina Mikhailovna," I'd asked, one day in the Solarium. "Forgive me, I'm jumping ahead a little. But I'm curious. What happened to make the KGB accuse your husband of treason?"

"Ah," she said, shaking her head. "Nothing happened! They told some story about Fedya spying for the Americans. But this was absurd. Even they knew it was absurd. They invented it out of thin air. Why did they kill him? I suppose they killed him because they felt like killing him."

"But surely there was *something* that made them—"

"No, Sonechka, there was nothing. Only their own brutality."

As dismissible as Irina claimed the KGB's suspicions to be, the idea stuck with me. Lara's father, spying for the Americans? The portrait of Fyodor coalescing from their stories—open-minded and inquisitive, sometimes at his peril—certainly made it seem possible. Could this be the link between his death and the death of Alexander Kurlansky, which I'd read about in the *Le Monde* archives?

But Lara meant what she said about sticking to chronology. When I brought it up, she responded, "In time, Sofie. We'll get there soon enough. Now, where was I?"

In the dining room and the kitchen, filled with the scent of Irina's cooking, and in the armchairs in the West Sitting Hall, bathed in wintry afternoon light: it was like we'd entered a different world. There was a sharp distinction between the public-facing portions of the White House and the private residential areas. Lara's husband may have been the president, but this was clearly *her* home.

There was a steady parade of visitors through these rooms. Irina liked to entertain, and she treated the entire White House residence like her living room. Lara told me how her mother played piano late into the night, added chairs to the dinner table for last-minute guests, forced her granddaughters to recite verses of Pushkin, just as she had forced her own daughters when they were little. Once, passing through the East Sitting Hall, I ran into a group of women, divided into tables of four. It turned out to be Irina's weekly bridge game.

"Come here, Sofie!" Irina commanded. "You must meet everyone. This is Tatiana Ivanovna, my dear old friend from Moscow who lives in New York now. And this is Betty. Do you know Betty? Her husband is in charge of the army." (By this, she meant that Betty's husband was the secretary of defense.)

Irina seemed happiest when she was holding court over this babelesque flock of elegant older women. There were expats like her dear old friend Tatiana Ivanovna: women whose husbands had made a fortune in post-1991 Russia, eventually fleeing when the government targeted those fortunes. There were friends from New York: Irina's Park Avenue neighbors, her tennis partner at the River Club. Then there were the Washington wives, Mrs. Secretary of State and Mrs. Majority Whip, who relished the minor misbehavior of gambling and gin and tonics on a Tuesday afternoon. Irina flitted around, refreshing drinks and spreading bits of gossip. She was eminently suited to the role of hostess; much more suited than Lara, who, after all, was the official White House hostess. I found myself wondering whether the First Lady minded this.

"Mind it?" Natasha said, during one of our interviews, when I posed the question. "Never. Lara is delighted that she doesn't have to do it herself."

Like Irina, Natasha spoke English with a thick accent. She was shorter than Lara, with darker hair and a rounder face. She was beautiful, perhaps even more beautiful than her supermodel sister, but in a subtler way. Her charm came from her constant laughter, her dramatic eye rolls, her frequent abandonment of English. I'd ask Natasha a question, and she'd search for the right word, scrunching her brow in frustration. Then she'd sigh, and start speaking in a fast stream of Russian or French.

"Stop, stop, I can't understand you!" I'd interrupt, laughing.

She'd smack her forehead. "Such an idiot! I forgot again!" she would say, laughing, too.

"Lara is reserved, you see," Natasha continued. "She always has been. Not like me, not like our mother, not like our father."

"Where do you think she got that from?" I asked.

Natasha shrugged. "God only knows. But this is why she likes you so much, I think."

"What do you mean?"

"She has me; she has our mother. With us, she can behave as herself. But this is not enough. Not in a long time has she had a friend like you."

I shifted in my seat, suddenly uncomfortable. "A friend?"

"She doesn't like to talk about herself. And how can you make a new friend if you never talk about yourself?" Natasha lifted an eyebrow. "But you, finally, are getting her to talk. I can see that she is letting you in. You are making her a little less alone. This is something no one else has done for her."

•

It was around this time, after I'd been invited into the sanctum of the Caine residence, that my old boss Vicky Wethers called me.

"I just had to see if the rumor was true," she said. "A little bird said you've been spending a lot of time in the White House."

"Well, hello, Vicky," I said. "Yes, I'm fine, thanks for asking. I miss you, too."

She laughed. "Forgive me, sweetheart," she said. "I'm just bursting with curiosity."

I hadn't exactly advertised the fact that I was working on Lara Caine's biography, but I also hadn't done anything to conceal it, and a journalist constantly coming and going from the White House would be noticed eventually. When I told Vicky that her little bird was correct, she let out a soft *Huh*. And then she went quiet for a while.

"Are you surprised?" I asked.

"Not exactly," she said. "I'm just processing."

"But?" I prompted. "You were hoping the rumors were wrong?"

Vicky laughed. "No, honey. I wasn't hoping for anything."

The ensuing silence was unsettling. It crackled with energy, like the air before a thunderstorm. Whatever she *really* wanted to say, she wasn't saying it. There was a screechy, echoey squawk in the background. "I should go," I said. "I think they're calling my train."

"Look," Vicky said, her voice lowering a notch. "I'm sure that whatever you have with Lara Caine—it's different from your old job. Fair enough. But make sure to keep your eyes peeled. She's the last part of the Caine administration that no one has been able to crack. I still think there's something there, and you—"

"I really have to go," I interrupted. "That's my train."

"Oh," she said. "Okay. Well, call me anytime, sweetheart. Let's have lunch soon."

As I walked down the platform, the deicing salt crunching underneath my boots, blood pounded in my ears. Feeling panicked and cornered, I'd lied to Vicky: there were still another ten minutes until the train left for New York.

Whatever you have with Lara Caine. She had said it with more than a hint of judgment. I told myself that there was a difference between intimacy and adulation, between trust and collusion. But the difference wasn't visible from the outside: and the outside is where everyone else stood.

•

Earlier, I said that the First Lady wasn't testing me with her silences—true. But she had other ways of testing me. With each passing week, she allowed me to witness a little bit more of her private life. The picture grew clearer. This mysterious woman began to make more sense.

It was both a gift and a burden. The world was thirsty for revelations about Mrs. Caine and her daughters, for the tidbits that turn figureheads into flesh-and-blood people. When I left the White House at the end of the day, a spectral presence seemed to hover just behind me: peering over my shoulder, watching to see what I did with this precious information.

Her daughters were especially juicy targets. Emily and Marina, the eleven-year-old fraternal twins, were already growing into different versions of their mother's striking beauty. The wider world knew almost nothing about them. (I found it surprising, and heartening, that none of the visitors to the residence ever said a word about the girls to the press.) Any nugget would have been worth a million clicks: the Harry Potter books Mrs. Caine was reading to them; their shared hatred of math class; the poster of Ariana Grande in Emily's room; the poster of Megan Rapinoe in Marina's room; the corner of the vegetable garden they were cultivating with their aunt Natasha's guidance; the French braids their babushka Irina often gave them before school. Every time I kept those nuggets to myself, every time those details *didn't* appear in print, the First Lady let me take another step closer.

It was an afternoon in late February when Mrs. Caine properly introduced me to Emily and Marina for the first time. We'd just finished for the day when the twins appeared in the West Sitting Hall, wearing their plaid school uniforms, en route to the kitchen for a snack.

Mrs. Caine called out, "Girls, please come here. I'd like you to meet someone."

Each of the girls shook my hand and looked me straight in the eye. Marina had a copy of *Island of the Blue Dolphins* tucked under her arm. Emily said, "I'm going to make cinnamon toast. Would you like some, Sofie?"

I smiled and said, "Maybe next time."

The twins seemed exactly their age, or possibly a little younger, with an innocence miraculous for eleven-year-old girls growing up in this nexus of power and wealth. It helped that Mrs. Caine was strict about screen time and social media. Despite Emily's and Marina's pleas that *all* of their classmates had phones, she'd held out.

The work absorbed me. Winter sped by. Our conversations grew longer. Eventually we started meeting two days a week. It became clear that the First Lady had a superhuman capacity for concentration. My conversations with her were never meandering and distractible, the way they were with Irina or Natasha. She remained so focused, so *present*. So on a Tuesday in March, when we sat down for lunch and Mrs. Caine seemed preoccupied, it surprised me. She'd never been like this before.

I asked, "Is everything okay?"

"It was Emily and Marina's birthday yesterday," she said. "And their father forgot."

"Oh." I winced.

"They're upset." She shook her head. "I explained to them that he didn't mean anything by it. He's just so busy, there are many people he has to take care of. Well—you can imagine. There were a lot of tears. They're young. Every birthday is such a big occasion."

"I'm sorry," I said. "That's hard."

"I reminded Henry this morning. He feels terrible. He wants to make it up to them, of course. Tonight we'll have dinner together, just the four of us."

Just the four of us: her tight tone indicated how rare that must be. President Caine didn't usually make it home for dinner. He preferred to eat with his staffers, or his old New York friends, or his billionaire-donor pals, all of them skilled in the art of attention giving. (The problem with children, of course, was that they expected you to pay attention in return.)

It was okay for her to admit that her daughters were upset. They were kids, after all. But Lara Caine would never admit her own upset. She shook her head again. "They idolize him," Mrs. Caine said, retreating into cool detachment. She might have been speaking about the behavior of animals in the zoo. "It's how children are. The power impresses them. My mother was a girl when Stalin died, and she wept for six days."

Wait a second, I thought. Had she just compared her husband, the president of the United States, to Stalin? But before I could wrap my head around that, the First Lady cleared her throat and spoke the words that always marked the beginning of the interview, the words that were like an iron gate clanging shut behind us: "Well, enough of that. Now where did we leave off?"

The following week, the girls were on spring break. This year they were staying put in Washington. Emily and Marina didn't mind the fact that their private-school classmates were skiing in Aspen and swimming in the Caribbean. They, more than anyone in the Caine family, adored living in the White House. They baked cookies with the chefs in the industrial-scale kitchen on the ground floor. They visited the basement, where there was a carpenter's shop, a flower shop, and a bowling alley. The White House was big enough for their boundless, earnest energy. So when I arrived in the residence that week, I was surprised to find them in the central hall, side by side on the couch, doing nothing. Or not doing nothing, exactly: rather, staring at matching gold iPhones.

Mrs. Caine appeared from around the corner. "Girls!" she snapped. "I said it already. That's enough screen time for the day."

Emily whispered something to her sister, and Marina giggled. Their eyes remained fixed on their phones. They made no sign of having heard their mother.

The First Lady stepped in front of them, hand outstretched. "Give them to me, please."

When they didn't respond, she started speaking in Russian, probably to spare me embarrassment. She snapped her fingers, and the girls finally looked up. Marina whined in Russian. Emily merely stared at her mother. Mrs. Caine grabbed the phones from her daughters. She spoke angrily and pointed down the hallway, toward their bedrooms.

Marina pouted and kept whining. Emily stood up and began stomping away, but then she turned around. "You're so *stupid*!" she shrieked. In English, so that I could hear everything. "Daddy gave us those phones! They're from *him*! And *Daddy* didn't say there were any rules."

Mrs. Caine didn't flinch when Emily slammed her bedroom door. A moment later, Marina slammed hers, too, in half-hearted imitation of her twin.

As we sat down in the kitchen for lunch, Mrs. Caine said, "It's been like that all week."

"I didn't know the girls had gotten phones," I said.

"Henry felt bad about their birthday. So he got each of them an iPhone, *and* a new laptop. Of *course* he didn't ask me." Her face was flushed. This was the closest I'd ever seen her to furious. "Look at how quickly it happened. Just look at them. They're addicted. And now I'm the monster who takes them away."

"Maybe the novelty will wear off?" I offered.

"No." She grimaced. "I doubt that."

When they arrived in Paris, the Orlovs were given an apartment on the rue de la Faisanderie, in the Sixteenth Arrondissement. They were across the street from the Bois de Boulogne, a stone's throw from the Arc de Triomphe, and a short stroll to the Eiffel Tower.

As part of his posting, Fyodor was granted use of a dark blue

Peugeot, but he preferred to walk. On Sunday afternoons, the family took meandering strolls, getting to know their new city. When Lara grew tired from those long walks, Fyodor would scoop her up and carry her on his shoulders. This vantage is where her version of her life story begins. She remembers the swaying motion with each step her father took, the smell of his cologne, the sight of the distant sidewalk and his creeping bald spot. Meanwhile, Natasha skipped ahead, endlessly energetic. Irina was grateful that her younger daughter didn't yet possess that energy. A four-year-old could only last so long. And thank God for that, otherwise Fyodor might have kept them out all night.

But could one blame him for his enthusiasm? They were in Paris, after all. Dating back to the time of Catherine the Great, the Russian upper class possessed a deep affinity for everything French. Despite the revolution in 1917, despite the overthrow of the decadent tsar and the Europhilic nobles, despite the cold demands of socialism, despite a harsh diet of Soviet ideology, the tradition continued coursing through Russian blood: an atavistic kinship with French culture.

Paris, Irina thought. *We're really here. Look at Fyodor. Look at the girls. Paris! And what is wrong with me? Why am I not celebrating like them?*

They settled into their new life. Eight-year-old Natasha was enrolled at the embassy school, her class filled with other children of the Soviet colony. Fyodor was, of course, absorbed by his secretive work at the KGB *rezidentura,* which lay hidden inside the depths of the Soviet embassy. For most of the day, Irina was alone in the apartment with Lara. This had been the case back in Moscow, too. Despite her new surroundings, her basic routine hadn't changed. She had her home; she had her husband and children to care for. So then why, during those first seasons in Paris, why did Irina feel so sad?

Their apartment was smaller than their home back in Moscow, with a cramped second bedroom shared by Natasha and Lara, and a meager kitchen, but Irina knew that she couldn't complain; many of the apartments in the Soviet colony were dim and dreary, with communal bathrooms and kitchens. At least the Orlov apartment was entirely private, with a big window in the living room that looked out over the street. They brought their best furniture and rugs from Moscow, making the space into a comfortable home. In good weather, Irina took Lara to a nearby playground in the Bois de Boulogne. The other wives in the Soviet colony were tight-knit, gathering daily for coffee and gossip and canasta. Irina joined their circle—it had always been easy for her to make friends—and this helped her sadness, but only a little.

Irina kept a journal intermittently while they were in Moscow, but when they moved to Paris, she began writing in it religiously. The entries were scrawled and abbreviated but also remarkably detailed—as if, in trying to pin down her own reality, there was so much to record that she couldn't waste time spelling things out. *N. home sick from school, fever 39 centigrade, higher than yesterday. Woke three times in the night. L. has not gotten sick yet but she will, I'm certain of that, this one will spread. L. has been whining, asking if N. can play with her. Made soup and N. ate half a bowl. She asked for canned peaches as a treat. F. will bring some home, he says. He spoils them, just like his father. Cloudy this morning, rain in the afternoon.*

It took Irina several months to understand this strange new feeling. As a teenager, when she was accepted to study at Moscow Pedagogical State Institute, she was more than glad to leave Leningrad, because there was nothing and no one in that city worth missing. But this was different. In Moscow, she had been happy.

"Fedya," she said. It was a weekend afternoon, the two of them sitting on a bench in the Bois de Boulogne, watching their daughters play. "Do you miss it?"

A gentle smile. "Sometimes," he said.

Her sentimental husband, offering a mere *sometimes*? She considered it. There might have been concrete reasons for Fyodor's lack of homesickness. Moscow in wintertime didn't inspire much nostalgia: the gray slog, the stench of cabbage and wet wool, the old babushkas shuffling along icy sidewalks, the omnipresent sense of resignation, from which not even the nomenklatura could offer protection. But there was something bigger, too. Here in Paris, Fyodor had what Irina didn't. A sense of belonging. A sense of purpose.

Her life in Paris was a half-life. As the wife of a KGB officer, Irina was expected to adhere to a strict set of rules. Rules governed everything, from whom one could see to where one could shop to what one could say. She might be living in France, but she wasn't even permitted to socialize with French people. Most Soviet wives flouted these rules, making themselves at home in their new city. But Irina—loyal, patriotic Irina—was far too cautious to risk such a thing.

◆

In the spring of 1975, after the Orlovs had been living in Paris for almost nine months, Natasha came home in a particularly bad mood.

"What's wrong, Nataschenka?" Irina asked. "Did something happen at school?"

Natasha shook her head. "Nothing ever happens at school."

"What do you mean?"

"It's horrible!" she burst out. "It's so dull. The teacher shouted at me because I fell asleep in class today. But what does she expect when the class is so boring?"

Irina had never once heard her older daughter complain of being bored. If anything, Natasha's imagination was usually *too* active for her own good. "Tell me more," Irina urged. "What have you been learning?"

Gradually, Irina pried out the truth. Back in Moscow, Natasha had attended an excellent grammar school. The instruction at her new embassy school lagged far behind. She was learning the same lessons she had learned the year before, or even the year before that.

"Sweetheart!" Irina exclaimed. "Why didn't you tell me sooner?"

Natasha looked up, her dark eyes brimming. "Because, Mama,"

she said. "What if you sent me back to my old school? I don't want to live in Moscow all by myself."

That evening, as Irina cooked dinner and bathed her daughters, her thoughts began racing. Lara was scheduled to start kindergarten in the fall, at the same embassy school as Natasha. Both girls would suffer from this poor education. But Irina had a sudden idea—a better idea. This made so much sense. What was the phrase? *Two birds with one stone.* This idea was contingent on Fyodor, and even if he agreed, it would require delicate string-pulling at higher levels. Normally, Irina climbed into bed early to read, but that night her brain was vibrating with possibility, so she waited up for Fyodor. (Working at the embassy required him to maintain an active social life. He was probably out at one of the many diplomatic cocktail parties that Soviet attachés, both real and fake, were expected to attend.)

"What is this?" Fyodor said, returning around midnight to find Irina in the kitchen, the table covered with papers.

For the last two hours, she had been writing furiously, filling notepads with ideas. She was getting ahead of herself, she knew—but the plans came so quickly and easily, and wasn't this itself a sign, that this was meant to be?

Fyodor smiled. "Ira, darling, what are you doing? Have you turned into Tolstoy all of a sudden?"

"Sit," she said. "I'll make us tea. Fedya, I've had an idea."

She talked, and he listened, and soon he began nodding along. He saw the wisdom in it, as she knew he would. She felt lucky to be married to Fyodor. Her kind, wonderful husband. Plenty of Russian men would have simply shrugged, saying, "Do whatever you want with the children, this isn't my business."

But Fyodor was devoted to his daughters. Of course he wanted the best for them. Of course he would do anything to make their lives a little bit better. "But this may be difficult," he cautioned. "It hasn't been done before."

"So you'll convince them, Fedya. I know that you can."

The real meaning of those words was mutually understood: *I know that your father can.* Whatever string-pulling was needed to obtain this particular favor, Fyodor didn't tell his wife about it. And so it came to pass, in the fall of 1975, that the names Natalya Fyodorovna Orlova and Larissa Fyodorovna Orlova were removed from the attendance lists at the embassy school. In a first for the Soviet colony in Paris, the girls would be homeschooled instead. Irina was returning to her original calling. She would be their teacher.

CHAPTER SIX

Passing through one of Irina's bridge parties in the White House, I'd spent some time chatting with Tatiana Ivanovna, her dear old friend from Moscow.

"Ah, you are Sofie!" she exclaimed. "Sofie the writer! Do you know, I read your biography of Raisa Maximovna? I knew her many years ago. Your book was good, but in reality she was much more calculating than you describe. That woman had her own agenda."

Tatiana, smiling a Cheshire cat smile, looked to be in her early seventies: an aging Russian beauty, blond and voluptuous. She wore a silk shantung jacket, the buttons straining whenever she took a breath. An air of deference surrounded her as she moved through the room. Irina might have been the hostess, but Tatiana was clearly the leader of the expat circle. That day, as I was making my way toward the exit, checking my watch, Tatiana called from across the room, "Sofie! You cannot leave without saying goodbye!"

She beckoned me over, opened her quilted Chanel purse, retrieved a card, and pressed it into my palm. "You live in New York, too, Irina says. You must come see me."

Embossed on the thick stock of the card was her name, TATIANA SOKOLOV, and a ritzy Fifth Avenue address. *Sokolov*, I thought, spinning through a mental Rolodex. *Sokolov*.

"You know the name," she prompted. "Yes. Boris Andreevich is my husband."

It clicked into place. Boris Andreevich Sokolov, I now remembered, was one of the original oligarchs. The first man to realize the potential of cellular technology in Russia after the end of the Cold War, a move that made him mind-bendingly rich. Then he had a falling-out with Yeltsin, and his family had to leave the country in a hurry. The deference accorded to Tatiana suddenly made sense.

"Call me," she insisted, kissing me goodbye. "We'll have so much to talk about."

•

On a Saturday morning in late March, Ben and I went running in Central Park. We jogged along the East Drive, weaving through other runners and walkers. Our steps were in sync, but I was breathing harder than Ben. He'd been a distance runner in college and had an effortless lightweight gait. He claimed not to mind that I slowed him down. Out of nowhere, as we were jogging north, he said, "It was, what, ten years ago when you started at Oxford?"

"Eleven in September. Why?"

"I just keeping thinking about it. You picked the subject, you wrote your thesis, and more than a decade later, it brings you here, to this"—he held his hands wide—"this crazy *thing*. That's a long payoff."

"Huh," I said. "I didn't really think of it that way."

"It makes sense that she wanted you to write this book. You already know the Russia angle, and the White House angle. The unknown woman behind the powerful man. But isn't it uncanny how it all worked out?"

"Can we stop for a second?" We were on the path around the reservoir. I bent over the water fountain, chest heaving. Ben stood upright, hands on hips, his breath calm and steady. After swallowing the icy water—the fountains had just been turned back on for the season—I asked, "So you think there's a kind of grand fate at work here?"

He smiled. "I wouldn't go that far."

After a few minutes, as we continued counterclockwise along

the reservoir, footsteps crunching on the gravel, gray water rippling in the breeze, Ben said, "But do you ever think there's something strange about it?"

This was why I liked running with Ben. It made me too breathless to talk much, which left room for his most ponderous thoughts. He was a good sounding board when I was grappling with something, but he could be neutral to a fault. Long stretches of quiet, like when we were circling Central Park, were needed for his own opinions to bubble to the surface.

"Strange how?" I said.

"That, of everything, this is what she's fixated on," he said. "Telling these old stories. Talking about her childhood. And meanwhile the country is falling apart. Worse than that, her husband is actually *destroying* it. She's a powerful woman. She could *do* something about it. But this feels like . . . like fiddling while Rome burns. Rearranging the deck chairs on the *Titanic*. That sort of thing."

We parted to navigate a double-wide stroller, and I stumbled slightly. Ben's phrasing had caught me off guard. Indulgent reminiscing, pointless fiddling: By working with Lara Caine, was I actually *encouraging* this? Was my presence in the White House distracting her from the big picture, from what actually mattered? It was an uncomfortable line of thought.

He isn't criticizing you, I told myself. But maybe he was, just a little.

"It seems like there are two possibilities," Ben said, as we rejoined and fell back into sync. "One, she doesn't give a shit about what's happening to the country. Two, she's actually happy about what's happening to the country."

"Or maybe she doesn't know what else to do. I think the biography might be like"—I gulped, trying to catch my breath—"like a control thing."

"Yeah," Ben said, though he didn't sound convinced. "I could see that."

We rounded the northern edge of the reservoir and looped south. Across the water, the skyline of Fifth Avenue stood squat and proper, like a line of dignified matrons.

"And what about Nikolai Gruzdev?" Ben glanced over at me. "Does she ever talk about him?"

I shook my head. "Never."

"You know, I keep wondering if her father knew him. It's possible, isn't it? Gruzdev was KGB, and around the same time. They might have overlapped. The KGB executed her father. Don't you think she must hate the guy?"

"Maybe. But she doesn't . . ." I was huffing and puffing, grasping for the right words. "It's like you said. She's so focused on the past. I don't think she even *thinks* about Gruzdev."

But as we circled the reservoir, Ben's words kept ringing through my head. Whether he was right or wrong about the Gruzdev animosity, that didn't matter: what struck me was that Ben had the perspective afforded by distance. He was seeing things I wasn't seeing; asking questions I wasn't asking. I was getting closer and closer to Lara Caine. But how close was too close?

In the apartment on the rue de la Faisanderie, the change in Irina's mood was like sunlight breaking through cloud. Yes: this was exactly what she had been missing. Even if she didn't admit it at the time, taking charge of their schooling was as much for Irina as it was for the girls.

Her life had unfolded as a series of tasks. Student, and then teacher, and then mother to two young girls. There was pleasure in these demands on her time, joy in this sense of competency. But as Natasha and Lara grew older, and more self-sufficient, a creeping malaise set in. What had been taut went slack. Very likely this change was happening even before the family left Moscow; but it was the move to Paris that made it obvious.

But now she was busy again, and happy again. Natasha and Lara would learn far more from her than from that lousy teacher at the embassy school.

Natasha, especially, was aware of the change in her mother. She recalls a particularly vivid memory from when she was ten years old. It was a winter day in 1976, the year after her mother began their homeschooling. Fyodor brought home a gift for Irina: a brand-new turntable. But for several days it just sat there, in their living room, because Irina had no records to play on it. Natasha fiddled with the needle and buttons until Irina scolded her to stop. "But, Mama," Natasha said. "When are we going to actually *use* it?"

Privilege can lead you in two directions. It can make you breezy and louche, certain that the ordinary rules don't apply to you. Or it can make you guarded and paranoid, fearing that the smallest misstep might cost you everything. Irina was one of the latter. Plenty of wives in her position were happy to exploit the material advantages of capitalism. A woman in her coffee klatch had a profitable racket going, smuggling suitcases full of Western clothing and cosmetics back to Moscow, where she sold them at a steep markup on the black market.

"Don't be so foolish," Irina said to her. "One day the DST will catch you doing this"—the DST was the French intelligence agency—"and they will blackmail you, and they will make you spy on your husband, and then what do you think happens?"

In response, the woman merely shrugged. "I'm careful about it, they won't catch me," she said.

"Idiot," Irina muttered.

The new turntable sat in the living room, shiny and seductive, but Irina was concerned about violating one of the many rules that dictated life in the KGB. Could she play French music? What about British music, or American music? She had no desire to get Fyodor into trouble. A few days later, she voiced these hesitations to him. In response, he laughed and kissed her. There was nothing to worry about, he said. No one would mind a little music. They were in Paris. By living here, they were already swimming with the devil.

The next day, after Fyodor left for work, Irina buttoned the girls into their coats. They began the long walk from their apartment: through the Trocadéro, across the Pont d'Iéna, beneath the Eiffel

Tower, down the rue de Grenelle. They walked right past the Soviet embassy (it would only be there another few months; it moved to a new location, in the Sixteenth Arrondissement, in 1977). Natasha and Lara waved at the building, imagining their father inside, although the real nature of his work meant that he was probably somewhere else: out on the streets, doing surveillance runs, meeting with agents. Finally, they arrived at a used record store, a few blocks off the boulevard Saint-Germain. Irina asked the clerk to recommend something.

Who knows what the clerk made of Irina? This serious-looking woman swathed in fur, dressed for Moscow temperatures, with only a halting command of French. This was 1976, the year of Diana Ross, and disco, and the Concorde. Irina, though only thirty-three years old, would have looked strikingly old-fashioned. As the clerk selected a record for her and handed it across the counter, maybe he thought it would be funny: that she wouldn't know what to make of the music. Or maybe—maybe—he saw a genuine glimmer of curiosity in her eye.

That night, after she put the girls to bed, Irina played the record for the first time. She kept the sound low, so as not to wake the girls, but it was just loud enough for Natasha to hear a faint echo in the bedroom. Natasha strained to listen, to make out the music. When she was sure that her little sister was asleep, she climbed out of bed and eased the door open.

Her mother sat in an armchair next to the turntable, legs crossed, one stockinged foot bobbing in time to the music. The doorway to the living room framed Irina like an image from a movie. She was swaying, ever so slightly, as she lit her cigarette. A trance had taken hold of her. Each song on the album—it was Serge Gainsbourg's *Initials B.B.*—gave way to another. Irina sat there, smoking and swaying, a dreamy expression on her face.

There was a scrape of keys in the front door. Natasha hurried back into the bedroom. A minute later, after her father walked past, she crept back into the hallway to resume her spying. With a cigarette still burning in her left hand, Irina changed the position of the needle on the record player. Another song began: "Bonnie and Clyde," her new favorite. She beckoned Fyodor to come closer. They hadn't exchanged a word, but they didn't need to. Fyodor smiled at his wife. He took the cigarette and lifted it to his own lips and wrapped an arm tight around her waist.

A hot blush rose in Natasha's cheeks. She had witnessed countless daily affections between her mother and father, nicknames and kisses and sweet gestures—but not until that night did she realize how much her parents truly loved each other. Truly *adored* each other. To be honest, up until that moment, she didn't think much about them. They were just her parents, after all, as constant as the sun and the moon.

It was later on the same March day that Ben and I had gone running in Central Park. The maid who answered the door of the Fifth Avenue penthouse was petite and dark-haired, wearing pressed khakis and white slippers. She ushered me into the living room and said that Mrs. Sokolov would be with me shortly.

The whole room screamed *money*. A fire crackled in the fireplace. The windows gave a sweeping view over the bare trees I'd been running through just a few hours before. Everything was opulent and overstuffed: the ceiling decorated with intricate plasterwork, the walls hung with gilt-framed oil portraits, the windows topped with heavy velvet valances.

Tatiana appeared and said, "Oh, Sofie, you're here! Welcome, welcome."

She smiled as she held my forearms and pulled me in, kissing me on each cheek. She wore black pants and a buttery-soft cashmere wrap sweater. "Come, you sit here," Tatiana said, tugging me toward a chair, pushing down on my shoulders. "I'll sit there"—she indicated a silk-upholstered settee—"but first I'll ask Josefina to bring us tea."

Tatiana disappeared into the hallway. She reappeared a minute later, this time trailed by a trio of Cavalier King Charles spaniels, jumping and yelping around her ankles. As she sat, she clucked at them. "These are my babies, but they are so badly behaved," Tatiana said. "Oh, yes, you three were sent by the devil to terrorize us. Weren't you? My husband hates these dogs. He would like to drown them in the East River."

Josefina came in with the tea, and Tatiana asked her to take the dogs away. After they left, she sighed. "Better. Now, Sofie. I'm glad you're writing about Larochka. She was always a special girl. A strong girl, thank God. One had to be strong to survive that situation."

"Which situation was that?" I asked.

"When Fedya was arrested," she said. "We all felt terrible about it. The idea of Fyodor Maximovich as a traitor, working with the enemy? None of us could believe this accusation. Of course, you couldn't say such a thing out loud. You must, in some way, *act* like you believe it. Poor Irina. Overnight she became an outcast. Their life back in Moscow was very hard."

"Tatiana Ivanovna, do you mind if I take notes?" I said, digging in my bag for my notebook and recorder.

She sat up, her chest swelling. "Of *course*," Tatiana said, evidently pleased at being taken so seriously. "You know, my husband was his oldest friend. Borya loved him like a brother. He would have done anything to help him, *anything*, but when the KGB decides you are guilty?" She clucked her tongue. "Well, really, what can be done?"

"What I've been wondering," I said, "is *why* they thought Fyodor was guilty."

"They had some proof that he was working with the Americans," she said, pouring the tea. "This is what I heard. Irina said that was impossible. My husband said the same thing. 'Never,' Boris said. 'Fedya had his criticisms, but he would never turn against his country.' Here, Sofie, will you have cream and sugar?"

I nodded.

As Tatiana stirred a generous helping into my tea, she continued. "People are declared guilty for all sorts of reasons. It was the late

1980s. A strange time in Russia. The wheel was turning. Fedya just happened to be in the wrong place at the wrong time."

"So you were close with the Orlov family in those years," I ventured. "How did Natasha and Lara cope with it?"

Tatiana sighed. "One must give thanks to God. Those girls were resilient. Lara, especially, was very practical. She worked hard. She kept the family going. Can you imagine what it was like? Going from their splendid life in Paris to such misery in Moscow? When they returned to Russia, they lost their old apartment, of course. They lost all the old comforts. You see, Fyodor's father was no longer alive, no longer there to protect them. Oh, those women were so thin and sickly. It was a terrible thing. Those were bad years."

I nodded. I was about to ask my next question (testing out Ben's theory: Did Tatiana know if Lara Caine had any strong opinions about Nikolai Gruzdev?), but Tatiana cleared her throat and said, "Now, Sofie. The reason I wanted to speak to you. Your book on Raisa Gorbacheva, it was very interesting. But I must tell you about the time I met her. I will never forget it. She was *quite* the little— Oh, look!" She suddenly sprang to her feet. "Look! Did you see that? Sofie, look, look. There, through the window."

I followed her pointing finger and saw—startlingly—a hawk, its dark wings swooping against the gray sky. Tatiana hurried over to the window, pressing her fingertips to the glass, her gaze following the hawk.

"Beautiful," she whispered. "How beautiful."

The hawk soared in elliptical arcs. Close, then far. North, then south. It came very close to the glass, so close that I could make out the individual feathers at the tips of its wings, and then—it disappeared.

"Oh no! No, where did he go?" Tatiana flattened her palms against the glass, craning her neck left and right.

There were three big windows in the living room, looking over Central Park. Tatiana was pressed up against the middle one. From where I sat, I saw that the hawk had alighted on the sill of the northernmost window.

"Look," I whispered. "He's right outside."

The hawk had dark wings and a proud white chest and beady black eyes. Handsome, but a little frightening, as his head swiveled around. The bird was so big, so *solid*, so out-of-place-looking in New York City. Tatiana stood with her hands clasped, her mouth agape.

"Oh my goodness," she whispered. "Sofie, quick, quick! Take a picture!"

If the hawk was bothered by our presence on the other side of the glass, he didn't show it. When Tatiana was satisfied that we had taken enough pictures, she stood very still, right next to the window. Whenever the hawk moved, turning his head or shirring his wings, she drew a sharp breath. Slowly, she lifted her hand, her palm facing out. Then she lowered it, seeming to trace the hawk's shape. It was like, in her mind, she was running her hand along his feathered back.

My heart flooded with a strange affection for Tatiana. This penthouse-dwelling socialite, this oligarch's wife—and here she was, reduced to the same childlike sense of yearning as anyone. Frozen by awe, struck silent with emotion, regarding the hawk with a tenderness that verged on melancholy. I sensed, for the first time, that I might be getting a glimpse of the real Tatiana, the person beneath the performance. For several minutes, we didn't say anything. We didn't need to.

The hawk finally took off, propelling himself from the windowsill with a few powerful wing strokes before gliding toward the park. Tatiana turned back to me, dabbing at her eyes with her fingertips.

"I hadn't seen him in over a year," she said, her voice husky with reverence. "I was beginning to worry he would never come back. Do you see what this means?" She clasped my hands, squeezing them tight. "This is a sign, Sofie. I knew you were special. Now we are bonded together forever."

After that, the atmosphere changed. We kept talking, but clearly I wasn't going to get much of anything concrete out of her. Tatiana had no desire to dwell on that time. Russia had stopped feeling like home even before they left. She often interrupted herself midstory to tend to the crackling fire ("I am very particular about this, you must use birch logs, only birch logs"), or to urge a plate of almond cookies upon me ("Have more, these are Josenka's special recipe"). The chatter washed over me. I felt drowsy and relaxed, sinking deeper into the armchair.

Tatiana mostly wanted to gossip about Raisa Gorbacheva, and to talk about her sons. Mikhail was raising his family in London. Vasily worked at Goldman Sachs. "Come see a picture of them," she said, tugging me to my feet and leading me to a table filled with silver-framed photographs. "See, look at my Vasily. So handsome! But a terrible playboy. He'll never marry. He has a new girlfriend every week."

But as I was nodding at the picture of Vasily, my eye caught on the frame beside it. I blinked and shook my head, and squinted to be sure I wasn't imagining it.

No—I wasn't. It felt like a cold bucket of water had just been dropped on my head.

"Pardon me, Tatiana Ivanovna," I said, heart pounding, pointing at the picture. "But what's this from?"

"This?" She picked up the frame. "Oh, this was very boring. One of those charity dinners where you donate a lot of money and then they give you a fancy award."

"But who are the people in the picture with you?"

"What was the name of it?" she said, scrunching her brow. "It was a few years ago. Oh, yes. The New York Foundation for Russian Heritage. I should know this better." She laughed. "That was the board of directors, I think."

Those people in the picture? No, she didn't really know any of them. She couldn't recall their names. She smiled, shooed me back to my chair, pressed another cookie upon me, resumed her storytelling. But I no longer heard what she was saying. Because right there in the photograph, standing only a few feet away from Tatiana and Boris Sokolov, with his gray mustache and familiar smile—there was my neighbor Maurice Adler.

•

"Sofie," Maurice said, opening the door to his apartment. "What a nice surprise. Would you like to come back a little later? I was just about to go out."

It was Sunday morning, the day after I'd visited Tatiana. Maurice always did his grocery shopping on Sunday mornings. He was already wearing his coat and hat, and beside him was a wire cart. A small part of me felt guilty for interfering with his routine, but a larger part was too curious to wait.

"I'll come with you," I said. "I need a few things from the store."

"Well." He smiled. "It will be nice to have the company."

Walking over, he said, "In fact, this is good timing. I'm reading a new book that you'll be interested in. I've been wanting to tell you about it."

Maurice and I spent a lot of our time talking about books. I knew almost nothing about the family he had left in Russia, or his love life, or his innermost regrets. ("Was he ever married?" Ben once asked. When I said I didn't know, Ben looked puzzled and said, "I thought you guys were close.") But I always knew what he was reading, and the ideas he was preoccupied with, and these were the things that mattered most to him. I didn't consider Maurice to be a mysterious man. At least I hadn't, up until that moment.

At the grocery store, we passed through the automatic doors and wended through the produce section. While checking an apple for bruises, he said, "This novel is quite extraordinary. The writer makes me feel as if I'm really there. The smells alone! He has this exquisite passage describing the meal that the narrator's mother once cooked. And yet he also allows you to see how sentimental the narrator is, and how unreal the memory. You must borrow it, my dear."

I followed him through the grocery store, which was exquisitely curated and crazily expensive. Sardines imported from Italy, twenty bucks. Regular old Heinz ketchup, eight dollars. A jar of organic pistachio butter, don't even ask. You were mostly paying for the experience: the lack of crowds, the opera soundtrack they played on Sundays, the genuinely friendly employees. Maurice took his time with his shopping, because, he told me once, that was the only way to feel that you were getting your money's worth. He carefully selected his fruits and vegetables. He stood before the dairy shelves and murmured, "Remarkable. Every week, a new kind of yogurt." He chatted with the man behind the deli counter, who shaved off a sample of *jamón ibérico* for Maurice.

And at the cheese counter, the cheesemonger called, "Mr. Adler!" He was a burly guy with a big grin. "And who is this lovely lady?"

"This is my friend Sofie," Maurice said.

"Sofie, you like manchego? We just got in a new kind. Here, both of you, try it."

He slid a piece of waxy paper across the counter, with two small wedges. The manchego was delicious, creamy and smooth and salty, but when the cheesemonger said, "Whaddya say? Quarter pound for the lovely lady?" I shook my head and smiled apologetically, because who even knew how much that would cost?

We were nearly at the checkout—Maurice was ordering a loaf of rye from the bakery counter, the last thing on his list—when he turned to me, looked at my empty basket, and said, "Didn't you need to get anything?"

"Oh," I said. "Right! Sorry. I'll be right back."

I went back through the aisles, grabbing whatever was at hand (a can of chickpeas, mango chutney, flaxseed crackers; Ben would think I was insane). I'd been too distracted to hew to my cover story. While Maurice spoke and shopped, and I waited for my opening, I'd been staring at him. Studying him. Overtaken by vertiginous doubt. Thinking: Was it possible that I'd gotten him entirely wrong? That he was *connected*, somehow? But connected to what?

As the clerk rang me up ($27 for some beans and crackers and jam?!), I turned to Maurice, who was carefully loading his grocery bags into his wire cart, and said, "Maurice, I have to ask you something. Do you know a woman named Tatiana Sokolov?"

He squinted into the distance. "Sokolov. Sokolov. Yes, why do I know that name?"

"Receipt?" the clerk asked, and I shook my head.

Maurice frowned to himself as he loaded his last bag. I thought: *He's stalling for time.* Then I thought: *You're crazy, Sofie. He's an old man. Give him a minute.*

Finally, he looked up. "Yes, now I remember. Tatiana and Boris Sokolov. They were involved with the Foundation for Russian Heritage. You remember, the one whose board I used to serve on. Why do you ask?"

"I had tea with Tatiana yesterday," I said. "I met her at the White House, actually. The Sokolovs are old friends of Lara Caine."

"Really!" Maurice said. "What a small world."

I held open the door, and we exited to the sidewalk. A taxi soared down the empty avenue. Sunday morning sleepiness clung to the neighborhood. Maurice turned toward home, the wheels of his wire cart squeaking, but I stopped in my tracks and said, "Maurice. I'm sorry, it's just—do you know Lara Caine?"

"Do I *know* her?" He laughed. "Sonechka, you're writing her biography. Don't you think I would have said something by now?"

"Well, have you ever met her?" I pressed. "At any of these events? It seems possible that your paths have crossed."

"Yes, it's possible." He nodded. "Entirely possible. You forget: she's famous now, but before Henry Caine ran for president, she was just another rich, beautiful Russian woman. There are plenty of them in New York City. Perhaps I met her and didn't even remember her."

"Okay," I said. "It's just that—"

"It's a strange coincidence." Maurice retrieved his gloves from his coat pocket and pulled them on. "I understand. An eerie feeling, isn't it? But when you're old like me, you see that these things happen all the time. Let's keep walking, Sofie. I'm getting a bit chilled."

We headed home, where I helped him unload his grocery bags. As I walked down the interior staircase to our apartment, I felt a sense of relief. His denial had put my suspicion to rest. The elegant old professor. The unassuming upstairs neighbor. A strange coincidence—yes, of course, that was it. What reason would he have to lie to me?

—~~—

Did they know how lucky they were? When Irina recalls those years, her nostalgia is almost painful. Everything was so easy. The girls were young and innocent, and Fyodor left for work every morning with a spring in his step, and it felt like life might always be this way. The Cold War had stretched on for so long that it seemed a bit silly, in fact, to call it a war. Perhaps it was just reality. Two superpowers, learning to exist side by side.

Not that Irina would have ever said such a thing aloud.

"Why do we hate the Americans?" Lara asked once, when she was six or seven years old.

Before Irina could answer, Natasha piped up. "Because they oppress their workers. They're greedy, greedy, greedy. They'll take a little girl like you and chop you up and sell each part of you. Would you like that?"

"No!" Lara said, horrified.

"Then you should tell the truth and be a good worker," Natasha said primly, looking to her mother for praise. As a girl, Natasha went through many phases. Around this time, when she was ten or eleven, she was fixated on the fable of Pavlik Morozov, the little Soviet boy who became a hero when he denounced his own parents to Stalin's police. She wanted to be just like him, shining and pure. (A year later, she would chuck Pavlik Morozov overboard in favor of a new idol—Mick Jagger.)

Their experience of the Cold War was also shaped by their geographic location. France wasn't *strictly* part of the Anglo-American alliance against the Soviet Union. The country was committed to the side of democracy, but France also followed her own agenda. For the men and women working in the KGB rezidentura, this meant they were able to enjoy their lives in Paris in a way that they couldn't have in, say, London or New York.

In England or America, it was dangerous to express any degree of affection for the country. But this was France: a historic ally of Russia, a country that would elect a self-declared socialist as president in 1981. It was a place of brackish overlap, a place where guards could be loosened. Affection for this country was much more permissible.

◆

Irina considered it one of her patriotic duties to remain well-informed about the workings of the enemy. She stayed abreast of the news, reading the paper and listening to the radio every day. In November 1976, she asked Fyodor what he thought about the outcome of the election in America. Surely the arrival of this new president, Jimmy Carter, would have an impact?

He waved away the question. "Oh, Ira, the men at the top change," he said. "But everything underneath them remains as it was."

Fyodor never worried much about how global events might affect his career. Many of his colleagues took the same approach. Fearsome reputation aside, the KGB was mostly filled with ordinary men and ordinary women. They understood how it went. You gain a little; you lose a little; you endure your mundane existence; the world spins on. True, there were occasional moments of cinematic drama, but for the most part, working for KGB meant that you were just a small cog in a massive bureaucracy.

In some ways, Fyodor was right. That fall of 1976, there was little to worry about. In the long arc of the Cold War, the 1970s had been a time of relative tranquility, when America mostly pursued a policy of détente with the Soviet Union. And Moscow didn't experience the same wild pendulum swings as Washington (Johnson, Nixon, Ford, and now Carter: Could the Americans never make up their minds?). So perhaps Fyodor didn't realize that a policy was only as durable as the person who implemented it.

But we know now that it was the last stretch of quiet before the final act. The war stayed cold. The world spun on.

◆

During her year at the embassy school, Natasha had a tight group of friends, and even after she left, she remained close with them.

Like her mother, she made friends easily. Lara, on the other hand, didn't know whether she shared this gift. She never set foot in the embassy school; she never had the chance to find out.

Does a child know when she is lonely? Or does language like that require the passage of time—because how does she know what loneliness is until she's experienced the opposite? As the years went by, Lara remained faithful to her mother's original observation. This girl was a good girl. She did her homework every day. She played quietly with her dolls. She dragged a chair beside the stove so that she could stand there, stirring the soup while Irina rolled out buttery pastry for pie. The easy baby became an easy child.

But there was a streak in her that Irina had overlooked.

In 1978, when Lara was eight years old, Irina decided that enough was enough: it was time for her daughter to learn to read. Oh, yes, Lara knew how to read in a literal sense, she could pronounce just about every word she encountered, but she wasn't a *reader*. The girl never thought to pick up a book. Irina felt that this was a referendum on her quality as a teacher, not to mention an insult to their heritage. Russia was the nation that had produced Tolstoy, Dostoevsky, Chekhov. For her younger daughter to be so utterly disinterested—well! Irina couldn't fathom that. She began assigning Lara thirty minutes of reading time, every night before bed. She also required Lara to memorize long skeins of Pushkin and Lermontov and recite the poetry aloud after dinner.

Lara quickly discovered that she hated this: the forced reading, the poetry, all of it. It was a disturbing sensation. In her eight years of life, she had never actually *hated* anything. She felt like she was being pushed toward the edge of a cliff, and even when she leaned back and dug her heels into the ground, the pushing continued. And the strangest part was that it was her *mother* doing the pushing. This woman who loved her, and who cared about her, was actually the source of this torture.

One night, that year of 1978, her parents hosted a dinner party. Irina and Fyodor saw it as their duty to entertain. With everything they were blessed with—this superior apartment, a growing record collection, caviar from Petrossian—it would have been selfish not to share it. Tempting fate, even, because if you don't share when the gods have smiled upon you, how can you expect anyone to return the favor in the future? Their parties became legendary within the Soviet colony. Irina would cook a feast, Fyodor would buy a case of vodka and put on the Bee Gees. He told stories about his adolescent misadventures in Moscow, and after dinner he urged everyone to dance, and for hours on end, laughter spilled through the open windows.

At these parties, Natasha and Lara were allowed to stay up as late as they wanted. Lara loved those nights, bodies squeezed around the table, listening to the confident voices of the grown-ups, basking in this delicious invisibility; often the adults seemed to forget that she was there. The night in question, after dessert had been served, just as Fyodor was pouring the cognac, one woman leaned forward and announced, "Irina Mikhailovna, did I tell you? We've just heard. My Alexei came top of his class at Bauman."

Irina smiled tightly, but Lara could detect her mother's irritation. Irina couldn't stand this woman, this arrogant and holier-than-thou wife of one of Fyodor's colleagues. Nevertheless, she lifted her glass graciously. "Bravo to Alexei."

"*Top* of his class! He must have gotten his mind for numbers from his father." The woman laughed shrilly. "He'll be working as a nuclear engineer in Pripyat. It's a very prestigious position."

"Wonderful, wonderful," Fyodor said, smiling warmly. He turned to this woman's husband. "Now, Volodya, you must tell us—"

But the woman wasn't finished. She interrupted Fyodor. "His professors said he was one of the most brilliant students to pass through Bauman in a decade."

"*Well*," Irina said, setting down her glass with a sharp *thunk*, red blotches appearing on her neck. "I'm sure your boy is very accomplished. But have I told you what my Larissa has done?"

Everyone at the table turned, in unison, to gaze at Lara.

"Lara has memorized 'Borodino' by Lermontov. The entire thing.

And she's just eight years old." Irina's voice was syrupy sweet, cloying and poisonous. "Lara, darling, stand up. Show everyone what you can do."

The room had gone silent. Lara stared down at the table, suddenly paralyzed. Dozens of eyes pressed upon her. She prayed for the moment to pass.

"Larochka, darling," Irina urged. "Stand up. You do it so brilliantly."

"No, thank you," Lara whispered.

A few of the guests chuckled. The silence stretched on. Lara finally looked up. Fyodor was gazing at his wife, a gentle pleading in his eyes, but Irina didn't notice. She was only looking at Lara. Her eyes flashed bright and hard.

"*Lara*," she said. This time, an edge in her voice. "Don't be rude to our guests. Everyone wants to hear the poem."

Lara knew how this would play out. Irina would push, and no one would intervene, because she was Lara's mother, and it wasn't right to second-guess her. But the idea of standing up, reciting this poem that she didn't even like, putting on a show that she had no desire to put on—could a person die from humiliation? Could they die from shame?

Lara stood. As she did, she noticed Irina's face relax. Finally, *finally*, her little girl was cooperating. This made it harder for Lara to do what she did next, but in a strange way, it also bolstered her. It had never occurred to her, until this moment, that she didn't have to do exactly as she was told.

She drew a deep breath and said, "Mama, I don't like reciting poetry. It doesn't make me feel good. Good night. I'm going to bed now."

An awkward silence hovered over the table as she walked down the hallway, but Lara no longer cared. The fire receded from her cheeks. She felt the relief that came from telling the truth. Behind her, in the dining room, Fyodor broke the silence. "Music! Music! What should we listen to next?"

Lara fell asleep listening to the vibrant strains of "Stayin' Alive," smiling to herself.

CHAPTER SEVEN

In April, two important changes occurred. The first was that the First Lady insisted I call her Lara. "Mrs. Caine" was much too formal, and we had grown too close for that. We ought to speak to each other like equals.

"Oh," I said. "To be honest, Mrs. Caine, I'm not sure—"

"*Lara*," she interrupted.

"I'm not sure I'm comfortable with that," I continued. "Because, with respect, we *aren't* equals. You're still the First Lady of the United States."

"And as First Lady, I'm going to insist. Please, Sofie. Don't fight this."

From then on, whenever I called her Mrs. Caine, she corrected me. "*Lara*," she said. Every. Single. Time.

Eventually I relented, but her name always felt unnatural in my mouth. I missed the formality of Mrs. Caine. The formality had served as an important guardrail. To call her Mrs. Caine was to remember who her husband was; to remember that, whatever happened in her childhood, *this* was who she was in the present.

But trading the knowns of Mrs. Caine for the unknowns of Lara—this seemed to be the price of admission for the second change, which was my increasingly unfiltered view of her world. Mostly we met in the residence, but some days, it was easier for Lara to meet in her East Wing office. I was now a permanent presence, rather than an appointment on her schedule. We would talk and talk, and when another obligation pressed in, she would say, "Stay a bit longer, Sofie. Don't leave yet." And so I sat there, watching her take phone calls, or answer questions from her aides, or dictate changes to speeches. Lara told her staff to treat me as she did, which was to say, as a trusted member of the innermost circle. A person whose discretion was absolutely guaranteed.

The first time it happened, Gabi glanced skeptically in my direction. "Are you sure, ma'am?" she said. "This is . . . somewhat sensitive."

Lara arched an eyebrow. "I trust Sofie. I expect you to trust her, too."

Trust: that was the only guardrail left.

One day in late April, President Caine's latest controversy was erupting. "You've heard about this?" Lara said to me that day, in her office. Gabi had just stepped in with an update. "This plan of my husband's? He wants to withdraw American troops from NATO bases in the Baltics."

"I saw that," I said. "People aren't too happy."

"Gabi," Lara said sharply. "Please keep me updated on this. Everything you find out."

When these controversies happened, as they did every week, the First Lady never issued a direct comment. Stepping into West Wing skirmishes only served to fan the flames. But that day, Lara seemed agitated. Once or twice, she cut herself off midsentence and stepped into the hallway to ask her staffers for the latest. Finally, she said, "Do you mind if I put the television on? I'll keep it on mute. I'd just like to see how this is going."

She wasn't really paying attention to my questions, her eyes fixed on the silent flash of CNN. Her energy felt intense, prickly, pent-up.

"You know," I finally said. "We could call it a day and pick this back up tomorrow. Does lunch still work for you?"

"Lunch, yes," she said distantly, staring at the TV, turning the volume back up. Pundits were arguing about the implications: how this Baltic withdrawal would benefit Russia and Nikolai Gruzdev, how it threatened the stability of Europe, how America was further abandoning her responsibility on the world stage and creating a dangerous power vaccuum. Then Lara suddenly snapped to attention.

"Gabi!" she called out. Gabi hurried in, and Lara said, "I'd like to move forward with the invitation for Mr. Cheban."

"Cheban?" Gabi asked, briefly puzzled. "Oh, right," she said. "Andrei Cheban. I didn't know we'd made a final decision about that."

"I did," Lara said. "Just now. I'd like to invite him for a special luncheon, in his honor."

Andrei Cheban? Despite my offer to leave, I stayed sitting in her office, now too curious to go anywhere. Why had that name suddenly popped into her head? Cheban was a fairly obscure figure. He was a Romanian intellectual, highly critical of the Russian government, fashionable among think tankers and the Davos set, but little-known beyond those rarefied circles. With his fierce opposition to the Kremlin, Cheban had long ago earned himself the hostility of Nikolai Gruzdev. Lately, inevitably, Cheban's criticisms had also extended to Henry Caine. *Nikolasha's little American friend*, he called him. *His little American puppet.* Caine wouldn't have the faintest clue who Andrei Cheban was, but once his staff looked up his name—

And that, of course, was exactly why it had popped into the First Lady's head.

"Are you sure, ma'am?" Gabi said. "Would it be better to run this past—"

"This needs to happen as soon as possible," Lara interrupted. "Today, in fact."

Gabi swallowed. "I don't think the West Wing will like how this looks."

"How it looks doesn't matter," Lara snapped. "We're inviting him. It's decided."

After Gabi left, Lara was possessed by an agitated energy, standing up, smoothing her dress, squaring the papers on her desk that were already perfectly tidy.

"I'm guessing the president didn't consult you on this NATO decision," I suggested.

She turned and gave me a grim look, but she stayed silent.

"If you disagree with him," I ventured, "why not say something? Why this veiled response? There's the possibility that you're misinterpreted."

Lara gestured at me. "Tell me, Sofie. How do *you* interpret it?"

"Inviting Andrei Cheban to the White House on the same day that President Caine announces a withdrawal of troops from the Baltics?" I said. "I think it shows that you agree with Cheban. He's been talking about this for years. That America needs to maintain a strong military presence in Europe, as a counterweight to Russia. Cheban is synonymous with that issue. Inviting him to the White House—that can only mean you think your husband's decision is foolish. Dangerous, even."

Her nostrils flared, ever so slightly.

"Maybe he would listen to you," I said. Even as I spoke, I felt a queasy lightness in my stomach. As a journalist, and as her biographer, I'd never crossed this boundary: giving advice, suggesting how the First Lady handle her affairs. What was I doing? I had no right to speculate on the nature of their private relationship. (Or did I? Was that exactly what my citizenship entitled me to—the right to pressure a politician, by any means necessary?) "And if you spoke out against the decision, it could empower other people to push back, too."

Lara shook her head. "I did it this way for a reason, Sofie. It's better to be indirect."

"But it's clear that you care about this issue," I said. "Forgive me, Mrs. Caine—sorry, sorry, Lara—but I can *tell* how much you care. You've got all this political capital, but you never use it. What are you waiting for?"

She shook her head again and looked away. I felt increasingly annoyed. This move with Andrei Cheban was cowardly. She was registering dissent without actually *owning* that dissent. Better to be indirect, she said. But why? To give herself plausible deniability? To maintain the image of the president and First Lady as a happy couple, in agreement on this, as on all things?

Lara Caine was a woman who told the truth. By this point in our work together, I was confident in that. That was ultimately the reason she never spoke to the press, or gave glimpses of her most private self. She didn't want to lie about those details. If she wasn't going to be honest, she preferred to say nothing at all.

But that day—that was the first time I knew she was being dishonest with me.

As we said goodbye, the mood was tense. I kept thinking about it as I rode the Metro back to Jenna and Sam's house. Lara's invitation of Andrei Cheban suggested that Ben might be right: perhaps because of her father's execution at the hands of the KGB, she disliked, even hated, Nikolai Gruzdev. Maybe she carried those old animosities with her. And maybe she was unwilling to say this bluntly in public—but why not in private, with me? She'd confided so much in me, by this point. Why did she draw the line here?

Because she's not your friend, I reminded myself. *You need to remember that.*

By the time I made it through the front door, a headache was creeping in. "Auntie Sofie!" Derek shrieked, barreling down the hallway. "It's taco night!"

"Wow!" I said. "Great!"

"Mom says it's because we did good at our soccer game." He tugged on my arm and dragged me toward the kitchen. "Luke got one goal and I got *three*."

Jenna was squeezing a lime into the blender. "Don't tell the boys," she muttered, beneath the whir. "But really it's just because I wanted a margarita."

"Long day?" I said, filling a glass with water and rummaging in the drawer for the stash of ibuprofen. "Me too."

Dinner was chaotic, as usual. Luke knocked over his milk, which spilled across Derek's plate, turning his dinner into a soaked mess. Derek retaliated by reaching over and smashing the hard corn shell of Luke's carefully composed tacos. Luke burst into tears. Derek started laughing. "You're an *asshole*!" Luke wailed. That word (when had sweet little Luke learned that word?!) shut Derek right up.

"Enough!" Sam snapped. "Cut it out right now or you're both going upstairs."

Jenna caught my eye and shook her head. *Kill me,* she mouthed.

The chaos didn't bother me. In fact, I kind of liked it. My presence at the dinner table had become routine for the twins. They took me for granted, behaving as their truest selves, in a way that felt flattering. Within a few minutes, Derek and Luke were happy as clams again. Jenna poured me another drink. Sam talked about the emergency appendectomy he'd performed that morning. I drank my margarita, loaded up my taco with shredded cheese and sour cream, and half listened to the chatter, but my mind continued to circle around what had happened that day in the East Wing.

Something was off. I just didn't understand what.

In 1981, Maxim called and said that he would like to come visit his son, daughter-in-law, and granddaughters in Paris.

"Of course you must stay with us, Maxim Ivanovich," Irina said on the phone. "No, no. A hotel won't be necessary. You *must* stay here. I insist."

Lara remembers the deadly look that Natasha, then fifteen years old, gave Irina as she hung up the phone.

"What?" Irina said. "Don't you love your grandfather?"

"There's no room," Natasha said flatly.

"There's plenty of room," Irina said. "Where is your heart, Naschenka? You would have him stay in a hotel? The poor man is lonely."

Fyodor's mother had died the year before. The sickness was swift, and Fyodor didn't have the chance to say goodbye. (Lung cancer, the doctors in Moscow said, though they were never quite sure.) Irina noticed that Fyodor seemed nervous in the days before his father arrived. His mother had always been the mediator, the peacekeeper. The pressure of Maxim's love could be like a vise grip. Family was everything, it was all he had—it was all that anyone had. For Maxim Ivanovich, sticking to this truth was the only way to survive in the Soviet Union. He was old enough to remember the day the Bolsheviks seized the Winter Palace. Old enough to remember when the tsar and his family were shot like dogs. Governments change; leaders come and go. All of this was beyond his control. The trick was to love what one could afford to love; to protect what one could realistically protect.

When Maxim arrived, Fyodor and Irina gave him their bedroom, and they slept with the girls. Natasha found this profoundly annoying. After the first night, claiming that she couldn't sleep because of her father's snoring, Natasha said that she would go stay with a friend, another daughter of the Soviet colony who lived in the same building on the rue de la Faisanderie. "If I were as rich as him," Natasha said to Lara, while stuffing clothes in a backpack with a bitter grimace, "I would be staying at the Ritz and swimming in champagne."

Lara was now eleven years old. Several years had elapsed since her grandparents had last visited the family in Paris. She remembered only a few things about Maxim: he was tall, and had a funny mustache, and always politely asked "May I?" before kneeling down on the carpet to join in their games.

On this visit, though, her grandfather was different. He was still tall, still had the funny mustache, but now he was more inclined to sit by the living room window and read. Sometimes he didn't even turn the pages of his book; he just left it open in his lap while staring at the leafy plane trees. It didn't make sense to her. Maxim, the grand old war hero, now seemed so painfully *shy*.

"Ah," Maxim said, turning to her. "Lara. You've caught me daydreaming."

"Daydreaming about what, Dedushka?" she asked.

He peered over his reading glasses. "Tell me, sweetheart: What have you been learning in school? Your mother is a good teacher?"

Lara nodded, although how truthful was that answer? She had no other teachers to measure her mother against, and Lara was a literal-minded girl. "My favorite is when we go to the museums," she said. "I like looking at the art. I'm getting better at sketching. I made a copy of *The Raft of the Medusa* and it isn't too bad. Would you like to see it?"

Blessedly, after the debacle of the mandatory reading and poetry memorizing, Lara was given the freedom to discover her real interest. She turned out to have both a passion and skill for visual art. That afternoon, when Irina returned from shopping for dinner, she found Lara and Maxim on the sofa, paging through her sketchbook, the girl narrating each image.

"Lara," Irina said cautiously. "Be sure not to bother your grandfather if he's trying to rest."

"Nonsense." Maxim was beaming. "Irina, my dear, you have an artist on your hands."

◆

One night that week, while Natasha was with her friends, the four of them went to dinner: Maxim, Irina, Fyodor, and Lara. Decades later, Lara could still recall the evening in detail. Her parents often dined out, but it was a rare treat when they brought the girls along.

They walked the short distance from their apartment to the restaurant on the rue de Longchamp. Lara wore her best dress and patent leather Mary Janes that pinched her toes. When they walked through the door, the maître d' lit up with a smile. He kissed Irina on both cheeks, shook Fyodor's hand, and ushered the family to their table. (Fyodor and Irina had been loyal patrons since the restaurant opened earlier that year—a restaurant that would go on to become world-famous—and the staff were loyal in return. The Orlovs were always given the best table.)

Lara craned her neck, taking in the scene. The room was exquisite and airy, with high ceilings, pale green walls, pink tablecloths, potted palms, and waiters in black tie. "Mademoiselle," the maître d' said, pulling out her chair.

As acclaimed as the chef was, Lara doesn't remember much about the food. In fact, the food seemed beside the point. What she does remember is how, in this beautiful place, her parents just *looked* different—how they almost seemed to glow. Lara regarded Fyodor and Irina with awe. With pride, too. She had come from these magnificent people.

Maxim appeared to notice much the same thing. After the wine had been poured, he said to Lara's parents, "Paris agrees with you both. I am almost envious."

"*Almost*, Maxim?" Irina teased.

"Almost," he said. "I am too old to envy it entirely. What you are doing requires the stamina of youth."

"And what is that, exactly?" she said.

"Living with contradiction," Maxim said. He turned to gaze at a nearby table, where a man was kissing the hand of a beautiful woman, adorned with glittering diamonds and cherry-red lipstick. "My God, just look at this. This city. This life you have. To fall in love with a place like Paris—for an old man like me, that would wipe the slate clean. It would make it impossible to ever return home. Once you've lived this kind of life, how could you ever choose anything else?"

He paused, holding his wineglass by the stem.

"But the nature of my son's work," Maxim continued, "means that you cannot feel that way. You *must* not. Instead, you must hold two ideas in your head at the same time. You can love all of this, but you must also understand that a place like Paris will never be your real home. In other words, you must accept that *love*—as real as it feels—is not *reality*, and it will never alter reality. Well, you see, an idea like this is difficult for an old man. But you are young still."

There was a brief silence, and then Irina said, "Maxim Ivanovich, do you—"

But Fyodor interrupted. "Papa, we understand."

Maxim smiled, grateful for his son's sublimated response.

"Fedya," he said. "Soon, when I die, I will be proud to leave our family in your hands."

"Don't say such things, Maxim Ivanovich," Irina scolded. "You aren't dying."

As dinner progressed, talk turned to politics. Earlier that year, the socialist François Mitterrand had been elected president of France. Irina took a certain glee in this. A socialist, in France, in the midst of the Cold War! Irina felt sure that the Americans must be frightened. She counted Mitterrand's election as a victory for the Soviets. "Perhaps Mitterrand can talk some sense into that cowboy," she said. "That warmongering fool."

Lara mostly stayed quiet through dinner. She only piped up when she was confused. "Cowboy?" she asked.

Fyodor reached over to smooth the back of his daughter's head. "She means the American president, Ronald Reagan. Before he was president, he lived on a ranch in California."

"Reagan is a madman," Irina said. "He'll get us all killed."

"Killed?" Lara repeated, her eyes going wide.

"Your mother is exaggerating, Larochka," Fyodor said.

Irina continued. "Well, I say if there will be a war, let there be a war."

"You don't mean such a thing," Maxim said. He glanced at Lara. "Irina Mikhailovna, think of your girls. You don't want them to endure that."

"Reagan thinks nothing of our girls." Irina spoke in a level tone. Lara's heart beat harder. Her mother was saying such horrible things, but she seemed so *calm*, so frighteningly calm. "Reagan thinks nothing of any child in the Soviet Union. He would sacrifice all of them in an instant. But when it comes to it, our girls will be brave. They will fight. They will stand up for what they believe in. Won't you, Lara?"

Her mother gazed at her. After a long moment, Lara nodded.

"Ah, wonderful," Fyodor said when the waiter appeared with their entrées. He quickly steered the conversation in a more benign direction. But Lara's pulse continued to thump in her ears.

She stared down at her plate, blinking, feeling a confusion of emotions.

Why had she nodded like that? She felt ashamed, felt like a liar. Her mother often did this, ascribing qualities to Natasha and Lara that neither girl actually believed herself to possess. Natasha is like *this*, Lara is like *that*. But just because Irina said it didn't make it true. Lara had learned this on the night of that fateful dinner party.

The difference, though: on that occasion, Lara had been certain of her disagreement. She was certain that she *wasn't* a reader, that in fact she *hated* poetry. Certainty allowed her to stand up, to assert herself, to walk away. But the declarations her mother made that night in the restaurant—was Lara brave? Or was she a coward? What was Lara meant to say? How was she meant to know?

CHAPTER EIGHT

"So how did it go?" Ben asked, after the waiter had poured the wine and recited the evening's specials. It was a Friday night in January, and the restaurant, a trattoria in the old part of Split, was lively enough to drown out our conversation.

"Okay," I said. "I think. It's hard to tell."

"What did she want to know?"

"Everything." My lunch with the television producer had been earlier that day. She'd leaned eagerly across the table, sensing the nearness of a good story. She was good at her job, which meant she had the uncanny ability to ask the questions I least wanted to answer. "How Lara picked me. How we worked together. Why she trusted me. But mostly, why I betrayed her."

"Because you had to," he said matter-of-factly. "You couldn't sit on a story that big."

"I said that, but I'm not sure she believed it."

"Why not?"

"Because of this!" I spread my arms. "Because a few weeks later, we uprooted our lives and moved to Croatia for no good reason. This, right here, is the part that doesn't make sense."

Ben looked puzzled.

"It doesn't track," I explained. "If I were a die-hard ambitious reporter, that would explain why I betrayed Lara. But a die-hard ambitious reporter would lean into the moment. She'd write the follow-up. She'd keep talking about it. She'd *milk* it. She wouldn't just, just . . . just run away from a story that big." I shook my head. "At a certain point, she could tell I wasn't going to say anything more. But she definitely suspects something."

The waiter returned to take our order. Branzino for me, squid ink risotto for him. Friday night was our standing date night; another week gone by. Those months in Croatia contained moments of stunning beauty: the ancient streets, the boats bobbing in the Mediterranean, the scent of salt and pine in Marjan Park, the quaint restaurants with flickering candlelight. But they also contained moments of crushing loneliness. I missed the anchors of our life back in New York. I missed the sense of being known. Here, washed ashore in a different land, we had to invest every little routine with outsize significance. If we didn't declare a thing to be meaningful, no one was going to do it for us.

"Well," Ben said calmly. "It's her job to be suspicious, right? And she has nothing concrete to go on."

"Not unless someone's been talking out of turn."

He shook his head. "They won't. They have more to lose than we do."

On our way home from the restaurant, Ben took us on a detour through the peristyle. We walked down the crooked streets, our shoes clipping on the flagstone. Split had once been part of the Roman empire, and the ruins of the emperor's palace still stood in the city center. The peristyle had been the inner courtyard of the palace. The rectangular courtyard was bounded by ancient Roman arches, glowing pale in the moonlight. At the far end of the flagstone expanse, resting on a pedestal, was a black granite sphinx, which the emperor Diocletian had brought from Egypt in the third century AD.

The peristyle was lively in the darkness: people lounging on the steps below the arches, leaning back on their elbows, legs extended. Smoking, laughing, drinking, kissing, flirting. Music playing from a tinny speaker. A man hawking plastic glow-in-the-dark necklaces.

"What would Diocletian think if he could see all of this?" I said. "Tchotchkes and Europop?"

"You know what I think?" Ben stood behind me, wrapping his arms around my waist. "Someday we're going to look back and be nostalgic for this."

I laughed. "Yeah? I'm *really* looking forward to that day."

"We should take it all in. Absorb as much as we can."

I craned my neck to look at him. "Seriously. How do you stay so optimistic?"

"Because there's a good reason we're here. What you did—it matters, Sofe."

As we kept walking, I finally realized what was bothering me. It was the past tense of that statement. *Did*, not *doing*. The year before, after everything with Lara Caine blew up, I'd had to pick a side. Those were their words: *pick a side*. Which had felt scary, but also *good*, and then it brought me here, and now—now what? Now I waited, and waited, and wondered if I'd got it all wrong.

The next morning, in the café, drinking my coffee while Mirko preached to me about the rookie the Bulls had just signed, Greta came in. She smiled at the waiters and waved at the other regulars. As she hung her coat on the back of her chair, her gaze traveled across the room. When our eyes met, for the briefest moment, her cheerful expression showed a flicker of seriousness.

Fifteen minutes later, standing up and leaving money to cover the bill, I said loudly, "See you tomorrow, Mirko. I'm just going to use the bathroom before I go."

After several minutes, Greta opened the bathroom door. "In the future," she said, turning to lock the door behind her, "no need to announce yourself like that. Assume that I notice exactly what you're doing."

Ignoring her brisk tone, I told her about my lunch with the TV producer the day before. That I had done what she asked, and it seemed to go fine, or at least, fine enough. Greta nodded. "Thank you, Sofie," she said. "Good work."

And then she turned away, back toward the door. It was now or never. I took a deep breath, holding out my arm to stop her. "Wait," I said. "I want to know who you are."

Greta frowned.

"I mean *exactly* who you are," I pressed. "You said you were a friend of our friend. That could mean anything. If you're asking me to trust you, I need more than that."

"Surely it is enough that we share the same goals," she said coldly.

"Not for me," I said. "I need to know. Either you tell me, or I start digging on my own."

She stared at me, her eyes glittering with suspicion. I was bluffing, of course. I had no plans to start investigating the woman known as Greta. And she was probably smart enough to perceive the bluff, but it didn't matter, because the line had worked; because, for the first time, I knew that Greta was seeing me. Me as Sofie Morse, not just a task that required servicing. Me as a person with agency, with opinions and desires that might not always be predictable.

Finally, in a quiet voice, she said, "Why?"

"Because," I said. "I'm tired of this. What am I doing here? I mean *doing*. Not just waiting, passing the time. I can't just stand on the sidelines. It's making me crazy. I need a *purpose*."

Greta folded her arms across her chest. "I see."

"I want to get back to work," I said. "Let me help finish what we started."

•

Springtime, the year before. With warmer weather, protesters descended upon Washington. On Pennsylvania Avenue, along the iron fence of the White House grounds, people shouted themselves hoarse. There was neon poster board and Sharpie writing, synchronized drumming against plastic buckets, chants rising and falling.

I watched the wave growing day by day. Parents brought their children, hoisting them on their shoulders to see over the crowd. The demands had grown simpler, and more powerful, as the Caine presidency wore on. Give us the chance to exist with less fear; give us the respect of being seen as individuals; give us our dignity back.

It wasn't about complicated legislation or polarizing policy positions. What brought the people there was something as basic and essential and ineradicable as the desire to live. There were days when the sight of the crowds—tense, electric, joyous—brought a lump to my throat.

There were the counterprotesters, too. And the opportunists, setting up tables to sell T-shirts and flags and water. But in the fluctuating crowd, there were a few permanent fixtures. One man stood in the same spot, day after day, whether in the pouring rain or the muggy heat, facing the entrance on Pennsylvania Avenue. His posture was military-perfect, and his baseball hat read USS *ABRAHAM LINCOLN*. He held a sign, impossible to miss as you approached the entrance: COLLABORATOR.

I told myself that nothing had really changed. The objectivity required by my old job at the newspaper would have taken me along this same path: noticing the protests without engaging in them; agreeing with the demands without acting on that agreement; crossing from the chaos of the sidewalk to the safety of the grounds. *You're a journalist*, I thought. *That's who you are.* Except that this felt different. Was this objectivity? Sitting in the First Lady's office as she complained about the situation? Where exactly was the line between attention and sympathy?

"No one can sleep," she said in a frayed voice, dark circles beneath her eyes. "Henry wants them to install new glass. Something more soundproof."

She'd been cooped up for several weeks. After a surge of death threats, the Secret Service had strictly curtailed her movements.

"It cannot go on like this," she said, wide-eyed. "It just cannot."

Every day, each White House employee had to drive past that angry roil. Protests had persisted through the Caine presidency, but now they were reaching a fever pitch. It had to be affecting the staffers, I thought. Maybe it would even drive a few of them to quit. One morning in mid-May, while I was waiting in the First Lady's office, Gabi Carvalho came in to leave a folder on Lara's desk.

"How's everything going?" I asked.

Gabi squinted at me. If she was suffering, it didn't show. Her skin was flawless as ever, her hair just as glossy and smooth. "Why are you asking?" she said.

"Because it's a polite thing to do," I said. "And I'm trying not to be a sociopath."

Gabi let out a sharp *ha*. "Do you actually want to know?"

I nodded at the window, at the outside world. "How are you weathering it?"

She tossed her hair over her shoulder. "Those people don't know me," she said.

"The protesters, you mean?"

"They don't know me *at all*," she repeated. "And you know what? They don't *want* to know me. I've been in this job for almost three years. Every article that mentions me says the exact same thing." She began ticking her fingers. "Gabi Carvalho, rich father, sugar fortune, prep school, party girl. Blah blah blah."

"To be fair, those things are true," I said.

"You know that guy, the one with the sign, right outside the gate?" Gabi said. "'Collaborator.' *That* guy. It used to really bother me. Like, it's just stupid. Does being one small part of an organization make you responsible for everything it's ever done? He was in the military. Does that mean I get to blame him for Abu Ghraib?"

Leaving aside her extremely tenuous analogy, I said, "It *used* to bother you? It doesn't anymore?"

"Well, it stopped bothering me when I remembered that man doesn't know me," she said. "He's never once tried talking to me. He has *no* idea who I really am. Or what I'm doing, or why I'm doing it. So he doesn't get to say what I am or what I'm not."

"But that's a slippery slope," I said. "Do you always have to know a person, like physically *talk* to a person, in order to make a judgment about them? That seems unrealistic."

"Well, how does it make *you* feel?" Gabi asked, arching an eyebrow.

"Me?"

"That word doesn't just apply to me. That man watches you coming and going every week. He's calling you a collaborator, too,

Sofie Morse. So I'm asking you. Are *you* happy about that? Does he get to call you a collaborator? Do you think that's right?"

A flat silence ensued, which seemed very satisfactory to Gabi. "I'd better go," she said, smirking. "I don't want to take up any more of your precious time."

I sat in the silent office. On this side of the building, the sound of the protest was more muted. I could hear only my pounding heart and snatches of conversation in the hallway. Duty carried out. The world spinning on. Lara had talked about her father like this: Fyodor as the diligent cog in the KGB machine, working away while the men at the top came and went. There were so many ways for a person to insulate herself. Gabi defiantly tossing her hair over her shoulder. Staffers turning up their music as they passed through the White House gate.

And me, sitting on the velvet couch in Mrs. Caine's office (no: Lara's office), waiting to begin another day. Nodding when Lara's secretary popped in to ask if I'd like a cup of coffee. *Splash of cream and sugar, right? I'll be back in a moment.* Smiling gratefully as she handed me the cup. *And—here—I got you a chocolate croissant from the Mess. I know it's your favorite.* Sitting alone in the sunny office. Wondering how it was that I had wound up on this side of the fence.

No: not wondering. Merely pretending to wonder.

Feeling queasy, I reached into my bag for my notebook and recorder and placed them on the coffee table. One might say that these objects were my defense, my reason for sitting here, but that was a paltry explanation. *I* was the reason I was sitting here.

Gabi was right: to the outside world, I looked just like the rest of them.

—∾—

As the years passed, their world began to expand.

They made good use of Fyodor's dark blue Peugeot, roaming through the countryside on weekends, often part of a larger caravan of Soviet families. Fyodor had fallen in love with life in France. The best wines in the Loire Valley, the briniest oysters in Brittany, the prettiest beaches in Normandy: he knew where to find them all.

They maintained the pretext of returning to Moscow someday, even if that "someday" was vague. In 1984, Natasha would turn eighteen. She had satisfied the rigorous coursework set by Irina, and now she was free. As her birthday approached, she was certain of two things: she didn't want to go to school, and she didn't want to return to Moscow. For the time being, Natasha chose to stay in Paris, taking a job at the embassy as a typist and translator, where her dual fluency in French and Russian was valuable. Her decision was an unspoken acknowledgment of reality: none of them really wanted to go back.

Although to Lara and Lara alone, Natasha said, "You cannot tell Mama, but the *real* reason I'm going to stay is because"—she paused dramatically—"because I'm in love."

Her boyfriend lived near the Canal Saint-Martin. He was a socialist and pacifist, and had been arrested several times at antinuclear protests. Lara had never met him, and Natasha didn't have a photograph of him (he hated cameras and had a paranoid fear of surveillance), but the image in Lara's mind was sharp and specific thanks to Natasha's swooning descriptions: his leather jacket, his battered copy of Milan Kundera, his nicotine-stained fingertips. Natasha said they would probably run away and get married, once they saved enough money. In the meantime, she moved out of the family home on the rue de la Faisanderie and into an apartment with other young women who worked as secretaries at the embassy.

Natasha no longer came on the family's weekend trips through the countryside, but that was okay; Lara had company in her sketchbook. As she grew older, and spent more time alone, she absorbed herself in observing the people around her—at café tables, park benches, bus stops—and rendering them in rapid pencil strokes. Irina was glad about this development. Her younger daughter had always been shy, which was part of why Irina had been so insistent on Lara developing a reading habit: because don't shy girls *always* like to read? Sometimes Irina wondered whether her daughter's quiet nature indicated a simplemindedness, or a great depth. When Lara's artistic talent became obvious, Irina felt relieved. So it was to be the latter, thank goodness.

◆

One of Lara's favorite trips took place in April 1984. The family left Paris in the morning. They arrived in Bayeux by lunch, where Fyodor was eager to show them the famous tapestry.

Her father was beginning to look older. His beard was graying, and his torso was thickening from years of French food, but his eyes still twinkled playfully. Inside the museum, he beckoned her over. "Did you see this, Larochka?" he said. "This tapestry has survived nearly a thousand years. Can you imagine that?"

"That seems lucky," she said, leaning to look closer.

"A thousand years!" Fyodor said. "Just think about how many people have watched over it. Who have kept it safe and intact, through so many centuries. Lucky, maybe. To me it seems like a miracle."

A thought occurred to Lara. "Well," she said. "It's out of self-interest, too, isn't it?"

Fyodor looked at her, quizzical.

"This tapestry is worth a lot of money," she continued. "If it belongs to you, you want to take good care of it, don't you? Otherwise it becomes worthless."

He nodded slowly. A minute later, he said, "You're a smart girl, Larochka."

Lara took another step closer. Her father kept mentioning bits of historical trivia, but Lara wasn't really listening; she was more taken with the tactile aspects of the tapestry. The dense texture where the figures were saturated with embroidery. The subtle tugging and puckering of the sheer fabric. Despite the childlike simplicity of the figures depicted, Lara found the piece to be curiously hypnotizing. Perhaps it was the scale of it. Or perhaps it was the strange feeling of recognizing a continuum. A thousand years ago, when this tapestry was created, the artists had relied on the tools available to them. They were working in the only way they knew how. It took the passage of centuries for other techniques to surface, which Lara now took for granted: perspective, dimension, shadow, depth.

She felt a shiver of pleasure as she gazed at it. In the year 1984, when Larissa Fyodorovna sketched the streetscape of the boulevard Saint-Germain (glimmering light on a glass window, wavy shadow of foliage), she was using tools that had been discovered sometime between that distant past and this present moment. It was one of the first times that she understood how she—how her brief life—was part of something bigger.

Irina came to stand beside her. If Lara was admiring the tapestry itself, Irina admired the intensity with which her daughter evinced this admiration, the unblinking purity of her gaze. In the past year, Lara had shot up like a weed. Irina squeezed her daughter's hand.

"These sleeves are short on you, darling," she said. "We need to buy you a new coat."

Sunday drives through the countryside. Shimmering fields of wheat. Leisurely lunches. Take your time. What do you need? A new coat, and here it is, just like that. Everything was so easy: that was the best word to describe it. There was a sense of liberation to nearly everything they did, because they were choosing this; because they never had to fear for their safety; and because they knew, at the end of the day, that no one was watching.

◆

One night during this spring of 1984, Fyodor came home after midnight and found Lara awake, sitting at the kitchen table with her sketchbook. In the past, he might have gently chided her for staying up so late, but Lara no longer had a bedtime. After Natasha moved out, the dynamic in the apartment had shifted: the remaining family members were suddenly, inarguably a trio of adults. Lara came and went as she pleased. Fyodor often worked late, and Irina often climbed into bed with a novel around 10:00 p.m. Their overlaps became rarer, and more precious.

Fyodor smiled at Lara, but he looked exhausted. He dropped his briefcase to the floor, opened the refrigerator, and stared for a while at the fluorescent interior.

"Is something wrong?" Lara asked.

He shut the refrigerator. "Yes, my dear."

"What is it?" she said.

"Oh, I won't burden you with it. It's very complicated."

This routine repeated itself the next night, and the next. Fyodor would come home and find Lara in the kitchen or the living room. He would sit down, drop his head into his hands, and release a heavy sigh. Then he would look up and run his hands through his hair, or smooth his beard over and over, staring into the distance.

Every night, Lara asked, "What is it, Papa?"

And every night, he replied, "It's too complicated, Larochka." Then, with a determined smile that broke her heart a little, Fyodor would change the subject.

"Larochka," he said. "Did I ever tell you about the night your mother and I first met?"

She nodded. "But you can tell me again."

He was glad for her company, glad not to be alone. She could see that much. Her father had always been a natural storyteller. It didn't seem to matter what he was saying; he just needed someone to listen. But then, on the fourth night—maybe when it became clear that Lara wasn't going anywhere, and wasn't going to stop noticing that something was wrong—he allowed himself to speak more truthfully.

"This is a hard business, Lara." He grimaced, shook his head. "We are told not to trust anyone. The problem is, then we cannot trust each other."

She sat up, alert. "What do you mean?"

With a sigh, he said, "Where do I begin? You know who Yuri Andropov was, darling?"

She nodded. Until a few months earlier, when he died in February 1984, Andropov had been the leader of the Soviet Union. Well, Fyodor continued, did she know what job Andropov held before becoming general secretary of the Soviet Union? Lara shook her head.

He explained: Andropov had been the head of the KGB. In that position, he had been convinced that a nuclear attack by the United States on the Soviet Union was imminent, especially with the madman Reagan at the helm. In 1981, Andropov had begun a program called Operation RYAN. Operation RYAN was designed to keep the KGB on high alert around the world, to seek out advance warning of such an attack, but this—according to Fyodor—was only making everything worse.

"Why?" she asked. "How does that make it worse?"

"It's a good way to make a man hallucinate," he said. "You don't need to hypnotize or drug him. You just tell him that danger lurks around every corner. That the enemy is out to get him. And then, suddenly, this man will see danger everywhere he looks."

Lara thought about it. "Like that time when Natasha wouldn't go swimming, because she kept seeing shark fins in the water."

Fyodor laughed. Yes, exactly, he said.

As Lara climbed into bed that night, after that first conversation, she felt her mind buzzing. She had never really thought about the work her father did. But knowing a little, she wanted to know more.

As a toddler, Lara had never gone through a "Why?" phase. Time for bed. *Why?* Brush your teeth. *Why?* Because I said so. *Why?* She was the easy baby, the trusting child. But perhaps Lara's curiosity just took a little longer to blossom.

◆

The Soviet ambassador had a country residence in Mantes-la-Jolie, about an hour west of Paris. During the summer, the families in the Soviet colony spent a lot of time there. The ambassador opened the home for parties, long days and nights of eating and drinking, volleyball and badminton. A few weeks after their trip to Bayeux in 1984, the Orlovs drove to Mantes-la-Jolie for the ambassador's May Day party.

The property was on the edge of town, a swathe of land surrounded by forest and tall fencing. Inside that perimeter, the windows of the old stone château were open to the May evening. These countryside parties followed a well-established script. The women socialized with women; the men socialized with men. Fyodor and the other KGB officers, all of whom worked under diplomatic cover at the embassy, gathered at a distant point on the lawn.

A permanent tension existed between the ambassador and the KGB faction. In the daylight, the Soviet ambassador and his staff were working to establish productive relationships with foreign powers. Meanwhile, in the shadows, the KGB spied on and undermined those very same foreign powers. The KGB officers necessarily stood apart from the rest of the group: their own tight little world, their own party within the party.

At first glance, the men standing with Fyodor looked similar enough. Serious Russians, shrugging at the fluctuations of the universe. But as they drank, their inner essences emerged. Almost all of them could be sorted into three categories. For men like Fyodor, the copious vodka made them red-cheeked and affectionate; they danced badly or burst into sentimental song. For other men, the vodka made them brash and boastful; they liked to recount violent exploits and challenge one another to arm-wrestling. But for the third group of men, the vodka only made them more serious. No matter how much they drank, it merely drew them into silence. They never sang or danced or bragged or boasted or planted inappropriate kisses on the cheek of a colleague's wife. There weren't very many of these men, but according to Fyodor, these were the ones to be feared.

The evening of the May Day party, Lara stood at the other end of the lawn, far enough that she felt comfortable staring at the group. In the last few weeks, as she learned more about the nature of her father's job, she began to understand that Fyodor took pride in his work, but it also made him miserable. During their late-night kitchen-table conversations, he shared some of his vague criticisms of the KGB. Many of the men he worked with were brave, and honorable, and doing their best. But there was also so much stupidity. So much craven self-justifying. And so much suffering, as a result.

As it happened, her staring hadn't gone unnoticed. A voice interrupted. "Is your father down there?"

Lara turned. There was a boy standing beside her, gazing in the same direction. Her recent growth spurts had put her at five foot ten inches, but this boy was even taller than she was. He was lean and angular, with smooth babyish cheeks and dark curly hair. Lara didn't recognize him. Because she was homeschooled, there were lots of people she didn't know, even in this closed-off world.

"I wonder what they're talking about," he asked. He was looking at the group, not her. "I wish I could eavesdrop on them. Although wouldn't that be ironic?"

She asked, "Who are you?"

He turned to her. He wore a curious expression, as though she were the one who had snuck up on him. "Sasha," he said. He extended his hand with a strange formality, like a skinny alien dropping into a new world. (She and Natasha had seen *E.T.* the year before.) "What's your name?"

"Lara," she said. "And, yes, that's my father there."

"And your mother?"

"She's up there, by the house."

"Do you like them?"

She laughed. "My parents? Do I *like* them?"

In a surprisingly graceful movement, he lowered himself to the grass, folding his long legs in a cross-legged seat. He patted the ground beside him. "It's a perfectly legitimate question. Most people never think to ask themselves: *Do I actually like these people?* We're meant to just *accept* it."

Lara sat down, too. "Is this how you begin every conversation?"

He smiled. (Later, Lara would think: *That smile is what did it.* That tiny barb, just enough to puncture his seriousness.)

"No, not really. But I can tell you're a curious person. Now you're going to ask, *how* can I tell that? And I'll answer, because you've been staring at those men for at least ten minutes."

Lara felt a sudden shyness. When she glanced over, she saw that Alexander wasn't looking at her; he was still looking at the KGB group. "Yes," she said. Already she found herself wanting to keep his attention. "I like my parents. They're wonderful."

He nodded. "You're lucky, then. Recently I realized that I don't like my parents. We're like oil and water. We just don't get along."

"Oh," Lara said. "That's sad."

"It was only sad for a little while." He shrugged. "Then it was useful. It's better to know these things. They work as clerks in the embassy. 'Work' is generous, though. They show up, they do nothing. They never really liked it here. They're going back to Moscow next month."

"Oh," Lara said again.

"But not me," he said. "I'm starting university here in September. Are you hungry?"

As they stood up and wandered toward the buffet, filling their plates with cucumber salad and black bread and pickled beets, they kept talking. And talking, and talking. They took their plates and sat on the grassy bank of the pond, at the edge of the property. Their intimacy was instant.

She had never heard anyone talk quite like Sasha talked. Here, right away, Lara was experiencing his greatest gift: his ability to find the urgency and importance in everything. She thought: *What teenage boy talks like this? Understands himself and the world in this way?* Of course, some of it was bullshit, designed to impress a pretty girl. But some of it wasn't.

And just when Sasha was growing especially serious, he tended to break into a wide grin. "Well, what does it matter, anyway?" he said, tossing a bit of bread into the pond for the resident ducks. "This world is such a ridiculous place." Then he would turn to Lara and ask her another question. "Do you like to read?"

"No," she replied. "Not really."

"I guess that's good."

She laughed. "Why?"

"Because they say that opposites attract."

By this time, twilight had given way to nightfall. Fireflies hovered above the lawn. The grown-ups had gone inside, drifting like fish through the aquarium of glowing windows. The music had gotten louder. Lara could imagine her father in there, teasing and coaxing her mother into dancing with him.

"Do you like to dance?" she asked, in return.

Sasha hesitated. Lara's heart gave a little thrum: he cared enough to not want to disappoint her.

"Actually, I hate it," he said. "I'm a terrible dancer."

"Another thing we don't have in common," she said. "I suppose we're doomed."

He smiled. "Star-crossed lovers," he said. "Like Romeo and Juliet."

The clear night, the bright stars. The melody of their native language, the mingled scent of lily of the valley and muddy earth. She was still only fourteen years old. Lara hadn't thought much about love, but when she did, she vaguely imagined falling in love with someone like her father. Bearish and boisterous and silly; the life of the party. And now?

There was a twinge to this; an abandoning of a belief that Lara didn't even realize she had been carrying. She looked over at Sasha, at the pale cast of his skin in the moonlight, his dark curly hair. He was unlike what she had ever imagined.

CHAPTER NINE

His arrival had tripped some invisible wire. When Lara spoke about him, it was obvious that the wound remained raw and exposed, that the decades had done nothing to dull the pain. Her intensity sometimes caused the hair on my neck to prickle. I was certain about this: Sasha, at last, was going to be the key to explaining Lara Caine.

"So that was the start of your relationship?" I asked. Glancing at the kitchen table, as I did every so often, to make sure my recorder was still running.

"Yes and no," Lara said. "The next time I saw Sasha was a month later."

"Why the gap?"

"He was busy with final exams. But he called me every night."

"He was smitten," I suggested.

"Smitten, yes." She smiled. "We both were."

But as Lara described meeting Sasha for the first time, it sparked a macabre countdown in my head. According to the newspaper clipping I'd read the previous fall, Alexander Kurlansky—Sasha to his friends—was found dead of suicide in December 1985. He and Lara met at the party in May 1984. As she reminisced, I found myself thinking: *Eighteen months from now, Sasha will be dead. Seventeen months. Sixteen. But why? What killed him?*

That day in the White House family kitchen, uncrossing and recrossing my legs, I said, "So the second time you saw Sasha. When was that?"

"Let's see." Lara tilted her head. "It was June fifth. I remember because it was Natasha's birthday. My parents had a party that night. Our apartment was so crowded, people were spilling into the hallway. Tasha was very pleased. My father bought cases and cases of champagne—he would have spent his last cent to see that look on her face. He adored her, you know. She was, she *is*, so much like our mother."

"What did Natasha's Marxist boyfriend think of all that caviar?"

"He was French, remember. Not Russian. So he wasn't allowed to set foot in that apartment, or anywhere inside the Soviet colony. We lived by the rules. There were *many* rules. It was a bad idea for Natasha to be dating a French boy. My mother would have been furious if she had known."

"And your father? Would he have been angry?"

"My father." Lara's gaze shifted into the distance. "My father would have told Natasha to end the relationship, of course. She had to. It was the only sensible thing. But he would have reminded her that every great love is inherently tragic. Ending the relationship didn't mean she had to stop loving him."

Lara closed her eyes for a moment. Months ago, she had drawn me a floor plan of the apartment on the rue de la Faisanderie. It was exquisitely detailed, right down to the furniture placement, with labels for the pattern of the wallpaper (yellow-and-cream damask) and the color of the drapes (oxblood red). She would often refer to that floor plan, pinning down a memory with her fingertip: *The mirror over the mantelpiece, that's where my mother would do her makeup before they went out, that's where the light was best*. Her past was like a series of rooms to be wandered through. While she spoke, I imagined her weaving among frozen figures, picking up sun-faded objects, running her hand across dusty surfaces.

"I'd invited Sasha to the birthday party," Lara continued. "I was nervous. There's that feeling when you've met someone, and you've had this connection"—she smiled, a little mournfully—"but you don't know whether it will last. What if it had only existed there, in that moment? But Sasha came, and he brought flowers for my mother and a gift for Natasha. A volume of poems by Mayakovsky. What she really wanted was a book by Sartre, to impress her boyfriend, but Mayakovsky was safer to bring to a KGB officer's daughter.

"Natasha, she flirted with everyone. She could see immediately why I liked him. Sasha looked beautiful that night. Beautiful, yes, rather than handsome. His pale skin and dark hair, and his heart-shaped face. And he wore this outfit, these acid-washed jeans and a white T-shirt and an enormous blazer"—she laughed—"it was ridiculous, and Sasha was skinny as a coat hanger, but he looked good in it. Sasha had gone to the embassy school, of course. He was the same age as Natasha, they had both just turned eighteen, they had mutual friends. She kept teasing him. 'You're so *quiet*, Alexander Alexandrovich. You're a man of mystery.' But her flirting had no effect. He didn't even blush. In the end, I think she found him boring."

"Did your parents realize who he was?" I asked. "I mean, that he was more than a friend—that he was a romantic interest?"

"Well." Her smile slackened. "Years later, my mother said to me, 'Lara, how was I to know how serious it was? How was I to know that you were *in love*?' He was four years older—though none of us cared about the age difference—and he was good-looking, so maybe they thought it was just a passing infatuation. You see, my mother, she had nothing to compare it to. By that point, Natasha had fallen in love a hundred times. We all knew how it looked. You could predict it. Oh, now Natasha is smitten. Oh, now Natasha is heartbroken. But for a person's first time—how do you know what it looks like on them? Maybe they're in love, maybe not."

"But *you* knew," I prompted.

"Yes," she said. "I knew exactly what this was."

In 1977, President Jimmy Carter sent a letter to Andrei Sakharov, the most important dissident in the USSR. Sakharov was a Soviet physicist who had once worked on the country's nuclear program but gradually became horrified by the ballooning dangers of the arms race. Carter's words, printed on White House letterhead, expressed sympathy with Sakharov's ongoing fight:

> *You may rest assured that the American people and our government will continue our firm commitment to promote respect for human rights not only in our own country but also abroad. . . . We will continue our efforts to shape a world responsive to human aspirations in which nations of differing cultures and histories can live side by side in peace and justice.*

These were beautiful words, but what did they look like, in practice? "To promote respect for human rights": What does this actually mean? "To shape a world responsive to human aspirations": How to make these sentiments into a concrete reality? Well, America had one massive advantage over her enemy, and she would use that advantage. America had money.

In those years, there was a flood of funding for the distribution and circulation of banned dissident writing. Funding for Radio Free Europe. Funding for book and magazine publishers. One of the beneficiaries was a small literary magazine in Paris called *Iskra*, or *The Spark*, founded in the early 1980s. *The Spark* published writers who were critical of the Soviet Union, whether they were living in exile or still inside the USSR (the latter always wrote under pseudonyms). The name was an ironic homage to the generations that had come before. "From a spark a fire will flare up": this had been the motto of the revolutionary Decembrists in 1825, and was later borrowed by Lenin during the years before the 1917 revolution. The editors and writers of this new *Spark* despised what Lenin had done to their country. They would take the impetus—a new spark, a new fire—and turn it against his inhuman ideas.

Youth was on their side. Older generations of Russians had cycled through belief and disbelief. Older generations had witnessed their country defeat the Nazis and send a man into space; but they had also witnessed Khrushchev denouncing Stalin, and Brezhnev strip-mining the state for personal profit. For the younger generations, disbelief was present from the beginning. It flowed through their veins like blood. They always knew the regime was corrupt. They never trusted the great socialist experiment. But if they were skeptical, they were also fearless: they hadn't been conditioned to crouch in self-defense, or to worry for their lives.

The small staff of *The Spark* worked out of a garret apartment on the rue Saint-Bernard in the Eleventh Arrondissement in Paris. They had two rooms crammed with secondhand desks, groaning bookshelves, and stacks of paper. There was one telephone line, used most frequently late at night, when the editors took coded dictation from writers inside the Soviet Union; that was the safest way for writers to avoid the censors and get their stories out. There were several old typewriters, and a TRS-80 computer, purchased by the magazine's generous backers. If one was to walk down the rue Saint-Bernard late at night in the year 1984 or 1985, the garret windows on the uppermost floor were always aglow. For a certain kind of person, those dusty rooms were a version of heaven.

◆

The rue Saint-Bernard was a sleepy street, narrow and crooked, with closed-up shutters and wooden doors concealing courtyards. Across the street from *The Spark* offices, there was a café where the editors ate their meals, kept on a running tab that they paid off with the generous subsidies from their American friend. Overly generous subsidies, in fact. One of the editors was in direct contact with the American, and he tried to protest: the money was too much, it was more than they needed. The American merely shook his head. "Just take the money," he said.

If you were to sit at that café on a cold winter night, as the front window grew foggy with interior warmth, you could rest assured that there wasn't much to see out there. The noise and bustle of Paris was far away. But if your curiosity persisted, and if you wiped clear a circle in the fog, you might see a young man leaving the building across the street. Dark hair, a heart-shaped face.

If you followed him down the rue Saint-Bernard, turning west along the rue Saint-Antoine, past the Bastille and then down toward the Seine, you might sense how he traversed every street and made every turn without really noticing where he was, preoccupied as he was with conversations back in the office. He crosses onto the Île Saint-Louis, then takes the narrow footbridge to the Île de la Cité, because he always prefers to approach the cathedral from behind, in a spirit of irreverence. He arrives in the plaza, striding past the entrance, and keeps his back to the building for a purposeful moment. Then, and only then, does he turn around and look.

The young man cranes his neck. The towering facade fills his vision. He claimed to appreciate Notre-Dame on aesthetic grounds, nothing deeper than that. But those who knew him could tell that, atheism aside, a change came over him in those moments. Maybe he wouldn't have used these words, but it filled him with a kind of awe. Especially at night, and especially when the plaza was empty. He could think of nothing else except what was before him. In this tumultuous world, the cathedral was a thing unchanging. Proof of devotion, old and new.

But as he lingers there, glancing at his watch, it becomes clear that he's expecting someone. For a long time, he remains alone. It's getting late. It's a cold December night. He hunches his shoulders higher, burrowing in his coat. He checks his watch again. And then, announced by the clipping sound of footsteps on flagstone, a girl finally appears at the edge of the plaza.

That winter, she has taken to borrowing a tall fur hat from her mother. A rich brown sable, a hat suited to an older woman, which should have looked odd on a teenage girl in the year 1984. But the girl was learning that it was easy for her to step into these other selves, to pull off these quicksilver changes. With her height and her bearing, with the fullness of her features and her gray-blue eyes, she wore the fur hat like a natural, like a woman much older than fourteen. In fact, it had spurred more than one person to comment that it was absolutely uncanny, she looked just like that beautiful actress. Surely she knew the one? Julie Christie, in the movie of *Dr. Zhivago*—and wasn't it even more uncanny that she, Lara, shared a name with the character?

But these compliments were always met with a blank stare, because she hadn't seen the movie nor read the novel, which were banned in her home country. Because even though she was in love with this young man—this young man with dissident ideas and dangerous friends—she was still a good girl. An obedient girl, who never sought out controversial works. A girl who had no desire to go against the rules that she had grown up with.

Not yet, anyway.

◆

In the past months, Lara had discovered what love does.

A heat wave in August, the streets deserted until the sun went down. Shops and restaurants are closed for the annual vacation. The sultry weather creates its own kind of privacy. There are evenings by the Seine, the stone pathway warm beneath their thighs, feet dangling above the water. To the passengers taking dinner cruises down the river, the shorebound teenagers are like indistinct shadows. In their hands, ice-cream cones from Berthillon, paid for by the generous magazine budget. Chocolate melting too fast, rivulets running down the cone and inside their wrists. There is the sense that none of this is an accident; that this is precisely where they are meant to be.

This is what love does: it makes everything matter.

Not long after that May Day party in Mantes-la-Jolie, Sasha's parents returned to Moscow. They were expecting him to return with them, but he had figured out a way to stay. Sasha was the brightest student ever to pass through the embassy school. When he won a competitive scholarship to a top university in Paris, the Soviet government embraced his achievement. Their young man had beaten countless Westerners! Proof, certainly, of glorious Soviet superiority! The apparatchiks were proud of him. They would allow him to stay in France for the duration of his studies.

In September, he moved into an apartment with several other university students. Sasha went to class, received excellent grades, wrote letters to his parents back in Moscow. He was the picture of a diligent student. He rarely talked about his work for the magazine. The Soviets would never have allowed him to stay in Paris if they had any inkling of what he was really doing. Lara herself only knew the vaguest outlines about *The Spark*. She didn't feel the need to pry. What she and Sasha had, just the two of them, was more than enough.

An autumn afternoon in the Luxembourg Gardens. The smell of woodsmoke in the air, the bright sun cutting through the cold. They sat in the mint-green metal chairs around the boat pond. Lara balanced her sketchbook on her knees, her rapid pencil strokes capturing the scene, while Sasha read the galleys of an upcoming issue (hidden within the cardboard covers of a textbook) and chewed absently on a red pen. Lara liked the challenge, attempting to render the glittering surface of the pond and the colorful flash of toy boats with simple graphite lines and curves. Occasionally she would look up, and then Sasha would look up, too. Cocking an eyebrow, grinning at her. It felt like her heart might burst.

What if we stayed here forever? she thought. *Will you remember this moment the way I remember this moment?*

Walks on winter nights, braving the cold until their fingers went numb. Their love mostly dwelled outside, because both of their apartments were off-limits. Lara would take the Metro to Notre-Dame to meet Sasha. She wasn't sure why this was their designated meeting spot, but she went along with it. From Notre-Dame, they set out on long late-night walks across the city. Eventually they ended back in the Sixteenth Arrondissement. In the Orlov apartment, Lara would turn on a lamp in the living room, her signal to Sasha that she was safe inside. On the sidewalk outside, he would lift his hand in goodbye, then begin his journey home.

◆

By the spring of 1985, Lara and Sasha had been together almost a year, but she still hadn't met his friends or roommates. His life was organized in tight compartments. This, he explained, was purposeful.

"Do you think the KGB would like an officer's daughter spending time with these radical French students?" Sasha asked. "Because that's who my friends are, Lara. Me, they can understand well enough. They can forgive you for falling in love with a nice Russian boy. My mother and father worked at the embassy, I lived in the next building over. But foreigners are different."

"Sasha," she said, laughing. "I doubt they're paying attention to me at all."

He frowned, but didn't say anything.

For all his talk of liberation, Sasha had an old-fashioned streak. He held the door for Lara. He paid for every meal. One day, as they were walking through the Tuileries, a little boy running ahead of his parents tripped and skinned his knee, just a few feet away from Sasha and Lara. The boy began wailing, turning red in the face. Lara quickly kneeled down and murmured to him. Almost instantly, the boy stopped crying. He sniffled shyly, and wiped away his tears. By the time his parents caught up, the boy was beaming. When Lara stood up, brushing the dirt off her jeans, Sasha smiled and took her hand. He said, "You will be such a good mother one day."

She looked at him, perplexed. "What if I don't want to be a mother?"

"Of course you do." He lifted her hand and kissed it. "You and I will have children together, and it will be beautiful."

He was open-minded, except where he was completely rigid. He was liberal, except where he was completely traditional. In a world full of murky unknowns, Sasha believed in certain incontrovertible facts. The KGB was always watching, women always wanted children, and so on. He could never quite let go of those bedrock assumptions.

On a sunny Saturday in March 1985, they were walking past a café in the Latin Quarter when someone shouted, "Comrade Kurlansky!" A group, seated at a table on the sidewalk, waved them over. The boys had patchy beards, the girls had long bangs. They wore faded Levi's and leather jackets. Lara felt a thrill in her stomach. These were Sasha's mysterious classmates from university, the ones he didn't want her to meet. Reluctantly, he returned the wave and walked with Lara over to the table, where his friends insisted they sit down.

Lara tried not to stare, but she was fascinated by these people, the ones who occupied the rest of Sasha's life. The way these young men and women spoke, raising their voices to be heard over one another—it almost seemed like part of a costume, just like their clove cigarettes and bitter black coffee. They were debating the outcome of recent local elections. Lara didn't know much about French politics. Even if she did, she doubted that she would become this animated about it. She glanced over at Sasha, who had stayed silent like her, watching the sparring. She loved that he didn't feel the need to exercise his intelligence in front of other people.

Then one of the girls started teasing him, saying, "*Alors*, Comrade Kurlansky, surely you have an opinion to offer."

Sasha began to open his mouth, then he paused, tilting his head for a long moment. The table erupted into affectionate laughter. Lara laughed, too. *We love him for the same reasons*, she thought happily. The painstaking care with which he chose his words, the almost-comical deliberation.

Finally, he spoke. Sasha had his criticisms of the French government, sure, but he quickly detoured to a bigger point. A few weeks earlier, Mikhail Gorbachev had been elected general secretary of the Communist Party. Gorbachev was the youngest and savviest Soviet leader they had ever known. Gorbachev spoke of perestroika, the need for economic restructuring and reform. Sasha conceded that this was a positive development. Better

Gorbachev than Gromyko, anyone could see that. But reforms weren't enough. The party was rotten to its core, it always had been. All of them—yes, even Lenin—were criminals and murderers and thugs. Gorbachev had to be pushed harder.

The sun was setting by the time they left. Lara was expected home for dinner. Their route took them down the rue de Grenelle, past the old Soviet embassy. The vehemence of Sasha's speech had surprised her. Lara felt uneasy. They were silent as they walked.

Finally, she said, "He was elected only two weeks ago. Are you not even going to give him a chance?"

Sasha shook his head. "It's important to draw a line, Lara. It's a matter of morality. We have to be clear about what we will and won't tolerate."

"But you called them, *all* of them, criminals and murderers and thugs. Sasha, how can you say those things?" Her voice was splintery and raw. Her father, her grandfather: Was he talking about them, too?

He opened his mouth, then shut it. Of course he was.

"Don't you think there's anything good?" she pressed. "Anything worth preserving?"

He shook his head. "Lara, you're asking the wrong question."

"What do you mean?"

"We're concerned with the future," he said. "Not the past. Not even the present. Our ideals are what matter. If we stay with those, everything else will unfold as it should."

She didn't reply. An agitated storm was surging inside of her chest. He noticed her downward stare, her hand clenched around the strap of her bag.

"Lara," he said gently. "I know you feel the same way. I can see it. Your eyes have been opened. And once that happens, you can't close them. You feel it too, don't you? The lies. The corruption."

She remained silent the whole way home, giving him a dry peck goodbye before heading inside. *But is this really true?* she thought. *Is this how I feel? Or is Sasha doing the same thing as always—assuming that I agree with everything he says?* Gradually, her uncertainty turned to irritation. In fact, she grew so irritated that she lay awake all night. She would have liked to push back at Sasha. To argue, even. Why this silence? Why this automatic agreement?

A few years earlier, when her older sister was still living at home, Lara had overheard Natasha begging their mother for permission to bleach her hair. *Everyone* was doing it. It was so chic, and Natasha would be an outcast if she didn't do it, too.

"It's a terrible idea," Irina said flatly. "It won't suit you. Dye your hair if that's what you really want. But do you even *want* to? You're a smart girl, Nataschenka. Smart girls make up their own minds."

Sometimes the advice that actually sticks is that which wasn't even intended for us.

That week, Lara read everything she could find about the newly elected Gorbachev and his reforms. The following weekend, when she and Sasha next saw each other, she had made up her own mind; she knew what she wanted to say. It was a beautiful Saturday afternoon in the Tuileries, the same place where Lara had comforted the little boy.

She asked Sasha to sit down with her. Then she took a deep breath and said, "You're being cynical. You're assuming that he is exactly like every leader that came before. But people are *different*, Sasha. Not cookie cutters. Why can't you see that?"

Sasha responded in a reasonable tone, but Lara pushed back. He seemed surprised by this, and then annoyed, and soon enough they exploded into argument. A full-fledged, raised-voices, day-ruining fight. But a small part of Lara, detached from the moment, was thrilled. *We're fighting*, she thought. *Our first big fight, but we're fighting about something real.*

It was getting dark. They were hungry. They had been arguing for hours, winnowing themselves down to certain essential differences. And that was okay; they didn't have to agree on every premise. Their love was strong enough to bridge that gap.

As they walked down the crowded rue de Rivoli in search of

something to eat, Sasha reached for her hand and squeezed it. Paris had given her so much: food, art, music, material comfort. But this was the real abundance. In that moment, Lara felt exhilarated. She, this child of the Soviet bureaucracy, could think and say—it struck her like lightning—*whatever she wanted.*

CHAPTER TEN

On a rainy day in early June, after getting soaked from a taxi ripping through a puddle on Fifty-Fifth Street, I stepped through the doors of a sleek Midtown restaurant. As I shook out my umbrella, I said to the hostess, "I'm meeting Vicky Wethers."

The restaurant was gleaming white: white walls, white banquettes, aging white media executives. The hostess led me toward the back, where Vicky was sitting in her usual booth, thumbing out emails as her reading glasses slipped down her nose.

"Sofie," she said, smiling. "Honey, thank you for schlepping to Midtown on this foul day."

"Careful, I'm wet," I said, as we hugged. Vicky even smelled the same, that familiar combination of powdery soap and Chanel N°5.

When the waitress arrived to fill our water glasses, Vicky said to her, "No need to do the specials, dear. I always get the same thing. And probably so does Sofie, because we're all so predictable, aren't we? Well, except for you. You changed your hair! I like it."

"I just got it cut yesterday," the waitress said, bemused. "So the Niçoise salad for you, Ms. Wethers. And for you, miss?"

"I'll have the tuna tartare," I said.

When the waitress left, Vicky leaned forward. "Tuna tartare, huh? That settles it."

"Settles what?"

"A few people in the office thought you were pregnant. I knew you weren't."

I smiled. "You always were clairvoyant."

"Enough," Vicky said, waving a hand. "Enough about what isn't happening. Tell me what *is* happening. How are you doing, sweetheart?"

From the first moment of my first interview for the job six years earlier, sitting in that same booth in that same restaurant, I adored Vicky. I'd never met anyone quite like her. When she offered me the job, I leaped at it—not only because of the work but also because it meant working for *her*. There was something special about her. There was a depth to her that I had wanted (and still wanted) to understand.

When Vicky was young, she had married a lawyer. He was a good man and a good father to their sons, but a dull husband. In her early forties, they divorced. She'd been happily single ever since. Marriage, she said, just wasn't right for her. She knew herself enough to know that. Her directness was one of her best qualities. It always made me want to tell the truth. During a heart-to-heart, one late night in the office, I'd told Vicky how I sometimes wondered whether I was doing the right thing, whether my life was unfolding as it was meant to, and how it felt lonely to wonder about this—lonely, even though I had so much. My marriage, my sister, my friends, my job. I was so lucky. This should be enough. Why did these questions persist?

She'd taken my hand, and said, "Oh, honey. I'm proud of you."

I'd laughed, baffled. "Why? Because I'm whining about nothing?"

She'd smiled. "Because you *should* be asking those questions."

Though she had plenty of war stories—first reporter into Kuwait during Desert Storm, front-row seat to the Clinton impeachment—Vicky rarely talked about the past. What good were the old stories? They only weighed her down. They only distracted her from what she loved. "Like my grandchildren," she'd said. "Or my dog. Or the cinnamon babka from Zabar's. Or showing up to this office every day. The things I love exist *here*, Sofie. Right here and right now. Nowhere else."

Where had she learned how to live like this? From what source did this spring? Vicky possessed a resilience that seemed wasted on twenty-first-century Manhattan. She ought to have been living on the frontier in the 1800s, building log cabins and arguing over water rights.

We talked and talked and talked. When the waitress said, "Can I interest you ladies in any dessert?" I looked up and was surprised to see that the restaurant was nearly empty.

"Yes," Vicky said. "We'll share the crème brûlée. And I'll have a cappuccino. Sofie?"

"A cappuccino sounds great," I said.

"The crème brûlée is really for you," Vicky said, after the waitress left. "I'm stuffed. You eat it, but go nice and slow. If we order dessert they'll leave us alone for a while longer. And there's something I want to ask." She squinted at me. "Level with me, Sofie. This whole Lara Caine thing. Did you always know this would be your exit ramp?"

I shook my head. "Nope," I said. "I had no plan when I left."

There was a long pause.

"*So?*" Vicky prompted.

"So what?"

"So tell me what she's like!" she said. "Sofie, come on! I'm beyond curious. No one has managed to crack Mrs. Caine's pretty shell. *No one*. And I know there's more to her than meets the eye."

"She's . . . ," I began, but what was the right word? The right adjective, the right metaphor, the right descriptor? "I don't know. I don't know how to say it."

Vicky cocked an eyebrow. "Why this false modesty? You've been there every week since December. Has she put the fear of God into you? Is your NDA *that* ironclad?"

At that moment, the waitress appeared, delivering our dessert. "Crème brûlée and two cappuccinos," she said brightly. "Enjoy."

Vicky gazed at me, waiting. I'd been on the verge of blurting it out—*I don't have an NDA*—but the interruption saved me. No: it was better to say nothing and let Vicky interpret my silence as she chose. Although, in that moment, it struck me anew just how bizarre it was. No NDA. Why had Lara left herself so needlessly exposed?

"Okay." Vicky finally nodded. She tapped her spoon and shattered the brittle caramel gloss, scooping out a drift of vanilla-flecked custard. "Okay. I promised myself that I wouldn't pester you too much about her. But I just have to ask you one thing. One tiny little thing I'm hoping you can confirm for us."

"But I can't—"

She held up a hand. "This won't cost you anything. It's a story we've been trying to pin down. You know that Andrei Cheban lunch she hosted back in April? We heard that FLOTUS had to fight the West Wing to make it happen. We've got a source confirming the story. That Mrs. Caine went rogue, basically. That no one wanted to do it except for her. We need one more person to confirm before we can run with it."

"Vicky," I said, taking a deep breath. "Why are you doing this to me?"

"Doing what?"

"Why are you putting me in this position?"

She laughed. "What position? It's a quick yes or no."

"It's more than that," I said.

"Sofie, come on." Her smile hardened slightly. "You're one of us."

I took a sip of cappuccino, avoiding her gaze, trying to talk myself free from my own sense of guilt. I *had* been one of them. Not anymore. Not since the day I walked out of that newsroom.

"You're kidding," she said. "You've been with her for, what, six months? Have your loyalties changed that fast?"

"It's not like that," I said, sounding both defensive and weak.

Vicky leaned forward. "I'm not asking you to *tell* me anything. Just to confirm. FLOTUS would have no way of knowing it's you. What's the big deal?"

I glanced at my watch. "It's almost three o'clock," I said. "I should probably get going."

She pushed the plate toward me. "You haven't even tried the crème brûlée."

"I'm not hungry," I said. "I'm sorry, but I have to go."

I was waving at the waitress for the check as Vicky opened her mouth. For a moment, it seemed like she was going to lose her temper and snap at me; and maybe, it occurred to me, I deserved it. But then she shook her head, and her expression changed.

"Okay," she said resignedly. "Okay, I get it. I'm sorry for pestering."

Silence endured for a while. Vicky took another bite of crème brûlée. I reached over to take a bite, too. A truce.

"You know it doesn't matter, right?" she said. "I push because it's my job to push, but it has nothing to do with you. I love you, Sofie. I care about you."

"I know," I said.

"And I'm always here," she said. "I'm not going anywhere."

•

A few weeks later, during summer's first heat wave. "I've had an idea," Lara said, as she walked me to the staircase on the second floor of the residence. We'd been sitting in the family kitchen, drinking iced tea. The air-conditioning in the White House wasn't all that great, and I felt my skirt sticking to the backs of my thighs, rivulets of sweat trickling down my breastbone.

"Emily and Marina are going to camp this year," she said. "Up in Massachusetts. But before they go, I'd like to take them to Connecticut for a few weeks. We've done it every summer. Our family tradition. And I was thinking—what if you came with us?"

I cocked my head. "Came to Connecticut?"

"We have plenty of room. I don't want to lose our momentum. It feels important to keep the work going. Don't you agree?"

"But it would only be a few weeks that you're gone, right?"

"I think it's a good idea," Lara said, in a firm tone. "I'd like this to happen."

It struck me as a strange request. A biography takes years to write; a two-week interruption doesn't matter. Even though we'd grown closer, this was crossing a whole other line: staying at her country house, captive to her hospitality.

"Can I sleep on it?" I asked.

"Fine," she replied, folding her arms across her silky sleeveless blouse. "But I'd have more time to give you in Connecticut. We could get through some very important material."

I thought about it as I walked down the carpeted stairs to the first floor of the residence. I turned into the East Wing, passed the windows of the East Colonnade, exited through the lobby, nodded goodbye to the guards. A strange request, but maybe it was concealing something else. Beneath those icy and imperious words, I could hear an appeal to my compassion.

"It isn't easy," she'd said, a few weeks ago. "Talking about him like this. It's been a long time since I let myself remember."

I could see it written on her face, how reliving those memories of Sasha was a source of joy, and also an exquisite form of torture. To talk about him was to remember, over and over and over again, that nothing could bring him back. *Help me finish this*, she silently pleaded. *Take this away from me.*

It was a Saturday in September 1985, during their second autumn together.

Lara and Sasha spent the morning in the university library. Because she wasn't a student, Lara wasn't technically allowed inside, but Sasha had befriended the security guard. The guard winked as they came in and said, "As long as you're sure she won't distract you, my friend."

When he enrolled at the university, Sasha initially planned to study political science, but during his first year he took a philosophy class that changed his mind. "This professor, Lara, I don't know how to describe him. But he *understands*. He can see every factor at once." Sasha seemed to idolize this professor. Hence this beautiful Saturday in the library, toiling at his essay for his ethics seminar. He wanted—no, he *needed*—to make it perfect. Meanwhile Lara paged through old issues of *Elle*, occasionally glancing up, impressed and amused by Sasha's unbroken concentration: his furrowed brow, his pursed lips.

When he was finally satisfied with the day's work, they set out across the river, toward *The Spark* offices in the Eleventh Arrondissement. He kept looking at his watch.

"Is everything okay?" Lara asked, hurrying to match his pace.

"They're going to call at one p.m.," he said. "I can't be late."

There were certain immovable pillars in Sasha's life. The phone calls from his writers inside the Soviet Union were among them. Every time these men and women picked up the phone and dialed the number for *The Spark*, they were risking their lives. The least Sasha could do was be there to answer the call. Miss it even once, and the writer might panic. They might never call again.

"I'll just barely make it," Sasha said, as they hurried past the Bastille. "Come on, Lara."

But as they approached the rue Saint-Bernard, Sasha stopped suddenly—so suddenly that Lara was several feet ahead before she turned around and noticed him. Pale, wide-eyed, frozen like a statue.

"Sasha?" she said. "What is it?"

He swallowed. "I need you to go without me," he said. "When the phone rings, you answer it. Tell them your friend was held up."

"Very funny," she said. Sasha didn't even like Lara visiting the office, let alone getting involved with the work itself. "Hurry up. You said one o'clock, right?"

But Sasha shook his head. "You need to take this call for me, Lara. I'll explain later. When you answer the phone, tell them you took the Metro to Ledru-Rollin and managed to get a seat. They'll know to trust you. Then write down whatever they say."

"But I don't understand," she said. "What's this all about?"

He took a key from his pocket and pressed it into her hand. "The other editors wouldn't get there in time. Wait for me at the office. I'll come find you. *Please.* I need you to do this for me."

The panic in his voice was new to her. Sasha would rather die than let one of his writers down. From the frightened look on his face, Lara knew that he'd seen something, or someone, that he wasn't expecting to see. "I'll explain later," he called over his shoulder, as he jogged in the other direction. "And, Lara—thank you."

She looked at her watch and started running. When she arrived, sprinting up the four flights of stairs, the office was deserted. Dust motes floated in the sunlight. The smell of stale coffee and cigarettes lingered. It was silent but for the blood pounding in her ears. She checked her watch again. One o'clock exactly. Was she too late? Had she already missed them?

But then the shrill ring of the telephone ripped through the quiet.

"Hello?" she answered breathlessly.

"Hello? Hello?" said the voice on the other end. A man, sounding fuzzy and distant.

"Hello," she repeated, more calmly. She drew a deep breath. Remembered her instructions. Gathered herself. "I'm afraid your friend got stuck, so I'm here instead. But don't worry. I took the Metro to Ledru-Rollin. Luckily I managed to get a seat."

There was a long stretch of quiet. "Is he okay?" the man finally asked.

"He is completely fine," Lara said with false confidence. "Now. How are *you*?"

She wrote down everything the man said: the weather in Moscow, the health of his mother and father, the lilacs blooming in the countryside. She nodded as he spoke, though she understood none of what he was saying and could only hope that Sasha would make sense of it. Then she remembered that this man couldn't see her nodding, so she began making reassuring *hmm* sounds to show that she was listening. He seemed to relax as the call went on. He spoke for nearly an hour.

Hanging up, she felt a rush of exhilaration. She'd done it! Even if she wasn't entirely clear what "it" was. She walked to the garret window, which looked down on rue Saint-Bernard. The café across the street was busy with the lunchtime crowd. Her stomach growled. She was starving. She badly wanted to go downstairs and eat something—but no. She told Sasha that she'd wait for him at the office. What if he came, and she wasn't here, and he panicked?

The afternoon went by. The sun sank lower. The office grew dim. Lara turned on a lamp. It was 6:00 p.m. It was 7:00 p.m. Her stomach was making crazy noises. She was tired, and hungry, and annoyed. Where was Sasha? He could have called; why hadn't he called? *But isn't this always how it goes?* she thought. *He never tells me the whole story. Wait for me, Lara. Do this, Lara. Do that, Lara.* Why? *No time to explain. You just have to trust me.*

Finally, *finally*, there was the sound of footsteps on the stairs. Sasha opened the door, looking calm and pleased. For some reason, this tipped her irritation into anger. "You're still here," he said. "I'm so glad. How did it go?"

"The notes are on the desk," she said, striding past him. "I'm leaving now."

"Lara, wait!" He caught her by the hand. "I'm sorry," he pleaded.

"Sorry for what?" she said, trying to wrest free of his grasp. "Sorry for abandoning me? Sorry for using me like a ridiculous errand girl?"

"I'm sorry for all of it," he said. He wouldn't let go of her hand. "Please. Will you just give me five minutes? I'll try to explain."

As they sat down, Sasha pulled a crinkling bag from his pocket. It smelled of butter and sugar. "I thought you might be hungry," he said, passing it to her. A palmier cookie: her favorite. "I didn't know that would take so long."

She shook her head. "What happened to you?" she said. "You looked like you saw a ghost."

His lip curled in a slight smile. "That's not the worst way of putting it."

Sasha began talking. Did Lara remember what he had once said about a man named Mr. Smith? Yes, of course: Mr. Smith was their American friend, the one who helped subsidize the magazine. Well, that's who Sasha had seen. Mr. Smith, standing there on the sidewalk, in broad daylight.

"So?" she said, crossing her arms.

So that never happened. Sasha and Mr. Smith rarely met face-to-face. It was too dangerous. And when they *did* have to meet, when it was absolutely unavoidable, it was an orchestrated effort. Cover of darkness, meandering routes, flushing out tails. You see,

Mr. Smith was more than just a financial backer. He helped Sasha with other things, too.

"Like what?" she asked.

Like strategizing over what the magazine ought to publish. Like connecting Sasha with dissident writers inside the Soviet Union. For everyone's safety, his real role at *The Spark* had to be kept secret. That was why Sasha was the only person who communicated with him. That was why it was highly irregular, and extremely alarming, for Mr. Smith to appear in such close and public proximity to the office.

"You understand, don't you?" His dark eyes were pleading, soft and puppylike. "You see why I was so alarmed. He would only risk such a thing in case of a true emergency."

"And was it an emergency?" she asked.

"Yes," he said quietly. "But we're figuring it out."

She wanted to press for more, but she knew she had reached the limit of what he would share. She picked at her cookie, the buttery flakes collecting in her lap. She was still angry. "That wasn't fair," she said. "You can't just spring that kind of thing on me. I have no idea what I'm doing. I'm not *you*, Sasha. I'm not capable of all this."

"I don't believe that," he said.

She looked up. Sasha was gazing at her with a new kind of tenderness.

"Lara, you're capable of everything I do," he continued. "You're capable of even more. Someday you'll start to see this."

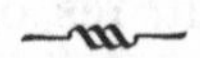

Jenna sat at the kitchen table, fanning herself, while I put away the groceries she'd just brought home. It was so hot that the orange juice carton had gone slick with condensation, the pint of ice cream soft under my fingertips. Bags of Goldfish, six-packs of strawberry yogurt, frozen chicken tenders: these little divergences in our lives often tripped me up. In the moments when it was just me and Jenna, gossiping or watching

TV or sharing a bottle of wine, nothing seemed to separate us. The same hair, the same mannerisms, the same laugh. Two sisters, two parallel tracks. But then I'd open the fridge and see the juice boxes; or open the medicine cabinet and see the Peppa Pig Band-Aids; and I would remember that if life is lived in the details, ours were nothing alike.

"How was your day?" I asked.

Jenna sighed. "Do you ever wonder what you're doing with your life?"

"All the time," I said, dropping baby carrots into the crisper. "Do you?"

"I treated this kid in the ER this morning," she said. "Six years old. He'd fainted, so his mother brought him in. Turns out he hadn't eaten in two days. What the fuck, right? At first I was so mad at the mother. I mean, I was *livid*. But then it turns out—she'd been kicked off SNAP. An issue with her job-training program. The government changed the rules, I guess. This little boy was starving, but he was pretending he wasn't hungry, because he wanted his baby sister to have enough to eat." She propped her elbows on the table, pressed the heels of her palms into her eyes. "This world doesn't make sense. And what can *I* do about it? You know? What good is treating the symptom without treating the cause?"

My stomach twisted into an awful knot. Packages of string cheese, jars of peanut butter, bags of apples—you couldn't even see the kitchen counter beneath this abundance of groceries. Jenna noticed my guilty gaze. "Yup," she said. "Exactly what I thought as I walked through Safeway."

I picked up the string cheese and paused. *The government changed the rules, I guess.* "The government" meant Henry Caine, and an hour earlier, I'd been drinking iced tea with his wife in the White House. There had been times, over the last months, when the disastrous effects of his decisions became too much to ignore, and I looked at Lara and thought, *You sleep beside this man every night*, and then thought, *Why are you tolerating this? People are suffering. You could do something about it. Why aren't you doing anything about it? Why are you making yourself complicit in this?*

I closed the refrigerator and stared at it for a long beat. But who, really, was the *you* I was talking to?

"Sorry, Sofe." Jenna sighed. "Didn't mean to kill the mood. Jesus Christ. I don't think I can cook in this heat. Not even for you. Want to order in?"

"Let's do Chinese," I said. "It's my turn to treat."

A half hour later, Sam got home with Derek and Luke. The twins were sweaty and hyper from T-ball practice. When they got like this, narrating the play-by-play of the game, they talked so fast that they barely made sense. (Jenna once joked they were like two coked-out bankers who had just closed a huge deal.) Sam flopped down beside Jenna, pouring himself a glass of wine with a heavy sigh. Derek and Luke started bickering and then scuffling, until Jenna barked loudly, "Boys!"

The whole house was in a hectic swirl when Ben arrived, a little after 7:00 p.m. The boys were setting the table, folding napkins into uneven triangles, arguing again.

"Ah, shoot," Ben said. "You didn't wait for me to eat, did you? I didn't mean to hold things up."

"Food's been ordered but isn't here yet," Jenna said. "Don't worry. This isn't politeness, just disorganization."

That week, Ben had arranged to work out of his firm's DC office. He told the partners in New York that he wanted extra face time with an important public-sector client, but truthfully, it was because the weeknight bachelor routine was getting to him. "I thought this chapter was behind us, Sofe," he'd said irritably, a few weeks earlier.

When I pointed out that I was only in DC two nights a week, which wasn't even that much, he said, "It's not that. It's that it seems like your *real* life is down there. And up here, you're only visiting. Haven't we done enough of this?"

A few minutes after that, he apologized for snapping. He knew how much this work meant to me. He didn't want to hold me back—he just missed me, that was all. So that week, the two of us came down to DC together, cramming ourselves in Jenna and Sam's spare room. In the mornings, we said Cleaveresque goodbyes on the doorstep, and in the evenings, we all ate dinner together. Despite the cramped quarters, it was surprisingly nice. The novelty of having their uncle Ben around made Derek and Luke even more energetic than usual. Ben, for his sins, was exceedingly attentive to the twins. Did he know that Derek knew how to do a cartwheel? He *didn't*? Did he want to see? Did he want Derek to teach him how?

Jenna and Sam and I sat at the kitchen table, surrounded by scraps of chow mein and barbecue pork, gazing through the window, watching Ben and the twins in the backyard. It was past eight o'clock, and the yard was filled with golden evening light. Ben made a show of rolling up his sleeves, turning up the cuffs of his pants, nodding seriously as Derek explained his cartwheel technique.

"He knows that he doesn't have to, right?" Jenna said, dipping the last dumpling in a puddle of sauce. "I'm not going back to the emergency room if Ben breaks his arm."

Outside, after Derek had demonstrated several cartwheels in a row, Ben assumed his position. He shook out his wrists, rolled his neck, drew in a deep breath. Jenna and Sam and I watched with an oddly respectful silence. Ben reared back, tipped his weight forward, and executed a perfect cartwheel.

Derek was applauding and beaming. Ben grinned at him and did it again, only this time, he suspended his body in a handstand. He walked several steps forward on his hands, and then several steps back, his torso and legs flawlessly vertical. By this point, Derek's and Luke's mouths were completely agape.

A moment later, the boys came bursting through the back door. "Did you see it? Mom! Dad! Did you see what he did?"

"Pretty amazing," Sam said, ruffling their hair.

"I'm tempted to call you a show-off," Jenna said, as Ben trailed them back inside. "But even I'm impressed."

"Where did you learn to do that?" I said.

Ben shrugged, grinning. "I've been going to yoga a few mornings a week."

When he went to the sink for a glass of water, Jenna caught my gaze. *Yoga*, she mouthed, eyes wide. Then she looked down, pinched her stomach, and frowned.

Jenna and Sam put the boys to bed and soon retreated upstairs themselves, because they had early shifts the next day. Their dishwasher was on the fritz, so Ben was washing the plates and glasses while I dried. When he'd finished the last dish, he yawned and shook his head. "I think I'm ready to crash, too," he said.

Through the whole evening, there seemed to be a ticking time bomb lodged in my rib cage. Ever since I'd reached my decision about Connecticut, the dread had gotten steadily worse. Part of me wanted to back out, turn down her invitation, say nothing to Ben, pretend it never happened. But I knew I couldn't do that. *Just do it, Sofie.* Why was I this nervous, anyway?

Drying the last plate, I thought of something Jenna had recently told me. "Remember how Mom would always feed us when she had bad news?" she said. "Because it's harder to be sad when you're eating a bunch of cookies? Well, the other day their teacher told the class about global warming. The boys went crazy, they had *all* these questions. So I made them brownie sundaes while we talked. And you know what? It totally worked."

Ben was looking at me, waiting. "Sofe? Should we head up?"

"Better idea," I said. "Let's have some ice cream."

In the stark white light of the freezer, there was the pint I'd unpacked. I'd go to the grocery store the next day, and replace it before Jenna knew it was missing.

"The good stuff," I said, shutting the freezer door. New York Super Fudge Chunk.

We took the pint and two spoons outside, to the back steps. The concrete radiated the day's heat, but there was the slightest relief in the night breeze. The ice cream was so deliciously cold that it hurt my teeth. I dragged my spoon along a thick ribbon of fudge and passed the carton to Ben.

I said, "I have to tell you something." I paused, looking down at my knees. *Say it. Just say it.* "It's Lara. She invited me to come stay with the family in Connecticut."

He arched an eyebrow as he scooped out a hunk of chocolate. "For, what, an overnight?"

I took a deep breath. "Longer than that. For two weeks, maybe three. Starting on Sunday. They go every summer. She doesn't want to interrupt the work or lose our momentum—which makes sense to me, and anyways, she needs an answer by tomorrow, so I'm sorry to spring this on you, but I wanted to make sure it was okay by you—I mean, I know I've been away a lot—and I'd have to miss your firm's summer party next week, and I know that's important to you, but this is just . . ."

I looked over at Ben, who was expressionless. After a beat, he said, "Sofie, it doesn't matter whether it's okay by me. You've clearly made up your mind. I'm not going to stop you."

"But I wanted to make sure—"

"You want me to endorse the decision?" He shrugged. "I can't do that. I don't know her well enough to know if this is a good idea."

"But I care about what you think."

"I know you do," he said quietly. "But whatever I think, it matters less than what *you* think. It might be a good idea. It might not. You have to make that call."

Another long silence. Ben dug his spoon into the ice cream, then passed the pint back to me.

"I don't know why I'm so nervous," I said.

The cicadas whirring softly. The blue flicker of a TV screen through a neighbor's window. The soccer ball in the moonlit backyard. An ordinary suburban night. At some point in time (When? Where was that threshold?), this had become a place whose every detail I could picture when I closed my eyes.

I said, "I thought you might be angry."

"Why would I be angry?" Ben said, mystified.

Because I'm worried you were right, I thought. *It's becoming my real life. When I'm with her.* What was I getting myself into? Where was this taking me? I could sense the ground shifting beneath me, but I couldn't articulate it, so I merely stared at my feet.

"Sofie." He laughed in bewilderment. "You thought I'd be angry because of the firm's summer party? Do you think I really care about that?"

No, I thought. "No," I said.

"This isn't going to last forever." Ben gestured for another bite of the ice cream. The sugary buzz coursing through my veins made me feel slightly ill. "Let's just remember that."

•

The air force plane landed in Hartford on Sunday, where a battalion of black SUVs waited for the First Lady and her entourage. Lara and her daughters rode in one. Gabi Carvalho and a few other aides were along for the vacation, and I started following them to their SUV, but then Irina called and waved for me to join her car.

"You're practically like family, Sonechka," she said. "So you ride with family."

The motorcade began its journey west, toward Litchfield County. "Family," for the next three weeks, didn't include Henry Caine. He would be staying in Washington. There had been long-standing rumors that POTUS and FLOTUS preferred to take separate vacations. Like many long-standing rumors, this one turned out to be true.

"Natasha says the honeysuckle is in bloom," Irina said, smiling at her phone in the back seat. She squinted through her reading glasses and tapped out a reply. Natasha had traveled to Connecticut a few days before, to get the house ready for the family.

"Did she get her green thumb from you?" I asked.

Irina shook her head. "From Fedya. At the dacha, he would spend all day in the dirt, tending to his plants, treating them like they were his children. This was something we both missed in Paris."

"Gardening, you mean?"

"More than just gardening," Irina said. "Our whole life in the country. Has Lara ever told you how this house came to be?"

As we drove, leaving behind the Hartford suburbs, Irina explained. Before they moved to Paris, the Orlovs spent many of their weekends at the family dacha in the countryside, outside of Moscow. Irina loved that dacha. When they were in France, and she felt lonely or homesick, she closed her eyes and imagined it. The linden trees, the lilacs, the long northern twilight. Afternoons spent foraging for mushrooms in the surrounding woods, which she fried in butter and served for dinner. The cherry trees near the house, heavy with dark fruit. The birch trees glowing a luminous shade of yellow in the autumn. There was a small river at the edge of the property. You could walk along the towpath and cross the river on stone footbridges that dated back to the era of Catherine the Great. Imagine that, Irina said wistfully. Imagine everything those stones had endured.

How easy it is, when you love a thing, to turn memory into myth. In the bleak years of the late 1980s and early 1990s, after the Orlov family returned to Moscow and Fyodor was killed, Irina felt a devastating sense of betrayal. She loved her country, she had never stopped loving her country—she had held strong, despite the many temptations of the West—but her country no longer loved her back. Their life in Russia was bleak and hopeless. Every comfort had been stripped away. Natasha had once asked, caustically, why their mother wanted to return to this godforsaken place. But even in her grief, Irina was loyal to her old memories.

"*No,* Nataschenka," she insisted. "You must understand. If you could see how it was before—"

During that bleak stretch she talked about it constantly, an endless stream of recalling the old days in Moscow, the old days at the dacha. If she didn't, who would? Almost everyone else who remembered those years was dead. Perhaps she was talking into a void. So be it. Her daughters could listen or not listen, she didn't care. Clinging to the past was the only way to keep herself afloat.

"But this is the thing about children," Irina said, as the SUV zoomed along the highway. "You may think they aren't listening, and yet they are listening all along."

When Lara Orlova married Henry Caine in 2002, she brought her mother and sister to New York, installing them in a large apartment next door to the newlyweds. And then, a few years later, when Irina was contentedly settled into her New York life, Lara told her mother that she had a surprise. The two women rode in the back of a town car, up the FDR and out of Manhattan, along the Hutchinson, and then to a series of small highways in northwestern Connecticut. Finally, the car slowed, turning into a driveway lined with an alley of sugar maples.

When the car approached the house, Irina felt a catch in her throat. "It's for you, Mama," Lara said, with a sudden shyness. "Do you like it?" The sight was uncannily familiar, right down to the lilacs planted by the front door. The house was set on a rise overlooking a vast field. There was a pond, fed by a burbling stream, with a grove of birches reflected in the rippling water. There was a handsome tree bearing dark, glossy cherries. Here it was, Irina understood. The shipwrecked salvage of a long-ago memory, painstakingly reassembled in a brand-new country. An invisible past made visible. Someone had been listening all along.

•

There were two symmetrical wings that branched from the central portion of the house, one with bedrooms for family, one with bedrooms for guests. Despite what Irina said, I was clearly in the "guest" category, assigned to a room along the same hallway as the First Lady's aides.

A soft knock came while I was unpacking. Lara stood in the doorway. She'd changed from her stylish outfit on the plane, now barefoot and in faded jeans and a sailor-striped boating shirt. I'd never seen her dressed so casually.

"I've always liked this room," she said, a fond gaze sweeping across the space. "I decorated this part of the house when I was pregnant. It makes me think of my daughters." And speaking of which, she said that she'd promised Emily and Marina that they would watch a movie together that night, so she suggested we start working the next day, after breakfast. In the meantime, if I needed anything, anything at all, I only had to ask.

The house had the feeling of a small, luxurious hotel. My bedroom came with spare silk pajamas, a tented card on the bureau listing the Wi-Fi password, a bathroom stocked with toothbrushes and toothpaste and expensive toiletries. The Secret Service had traded their dark suits for khakis, but they still wore their earpieces and serious expressions as they rotated in and out of the house. That first evening, a slim man wearing Nantucket reds and a white polo shirt introduced himself to me as the manager of the property. It turned out he was the captain of an entire assemblage of domestic staff: housekeepers, gardeners, cooks, handymen. Natasha liked to putter with her lilies and zinnias, and Irina liked to make borscht and sirniki, but there were plenty of professionals around to do the heavy lifting: the weeding and mowing, the grocery shopping, the relentless preparation of three meals a day for large crowds.

In the morning, when I came downstairs for breakfast, there was already the distant buzz of activity throughout the house. Phones chirped with alerts, snatches of conversation drifted through open windows, a walkie-talkie issued a staticky crackle. For Lara's aides, these weeks in Connecticut were definitively not a vacation. They moved through the house in the same grooved patterns as in the East Wing: walking, stopping, talking, retracing, heads on a swivel in case the boss appeared. Gabi Carvalho was standing on the porch, phone pressed to her ear, coffee in one hand. Her sharp voice traveled through the screen door: "I don't give a shit what you heard. It's not true. Okay? Mrs. Caine never said anything about that anti-vaccine crap. That's her husband. Not her."

Breakfast was laid out in the dining room: platters of tropical fruit, a silver coffee urn, bacon and eggs kept warm in a chafing dish. I took my plate outside, into the sunny late June morning. Behind the house was a formal garden with sculpted hedges and gravel paths. Past that was a windbreak of tall birches, the breeze billowing through their high crowns of foliage. It was one of those bright blue days that saturated everything with extra color and depth. Walking across the gravel path with my breakfast and coffee in hand, I smiled in recognition. These weren't just Irina's treasured memories. The mint-green metal chairs scattered through the garden were exactly like the chairs in the Luxembourg Gardens that Lara told me she and Sasha had sat in, decades ago.

"I love it," Lara said, looking up from the page. "Sasha, this is fantastic."

In the café on the rue Saint-Bernard, Sasha waved a dismissive hand. "Well, it's fine. It's adequate." It wasn't that he disagreed with Lara—he'd worked hard on that essay, it had taken him months—but too much praise tended to make him uncomfortable.

It was a Friday night in October 1985, and the latest issue of *The Spark* had just been delivered from the printer. Lara came into the office to help with unpacking the boxes and sorting them for distribution. She loved those delivery days: ripping open the tape, flipping through the pages, inhaling the scent of fresh ink. Upstairs in the office, she scanned through the table of contents. "This issue has your new essay, doesn't it?" she said. "Here it is. Oh, wow, Sasha, it's so long! It's—"

But before she could start reading, Sasha had hurried her out of the office, to the café across the street, a fierce heat rising in his cheeks. The embarrassment of his girlfriend reading his work in front of all his colleagues, exclaiming at his brilliance, might well have killed him.

"I mean it," Lara said. "You should be proud of this."

Sasha shrugged. He picked up the magazine and began turning the pages, squinting for any typos that might have slipped through. Lara smiled. If he wouldn't allow himself this moment of pride, she would be proud for him. In the month since she took that coded phone call, Sasha had allowed her to witness more of what he did at *The Spark*. Lara felt that she was well-suited to this job of spectator and cheerleader, but lately, this was beginning to bother Sasha.

"I don't like it when you say these things," he'd said, a few days earlier, as they rode the Metro back toward the Orlov apartment.

"I know," she'd said. "Because you never learned to take a compliment."

He shook his head. "No. When you say these things, it's like you put me on a pedestal. You suggest there's some great difference between me and you."

She frowned. "But there is a—"

"*No*," he interrupted sharply. "Lara, listen to me. You've come to understand this work, my work, in an important way. When you read what I write, you grasp the real essence of it. When you talk about it, I realize: yes, she has *heard* me."

"Because you're a good writer!" she exclaimed. "Why do you think it's so hard to understand what you're saying? The argument you're making is obvious, Sasha. It's so . . ." She paused: What if he took it as an insult? But Lara was getting annoyed. If this injured him, so be it. "It's so *simple*," she said.

"I know," he said. "But not everyone can see the simplicity."

"You're just telling the truth," she shot back.

"I know," he repeated.

"It just makes *sense*."

"I know," he said again.

She stared at him, puzzled. "Then I don't understand what we're fighting about."

He grinned. "You're very beautiful when you get mad, do you know that?"

She rolled her eyes. He reached for her hand and kissed it. Their arguments were like quicksilver, short and specific, never the same and yet always the same. She didn't like being told what she was, or who she was. She didn't like Sasha pushing her. But he was stubborn, and didn't seem inclined to stop.

◆

"You've done this before," she'd said. Sasha brushing his lips against her neck, running his fingertips along her spine. This was a few months earlier. A Saturday afternoon in her childhood bedroom, a weekend when her parents were out of town. She shivered slightly: the unfamiliar feeling of so much bare skin.

"Yes," he'd said quietly. "But this is different."

She was nervous. They'd always been so happy together. What

if sex changed it, or ruined it? But she loved him, and she was ready even if she wasn't ready. In the beginning she kept her eyes closed, too bashful to meet his gaze, but soon she opened them. He was looking right at her. Her shyness softened, and as it did, she realized something both obvious and profound. This wasn't about a fulfillment of physical lust. This was about trusting one another; a trust deep enough to wipe away any shred of self-consciousness.

She grew to like sex, then to love it. As they wandered museum galleries or browsed bookstore shelves, Lara looked at Sasha and thought: *In this room full of people, I'm the only one who knows about those starry moles on his shoulder blade.* Or about the way he liked to trace delicate lines across her body, down the ridges of her rib cage, around the rise of her breast. Or about the tender gaze on his face when he asked if this was okay; if this felt good.

After they had sex, Sasha wrapped himself around Lara, buckling her body tight against his chest. His arms were thin but strong. Sometimes he squeezed so hard that it made her squirm.

"Easy." She laughed. "I'm not going anywhere."

But despite how tightly he held her, there were moments when he seemed to slip from her grasp.

On that Friday night in October 1985, he finally finished reading through the new issue of *The Spark*. He looked up at her with a slightly dazed expression, which he always wore after resurfacing from work. She gave him a coy smile. "They've left by now," she said. They had to steal their intimacies whenever they could. "Remember? My parents are away this weekend."

Sasha shook his head, summoning himself back to the present. "I'm sorry, Lara," he said. "I can't. I have things to do."

Lara's smile disappeared. "What things?"

"Do you know what I realized recently? *The Spark* isn't reaching the people it needs to reach. I've asked myself who this is for." He picked up the magazine and held it aloft. "And it's not for Parisians. Not for Westerners. The people who need to read this—they're back home, in Moscow. Or in Kiev, or Minsk. They're the ones we need to reach."

"Okay." She crossed her arms. "Was this your idea? Or was it *his* idea?"

His meaning the man who called himself Walter Smith. Since his initial disclosure in September, Sasha wouldn't tell her anything more about his relationship with the American. ("I can't," he said. "It's too dangerous for all of us.") This only intensified her curiosity. Her skepticism, too. Who was this man, anyway? And why did he have such a sway over her boyfriend?

"Of course it was my idea." He frowned. "Lara, this is serious. This isn't some plaything. This issue alone, we have a dispatch from a nuclear physicist in Canada, and we printed sections from Solzhenitsyn's new novel. It deserves a bigger audience."

"So this is how you'd rather spend your weekend," she said.

He either failed to hear the genuine hurt in her voice, or he chose to ignore it. "I made it clear to you," he said coldly, standing up from the table. "How important this work is. I thought you understood."

"Sasha!" she shouted after him, but he was already halfway across the café.

◆

The next day, he stood outside the apartment on the rue de la Faisanderie, holding a bouquet of daisies. "I'm sorry," he said. "I ruined the weekend. I'm sorry, Lara."

It wasn't that he was blind, he explained. He knew exactly when Lara was irritated, or jealous, or frustrated. But sometimes it was like there were two movies running in his head. His life with her; and his other life. Each one flickered and beckoned, side by side.

The first time they met, at the May Day party in Mantes-la-Jolie, Lara was struck by how well Sasha knew himself. He could explain to her exactly how he came to believe or think a certain idea. She mistook that for transparency. They aren't remotely the same thing.

That fall of 1985, he worked like a maniac. He grew too thin, and had perpetual dark circles beneath his eyes. Sasha and Mr. Smith had found someone willing to smuggle *The Spark* into the Soviet Union. The package would have to take a circuitous route, with trucks and trains and false-bottomed suitcases, but by the end of the year, there would be thousands of copies in Moscow and Leningrad. And not a moment too soon: the situation at home was only getting worse.

"Shh, Sasha, be *careful,*" Lara said. They were at a quiet café in the Marais, and his loud voice had startled the other patrons. He shook his head. *No, Lara, listen:* there was so much to be furious about! Poverty in the Soviet Union was worse than ever. Afghanistan was a travesty. Sasha's cousin had recently returned from serving in the Afghan-Soviet War. The young man was in such despair about the atrocities he had witnessed—the atrocities he himself had been a part of—that he shot himself in his mother's living room.

"Do you see this?" He grabbed the bread basket on their table and shook it. "There are children dying from malnutrition and starvation. In a world where you and I can eat like kings, tell me—how does this make sense?"

"I agree with you," she pleaded. "But *please*, Sasha. Everyone can hear you."

"Good." He looked around the café, eyes flashing like steel. "I want them to hear me."

◆

Fyodor and Irina had met Sasha a grand total of twice. The first time was at Natasha's birthday party in 1984. The second time, they had him over for dinner. Sasha was polite and thoughtful, complimenting Irina's cooking, eating seconds and thirds of everything, and (he wasn't stupid, after all) completely avoiding the subject of politics.

Natasha, in her teenage years, had a long string of boyfriends, which had inoculated Fyodor and Irina against excessive curiosity or caution. Her parents didn't pry into Lara's new relationship. They were happy to see her happy. That was enough.

It didn't feel honest to her, but Lara was learning to reconcile herself with dishonesty. Her parents had taught her to trust her own intelligence. Sasha had taught her to give voice to that intelligence. But if she did that—if, on any given night at the dinner table, Lara said exactly what she thought—then Fyodor and Irina would wonder about the source of these ideas, and that wonder would soon turn to suspicion. Keeping Sasha safe meant keeping her mouth shut.

One night that fall, while the three of them ate dinner, Irina was getting worked up. "All of this change," she said, raising her voice. "And what for? What's the point of all the sacrifice if he just throws everything away?"

"He won't throw everything away," Fyodor countered in a reasonable tone. He splashed more wine into his glass. "Mikhail Sergeyevich is a wise man."

"Mikhail Sergeyevich is weak," Irina said. "No, no more wine for me, Fedya. I have a terrible headache."

The subject of Gorbachev always made Irina snappish. With his housecleaning of the Politburo and his talk about perestroika, Irina thought he was going too far too fast. No matter what the general secretary said or did, she managed to find the bad in it. When he talked about reform, she saw cowardice: he merely wanted the approval of the West. When he took a hard line, she saw trickery: he merely wanted to fool people into thinking him strong. Time after time, Lara watched her mother contorting herself into these knots, and wondered how anything that required such an elaborate explanation could possibly be true.

After Irina went to bed with her headache, Fyodor and Lara cleared the dinner dishes. In the kitchen, as he washed and she dried, Fyodor said, "Your mother is a patriotic woman."

"I know," Lara said.

"If a person has lost both of her parents to a cause, it's very hard to abandon that cause."

Fyodor handed his daughter the crystal wineglass from which Irina had been drinking. In the living room, a Phil Collins record spun on the turntable. Lara was wearing Calvin Klein jeans, and Fyodor had a TAG Heuer watch on his wrist. Their life contained so many luxuries. What Fyodor didn't say, in that moment, was how easily the luxuries could vanish if the winds changed. Irina had traveled far from the deprivations of her childhood, but she knew how contingent these privileges were. The system, such as it was, had been working for her. Why would she want it to change?

"This is one reason we're lucky to have lived here," Fyodor said, drying his hands. "If nothing else, I wanted you girls to see the world with your own eyes. To make up your own minds. Do you know, back in Moscow, what people think of the West? They teach you that the other side is full of crazed murderers." He smiled. "How disappointing to get here and realize that these men and women are perfectly ordinary. Well, my darling. Do you have plans tonight? Or will you keep this old man company for a little longer?"

The two of them settled into the living room. Fyodor sat in the brocade armchair, a stack of files in his lap. He dropped each file to the floor when he finished reading it. ("So much paperwork!" he often exclaimed. "No one ever tells you how much paperwork this job requires.") The room was quiet, just the ticking grandfather clock and the swish of Lara's pencil in her sketchbook. At one point, Lara looked up and noticed that Fyodor was frowning, scratching his temple with the end of his pen. He must have felt her gaze upon him, because he looked up, too, and gave a tired smile. "It never gets easier," he said.

"What doesn't?" she asked.

"There's a big meeting later this month," he said. "Between Gorbachev and Reagan."

"Oh, right. In Geneva," she said. Sasha had been talking about it.

Fyodor looked surprised. "That's right," he said. "In Geneva."

He explained: in the run-up to the summit, the Americans and the Soviets were both stating that they sought a reduction in nuclear arms. The KGB had no intelligence to suggest that the Americans were being disingenuous. And wasn't that a novel concept? (Fyodor said, with an ironic grimace.) That our leaders might actually desire a more peaceful world? The best thing would be for the Soviet Union to approach the summit in the spirit of genuine cooperation. And yet that old bugbear, Operation RYAN, kept the KGB on high alert for a nuclear attack.

"They're convinced the Americans have a grand plan to attack us. Do you know what they have us doing?" Fyodor removed his glasses, rubbing the bridge of his nose. "Monitoring hospitals, to see if the West is filling their blood banks. Watching slaughterhouses, to see if they're stockpiling beef. My God, we're even watching their priests and bankers, to see if they receive some advance warning. Apparently this is how we'll know that the West is preparing for nuclear war. Blood and hamburgers. We're looking for things that aren't there. We're wasting our time on absurdities when there's real work to be done."

Fyodor no longer had the discipline of a young man. He often disregarded the most basic parts of tradecraft. When he stood up from the armchair that night, his papers were scattered across the living room floor; papers containing secure information, which ought to have been stored in a safe somewhere, or at the very least within his locked briefcase. But Fyodor, tired and weary, no longer seemed to care about protocol.

As he talked and talked, Lara found herself wondering: *Why is he telling me this? Why* me*? Why not our mother, or Natasha, or one of his friends?* Maybe he was just talking because he needed to talk: to unburden himself, and Lara happened to be sitting there. She hoped that was the case.

It was clear that the work was weighing on him. That he no longer believed the KGB was making their country a safer place. But what did he expect her to do about it?

CHAPTER ELEVEN

We met for lunch on the porch overlooking the pond. As we sat down, Lara said, "I saw you in the garden this morning. You looked so peaceful."

I smiled. "I can see why you love this place."

"These men and women"—she tilted her head at her Secret Service agent, a dozen feet away—"they would prefer we go to Camp David instead. It's more secure, and easier for them. I know this is a hassle. But I can't tell you how good it feels to be home."

Lara gazed out over the pond. In the rowboat, bobbing in the water, Emily and Marina had hooked bait on their fishing rods, following their aunt Natasha's instructions. The boat wobbled when Marina stood to peer over the edge as the sinker tugged the wire taut. Lara slowly turned her attention back to the table, placing her napkin in her lap and smoothing a crease in the tablecloth. When she lifted the bottle of Pellegrino to fill our glasses, her hand was trembling.

"I suppose I'm nervous," she said. "I've never told anyone how Sasha died. My parents and Natasha only ever knew part of the story."

I nodded. "I understand."

"Oh, Sofie." Her eyes were soft. "I hope you do."

—∞—

On a Sunday evening in December 1985, Sasha and Lara met in the Bois de Boulogne. Christmas was only a few days away. Paris was glittering and festive.

As they sat on a bench in the park, Sasha was more animated than usual. His cheeks were red, his eyes shining with excitement. "I have good news and bad news," he said, slightly breathless. "The package made it to Russia."

Lara smiled. She knew how hard he'd been working on this. "Sasha! That's—"

"Except." He held up a hand. "We only managed to distribute a small portion. Maybe a hundred, two hundred copies of the magazine. The rest were sitting in an apartment in Moscow, waiting for distribution. Until three days ago, when the building went up in flames."

"What?" she said. "What do you mean?"

"Gone." He snapped his fingers. "The whole building, just like that. They're saying it was an accident, from the faulty electrical wiring. But don't you see what this means?"

She shook her head.

"They're scared!" he said. "They're so scared that they'll burn down a building, an entire *building*, just to get rid of a few honest words."

Except that fires happened all the time, she thought. Especially in those shoddy old Moscow buildings. But she didn't want to turn this into a fight, so she reached for his hand, and said, "I think it's amazing that you tried."

"*Tried?*" he said. "No, no, you don't understand. We already have another source helping us to smuggle another package into Moscow. It's happening right now."

"But isn't that stupid?" she said. "If you think they burned down a building to stop you?"

"I don't *think* they burned it down." He frowned. "They *did* burn it down."

"Well—that's not the point. If they did that, what do you think they'll do next?"

"It's a game, Lara!" he exclaimed. "We can't stop now. We make a move, they make a move. Now we make a move again. I'm not quitting just because of this."

"But where does it end up?" she pressed, as he stood from the bench. "Sasha! Where are you going?"

From where she sat, he towered against the sky. Behind Sasha was a beautiful winter sunset. For a moment, it distracted her from the churning dread in her stomach. It was almost heartbreaking to behold: pale lilac sky, watery blue shadows, clouds tinted gold, trees etched like a wood carving. *Look!* she thought. *Turn around. Look at this world, Sasha. Give yourself a chance to see what's already here.*

"I have to go," he said firmly. "There's too much work to be done."

◆

They had been planning to get dinner that Tuesday night at the café on the rue Saint-Bernard, but when Lara arrived, Sasha wasn't there. She climbed the stairs to the magazine office and knocked on the door and asked the other editors, but they just shrugged. They hadn't seen him since Monday, the day before. Maybe he was sick. Maybe he was busy with schoolwork. They weren't worried. Sasha never told them the particulars of his schedule.

Sasha's apartment was a few blocks away from the office. Lara walked quickly, her footsteps ringing against the sidewalk. That Tuesday night happened to be Christmas Eve. Like any good Soviet family, the Orlovs didn't celebrate Christmas. But the rest of Paris did, and that night, Parisians were gathered inside, embarking on the réveillon feast. They would stay awake into the small hours, plates piled with foie gras and *buche de noel.* During their years in France, Lara had grown to love the trappings of Christmas. The sparkling lights, the aromatic pine needles, the decorated patisserie windows. She knew it was wrong, but she couldn't help herself.

She turned down a small street. She was almost there; the next block was Sasha's. With everyone gathered inside, the streets were deserted. From an apartment high above, a clamor of voices carried through an open window. Lara craned her neck to look up. The sound was comforting, and it eased her nerves a little. Too many people in too small a room with too much to drink. The sound of joy; of lives being lived.

When she rounded the corner to Sasha's street, she initially thought that the lights were part of the holiday festivities. Someone must have hung a strand of flashing red-and-blue bulbs outside his apartment. But—no, this didn't make sense—they were too bright and persistent. This wasn't the holiday. Lara had gotten it all wrong.

Three cars were parked at skewed, urgent angles outside Sasha's building. The flashing lights came from beacons on the roof of the cars, beacons that continued to rotate even though the sirens had ceased, because the police had come too late.

◆

Later, the explanation would be suicide. An overdose of sleeping pills from the bottle he kept on his nightstand. A few months ago, a doctor had written a prescription to help Sasha with his insomnia. Sometimes his mind simply ran too fast, and he needed the pills to sleep at night. See, there was his name, right on the label: Alexander Alexandrovich Kurlansky. Yes, the prescription was legitimate; yes, the doctor remembered this young man. The police were satisfied with these conclusions. There was no reason to question the story.

The body was already wrapped in a heavy plastic bag when the medics carried it out on a stretcher. "Please," Lara said, trying to push past the police officer. "Please, please let me see him."

"That is not possible," the officer said to Lara.

"But why?" Lara said, anguished. "How do I even know it's him?"

Sasha's roommates were there on the sidewalk, too, stricken and pale. One of them stepped forward and placed a hand on Lara's arm. This was the boy who had found Sasha, who broke down his locked bedroom door, saw the eerie pallor and unnatural angle of his limbs, and called the police.

The roommate said quietly, "It was him, Lara."

What was meant as reassurance only made her frantic.

"No," she said. "No, no, *no*. It can't be him. I just saw him. He was alive. He was *alive*."

The police officer instructed the roommate to escort Lara home. Surely this was a trick, she thought. This wasn't real. The body bag, the stretcher, that wasn't Sasha. He couldn't just be *gone*, not like that. It was fake, like a movie. Nothing this big happened this suddenly. She would walk into the apartment on the rue de la Faisanderie, and her parents would be there, and they would announce that there had been a misunderstanding. Maybe Sasha would be waiting there, too, sitting in the living room. The three of them would laugh at the look of relief on Lara's face. A misunderstanding. Yes. That's what would happen.

Even though Lara had grown up in the past year—falling in love, having sex, finding the seeds of her confidence—she was still only fifteen years old. Still young enough to believe that her parents possessed magical powers; that they could fix anything. The whole way home, she played this scene in her head, as if repetition could make it real. She would walk through the door, and her parents would say, *Thank God you're here, Larochka. There's been some terrible mix-up.*

But when she entered the apartment, her parents were immersed in a game of canasta, like any ordinary Tuesday night. Without glancing up from her cards, Irina said, "Were you warm enough in that jacket, Lara?"

"Join us, darling," Fyodor said. "Your mother is walloping me. Help me fend her off."

"Lara?" Irina said, finally looking up. "Lara, what's wrong?"

◆

The burial took place a few days later, in a cemetery in a distant corner of the city. It turned out that Sasha's dutiful letters back to Moscow had long since ceased, and his relationship with his parents had dwindled into nonexistence. No, his mother and father wouldn't come to Paris. No, they wouldn't bring his body home. Both measures were far too expensive for a boy they now regarded as a stranger.

It was cold and drizzling that day, the cemetery grass sodden with rain, the weather clinging to the earth in misty shrouds. A handful of people gathered around the grave: a priest, the editors from *The Spark*, his roommates, his friends from university, his favorite professor. Lara stood apart from the others. She knew how terrible she must look, with her puffy face and unwashed hair. It felt like her duty to spare the others from the contagion of her anguish. There were rituals in place for a thing like this: the priest in his long robes, the dirt scattered on the casket; small ways of comforting the living. But, for Lara, none of the rituals were working. The grave was a raw scar in the earth. The feeling was too enormous to be managed.

She stared numbly at Sasha's friends. Even in their devastation, these young men and women seemed to accept the reality of what had happened. They saw no reason to question it. Sasha was a human being, after all. Human beings can surprise us at any time. Would any of them have predicted that Sasha would commit suicide? No, certainly not; but he was prone to deep sadnesses; and they hadn't realized the true depths of his despair.

His friends bowed their heads, blinking back tears. They took turns stepping forward and sharing stories about Sasha. Occasionally they laughed between sobs. His friends were beautiful, Lara thought. The boys with patchy beards, and the girls with long bangs, shivering in their rain-soaked jackets. So sad, and yet so beautiful in their grief.

But to resist grief is to reveal its true and ugly power, its battery-acid ability to strip everything of meaning. *Who called the priest? Sasha didn't believe in any of that. This priest is just a man in a robe*, Lara thought. *And this cemetery is just a lawn with big rocks. Sasha would hate this.* Lara watched his friends across the open grave. Would she have traded this awful feeling—this bitterness, this aloneness—for their more dignified version of grief? But that wasn't an option. She hadn't reached that place of acceptance. Because even if they couldn't see the truth, Lara saw it plainly.

Sasha hadn't committed suicide. Sasha had been murdered.

The professor from Sasha's university wanted to make a few remarks. He was a tidy-looking man, with a trimmed mustache and a trench coat. Before he spoke, he removed his hat. Sasha was one of the brightest students he'd ever taught. Sasha was brave. Sasha always wanted to know more, and more, and more. Lara found reassurance in the professor's presence: yes, this really had happened. The grown-up world was acknowledging the loss. After his remarks, he invited everyone to lunch at a nearby bistro, where they could continue their remembrance of Sasha.

The professor donned his hat. He stood before Lara and extended his hand. "Larissa Fyodorovna." His French was precise and correct, but carried a heavy foreign accent. "You surely know how much Sasha loved you," he said. "But I hope you know that he admired you, too. He often told me how remarkable you are."

Lara didn't know what to say. She nodded and thanked him, but declined the invitation to lunch. She wasn't ready to leave; not yet.

Two men in coveralls stood at a remove from the grave, shovels in hand. As the group departed, Lara turned to the workers and said, "Can I stay until you're finished?"

The men were efficient. The plain wood of the casket quickly disappeared under the accumulating dirt. Shovel after shovel was dropped into the grave. Lift, *thunk*. Lift, *thunk*. Soon the grave was filled, but the men kept shoveling, piling the dirt higher and higher. The worker, seeing her confused expression, explained, "The soil will settle over time. In a few weeks, this will become level, and then we can lay the sod."

"Oh," Lara said.

"It's like anything," he said. "Gravity does its work."

Eventually the men left. Lara stood there, gazing at the mound. The drizzle had turned to rain, drops pattering steadily against the grass and the headstones. Gray fog erased the rest of Paris.

It was the first time the two of them had been alone since he died. Sasha's body had passed from one custodian to the next: the police, the medics, the coroner, the undertaker. Now it was just her, and when she left, he would be entirely alone. Sasha—just a week ago, talking and laughing, holding her hand, brushing the hair from her eyes—now abandoned to the earth. She imagined the terror of it, of Sasha realizing that he was now completely alone. How long could she stay? Did they lock the gates, eventually? Or maybe they would take pity on her, and let her sleep here? She didn't mind the dirt, the rain, the cold. The mounded earth looked soft and inviting. She wanted to lay herself across it, and spread her arms wide, and turn her cheek to the dirt, and close her eyes. She wanted to feel his body, even with the ground between them. She wanted to breathe the same air as him.

"Sasha," Lara whispered.

She wanted just a little more time.

The rain continued, dripping from tree branches, muddying the earth. An hour might have passed. Or two, or three. But then, at a certain point, she felt something change. An interruption of their privacy. Someone else was here. The physical awareness of it pressed upon her, as visceral as her sodden shoes and frozen fingers.

She looked around, scanning back and forth. The man was hard to see, partially hidden among the trees. He was standing still, as if waiting for Lara to notice him. Her pulse accelerated. Then he took a step forward, then another, and his figure became more distinct. He was tall, and he had dark skin. He looked—even from afar, she could tell—like an American.

A few days later, sitting in the veranda. A gusty summer breeze billowing through the oak trees, carrying the scent of honeysuckle and mown grass. Birds chittering above us. Flies grazing at the crumbs on our plates. Lara had been looking into the distance while she talked, in the vague direction of the house, but she suddenly stopped, her gaze snapping into focus.

I turned to see Gabi striding across the wide green lawn that separated the veranda from the house. She clutched a piece of paper, a serious expression on her face. She walked up the stairs and started to say, briskly, "Pardon me, ma'am, but there's an issue with"—when Lara cut her off with a sharp shake of her head.

Gabi stopped in her tracks. I'd never seen this happen before. The First Lady adored Gabi. She *loved* her. Gabi was sharp, and efficient, and understood Lara on a molecular level. President Caine had tried to poach her for a top position in the West Wing, but Lara wouldn't have it. "You can have anyone else," she reportedly said. "But not Gabi. *Never* Gabi."

Lara gave her most loyal aide an icy stare. "I clearly said that I didn't want to be interrupted."

Gabi looked confused. For a moment, it seemed like she might push back. She glanced down at the paper in her hand, but then she looked back up, and nodded tightly. As Gabi retreated down the veranda stairs, Lara said, "We need privacy for this, Sofie. This is very important, what I'm telling you.

"I knew it was him," she continued, after Gabi was out of earshot. "That man at the cemetery was Mr. Smith. He was just as Sasha had described: tall, Black, glasses. It seemed strange that he revealed himself like that. Surely he noticed me lingering, and he knew that I would see him. But then I realized, he *wanted* me to see him."

I felt my heart beating harder. "Why?"

"It was more than the magazine," Lara said. "The KGB wouldn't murder Sasha over a handful of critical articles. They were after him for more serious matters. The magazine was just the pretext, you see. Sasha was *working* for Mr. Smith. And Mr. Smith wasn't some ordinary American. He had a cover story, of course. To the wider world, he was just a junior diplomat processing visas at the embassy."

"A cover story?" I said. I paused, and then it clicked. "But that would mean—"

"It means," Lara said, "that Sasha was working for the CIA."

Lara spent New Year's Eve curled up in her bedroom, pretending to be asleep, ignoring the voices in the living room, wishing the clock would never reach midnight, because the next year would be a year in which Sasha had never existed.

She rarely left the apartment. She had lost her love of the most ordinary things: the cracking spine of a fresh sketchbook, the scent of her mother's cooking, the buttery *kouign-amann* from the patisserie down the street. She felt clumsy and frustrated when these consistent pleasures failed her, because the failure seemed to lie within herself. The kouign-amann, for instance, looked and tasted exactly the same. She knew this intellectually. Why, then, was she unable to find solace in it—in any of it?

It was like her insides had been scraped out, leaving only hollow blackness. She was a mere body moving through the world. In January, when she got her period, she felt a fresh wave of loss. On some secret level, as inconvenient and scandalous as it would be, she had been hoping that she might be pregnant with Sasha's baby. But her body kept breathing, and sleeping, and eating, and charting the passage of time; and all of this felt like another betrayal.

Death held a new curiosity for her. The choice became stark. What was she meant to do? She could keep living, or she could kill herself. Those, really, were the only two options. She considered it, and realized that, despite the pain, she had no desire to die.

So she went through the motions, propped up by her own self-consciousness. This was her burden to bear, hers and hers alone. She didn't want to make life harder for the people around her. So she did the homework that Irina assigned, and she ate regular meals, and she allowed Natasha to drag her to the movies. Weeks went by. In late January, one of Sasha's friends called and invited her to a party. She said no—she couldn't bear the thought of being surrounded by all of them—but then he invited her again in February, and again in March. Relenting was eventually easier than making up another excuse. The party was fine. His friends were nice. It was hot and uncomfortably loud, but it was no worse than another night spent alone in her bedroom.

In the quiet moments, when they thought she wouldn't notice, Fyodor and Irina gazed at their daughter. They met each other's eyes, exchanging the helpless question: *But what do we do?* Lara could sense their stares. She hated the feeling. She hated, too, their attempts at consolation. *Think of it, darling. He must have been in a great deal of pain, to do what he did. At least his soul is now at peace.* No. No. If she couldn't have Sasha, Lara only wanted one thing: she wanted another person to see the same truth as her. Just one single other person.

You're not crazy, Lara. Sasha was murdered. Of course he was murdered. Was that asking too much? It was so blazingly obvious. Why would the universe withhold this simple relief?

But she was a daughter of a high-ranking KGB officer. Perhaps her father even knew the men who had murdered Sasha. (But he wouldn't have had anything to do with it, would he? No, it was impossible: not her father, who loved her beyond words. *But how can he tolerate that terrible place?* she argued with herself. *How can he allow himself to live like that?*) She had no one to talk to about these things. She had no one in her life to trust with her heartache.

Spring arrived. The apartment on the rue de la Faisanderie began to feel claustrophobic. As the weather grew warmer, she began venturing outside. She walked into the Bois de Boulogne, sat on a bench, and sketched for an hour. Each day she went a bit further, like an animal testing the radius of its tether. Her mother was pleased by this progress. She offered gentle words of encouragement.

"You're so young, darling," Irina said. "There's so much time. You'll fall in love again. You'll see."

These suggestions were upsetting, more than anything. *So much time*: but she didn't want time to heal her wounds. She didn't want to lose this feeling that burned in her heart. There was something clarifying about this anger. The constancy; the purity. It was a thing she could depend on.

At the dinner table, when Fyodor and Irina talked about the situation at home, Lara wondered why she continued to keep her mouth shut. Why not speak the truth aloud? Why not call the system what it was? Were she braver and bolder, like Natasha, she would have spoken her mind. *And I don't have to protect Sasha anymore. The KGB took care of that.* But then she could only think: *What good will it do?* It wouldn't bring him back. What would it change, where would it get her?

Every day, Lara woke up early. She stared at the light edging her curtain until it grew bright and clear. The sun rises every morning and sets every night. Laws like this hold the universe together. *And me?* she thought. *What am I meant to do?*

One day in early April, she ventured as far as the boulevard Saint-Germain, to the café she had once frequented. The waiter remembered her, the girl who used to linger with her sketchbook. Of course, he had no idea who Sasha was, or what had happened to him. Strangely comforted by this, by the invisibility of this facet of her life, Lara found herself returning his smile. She sketched the streetscape and sipped her coffee. The old habit felt good.

She returned to the café the next day, and the next. Her thoughts became clearer. The anger and grief burning in her heart: they would be her companions forever. She must learn to live with them. Lara knew that she was immensely lucky. She was young, and healthy, and privileged. She had a good home and a loving family. You must see yourself clearly before you can see the world clearly. That's what Sasha liked to say. At certain moments she could almost hear his voice; could almost imagine him sitting across the café table. She could hear him warning her against self-pity. *This is the hand life has dealt you, Lara.*

"*Et voilà*," the waiter said, on a late April day at the café, depositing a tulip-shaped glass of strawberry ice cream at her elbow.

"Oh, no," Lara said. "There's been a mistake. I didn't order this."

"No mistake, mademoiselle." The waiter smiled. "It comes with compliments from that gentleman over there."

She glanced around at the other tables on the sidewalk—and then she spotted him. Despite the warm afternoon, a shiver ran up her spine. It was him. The tall man with dark skin from the December day in the cemetery. He was gazing directly at Lara. There was a matching glass of strawberry ice cream on his table. He lifted it slightly, like a salute.

Lara looked away, heat flooding her face. She didn't know much about Mr. Smith, but she knew enough to realize that he was dangerous. That it would be foolish for her to be seen in public with him. When she eventually looked back up, he was counting out coins, standing from the table. And then he was walking away, vanishing into the crowd along the boulevard.

Was that it? Was she never going to see him again? She realized, suddenly, just how many questions she had for him.

But then, beneath the tulip glass, she noticed the paper doily. Instinct told her to slide it out and turn it over. There, written in the faintest pencil: *Saint-Germain des Pres. 30 minutes.*

◆

"Who are you?" she whispered. The church was empty, the stained glass glowing like bright jewels. They both gazed straight ahead, sitting several feet apart, in a pretext of separation.

"I was a friend of Alexander's," he said. "I'm sorry if I startled you that day at the cemetery. I thought everyone would be gone by that point."

"You speak Russian," she said, her heart hammering.

"You're Lara, aren't you?" His voice was very calm. "Alex told me a lot about you."

"Yes," she said. "And I know that you're his friend, the one who pays for the magazine, but what I mean is—who *are* you?"

"I can't really answer that. But I'm glad you came. I think you're owed the truth."

He turned to look at her, his forehead creased in sympathy. He wore rimless glasses. His cheeks were rounded and youthful. He looked pleasant, and ordinary, like a traveling businessman on a plane or a train, with a kind face that was easily forgotten.

"Lara," he said. "Do you understand what happened to Alex?"

She blinked several times. For the first time, she said it out loud: "They killed him."

"Yes," he said. "And do you know who they are?"

"The KGB." After a long silence, she added, "He was stubborn. All those plans, and that talk about smuggling. It was dangerous. He needed protection." Her anger was swelling. "*You* should have protected him."

He didn't flinch at her tone. Instead, he said, "Lara, would you like to hear the whole story? It wasn't just the magazine. There was more to it than that."

◆

Sitting in the gloomy church, Mr. Smith explained, "We've never been much good at understanding what happens in Moscow. We don't have anyone there who can tell us what it's like. What it's *really* like. It's not easy to cultivate sources inside the Soviet Union. And we're not good at blending in. Americans always manage to stick out.

"Alex cared about *The Spark*. It was the real deal. I wanted it to succeed, too. The magazine was how Alex and I got to know each other. He told me about their network of writers in the Soviet Union, and the system they developed. The editors took dictation over the phone in code—that was how they avoided the censors. People could describe what was really happening back home.

"And the people back in Russia, they knew more than what could fit in the magazine. Details that might not be interesting to general readers, you know, but details that were useful—the kind of thing we've always been lacking. It was simple enough. Alex picked a few code words, and made sure the writers had them, too. When he took their phone calls, he wasn't just taking dictation for the magazine. He was gathering information for us, too."

Lara's stomach twisted as she processed what he was saying. "So you used him," she said. "And then you let him take the fall."

He shook his head. "We didn't ask him to do anything. This was his idea."

"I'm not stupid!" she snapped. "What choice did you leave him? He cared about the magazine. He must have known you wouldn't help him with the funding unless he did this . . . this *other* thing for you, too."

"It was a risk," Mr. Smith said. "But Alex wanted to do it."

"If it was such a risk, why didn't you stop him?"

"I just told you," he said patiently. "He *wanted* to do it. He could have stopped at any time. There was nothing to force him to do anything. Lara, I'm sorry, but the idea that we'd take this young man hostage over such a small amount of money—it just wouldn't be worth it. The United States government isn't even going to notice the budget of something like the *The Spark*. He died for something bigger than himself. But he was willing to take that chance."

She shook her head. "But he never told me about this," she insisted. "About any of this. Why would he lie to me about . . . about all of it?"

"To keep you safe," Mr. Smith said. "He loved you too much to put you at risk."

There was a stretch of silence. She blinked, her throat aching. She refused to cry in front of this strange American man. She missed Sasha; she loved Sasha; she hated Sasha. Walking away from her. Lying to her. *I have to go. There's too much work to be done.* Had she even really known him?

She said, harshly, "You don't actually know that."

"Don't know what?"

"That he loved me at all."

Mr. Smith gazed at her. "We offered to bring him to America," he said. "We knew that the KGB was watching him. That it was only a matter of time. He would have been safe in America. We had a spot for him at a university, the paperwork sorted out—it was a good plan. I thought he should do it. But Alex refused to go. He said he would never leave you."

Lara closed her eyes. The sound of traffic drifted into the church. His secret, separate, invisible compartments. She could almost see it—this other life, this other self—but not quite. It lay behind one more closed door.

She was sick of those closed doors. She wanted to pry it open.

"Tell me how it worked," she said. "What he did for you. How often did you see him? What kind of information did he pass along?"

He shook his head. "I can't tell you that."

"Why?" she asked, frowning. Then it occurred to her: Mr. Smith surely knew who her father was. "Is it because you think I'd betray you to the KGB? But how can you think that?" Raw frustration overtook her. "They killed Sasha. I *hate* them."

"I'm sorry, Lara," he said. "There are rules."

The church bells began pealing. He glanced at his watch. As he stood up from the pew, she felt a sudden desperation. For the first time in months, the bracing clarity of the truth swept through her; for the first time in months, she didn't feel like she was losing her mind. A breeze in an airless room. She'd missed this feeling. How was she meant to live without it? "But what if I need to talk to you again?" she said.

He paused, regarding her through the dim afternoon light. For a moment, it seemed like he might simply walk away. What must he think of her? This silly girl, asking questions that were better left unanswered.

But then, finally, he said, "I have a weakness for strawberry ice cream. The craving hits at the same time every week."

◆

On the last day of April, Lara turned sixteen. For the occasion, Irina baked a *medovik*, an elaborate honey cake with eight slender layers and pillowy sour cream frosting. She was determined to make her daughter's birthday special. Irina was an excellent cook, although the finicky medovik had taken her several hours and was probably more trouble than it was worth.

The table could barely hold the bounty of food. Irina had planned to invite their friends and neighbors to the birthday dinner, but when Lara said she didn't want anyone else there, Irina took heed, because Lara never insisted on anything. It was just the four of them around the dinner table; a rarity, in those days, as Natasha was usually out with friends.

While they ate, Natasha kept them entertained. She was always getting into arguments, breaking up with boyfriends, making broad declarations. For instance: Americans were greedy warmongers, but their music was excellent. Prince was the best of them all. His new song was stuck in her head. " 'You don't have to be rich to be my girl,' " she sang, in clumsy English. Then she laughed. "What does this mean? How can they allow him to say this? How un-American. I'll get the album for you, Larochka. You'll love it."

Natasha made decent money as a typist at the Soviet embassy. Her ideological loyalty to socialism didn't extend to the clothes she wore, the music she listened to, the food she ate. She was the one who bought Lara her designer jeans, who took her to see *Back to the Future*, who introduced her to Big Macs. Her knowledge might not have gone very deep, but Natasha knew about a lot of things. Lara had always admired her sister's outspokenness.

Toward the end of the meal, after the family had second and third slices of the medovik, Natasha said, "Papa, I was reading in the paper about the accident. It's getting worse, isn't it?"

Fyodor frowned. Irina said, "Lara, more cake?"

"I don't know why they keep lying to us," Natasha continued. "When all of us are capable of reading *Le Monde* and seeing what's really happening."

"You shouldn't read that rag," Irina interjected.

"What accident?" Lara said.

Fyodor turned to his younger daughter. "There was a fire at a nuclear reactor. Near Pripyat, in Ukraine. It's very serious."

"Not that the government will admit it," Natasha said. "It makes them look like such idiots. Cowards and idiots."

"Watch your tongue, Natasha!" Irina snapped.

Fyodor shook his head. "Ira, it's fine. She should be asking these questions. Natasha is right. It *is* getting worse."

He explained what was happening. That day, April 30, 1986, the Soviet government had gone so far as asking other nations for help containing the fire at the reactor. Although it had been several days since the fire, the government wouldn't share even basic details about the accident. They refused to admit to the seriousness of what was happening. As far away as Sweden, there was detection of heightened radioactivity in the atmosphere—but in Kiev, just eighty miles away from the accident, impending May Day celebrations were scheduled to go on. Like his daughter, Fyodor had learned this by reading Western newspapers. To rely on the word of their government was to know essentially nothing. Two people dead from the fire, that was all the Soviets would say.

As an officer in the First Directorate of the KGB, Fyodor had carte blanche to read Western newspapers and magazines and books. He absorbed the information and dispatched long summaries back to the center in Moscow. Perhaps this wasn't intelligence-gathering in the traditional sense—he was reiterating information that anyone in the West had access to—but it was enough to keep his superiors happy.

And how painfully ironic it was: sitting in the embassy in Paris, reading *Le Monde* and *Der Spiegel*, Fyodor had a clearer idea of what was happening in Chernobyl than did most people who actually *lived* in Chernobyl. In fact, he probably knew too much. This would prove to be a critical flaw in the system. If the theory of glasnost was just beginning to circulate in Moscow—the idea of greater openness, and wider dissemination of information—the practice of glasnost had long since arrived in the Western outposts of the KGB. People like Fyodor, people charged with protecting the Soviet state, were the first ones to truly see the state's weakness. They were the first ones to realize the tragedy of their own government.

"What happens to the people in that town?" Lara asked. Fyodor had been explaining that the radioactive debris from the nuclear plant could be lethal. "It's dangerous to be there. Shouldn't they evacuate?"

"They probably should," Fyodor said. Lara waited for him to say something else, to do what he usually did, to mitigate and soften this horrifying idea of inaction. *But there's an order to things, Larochka,* he would surely say. *First this needs to happen, and then this.* But this time, there was no such mitigation. Fyodor was only silent.

◆

There were fleeting moments when the pain of Sasha's death became weightless. Most of the time, Lara felt trapped within the lonely boundaries of herself. But other times—

Other times she would sit on the steps of Sacré-Coeur in Montmartre, sketching the skyline's jumble of cornices and garret windows, and think of nothing but capturing every intricate detail. Or she would go to the patisserie to buy a kouign-amann and lose herself in the glassy caramelized crust, the flaky layers of pastry, the rigorous perfection of this small exquisite thing, and remember why she loved it so much.

Something was coming back to her.

In the church that day, Mr. Smith had called him Alex. Such a sprightly, energetic, American-sounding name. Strange to think of Sasha as *Alex.* The word was like a beginning. It gave birth to a new universe in her mind. She imagined Sasha living by this different name, choosing this different path, studying at university in America, bopping around to his Walkman. She could almost imagine him alive: alive as Alex, happy and healthy, thousands of miles away, on the other side of an ocean.

What did she owe to Alex? she wondered.

And what did she owe to herself?

When I look back, I'm surprised by how long it took me to put the pieces together. The truth was right there, glowing like neon in darkness. But, so often, we see what we want to see. When you're expecting one thing, you can easily fail to notice what is right in front of you.

As Lara talked and talked, I thought: *How is this going to add up?* Fyodor had been accused of spying for the Americans. It made sense, based on what she had told me about her father. Take an intelligence officer with natural exuberance and curiosity, and saddle him with growing frustration and despair: certainly Fyodor could turn against his country. But how did we get to there from here?

The two of us often stayed up late, long after the rest of the house had gone to bed. Nighttime on the porch, flickering candles. She talked in long streams, as if, once she had started, she was unable to stop.

One afternoon, during our final week in Connecticut, I walked barefoot across the lawn to the veranda, the grass soft and warm from the sunshine. The table was set, the water glasses filled, the food covered in cling film to keep the flies away. Lara was already there, lying on the lounger, papers dropped to the floor, her eyes closed. She was fast asleep.

"Lara?" I said quietly, but she didn't stir.

I considered waking her, but then I thought: *Have a little patience.* She looked so peaceful. And we had time, didn't we? If you don't have to break the spell yet, why would you?

Surveillance was a fact of life, even in Paris. During one of their late-night conversations, Fyodor had told Lara how it worked. A man like Fyodor always had a fellow officer on his tail, an officer from the Second Chief Directorate of the KGB. This directorate was responsible for the internal security of the KGB. It was their job to prevent infiltration of the KGB's own ranks, and the Soviet colony as a whole.

The work of an intelligence operative is extraordinarily delicate. It was Fyodor's job to cultivate agents in Paris: men and women who worked in government, or business, or rival security services like MI6 and the CIA; men and women who might share helpful tidbits of information with their Russian friend. His cover, as an attaché in the Soviet embassy, meant that he and Irina were regulars on the diplomatic cocktail party circuit. These parties and dinners gave him plenty of chances to meet useful foreigners. Perhaps Fyodor and a useful foreigner would make a date for lunch. Perhaps they would become friendly, playing tennis and drinking cognac and commiserating over how fast their children grew up. This was all permissible, of course. It was Fyodor's job to enact this seduction. But to spend so much time with the enemy also opened one up to the possibility of reverse seduction. What if MI6 or the CIA tried to recruit *him*? The Second Chief Directorate had to watch men like Fyodor to be certain that this wasn't happening.

"I've grown used to it," Fyodor had told Lara. "They should be invisible, of course. Surveillance isn't much use if the target is aware of it. But these men are sloppy. If I want to lose my tail, I can."

These men were scant in number, too. The Second Chief Directorate couldn't possibly monitor everyone. They relied on the wives and children to police themselves, to abide by the rules. If this degree of trust was a risk—well, the wives and children were just ordinary people, after all. They had no access to valuable secrets. Who would bother targeting them?

Even so, on the day she planned to return to the café, Lara took a deliberately meandering route. She looped through side streets and made use of reflections in store windows. She entered the Bon Marché through one door, wandered among the floors for a while, and left through a different door. Eventually, she was confident that she wasn't being watched. This anonymity wasn't like loneliness; it was more like freedom. She pictured herself as a cosmonaut floating through outer space.

That day, the café on the boulevard Saint-Germain was bustling. She drank her coffee, and tried to concentrate on her sketching, but it wasn't easy. She kept glancing up, worried that she might not spot him amid the crowds, or that he might not spot her. The waiter brought her more coffee and asked if she needed anything. She shook her head.

And then she saw him, several tables away. Slacks, polo shirt, sunglasses. Leaning back in his chair, reading his newspaper. He had materialized in the middle of the busy café, silent as a ghost.

Several minutes later he stood up, folded the newspaper and tucked it under his arm, and left a few coins beside his coffee cup. He strolled across the boulevard, like an unhurried tourist enjoying his vacation.

Five minutes later, Lara stepped inside the dim church. The air was cool, and smelled of beeswax. She sat in the pew beside him. She drew a deep breath, and began. "Mr. Smith, there's something I wanted to—"

"You really don't have to call me that," he interrupted. "You can just call me Walter. I never understood why Alex insisted on addressing me that way."

"Okay. Walter," she said, trying it out. "Walter Smith."

He nodded. "Better."

"Funny," she said. "Sasha never once called you Walter. He was very formal, you know? He always had to hold the door for me. *Always*. It could be annoying." Lara smiled, and then, realizing what she had just said, she cringed. "No, no, I don't mean that, I don't—"

"It's all right, Lara." Walter smiled, too. "He wasn't perfect. No one is."

After a beat of silence, he prompted: "So. Is there something on your mind?"

"I can't stop thinking about it," she blurted out. "You said he gave his life for this cause. But I don't . . . It doesn't . . . What *is* that cause? What does that even mean? He always talked about the problems in our country. Everything that was wrong with our country. But is that it? Was he willing to die just because . . . because he *hated* it so much?"

Walter shook his head. "Exactly the opposite. He thought that he could work to improve the situation. Alex didn't want to destroy anything. He wanted it to be better."

"But this is a war." She gestured at the two of them. "We're enemies, aren't we?"

He gazed right at her. "Do *you* think we're enemies, Lara?"

"I don't know," she said. "I guess that I just . . . have a lot of questions."

"And I wish I could answer all of them," he said. "But you remember what I—"

"Yes, yes," Lara cut him off. Then she sighed. "Why can't you just trust me? I promise that I won't tell anyone. It's only for me."

"Because there are repercussions," he said. "My gut says to trust you. Of *course* I want to trust you. But think of who your father is. I don't want you to have to lie to him. That's a dangerous position to be in."

"So that's it," she said irritably. "Great. Thanks a lot."

Behind his glasses, Walter blinked calmly. He seemed unbothered by her fluctuating moods. Lara was surprised to find that she liked Walter, that she trusted him instinctively, even when he withheld so much from her. *What a bewildering man*, she thought. She knew that she ought to stand up and walk away—because what was the point of this conversation?—but something kept her there.

Finally, he said, "Would you like to hear a story?"

"Is it about Sasha?" she said, perking up.

"No," he said. "This was several years ago, in Berlin, during my first tour abroad. One night, a man walked into the embassy. He had a thick Russian accent. I was the only officer on duty who spoke Russian, so I met with him. He said he was KGB. He was a serious-looking guy. The fedora, the whole getup. I thought he was the real thing. Everything he said corresponded exactly with what we knew about the KGB. I couldn't believe my luck. My first station abroad, and the white whale walks through the front door. Well. Can you guess what happened next?"

Lara shook her head.

"I told my boss. He gave me a little smile, and said, 'Ask this man to bring you something useful. A classified document, a memo, a list of KGB agents. Anything to prove that he means it.' So I went back and asked the Russian for some documentation. 'Oh sure,' he said. 'No problem. Give me twenty-four hours.' But he never came back. He vanished right back into the life he'd always been living. You see, he never really meant it."

Silence, as he arched one eyebrow. "Do you understand what I'm saying, Lara?"

◆

The next evening, Fyodor yawned and said good night, leaving Lara alone. The living room was a mess. His briefcase was unlocked and splayed open, his papers scattered everywhere. Irina had often scolded him for this habit. While vacuuming the other week, Irina had found an old memo marked TOP SECRET crumpled beneath a dusty corner of the sofa.

Lara did it without even thinking about it.

The next week, Walter studied the piece of paper she handed to him. He nodded slowly. "Okay," he said quietly. "This is good."

Her pulse was pounding. Finally, the last door of Sasha's life, creaking open.

Walter looked up. "Lara, how old are you?"

"Eighteen," she lied. Where did that lie come from? But she somehow knew it was necessary.

"Eighteen," he repeated. "Are you going to university in the fall?"

"No," she said, thinking quickly. "We didn't go to the embassy school. My mother homeschooled us. We don't have any proper tests or transcripts."

Walter squinted at her. "So what will you do instead?"

"I help her around the house," Lara said. "I babysit. I do odd jobs for other people. I might start taking art classes."

"Hm," Walter said. He looked down at the paper. Then he handed it back to her.

"Don't you need to keep this?" Lara said, surprised.

"Put it back where you found it," he said. "As soon as possible. You don't want your father to notice that it's missing. I have to go now. I need to check a few things. But if it looks okay, I'll keep my end of the bargain."

"You'll tell me how it works?" she said.

He nodded. "I promise."

◆

The next time they met, a few weeks later, Walter said, "You trusted me, so now I'll trust you."

He told her the things that Sasha had always withheld: the kind of information he got for Walter, the methods of passing along that information. There was a dead drop—a place he could safely leave messages, Walter explained—in the garden behind Notre-Dame cathedral. Sasha had a method for signaling Walter, and vice versa. (*So that's why*, Lara thought. *That's why we always met at Notre-Dame.*) To each of her questions, Walter gave patient and thorough answers. She craved the mundane details, the ordinary habits, the granular information that allowed her to picture Sasha's movements. *There's so much I didn't know*, she realized. But what a strange gift, too: discovering the unread chapters of a story she once thought finished.

"Alex was good at it," Walter said. "A natural. Sometimes I forgot that he was only twenty years old. Too young for that much responsibility."

"But he wasn't too young," Lara replied. "You said it yourself. He wanted to do it."

"Both things are true. He did want to do it. He was also too young."

"That's stupid." Lara bristled. "Are you saying that *I'm* too young to make a difference? I'm too young for so much responsibility?"

Later, she would realize what an easy mark she'd been. He saw the stubbornness that lurked beneath her surface, the pent-up frustration that came from months of inaction. He knew exactly how to bait the trap. Whether Walter actually believed that Lara was eighteen years old, he had chosen to accept her lie and advance to the next step in the game.

"I didn't say anything like that," Walter said.

"Well," Lara said sharply. "You have no idea what I'm capable of."

For a while, Walter gazed into the distance. "It was a big loss for us," he finally said. "When Alex was killed. He was a critical source of insight. He believed in this work. He gave his life for it." He paused. "He would have wanted it to continue."

She felt her heart skip. She suddenly knew what he was about to ask, and it terrified her.

"What you brought me last week," Walter continued. "That memo. It was very useful. Would you be willing to do that again?"

She thought of her father and mother. Her family loved her. They wanted to rescue her from her grief. They tried as hard as they could. But it was like they lived on the other side of a thick pane of glass, and it kept them from sensing that bright flame burning in her heart. Sasha had known Lara: the real Lara. To have her true self seen; to have her true self loved; to lose that feeling. What could fill such an impossible void? She had never known that she could be this lonely.

But it was strange. With every revelation she learned, she felt Sasha drawing a little closer. To follow in his footsteps—to complete what he couldn't—to finally believe his declaration that she was strong enough for this—it terrified her, and yet it was the only thing to do.

Lara drew a deep breath. "Yes," she said. "Yes, I would."

—∾—

"Wait a second," I said. "Wait—he asked you, flat out? And you told him yes?"

My exclamation seemed to startle her. Lara turned to look at me, and for a moment, her eyes flickered with hesitation. Maybe she would back away, and wait until the clear light of morning, heeding a scheherazadian impulse toward self-preservation. It was well past midnight. The darkness was filled with rasping crickets and distant frogs.

But then I saw something change. Determination pushed aside fear. My heart was thumping. I think hers was, too.

"Yes," she said. "I told him yes."

"So, wait," I stuttered. "This means that—it means that—"

The First Lady cleared her throat and said, "It means that, beginning in July 1986, I was an agent working for the CIA."

CHAPTER TWELVE

"Hang on," Ben said. He was standing inside the front door, having just gotten home from work, on my first night back in the city. It seemed risky to say it by phone or text, so I had waited three agonizing days to tell him in person. Was that paranoid? Yes. No. Yes. I didn't care.

"Hang on a second," he repeated, closing the door behind him. "She worked for the CIA? Lara Caine, as in the First Lady of the United States? Lara Caine, as in the wife of *Henry* Caine?"

After that late-night revelation, Lara glanced at her watch and said, "Time for bed, I think." As she bade me good night and we retreated to opposite wings of the house, I felt certain there was a misunderstanding. Surely, *surely* she hadn't meant what I thought she meant. I spent the whole night tossing and turning. But the next morning, as we sat down to breakfast, Lara was bright-eyed and fresh. Apparently she'd slept just fine.

"So," Lara said, stirring milk into her coffee. "Walter Smith and I worked together for less than two years. Not very long, in retrospect. But we got a lot done."

"Lara." I swallowed. "I just . . . Does the president know about this?"

"No," she said matter-of-factly. "He has no idea. So, as I was saying. We got a lot done. Your recorder is on, yes?"

Those last few days in Connecticut passed in a blur. I was barely aware of what Lara was saying (thank God for that recorder). My mind was already racing ahead: President Caine, constantly railing against the deep state, lashing out at the intelligence community, was *married* to a former CIA agent? And he didn't know it? How the hell was he going to react to this news?

Ben shook his head. "I don't know what to think," he said.

"Me neither," I said. "Jesus Christ! What am I supposed to do with this?"

"Well," he said. "She probably hopes you'll do nothing. Right? Hasn't she always wanted you to just keep writing?"

"Right," I said. "But this is a completely different ball game."

Ben and I spent most of the night debating what I ought to do next. If I wanted to, I was free to publish this. It would be a life-changing scoop. My career as a journalist had never quite achieved escape velocity, but a story like this would open doors in every direction. I was thirty-six. This could set my career in a whole new direction. Without question, this would be my big break.

Except there was Lara. If I went through with it—if I exposed the secret she'd kept for over three decades—if I violated the trust we'd built together—what would she think of me? Would she ever speak to me again? Reprisal wasn't what I feared. (For all of the administration's anti-journalist vitriol, they never really did anything about it.) What I feared was having to live with myself in the aftermath.

"Sofe, this isn't my expertise," Ben said. My second night home and we continued talking in circles, rehashing the same upsides and downsides. Even when asked point-blank what he would do in my shoes, Ben was, predictably, too thoughtful to give a straight yes/no answer. "You know who you should *really* be having this conversation with," he said. "Vicky would know what—"

"No," I said sharply. "No. I know exactly what she'll say."

Vicky, of course, had been the first person I thought of. But Vicky wasn't the person you called when you were wrestling with whether to load the cannon. She was the person you called when you were ready to take aim.

•

And then Lara Caine stopped returning my calls.

As we were standing in the driveway in Connecticut, saying goodbye—the black SUVs loaded with luggage, the staff closing up the house until her next visit, the air force plane in Hartford awaiting the motorcade's arrival—Lara said that her schedule for the next few weeks was in flux. She wasn't sure when I should plan to come down to DC next. Maybe the coming week, maybe the week after. In any case, Gabi would be in touch. She squeezed my hand and smiled tenderly.

"Thank you for agreeing to this, Sofie," she said. "This was a good idea, wasn't it?"

I returned to New York. Several days passed. But Gabi never called.

"Hi, Gabi," I said, leaving my third voice mail in as many days, trying to sound nonchalant. "It's me again. Just wondering what the First Lady's schedule looks like this week. I can come down anytime. Call me back?"

I called. I texted. I emailed. But Gabi Carvalho, who had always been the world's most reliable returner-of-messages, didn't respond to any of them.

"What did I do?" I asked Ben, during that stretch of silence. Since beginning the biography, I'd been in touch with Lara Caine's staff on a daily basis. Now it had been ten days—ten days!—without the slightest communication. "Oh God. Do you think it bothered her when I asked if the president knew? Do you think she thought that was, like, too *personal*?"

Ben shook his head. "She's gotten way more personal than that, hasn't she?"

I gnawed on my thumbnail. "Maybe I should just go to DC and figure it out. I can wait for Gabi outside the entrance, and when she gets there, I can—"

"Sofe." Ben took my hand, gently tugging it away from my mouth. "You know that won't work. It's not actually Gabi you have to worry about."

"But what did I do?" I said, again and again. "Ben, I don't get it! What happened?"

Maybe Lara needed a break after the intense intimacy of Connecticut. Maybe she was overscheduled with meetings and receptions and events. Maybe Irina had gotten sick, and she was nursing her back to health. But my mind dismissed these explanations as quickly as it conjured them. No, no, no. This couldn't be a coincidence. Lara Caine shared this revelation, and then she vanished. And there was the factor that had always nagged at me: the lack of an NDA, her foolhardy decision to give me that free rein. It all seemed to suggest *something*, some invisible game that I couldn't see, a game that had suddenly changed.

But then it occurred to me: What if nothing had changed?

Was this merely a heightened version of the test she'd been administering all along? Was she using this to measure the true depth of my loyalties?

Take another step closer. Peel back the next layer. And what will you do with the truth? Will you keep trusting the person telling you? Will you hold your fire for the promise of what comes next?

•

"The boys keep asking for you," Jenna said. "When are you coming down?"

With the weeks I'd spent in Connecticut, and the ongoing lack of response from the East Wing, it had been well over a month since my last trip to Washington. "I'm not sure," I said. "Soon, hopefully. I think it's, uh, a busy time for her."

I found it less shameful to tell Maurice the truth. Or maybe it was just that physical proximity made it harder to conceal things from him.

"Is something wrong, Sonechka?" he asked. It was a hot July day in the backyard. He wore a sun hat and had zinc oxide striped down his nose. I sat on the edge of the garden bed while he checked the cherry tomatoes. Listlessness had drawn me to follow Maurice into the yard. The feeling reminded me of those long childhood days of summer, those bored and empty days, when I trailed Jenna from room to room for lack of anything better to do.

I squinted up at Maurice. "Is it that obvious?"

"It's the contrast, my dear," he said. "You don't seem like yourself."

So I told Maurice what happened with Lara Caine. Not all of it—I said nothing about the exact nature of her revelation—but enough to explain why I was sitting here, looking so worried; that, at the bottom of it, I was haunted by the notion that I had brought this upon myself.

"I don't know what to do," I said. The words sounded pathetic. "I don't have any idea. I just wish she would call me back."

"But Mrs. Caine will either call you, or she won't call you," he said. "That decision is hers to make. You can't control it. And you can't put your life on hold because of a circumstance that exists outside of you."

"But . . ." I trailed off, staring at Maurice as he bent down for the watering can. What on earth did he mean? My life? But this *was* my life: my work with Lara, my days with Lara. I bit my lip and looked at the ground, blinking back tears of frustration. Her withdrawal had stolen something from me. Something essential; something deep.

I hate her, I thought, and then felt shocked by the thought.

"Oh, my dear Sonechka," Maurice said, noticing my expression as he watered the tomatoes. Droplets suspended briefly in the sunlight, like a glittering waterfall, before soaking into the soil. "Life has a cruel way of pulling out the rug from beneath us. But what can you do? You must keep going. You must simply do whatever you can do."

•

Certain people dazzle you in a way that is entirely out of proportion. Years earlier, I'd had a helpless crush on a boy in graduate school.

This boy had long hair that flopped across his forehead, he wore shabby wool sweaters, he mixed a perfect martini. He was brilliant, and estranged from his family, and I could never figure out whether he was extremely rich or extremely poor. Our fling lasted a few weeks: long nights in low-ceilinged pubs, the sun flooding through his bedroom window at 6:00 a.m. because he never bothered to buy curtains. And then one day it ended. It ended in the most predictable possible fashion: He stopped texting me back. He avoided the library, where we'd so often crossed paths. He found new pubs and coffee shops to frequent.

In the wake of his ghosting, I developed a split personality. Fake indifference concealed stinging shame. *Oh, him? I didn't even really like him.* Outwardly, I laughed, shrugged, flirted with other boys, pretended to move on. Inwardly, I was completely obsessive. *Where is he? Where is he? WHERE IS HE?* Looking for him everywhere. Finding excuses to walk down his street, past his apartment, checking every possible place he might be lurking.

That's exactly how I felt in those agonizing weeks after Connecticut. Raw and desperate, waiting for a sign, hearing nothing. *Where is she? WHERE IS SHE?* Theoretically the power was in my hands. I could reveal everything. But was I ready to take that decisive step, and end this chapter forever? Had I even understood the situation correctly? Maybe Lara regretted being so candid. Maybe her silence came from fear. She'd trusted a stranger with a fraught truth. How could she help feeling doubtful, uncertain, hesitant?

Looking for her everywhere. Refreshing the news, refreshing my feeds. And then, one morning, after two weeks of silence—two weeks that felt more like two years—there was a short item in *Politico* Playbook:

> **SPOTTED . . .** First Lady Lara Caine, having dinner at Le Diplomate with the *NYT*'s Eileen Bates. The two women dined in a private room, noshing on king crab, dover sole, and *gougères*. Bates is currently on book leave from the *Times*.
>
> **AS WE REVEALED IN PLAYBOOK** last week, Bates is re-

portedly at work on a biography of the First Lady. No word yet on when to expect the book, which would be the first major biography of Lara Caine.

•

"Let's go out," Ben said, shutting his laptop. His papers were spread across the dining table as he worked on a brief. I was on the couch, staring at my phone. My mood had been mounting ever since reading the *Politico* piece that morning. *I dare you*, I thought. *I dare you, Lara. Call and explain yourself.*

"I'm getting cabin fever," he said. "Let's go out for dinner. I bet we could get a table at Elio's."

"But what if—"

"It'll be okay," he said, prying my phone from my grasp. "Just leave it here."

The light was long and golden as we walked up Second Avenue. Saturday evening in July, and the Upper East Side was a ghost town. "I don't get it," Ben mused. "Why would you choose to sit in traffic all weekend when there are so many perks to staying put?" He held open the door and ushered me inside. Though it was usually impossible to get a table, that night we walked right in.

"Well," I said. "For one thing, the beaches. For another, the ocean. And I bet it doesn't smell like hot garbage out in the Hamptons."

He rolled his eyes. "Come on, Sofe."

I sighed. "I know. I'm sorry. I'm just stressed."

Ben did his best to keep the mood light, bantering with the waiter, asking me questions that didn't leave room for objection. Did I want the Chianti or the Nero d'Avola? Should we share the caprese or the bresaola? But poor Ben was fighting an impossible battle. I saw right through his tricks. *That's nice. He's trying to cheer me up. But I've seen this one before.*

"I just can't get over Eileen Bates," I said, as our entrées arrived. I picked up my fork and knife and started attacking my chicken Milanese. "I mean, Eileen Bates? What could Lara possibly see in her?"

"Maybe her three Pulitzer Prizes?" Ben said.

"Oh, *thanks*," I said acidly. I was angry. It felt weirdly good to get angry. "I've been working like a dog all year. Now Eileen Bates and the *Times* are going to swoop in and get the glory? You know I met her once, at a party down in DC. We talked for almost an hour, and she had spinach stuck in her teeth *the whole time*." I grimaced. "I bet Lara can't stand her. She's probably just doing this because . . . because . . ."

"Sofie," Ben said, reaching for my hand. "Please. Just stop."

"Stop what?"

"I remember the time you met Eileen Bates," he said. "You came back from that trip and you were practically *giddy*. Don't you remember? You idolized her. You said she was a legend."

"Yeah, well. That was then. That was before—"

"Before what?" he interrupted. "Look, I get it. Lara Caine has gone AWOL, and you're frustrated, and that's completely valid. I'd be angry, too. But why are you mad at Eileen Bates? She's just doing her job. Put yourself in her shoes. You'd do the same."

The waiter swooped over to ask how everything was tasting. "Delicious," Ben said, smiling. "You were right, the ragu is fantastic."

I stared down at my chicken. The heat was gradually receding from my cheeks. "Keep going," Maurice had said. "You'd do the same," Ben had said. But how? How? How, when my life had become my work with Lara?

And then—then it happened. Maybe the mental chatter had simply exhausted itself. Maybe I saw the dead end. In either case, something unclenched. It let go of me, or I let go of it. I took a deep breath. The sensations of the moment flooded in. Here I was. Sitting in an Italian restaurant on the Upper East Side, Ben on the other side of the white tablecloth, inky sediment streaking the wineglass. With a strange detachment, I watched my hand reach for the wineglass and guide it to my mouth. I took a sip, and thought:

My life is right here. Not anywhere else. I'm free to do whatever I want.

And I want to do my job.

I would never forget how good that moment felt.

That night, as soon as I got back to the apartment, I called Vicky Wethers.

"See this?" Walter Smith said. "Do you know what this is?"

Lara took the object from him and turned it over in her palm. Plastic casing, yellow Bic logo. She pressed her thumb down and a flame sparked to life. She looked up at Walter. "It's a lighter."

"Yes," he said, taking it back from her. "But see when I open up this part? It's also a camera. I'm going to give you a length of thread. You can tack the thread to the bottom of the lighter with chewing gum. And then use the thread to get the right distance between the paper and the camera. It needs to be exactly eleven inches for the focal length to work. Do you smoke?"

Lara shook her head.

"You should start. Or at least pretend, even just a few cigarettes a day. Enough so there's always an excuse to have this with you."

It was September 1986. From where she and Walter sat, on a bench in the Luxembourg Gardens, Lara could see the boat pond. She and Sasha had spent so many afternoons in those mint-green metal chairs. Sunlight danced on the surface of the pond. Bright triangles of color wobbled across the water. It had been almost nine months since he died. She shook her head again, focusing on Walter, who was explaining how to use the camera, how to unload and reload the miniature rolls of film. She slipped the lighter into her purse and made a mental note to buy cigarettes on the way home. Fyodor and Irina wouldn't care about her new habit. Everyone in her family smoked.

"Let's go over it again," he said. "When the film is ready, how do you get it to me?"

"The bathroom in the back of the art store on rue des Beaux

Arts," she said. Lara was in that dusty old store at least once a week, buying paper and pastels, which made it ideal for a dead drop: if anyone was watching, there was nothing unusual about her going there. The store's musty bathroom was rarely used. "I'll tape the film behind the toilet tank. I'll signal that it's ready by leaving a chalk mark on the lamppost on rue de Longchamp."

"Good. Someone will be checking the lamppost every day. And if you need to meet in person?"

"I'll go to the market on rue Cler on a Sunday," she said. Again, chosen for maximum plausibility: Lara was there every weekend, shopping for Irina. "If I need to see you, I'll wear a purple sweater, I'll have my bag on my left shoulder, and I'll be holding an ice-cream cone. And then we'll meet here, three days later, on a Wednesday afternoon."

"Good, Lara," he said. "You've picked it up fast."

Walter glanced at his watch. She felt a thrum in her stomach. This part, talking to him, felt easy because it was honest. But in a few moments she would stand up from this bench, say goodbye to Walter, reenter the slipstream of ordinary life—and that's when the deception would begin.

"We won't be seeing each other as much, going forward," he said. "It's too much of a risk. Better for us to rely mostly on the dead drop."

She nodded. *You're okay,* a voice in her head said. *You can do this.*

◆

She was eager to make use of this nervous energy, to convert it into something tangible. But as luck would have it, weeks had gone by without one of her late-night conversations with her father. Through September and October, Fyodor was leaving the house before dawn and coming home well after midnight, trudging straight to the bedroom without bothering to set down his briefcase.

The first time, acting on impulse, it felt easy to take that paper from his briefcase. But this was infinitely harder: as she waited and watched, she was acutely aware of what she was doing.

Finally, in mid-October, Fyodor was home in time for dinner again. While they ate, he cracked jokes and told long-winded stories, and after they cleaned up the kitchen and Irina said good night, he and Lara retreated to the living room. The grandfather clock ticked quietly, chiming on the hour. Their old, peaceful routine. Lara was tempted to let this comfortable silence endure.

But after a few minutes, she ventured, "Papa, was there something going on, these last few weeks?"

"Ah, so you did notice. Yes, Lara, and thank God it's over."

"What was it?" she said. (To Fyodor, there was nothing odd about her inquiry. A year ago, she would have asked this question out of innocent curiosity. Now it made her feel queasy: using the patterns of the past to create a smoke screen in the present.)

"Last week there was a summit in Iceland," he said. "Reagan and Gorbachev met, to talk about nuclear disarmament. We were busy preparing for that. You see, it's helpful for the general secretary to know ahead of time what the other side is thinking and wanting. That's where we come in. It's our job to find these things out."

And did it work? Well, Fyodor explained, the two sides made good progress, but at the last minute, the talks collapsed. Everyone was very depressed. Both the Americans and the Russians blamed the other side for intransigence. But Fyodor wasn't so sure. Give it a few months, give it a year. This might yet prove to be a turning point. Around midnight, he stood up and yawned. "Off to bed for me. See you in the morning, Larochka."

◆

Faucet running while he brushed his teeth. Humming while he flossed. Toilet flushing. Door closing. Springs squeaking as he settled into bed.

Lara watched the ticking hand of the grandfather clock. Half an hour passed. She stood up, tiptoed down the hallway, and pressed her ear to the bedroom door. She could hear the thick sound of her father snoring, his breath dragging in and out, regular as a metronome.

His unlocked briefcase sat on the floor, next to the armchair. His papers peeked from the top. Lara slipped into her bedroom and retrieved the Bic lighter from her purse. In the living room, she knelt down on the carpet beside the briefcase. Every fiber of her body strained to detect movement or sound.

She laid the first piece of paper flat on the carpet. Walter's instructions ran through her head. She stuck the eleven-inch thread to the bottom of the lighter. She drew the thread taut, positioning the camera directly above the paper.

The first time hadn't felt like betrayal. It was merely the cost of getting the truth about Sasha. But this, right here and right now—this was different. This was the bright line between guilt and innocence. Between loyalty and treason. She paused, her heart pounding. She could call it off, chuck the lighter in the trash, never see Walter Smith again. She didn't have to press that button.

No, she didn't have to. No one was making her. She did this for him because (she realized) she *chose* to do this for him.

The camera made a tiny click when she pressed the button. Her palms had gone slick with sweat. She put down the camera, shook out her wrists, wiped her hands on her jeans, and drew a deep breath. *You're okay*, she thought. *You're okay.* She moved as fast as she could. Keeping careful track of the order in which she withdrew the papers from the briefcase, she took picture after picture. It took less than five minutes to photograph everything. She didn't linger. Lara paid no attention to what was written on each page. She didn't really want to know.

◆

The bell on the front door of the dusty old shop on rue des Beaux Arts jingled when she walked in. Lara took her time, browsing among the aisles, asking the clerk whether they had a certain kind of India ink. After her purchase was rung up, as the clerk was wrapping the bottle of ink in brown paper, Lara twisted her face into a theatrical expression of concern and said, "Oh, before I go, I'd better use the restroom." The clerk shrugged, indifferent. (Next time,

Lara thought, she wouldn't bother announcing her movements like that.)

The whole thing was shockingly easy. Taping the used film to the back of the toilet tank, untaping the new film that had been left for her. On her way home, dragging a bit of chalk along the lamppost. *Just like that*, she thought.

The most important thing, Walter Smith told her, was not to draw attention to herself. Don't alter her usual routines. Don't suddenly act like a different person. Keep up the old habits. This meant that Lara only had so many windows of opportunity to take her photographs. A few nights a week, she went out with Natasha and her friends. And the nights she stayed in, Fyodor didn't always leave his briefcase in the living room.

Her next chance came in late November. The second time was a little easier. Waiting for him to fall asleep, staying alert to every sound, moving quickly through his papers. The nerves remained present in her sweaty palms and thudding heart, but her mind was calm and clear.

Papers placed back in the briefcase, exactly as they were before. Lighter tucked away in her purse. Switching off the lamp in the living room, leaving her sketchbook and pencils on the coffee table: a reminder for her parents, in the morning, of why she had been up so late. Hanging up her sweater, folding her jeans, smoothing out the creases. Sasha used to tease Lara for how fastidious she was about her clothing. It was true: she hated getting stains or tears. Her problem was that she remembered the way it had looked before. It was hard to accept imperfections when the memory of the perfect burned so brightly in her mind.

In her bedroom, she pulled back the blankets and climbed into bed. Natasha's old twin bed was still there, across the room. Lara turned to face the other way, curling her knees toward her chest, pressing a fingertip against the wallpaper, which was faded and peeling, air-bubbled from the passage of time. The wallpaper had been there for the last twelve years, since they moved into this apartment in 1974.

Would her younger self have recognized the Lara of this moment? Would Natasha have recognized her? Would Fyodor, or Irina? This was so unlike her: taking advantage of her father's trust, exploiting her family for the sake of . . . of America? A country in which she had never set foot; a country to which she owed absolutely nothing.

When you become a stranger to your past self, what do you call that?

But she felt so *alive.* Alive in a way she hadn't felt since Sasha was killed.

◆

December 1986, the week before Christmas. The Luxembourg Gardens were nearly empty. She had been sitting on the bench for over an hour, jiggling her knees to stay warm. Fyodor had once explained how losing a tail required elaborate movements and maneuvers, which could take several hours. Lara knew that this was true on both sides of the game, and that Walter Smith was carrying out that same procedure right now—"dry cleaning," as the lingo went—to ensure he hadn't been followed.

When Walter finally appeared, he looked like a man out for a casual stroll on his lunch break. Dark overcoat, tartan scarf, earmuffs, calm expression. His mood never seemed to change. A muted acceptance that might have verged on indifference, were it not for the warm quality of his voice. During an earlier conversation, Lara had asked him: "Do you like living here?" And he responded: "I like how comfortable it is. In a lot of the world, a man with my skin color gets looked at. But Paris is different."

Walter sat on the bench beside her and said, "You're doing excellent work, Lara."

She felt a flush of satisfaction, an expansion in her chest.

"They're very pleased with what you've gotten," he said. Walter always referred to his bosses as *they*, not *we*. An entity separate from him. "The only problem is, now they want more. As much as you can get. You've uncovered something big, do you realize that?"

She shook her head. "I haven't been stopping to read anything."

"Well, good. That's smart. But, Lara, it looks like your father has access to a program called FOLIANT. Have you heard of this?"

Again she shook her head, so Walter explained. Fyodor had recently recruited a scientist from France's top research institute. This scientist was an expert in a particularly useful kind of chemistry. He was now working as an agent for the KGB, sharing his expertise with Soviet scientists, as they proceeded with operation FOLIANT.

"But what does that mean?" Lara said. Her mouth had gone dry. "What is FOLIANT?"

"We don't know yet," Walter said. "We're hoping you can help us find out."

◆

Well, what was she meant to do? She couldn't exactly bring it up with Fyodor. *By the way, Papa, I was looking through those papers in your briefcase—you know, those ultra-classified, top secret papers—and I wonder, what's this thing called FOLIANT? Can you tell me all about it? And all of the technical details, please?*

There was a constant tension to this work. *Don't draw attention to yourself, don't take any unnecessary risks. But give us as much as you can, the sooner the better.*

She seized every opportunity she could. On the nights when Fyodor happened to carry his briefcase into the bedroom, she grew frustrated. *Why does he do that? It's not like he can work while he sleeps. What a stupid thing to do.* It surprised her, how easily her thoughts turned nasty like this. When she began this work, Lara had been very clear with herself: she was doing it *for* Sasha, not *against* anyone. Not against her father, not against her home. Sasha had led her to see the flaws in the Soviet system; but even still, she belonged to that system. That system was the only home she'd known.

Her failure to make progress meant she was letting Sasha down. That was the worst feeling in the world. She stood in the hallway, wondering what to do. Ear pressed against the bedroom door. The sound of Fyodor snoring. The work was easier to justify when her father left the papers scattered everywhere. His carelessness wasn't her fault. But this was yet another layer of calculation. Every time you cross one line, she realized, the next line awaits.

Lara thought of her sister. When she lived at home, Natasha used to play Michael Jackson and the Rolling Stones well into the night, dancing and singing and thumping around. Their parents never awoke. *If they could sleep through that*... Lara thought. And then she placed her hand on the doorknob.

CHAPTER THIRTEEN

How many times does life hand you a winning lottery ticket? Of course Vicky wanted to publish the story. *Anyone* would have wanted to publish the story. On the late July day when I walked back into the newsroom and sat down at the conference table across from Vicky, I reminded myself: *This should feel exciting*. But it was harder than I'd anticipated, telling her the story of the past seven months.

I talked, and Vicky listened. When I finished, she sat back in her chair, removed her glasses, closed her eyes, and rubbed the bridge of her nose.

"Just need a second," she murmured. "I'm thinking."

A minute later, she opened her eyes. She leaned forward, reaching across the table for my hand. "You realize, sweetheart. This story is going to change your life."

•

And she was right, of course, but not in the way either of us had expected. Six weeks later, Ben and I left New York without knowing when we'd come back.

Most people who read my story took it at face value: here was the shocking truth of Lara Caine's past, and wow, wasn't that something? But a much smaller subset of people—those trained to be skeptical of appearances, even the most plausible of appearances—looked at the nature of that truth, and the institutions involved in that truth, and wondered if there wasn't something else afoot. The man standing in our living room—an ambassador from that parallel world—was trying to explain the danger this posed.

"But why do we need to leave?" Ben asked.

"I have no way of protecting you if you stay," the man said. "Our charter doesn't give us those powers. And there aren't many people left who we can trust. If you go abroad, to a country without an extradition treaty, you'll be safer. And we'll have certain friends who can help you."

Ben shook his head. "But what . . . what are we going to tell people? My bosses? Our friends and family?"

"Whatever you want to tell them," he said. "You'll be surprised by how easily people believe you. How much they *want* to believe you."

For the most part, he was right. He helped us come up with a simple cover story. I'd been tipped off to a subject in Croatia that might form the backbone of my new book; Ben needed a break from all those billable hours; both of us craved a change.

"Cool!" our friends said. "Good for you guys." Maybe I shouldn't have been surprised at this lack of surprise; at their easy willingness to let us go. Look at it from their perspective. Ben and Sofie never wanted children, did they? And they've always liked to travel. In any case, flights were so cheap these days. Croatia wasn't *that* far. They would come visit! Was it true that Dubrovnik looked like Disneyland?

In Croatia, the months went by. Winter turned to spring. The bora tapered to a gentle breeze. We had our routines, our mechanisms for staying sane. Every Wednesday afternoon, I had a weekly FaceTime date with Jenna and the boys. Afternoon in Split was morning back in DC, and my efficient sister had realized that the sight of my face on her propped-up iPad kept Derek and Luke distracted while they ate their breakfast and she ran around the kitchen, packing lunch boxes and cleaning up last night's dishes.

On a Wednesday in April, my laptop chimed and their faces blossomed to fill the screen. The boys were growing like weeds, getting bigger from one week to the next. Derek had a bright red gash above his eyebrow.

"Oh, sweetheart! Ouch! What happened?" I said, leaning closer to the screen. Derek said proudly: "I fell off the jungle gym!"

"And what did we learn from that?" Jenna called, somewhere off-screen.

"That we should always hang on with *two* hands," Derek said. Then, with great effort, and bearing an uncanny resemblance to his handsome father, he winked.

The boys chattered for a while about their school projects and soccer games, about their ongoing campaign for a family dog. And, as always, they asked when I was coming home. The words Jenna used in her explanation of where Auntie Sofie had gone—*Croatia, temporarily*—meant nothing to them. "Will you be back in time for our birthday party?" Luke asked. "We're getting an ice-cream cake and pizza, and Mom is doing a scavenger hunt."

"I don't know, sweetie. Maybe." Their eighth birthday was in two weeks.

Sam appeared on-screen, waving blurrily in the background. As he hustled the boys out the door, Jenna and I were left alone. A sudden silence descended. She sat down in front of the iPad, her hands wrapped around a mug of coffee.

"So do you mean that?" she said. "That 'maybe'? Or are you just being nice?"

I sighed. "Are we really doing this again?"

"Oh, *sorry*, Sofie. Just trying to get a handle on the truth here. Just trying to figure out whether you're lying to my children."

"You act like I'm enjoying this," I said peevishly.

She rolled her eyes. "I'm kidding. You know I don't give a shit if you lie to them. I lie to them ten times a day."

She was kidding, sure, but only on a certain level. For several months, a rawness had persisted between us. *Don't lie to my kids*, Jenna said. What she wanted to say, but wouldn't, because she was too tough for that, was: *Don't lie to me.*

It had been my very first question. "What about my sister?" I'd asked, on the day when we were advised to leave New York. "Can I tell her the truth?"

"That would be unwise," he'd said. "If you do, you'll be putting her at risk, too."

Jenna didn't buy our cover story. Not for one second. "What the actual *fuck*, Sofie?" she said when I told her, just before our red-eye to Europe. "What? You just decided to do this? You just woke up yesterday and thought, *Hmm, I'll move to Croatia*?"

"I know it's really far," I said. "But, Jen, I've got this opportunity, and the time feels right, and—"

"I don't give a shit how far it is," she snapped. "Live wherever you want to live. Do whatever you need to do. But at least tell me the *truth*."

She was angry, and I was a liar, and though there was a good reason for lying, that didn't make our terse texts and calls any less painful. But even if I'd wanted to tell her the truth—how could I? Our apartment and cell phones were likely bugged. Those first weeks in Croatia were horrible, lonely and silent and dead-ended. I wanted to believe that I had done the right thing, in publishing the story; but if this was part of the result, had it really been worth it?

And then one day, standing in line at a convenience store in Split, staring vacantly at the shelves behind the cash register, it jumped out at me. An impulse. "I'll take one of those," I said, pointing to the array of prepaid cell phones.

I texted Jenna from the burner. *It's Sofie. We have to talk. I'll call from this number later today.* I spent hours crisscrossing the city, taking buses in random directions, exiting shops through back doors. When I was confident that I hadn't been followed, I found a secluded corner of Marjan Park. The sightlines would keep anyone from sneaking up on me, and the rustling trees would cover the sound of my voice.

Jenna picked up after the second ring. "Jesus, what's wrong!" she exclaimed. "What's this all about? Did you lose your other phone? Is everything okay?"

At the sound of her concern, I burst into tears.

"Sofie!" she shouted. "Sofie, you're freaking me out! Are you okay? Is it Ben? Tell me!"

"I'm fine," I said, crying. "I just need to tell you something."

She was right, I said. She was right, I wasn't being honest. And I wanted to tell her the real story—I wanted that so badly, she couldn't even imagine—but I couldn't. She just had to trust me. Did she trust me?

"Oh, Sofie," Jenna sighed. "Of course I trust you." For a long moment, she was silent. "This is something to do with Lara Caine, isn't it?" she asked. A pause, and then: "Never mind. You probably can't answer that."

Our relationship hadn't quite gone back to normal. Maybe it never would (a thought that sometimes visited me in the middle of the night, which I hated, but couldn't deny the possibility of). But her forgiveness was the first step, and for now, that was enough.

That April day, Jenna sipped her coffee and we chatted about the boys. Jenna had learned not to ask too much about my life in Split. What could I tell her, anyway? That day, she was narrating the latest PTA drama ("I swear to God, this woman acts like she's the General Patton of bake sales") when the phone rang in the background. "Oh, shit. Do you mind if I get that? It's probably the school, they always call the landline. Hang on—" Jenna jumped up to answer the phone, disappearing off-screen.

The iPad was propped up on the kitchen table, capturing the same perspective I would have had if I were there in person, sitting across the table from my sister. I leaned closer to the pixelated video, searching out the familiar details. The box of Cheerios, top flap still open. The gallon of milk on the counter. The peeled, half-eaten banana. The refrigerator covered with crayon artwork and soccer schedules. Amid this, I spotted a familiar-looking postcard. Bright blue water, red-roofed buildings, mountains in the background. GREETINGS FROM SPLIT! I remembered what was scribbled on the other side. *Miss you. It's beautiful here.* It gave me comfort, knowing that sliver of me—paper I had touched, ink I had shaped—had winged its way across the world and come to rest.

•

Every day without fail, the Russians sat in a black Mercedes at the end of our block, watching us come and go. They arrived at seven in the morning and left after our bedroom light went out. To test the theory, I varied my bedtime for a few weeks, standing in the darkness and watching through the curtain. Thirty minutes after our light went out, the Mercedes departed. It happened like clockwork, I told Greta.

"Good," she said. "They're predictable. It's useful to know that."

"How much do you think they know about me and Ben?" I asked. "About our lives?"

"Plenty, if they're any good at their job."

"Do they know about you? About us?"

She shrugged, indifferent. "Assume that they do. They suspect the connection, certainly."

Tuesday mornings were when Greta and I overlapped at the café. A glimpse across the room was sufficient to establish that we were both alive and well. Most of the time we communicated by dead drop. If we needed to speak face-to-face, one of us would stand up, put on her coat, and walk to the bathroom with a newspaper tucked under her left arm. Five minutes later, the other one would follow.

After my ultimatum—slightly dramatic, but hey, it had worked—Greta had given me a series of tasks. The Russians who watched me, I now watched in return. Peering through the window at the car down the block, glancing over my shoulder as they followed me on foot, I kept a meticulously detailed log of their movements: the arrivals, the departures, the color of their clothing, the candy they ate, the soda they drank. Each week, I left this log, rendered in code, taped to a dumpster in an alley behind a restaurant in the old city. Greta insisted that there never be any form of digital contact between us.

Often I caught the Russians staring directly at me, unafraid of being spotted, perhaps even *wanting* to be spotted. My one safe haven was the café; they never came inside. Instead, they stood across the plaza, wearing their dark leather jackets and heavy boots, smoking cigarette after cigarette, waiting for me. Greta explained that the café owner had a long-standing grudge, and unwritten ban, against the Russians. Decades ago, several of his family members had died at the hands of Tito's regime, and to this day, he hated any form of authoritarianism. (He's a stubborn old bastard, she added, with quiet respect.)

I carried out this work without being exactly sure *why* I was doing it. How was this connected to what was happening back in Washington? How were these mundane details going to help? During our walks through the city, our rare moments of true privacy, I sometimes mused about this to Ben. Was I actually accomplishing anything tangible, or was Greta just indulging me?

"Maybe," he said slowly, "that part matters less than we think."

"What do you mean?"

"Well, why did you ask for this work? Because you needed *something* to do. And they'd rather keep you busy on their behalf than let you . . ." He trailed off, shrugged. "I don't know. Then let you have second thoughts."

I frowned. "But I'd never have second thoughts."

"Yeah," he said. "I know."

We walked in silence for a while. I wouldn't have done this any differently: that was the truth. But I didn't like saying that out loud. I had traded certain things, meaningful things, to get to this point. To say that it was worth it was true; but there was a coldness to those words; a coldness that I hadn't really known that I possessed.

•

Another morning in April, in the café. She stood up, a copy of *Der Spiegel* tucked under her arm. I looked back down, pretending to study my phone.

Five minutes later, in the bathroom. I locked the door. Greta turned on the faucet. "He's here," she said abruptly. "Hotel Danica, room 507. Be there at noon today."

"Today?" My heart thumped like a drum. "What's going on?"

"This is why you're going to see him. He'll tell you himself."

Is it finally happening? I thought, as Greta exited the bathroom. *Is this it?*

You see, even the most careful person—even the person who has the most to lose—will eventually trust someone they shouldn't trust.

The investigations hadn't worked. Impeachment proceedings had sputtered out. His luck kept holding. But there was one last place where Henry Caine had left himself exposed.

We had gone abroad to put ourselves beyond the reach of our own government. *What we're talking about is treason.* But this was the calculation we had made; this was the reward for our trade-offs. I was part of the plan to end the Caine presidency.

1987 began. It had been over a year since Sasha died.

Sasha, she realized, had given her everything she needed. The thrill of his hand against her naked body. The lively sparring over ideas. The quiet companionship of side-by-side work. A whole universe of satisfaction, contained within a single person.

To meet one person like this, in the span of a lifetime, is luck beyond measure. Lara knew that she would never meet a second. She wouldn't ever try to replace Sasha. Instead, she would rely on a constellation of people to fill those needs.

Among the moody young Russian men who worked with Natasha at the embassy, there were always a few who were eager to date Lara. She went drinking and dancing with them, stayed out late and got blisters from her high heels. There was a rough kind of pleasure from their bid for her attention, from the grip of their arms around her waist. She let these men walk her home, and sometimes she let them kiss her, and then she pushed them away, saying a firm good night. Anything more, she thought, wouldn't enhance this feeling. It would only cause trouble.

One morning in February of that year, the phone rang.

"Will you get that, Lara?" Irina shouted, her hands submerged in soapy water as she washed the breakfast dishes.

Lara picked up the phone. A voice said, "Is Seryozha there?"

She took a deep breath. "No," she said. "I'm afraid you have the wrong number. There's no one called Seryozha here."

"Who was it?" Irina said, as Lara walked into the kitchen.

"No one," Lara said. "Wrong number. I'm going out for a bit, Mama. I'll be back soon."

Lara's fingers were trembling as she buttoned her coat. *Seryozha* was one of several code names that Walter Smith could have given. Each one referred to a specific meeting point. This one indicated the middle of the Pont des Arts. Right? The Pont des Arts? She was nervous, certain that she was going to make a mistake. But when she arrived, there he was, exactly according to plan.

She stood beside him, at the railing of the bridge, both of them looking out over the Seine.

"Did you have trouble getting away?" he asked.

"No," she said. "It was easy enough."

"I'll only call the apartment when it's absolutely necessary," he said. "I want to tell you something, Lara. We're getting a clearer picture on operation FOLIANT."

"What do you mean?"

Walter glanced over. "Have you heard of a place called Sverdlovsk?"

"It's a city in Russia."

"There was an outbreak of anthrax in Sverdlovsk eight years ago. About sixty or seventy people died from it. The Soviets have always said the outbreak came from contaminated meat, but this never made sense. The way it spread, the number of people who got infected, the anthrax had to be airborne. It had to be that the Soviets were manufacturing anthrax—which is illegal—at the scientific complex in Sverdlovsk. We suspect there was an accident at the complex, which spread the spores into the city."

Lara's mouth had gone dry. "Is this what you learned from my father's papers?"

"No," Walter said. "We were already fairly certain about Sverdlovsk. But that outbreak put us on high alert. What if there was more than just anthrax? What if the Soviets have been working on other weapons, too? This is what operation FOLIANT seems to be. From what we can tell, it refers to a comprehensive chemical weapons program. This is what we've been learning from your father's papers."

She felt a sudden wave of dizziness, and had to grip the railing to stay upright. Ringing heat filled her ears. For the first time, she felt that this might have been a stupid idea. A very stupid idea. She was a little girl playing a dangerous game. Maybe she ought to leave right now. Run away, back to the safety of home.

"Lara?" Walter's voice sounded distant. "Lara, I know this is something of a shock."

Finally, she shook her head. "Why did you tell me? I didn't *want* to know these things. That's why I never stopped to read his papers."

"It's your decision whether to continue," he said. "It's always been your decision. But you deserve to know what your involvement has meant to us. This information will make a real difference."

She felt that he was making assumptions—about her loyalties, about her desires—which he had no right to make. Something hardened in her.

"A difference to who?" she said sharply. "Not to me."

"Lara," he said. "Do you mean that?"

◆

At dinner that night, she was especially quiet. "Is something the matter, Larochka?" Fyodor said.

"I'm just tired," she said.

Fyodor and Irina exchanged the briefest look, but they left it alone. Her parents never sought to interrogate her moods. Sometimes, she thought mordantly, it was useful to have a dead boyfriend.

As she watched her parents eating and drinking, carefree as anything, there was bitterness in her mouth. At this table, less than a year ago, Fyodor had spoken so gravely about the accident at Chernobyl. People dead from radiation. Poison leaching into the ground, the water, the crops. *Playing with fire*, he called it. The carelessness. The tragedy.

Did he mean any of it?

Earlier that day, when she walked away from Walter Smith on the Pont des Arts, she wasn't sure if she would ever see him again. She wasn't sure how much more she wanted to find out. A flimsy wall separated her from the darkness—as flimsy as a few papers in a briefcase—but maybe that was better than no wall at all.

Or maybe it wasn't.

What do I do? she thought, lying in bed that night, curled into a ball. *Do I have to pick a side?*

Tell me, Sasha. I've only ever done this for you.

◆

One spring morning, a couple of months later, Irina opened the bedroom door. She sat down on Lara's bed, and gently shook her awake.

"Happy birthday, Larochka," she said. "My wonderful girl."

As a treat, Irina took Lara to lunch at a neighborhood brasserie. Lara had just turned seventeen. In a year, she would be free to leave home, free to do whatever she wanted. They had never really talked about Lara's future before. But now—Irina pronounced, as she poured wine into her glass, and a little bit into Lara's, too—now was the time to talk about it.

"You're a very bright girl," she said. "You know that, don't you? You've always been shy, I suppose that can't be helped. Your sister never had an interest in university. But you, Lara, you must continue your studies."

Lara nodded as her mother spoke, but didn't say a word.

"Now," Irina continued. "There are many excellent universities in Moscow. We've already asked your grandfather, and you can live with him. You remember your grandfather's apartment, darling? On Kutuzovsky Prospekt? Oh, you loved it as a little girl. You loved it. Just think! Soon you'll be back there, and . . ."

This moment had to come eventually. Lara was prepared for what she had to do.

When Irina finished describing everything that awaited Lara, she smiled and said, "So, sweetheart. What do you say? It's a good plan, yes?"

"It's a lot to think about, Mama." Lara spoke with deliberate slowness, as if considering everything in real-time. "There are other good universities besides those in Moscow."

"True," Irina said. "There are excellent schools in Leningrad, or Tomsk, or Novosibirsk, or—"

"No," Lara interrupted. "I mean there are good universities outside the Soviet Union."

"Oh." Irina's eyebrows shot up. After a pause, she said, "I see."

Lara had said nothing to her parents about wanting to attend university in another country; she had said nothing to them about *any* future plans. But over the past few months, she had given it plenty of thought. Recently, she had made up her mind.

Several weeks prior to that birthday lunch, Lara went to the market on rue Cler to signal that she wanted a meeting. Three days later, she sat waiting on a bench in the Luxembourg Gardens. Walter arrived, walking at a fast clip. Lara had never used that signal before. "Is everything all right?" he said, slightly breathless.

"How does this end?" Lara asked. She gestured at the two of them. "What happens to me?"

"Oh," he said.

"I know it can't go on forever," she said. "So what happens to me when it ends?"

"Well." He sank to the bench beside her. "It largely depends on what you want."

It had been churning through her mind, ever since their meeting on the Pont des Arts. She knew, in the abstract, that she was betraying the Soviet Union by giving this information to the CIA. But did that mean she was automatically on America's side? No, she wasn't as grand as all that. She wasn't part of any larger historical narrative. This wasn't about ideology. Her broken heart had led her down this path.

And so when this ended—as it had to, eventually—how was she supposed to pick a side? Where would she make her home? The notion of operation FOLIANT, and the work her father was doing at the KGB, horrified her. These were the men who had murdered Sasha. But the other side? Walter Smith was nice enough, but the country and ideology he represented meant nothing to her. America was an alien land. Lara was doing her best to live in a way that would have made Sasha proud. But what would Sasha have wanted from her, wanted *for* her, once this ended?

Maybe it wasn't possible to know. Or maybe—she thought—maybe he would have wanted her to take the path he never had the chance to take.

Maybe the unknown was better than the known.

"I want to leave," she said to Walter. "You were willing to arrange that for Sasha. Have him attend university in America. Give him a new life. Can you do the same for me?"

Walter nodded slowly. "I think we can."

CHAPTER FOURTEEN

That July and August, back in the newsroom, during the weeks I was working on my story, Vicky had me sitting in my old cubicle, the one I'd packed up right after Henry Caine's reelection.

"What did I tell you?" Eli said cheerfully. "Knew you couldn't stay away, Morse."

Vicky stopped by constantly, delivering a steady stream of coffee, snacks, and encouragement. "You got everything you need?" she said, as I attempted to translate my sprawling notes into a coherent story. "Is the light okay? Do you need another desk lamp?"

At the end of that first week, on a Friday afternoon, Vicky gestured me into one of the small conference rooms, where we could have some privacy. "Just wanted to check in," she said quietly, closing the door behind her. Eli and the others didn't yet know why I was back. "You know that we'll need to get the lawyers involved at a certain point."

"I know," I sighed.

She raised her eyebrows. "Cold feet?"

"No, nothing like that. But this story is . . . complicated. I still haven't figured out how to tell it. Where to start. How much to put in."

At this, Vicky smiled and shook her head. "Sweetheart, this is your signature move."

"What is?"

"You say, 'I can't do it, I can't do it, I can't do it.' And then you wake up one day, and there: you've done it. I'm not worried in the least."

Vicky offered to read whatever I'd written, no matter how rough it might be, but I wasn't ready for that. There were things in this story I needed to figure out on my own. What was the perspective? Lara Orlova had once betrayed her country for the sake of love. But how did that teenager in long-ago Paris connect to the woman in Washington today? What, in the end, did it add up to?

At the end of the second week, Vicky summoned me back into the conference room. Only now, every seat at the table was filled. "It's time," she said. "Everyone here is on your team, Sofie. They're going to get you across the finish line. Start looping them in on everything."

I recognized the people at the table—the fact-checkers, the researchers, the lawyer—but the sight of them assembled together was new. My other stories at the newspaper had never gotten this treatment. The stakes had never been quite high enough.

Vicky touched my elbow, gently prodding me forward. "Go ahead," she said. "Tell them what we've got in store."

•

We'd been working on the story for nearly a month. One day in late August, Vicky sent an intern to Pret A Manger to pick up our lunches.

"I'm *not* getting ahead of myself," she insisted, unwrapping her Caesar salad. "I've been in this business a long time. This is going to be the biggest story we've ever broken. So how are you feeling? Are you ready?"

I nodded. Later that day, Vicky and the lawyers would be calling Lara Caine's office for comment on the story, which clocked in at nearly ten thousand words. After many stops and starts, I'd finally seen that there was no way for me to leave myself out of the article. This was Lara's story. It was also the story of her telling me her story. I didn't relish the feeling, but I'd have to appear in the narrative.

History would eventually forget this, of course; as a minor character in the Lara Caine saga, I'd be relegated to a footnote. That was fine by me. Actually, it was better than fine. I was ready to let go of this. I was ready to get back to my ordinary life. Write it, edit it, release it. Just around the corner: freedom.

But even when I was this close, even after all this time—something felt off.

•

The East Wing responded to our call with a blunt, haughty *No comment*. They had no interest in addressing these ridiculous allegations point by point.

"Allegations?" I said. "But I'm writing exactly what she told me!"

Vicky waved her hand. "Take heart, Sofie. This means all of it was right."

"Well, yeah, I *know* it was right," I said, annoyed. As unrealistic as the desire was, I wanted *them* to admit the rightness, too. But I kept my mouth shut.

An hour later, the team huddled around Vicky's desk in the newsroom. "One last time?" she said. I stepped toward the computer screen. All of us, the editors and researchers and fact-checkers and lawyers, scrolled through the story. I felt a surge of pride. This, right here, would be a dividing line. This was the moment when another brick was added to the greater structure of historical truth.

"Enough already," Vicky said. "Sofie, you do the honors."

The cursor on her computer screen hovered over the button that read PUBLISH. I clicked, and the screen reloaded. A moment later, the story appeared on the newspaper's website, waiting for the whole world to see.

•

Just as Vicky had predicted, there was a deluge.

Town cars whisked me into Midtown. Makeup artists powdered my forehead. Producers clipped mics to my lapel and ushered me onto cable news soundstages. I made an emergency trip to Ann Taylor when I ran out of TV-ready outfits. The story led the morning shows and evening news. I phoned into several NPR programs, running upstairs to borrow Maurice's landline because it was a more reliable connection than my cell phone. In green rooms, other guests recognized my name, lighting up with curiosity. *Sofie, right? Wow. Quite a story. I always knew there was something strange about the First Lady. So what do you think? Did the president know about this? Or is he just as shocked as the rest of us?*

Immediately, Gabi Carvalho issued a scathing press release: "The journalist Sofie Morse had entered into a private arrangement with the First Lady to work on a biography. This work was intended to last for several years, with publication to occur long after the president and First Lady leave the White House. Unfortunately, in a desperate bid for attention and profit, Ms. Morse chose to violate that trust and cherry-pick the most salacious details for publication. Ms. Morse has twisted the First Lady's story, taking it out of context, and has done a grave disservice to the truth. The First Lady will not be dignifying this lurid story by responding to specific details. Needless to say, she no longer has a relationship with Ms. Morse."

I tried to get in touch with Lara after the story broke, but no surprise, my messages went unanswered. Almost eight weeks had passed since my return from Connecticut. In that whole stretch, the East Wing had been completely nonresponsive. It continued to baffle me. If the silence had been Lara's way of testing me, why had she let it go on for so long? And why would she risk that public lunch date with Eileen Bates, and the rumors about another biography?

A nagging question kept returning. Lara had to know I'd panic. What if she *wanted* me to panic?

"She canceled another event," I said to Ben, scrolling through my phone. It was Saturday afternoon, nearly a week after the story had published. The First Lady was supposed to attend a performance at the Kennedy Center that night. But, as was true for all of her events for the past week, she dropped out at the last minute.

"I can't blame her," Ben said. "Can you imagine what a feeding frenzy it would be?"

"But she can't hide out forever," I said. "Why not rip off the Band-Aid? The longer she keeps this up, the hungrier the media gets."

Lara Caine liked to control her own narrative. And here she had allowed herself to lose control, in the worst way possible. The media swarming. Reporters digging further into her past. Rumors of her husband losing his temper. And why? To what end? No, that nagging question didn't make any sense: she couldn't possibly want any of this.

•

The next day, on Sunday afternoon, Lara Caine finally appeared in public. The *Daily Mail* was the first outlet to have pictures up online:

> ***WITH A CHERRY ON TOP!***
>
> First Lady Lara Caine is all smiles as she and her daughters make a trip to Thomas Sweet in the posh Washington neighborhood of Georgetown—one week after the explosive revelation about her past as a CIA agent.

I'd never been so grateful for the psychotic thoroughness with which the *Daily Mail* chronicled the lives of the famous. There were dozens of photos of Lara, Emily, and Marina entering and exiting the ice-cream shop in Georgetown. I squinted, zoomed in, scrolled and rescrolled. Lara appeared happy and relaxed. It was a bright summer day, but she wasn't wearing sunglasses or a hat, as if she wanted to give the paparazzi a good long look.

In the photos, Lara was holding an ice-cream cone, tanned and smiling, her hair wavy and loose. She looked—and this was a rarity—strangely *relatable*, wearing sandals and white jeans and a soft lavender cardigan. Yes, granted, that was a Birkin bag hanging from the crook of her elbow. But the overall impression was that of a normal mother spending a normal August afternoon with her daughters. A normal mother, focused on her family, not on the wild media coverage of her long-ago youth.

So this, I thought, was her strategy. Refuse to give the story any oxygen. Just keep living. Let them write what they write. Pretend it never happened. It was one way to handle the situation, and honestly, there were worse ways. When those pictures appeared, I gave up hope of ever hearing from Lara Caine again.

But two days later—just as the news cycle was moving on, just as the flood of interview requests slowed to a trickle—the radio silence abruptly ended.

An email in my inbox, from Gabi Carvalho:

> Hi, Sofie. Mrs. Caine will be in New York for an event on Thursday night. She'd like to come see you and your husband at your apartment. Could you make yourself available that afternoon?

•

The knock on our front door came promptly at 3:00 p.m. on Thursday. I opened the door to find two Secret Service agents in dark suits.

"Afternoon, ma'am," one of them said. "We'll need to do a sweep before the First Lady enters the premises."

I stepped aside and gestured them in. The men worked quickly, scanning the space for potential dangers and weak points. One of them held his wrist up to his mouth and muttered into his radio. He nodded at the other agent, who headed toward the back door.

"The First Lady has requested complete privacy for this conversation," he said. "My colleague will be out back, in the garden. I'll be just outside the front door."

"Um, sure," I said. Through the window there was a trio of dark SUVs. No motorcade, no sirens or flashing lights. The Secret Service agent was now opening the door to the middle SUV.

I glanced over my shoulder at Ben. "It's okay, Sofe," he said, nodding at me. "It doesn't matter what she says. You did the right thing."

I didn't understand why Lara wanted Ben to be at the meeting (and when asked for clarification, Gabi didn't give any), but I went along with it. In any case, it was comforting to have him there.

I waited in the hallway, facing the front door. A moment passed. I could hear my pulse pounding in my ears. The door creaked slightly as it opened. She was in the doorway, backlit by the sunshine. Gradually she came into focus: Lara Caine, standing on our doormat, right next to our flimsy coat hooks and framed Rothko prints and cheap Ikea bench. It was one of the more bizarre sights I'd ever seen.

"Hi, Sofie," she said, turning to close the door. She took a step forward and extended her hand. "And you must be Ben. It's nice to meet you."

"Um, you as well," he said, his voice pitched higher than usual as he shook her hand.

"I'm sorry for all this fuss," Lara said. "May I come in?"

There wasn't a trace of anger in her expression. In fact, she looked entirely peaceful. She walked toward me and grasped both of my hands in hers.

"Sofie," she said. "Thank you. You've done everything beautifully."

My stomach did a somersault. "W-what?"

As she squeezed my hands, I glanced down and noticed that she wasn't wearing her diamond ring. "Sofie, please look at me," she said. "*Thank you.* I mean that. I mean that with every part of my being. Thank you."

No, I thought. *No, no, no. I don't understand.*

I don't want to understand.

"We don't have much time," she said, releasing her grasp. "An hour at most. Now, there's a staircase in this apartment, isn't there? It connects to the apartment above yours?"

Lara surveyed the space, just as the Secret Service agents had done. She spotted the door, and pointed at it. "This is it? The staircase is behind here?"

Why the staircase? But in my silent shock, I just nodded.

Ben took a deep breath. "Excuse me, Mrs. Caine, but is there something—"

"Quiet, please," she said, holding a finger to her lips. She stepped closer to the door. Turned and pressed her ear to it. The apartment was silent. She knocked softly. A few moments passed. There was a returning knock from the other side of the door.

Someone was inside.

Lara reached down and unlocked the dead bolt. "You can come out now," she said.

A moment later, the handle turned. The door opened. Though I'd never seen him before, the man who stepped out looked familiar. Dark skin, rimless glasses, gentle eyes. A character from a long-ago story, just as she had described.

"Walter," Lara said softly. "It's you."

—w—

At their next meeting, in May 1987, Walter Smith described the plan. The CIA was given an annual quota of one hundred green cards, to dispense to agents who needed them. Lara would receive one of these green cards. When she arrived in America, her future would be of her own choosing: she could attend university, she could work, she could do whatever she wanted.

There was also a bank account, into which the CIA had been depositing her monthly salary. The money would be waiting for her.

"A salary?" she said.

Walter nodded. "Most of our agents want to be compensated for the significant risks they're taking. They're motivated by money. But even when they aren't, we want to be fair."

"Fair? What does that mean?"

"I've been approved to pay you ten thousand American dollars a month for the work you've been doing. We're backdating the pay to last year."

She blinked in bafflement. Ten thousand American dollars a month? It was a number so big that she couldn't really understand it. But she grasped one thing: the number meant freedom. It meant independence, and choice. She shook her head, setting it aside for now, forcing herself to focus on what Walter was saying.

Given that they were in Paris, the actual process of exfiltration was simple. "It would be a different story if we were in Moscow," Walter said. "It would be virtually impossible to get you out of Moscow. But here, you'll just walk out the front door like it's any normal day—no luggage, nothing. Follow protocol to make sure you aren't being tailed, and then a car will pick you up and take you to De Gaulle. We'll book your ticket to Washington under a different name. You'll carry identification in that name. If anyone at the airport asks, you're a student, and you're visiting a cousin who lives in Virginia."

"And then?" Lara said, swallowing hard.

"Once you've arrived, the agency will take some time to debrief you. Assuming you still want to go to university, we'll get you enrolled somewhere for the fall semester. We have connections at several different schools."

She tried picturing all of these things—the airplane, the airport, Washington, Virginia—and found that she couldn't. The words meant nothing to her. The unknown was too immense.

"When will this happen?" she asked. "Will it be soon?"

Walter shook his head. "Next spring," he said. "About a year from now."

"Why?"

He hesitated for a moment. He looked down at his hands, then back up at her. "You're very valuable, Lara," he said. "What you've uncovered is some of the best intelligence we've had in years. It's being used at the highest levels. They'd like to keep you where you are."

With a twist in her stomach, she asked: "But is it safe for me to stay here?"

He nodded. "I promise. If it wasn't safe, I wouldn't let you stay."

After a long silence, Walter added, "I know you might be disappointed."

Another year of lying. Another year of betraying her father while living under his roof; of not understanding how she was meant to feel. She detested what her father did, and the organization he was a part of. But she loved him—she loved her mother, she loved her sister—she loved her family because they were the very essence of her. How was a person meant to endure this mixture? And yet the path unfurling before her felt inevitable. She would wait another year because she had to wait another year. She would leave them because she had to leave them. This was the awful, heartbreaking cost of her freedom.

But her soul rebelled against this calculation.

"Can they come with me?" she asked. "My family?"

"Well," Walter said. "They *could*, theoretically. If they wanted to."

But, he continued, did they want to? Did Fyodor and Irina and Natasha feel the same way as her? Would they accept and condone the nature of her betrayal? Were they ready to say goodbye to the only life they had ever known? To cross that permanent line and leave their country forever? Because make no mistake: once Lara set this in motion, she could never go back to Russia.

This wasn't exactly a conversation for the dinner table. Lara couldn't possibly ask her parents and sister about this without showing her hand, and endangering everyone in the process. But she could guess what they would say. Actually, she could do more than guess. In her heart, she was certain: no, they wouldn't want to go.

"But next year, when I leave," she said. "I can say goodbye to them, can't I?"

"I'm sorry, Lara," Walter said. "It's too risky."

If they knew she was leaving, they could tip off the authorities. Even if the window was just a few hours, that would be enough time for the KGB to spring into action and intercept her. And besides, Walter added: when her departure was eventually noticed, the Orlov family would be thoroughly questioned. The less Fyodor and Irina and Natasha knew about Lara's disappearance—the less they were forced to lie—the safer they would be.

◆

Spying required a great deal of stamina. One must remain alert at all times. She learned to seize her openings. She developed a knack for gathering stray bits of information, for making the most of her position, for going above and beyond what Walter asked of her.

Fyodor and Irina continued throwing their famous dinner parties. Toward the end of these dinners, when the husbands were good and drunk, Lara always offered to clear the dishes.

"Such a lovely girl. Truly, she's a credit to you, Irina Mikhailovna," one of the wives remarked. Irina smiled, proud of her sweet and helpful daughter.

The women moved into the living room, and the men remained at the table, where they complained about work, tongues loosened by vodka. Standing in the kitchen, as long as she didn't clatter the dishes too loudly, Lara could hear every word the men said. Afterward, she stayed up late into the night, flashlight beneath her blanket, transcribing the conversations in minuscule handwriting. She taped those handwritten pages behind the dusty toilet in the art store, along with the film.

Walter told her that her work was making a difference, that it was appreciated by the powers back in Langley—but what did those words mean to her? She lived on a thin diet of hope. Gratification was still in the future. Next spring, to be precise, when she would leave for America.

A clean break. A chance at total independence. A life completely on her own terms. The idea terrified her; but it was also the most thrilling thing she could imagine.

◆

From the outside, 1987 might have looked like an unremarkable year for Larissa Fyodorovna Orlova. She was a teenage girl, doing normal teenage things. The people closest to her saw nothing amiss. But the most important changes were occurring in the silent parts of herself.

This is how real change happens, after all. A surface appears placid for the longest time, until it suddenly begins to boil.

In February 1987, the dissident Andrei Sakharov appeared in public for the first time since returning from exile. He spoke at a conference on nuclear disarmament. He was treated less like an academic physicist and more like a dazzling global celebrity. Sakharov's ideas, dismissed for so long, were finally gaining traction. Maybe the two superpowers didn't have to be locked in an arms race until the end of time. Maybe there was another way.

In June 1987, the liberal Solidarity movement in Poland seized the TV airwaves. They urged supporters to take to the streets to demonstrate against the repressive Communist regime. Just a few years before, these protesters had been crushed by Soviet tanks. But now, the opposition's power was unmistakably real, and it was growing.

In September 1987, the sound of American broadcasters could be heard on Moscow radio waves for the first time in decades. The Communist Party had been jamming the signal of the BBC and Voice of America since 1949, in order to protect its citizens from poisonous Western propaganda, but it had finally given up on this fruitless fight.

And every month, every week, every day of that year, glasnost did its work. The water of truth began flowing more freely. One memory at a time, the past was allowed to return.

◆

A January night, early in 1988. Irina and Lara were sitting at the kitchen table, where Irina was correcting Lara's essay about *Anna Karenina*. "You see, Larochka, you have not *explained* here what you mean by Vronsky's guilt. Guilty for what reason? Why can't we assume that Anna Arkadyevna brought this upon herself? If you look here, then—"

Irina paused at the sound of the front door opening. When she smiled, she looked as lovestruck as a schoolgirl. It remained the best part of her day, the moment when Fyodor walked through the door.

"Fedya, darling," she called out. "Did your girl pass along my message? We need more milk for the morning, did you get it?"

But there was no response. Irina wrinkled her brow. "Fedya?" she called again.

Footsteps came quietly down the hallway. When Fyodor appeared, his face was pale. "It's my father," he said. "He had a heart attack."

◆

Fyodor and Irina decided it was best for Natasha and Lara to stay in Paris while they attended Maxim's funeral. Plane tickets to Moscow were expensive. "It's just three days," Irina said to them, stroking their hair nervously. "You'll be fine, won't you?"

Those three days passed in agonizing slowness, in oppressive quiet. Lara found it hard to sleep. When her parents finally returned—hugging her fiercely, kissing her over and over—something inside her unclenched. She couldn't admit it to herself, not until that moment, but she had been terrified that Fyodor and Irina might not come back. Her grandfather Maxim had always been the one who protected them, who ensured the state's hammer didn't come crashing down; who allowed the Orlovs to feel invincible. What would happen now? She burst into tears. "Oh, sweetheart, I know," Fyodor said, drawing her into his arms. "I miss him, too."

If it wasn't safe, I wouldn't let you stay. Walter had told her that. But what would Maxim's death change?

Later that evening, after her parents had said good night, Lara could hear the sound of their voices behind their bedroom door. She tiptoed down the hallway. If she leaned close and concentrated, she could just make out what they were saying.

"It will be totally different, Fedya, can't you see that? This will change everything."

"Now, we don't know that. I've always done good work for them."

"Oh, please. Don't be naive. Your father was an important man. Why do you think we've always had such a nice life?"

"My father was an important man, yes. And I am my father's son. They will respect that. They trust me."

"They! They! Here is the other problem, Fedya! This *they* you talk of. *They* won't have the power, from now on. *They* won't be able to protect us. You saw what it was like in Moscow. It's a different world. Everything is changing. No more favors for us, that's certain. They'll take this whole life away. Take your job away. Send us back with no explanation."

"So what if they do? Then we'll go back to Moscow. It will be fine."

"Fine! You are talking like a fool. What kind of job will you get? How will we eat, hmm? How do we live? People are starving to death. There's no food on the shelves. Don't you see, Fedya? Our time is up. We'll be thrown away. Mark my words. We'll be thrown away like an old heap of rags."

◆

"What if my mother is right?" Lara asked.

It was a few weeks later, in February 1988. Lara wiped away a thin dusting of snow before sitting down on the bench in the Luxembourg Gardens. She jiggled her knees to keep warm.

"You'll be okay," Walter said. "You only have to make it a few more months."

"But that's the point!" Lara exclaimed. "They could recall him at any time. Especially now that my grandfather is dead."

"I doubt that," Walter said. "Operation FOLIANT is highly sensitive. And it appears your father has been making real progress on recruiting another important source. The KGB won't pull him off that. Think back to when they were arguing. How did your father sound? Did he seem worried?"

Lara closed her eyes, summoning the memory. "He sounded . . . normal."

Walter nodded. "Exactly. That's the best way for you to act, too. Remember that we have someone stationed at the rue Cler every Sunday. Keep going to the market. We'll know that you're safe. If something is wrong, signal for a meeting. We can always activate your departure early."

◆

Winter turned to spring, and it appeared that Walter was right.

February went by, and everything was fine.

March went by, and everything was fine.

The date of her departure drew nearer. Lara was planning to leave on May 1, 1988, just after her eighteenth birthday. Her parents would be gone that day, attending the ambassador's annual May Day party at the country house in Mantes-la-Jolie. It was an ideal date to make her escape. The entire KGB rezidentura would be at the party.

She liked the symmetry of it, too. May 1 had always been an important day. She would be leaving Paris exactly four years after she first met Sasha.

And then it was April. She had less than a month left.

◆

It was a Saturday morning when the phone rang in the apartment on the rue de la Faisanderie. Lara answered it, but the call was for her father.

"I have to go in for a bit," Fyodor said, after hanging up. "Some silly issue."

"Don't forget, Nataschenka is coming for lunch today," Irina said.

"Of course. I won't be long," he said, and kissed his wife goodbye.

Fyodor returned a few hours later, just after Natasha had arrived for lunch. But when he walked in, he was very pale—even paler than the day Maxim had died. Irina looked at him and froze. Then her hands began trembling. The plate she had been holding shattered against the floor.

"My dears," Fyodor said, in a hoarse voice. "We need to pack."

"Pack?" Natasha said. "Why, Papa? Where are we going?"

Irina shook her head. She took a deep breath and drew herself upright. "Back to Moscow," she said abruptly. "Lara, will you please get the broom and dustpan? Natasha, you can leave that chopping alone. We won't have time to eat."

"What do you mean?" Natasha pressed. "When are we leaving?"

"Tonight," Fyodor said. "They need me back at the center immediately."

"Okay, but why do *we* have to go?" Natasha whined.

"Because we're a family!" Irina snapped. "Now, stop asking questions. You'll need to pack your things. One suitcase each. The rest of it can be sent later."

Natasha turned around and glared at Lara. "Well, *you're* being very quiet. Don't you even care? Good little Lara. Never says a word. Never complains about anything."

"You could take a lesson from her!" Irina shouted as Natasha stormed down the hallway.

Natasha slammed the bedroom door. But just a few minutes later, she emerged in much better spirits. "You know what?" she said cheerfully. "I've decided to be glad about this. Just imagine what Arkady will think when I'm not at work on Monday. He's in love with me, you know. He'll be devastated. He might even kill himself."

She laughed. Then she caught a glimpse of Lara and looked horrified. "Oh, Lara, forgive me. God, I'm such an idiot! I'm so sorry, I didn't mean that. I didn't mean—"

"It's fine," Lara said stiffly. "I need to go pack."

In her bedroom, she knelt down on the carpet and dragged the suitcase out from beneath her bed. From the living room, she heard Irina giving Natasha permission to return to her nearby apartment to pack her things, as long as she was back in an hour. After Natasha left, Irina said quietly (but Lara's ears were as alert as ever): "Did they say anything else, Fedya?"

"No," he said. "Nothing."

"Fourteen years!" she said. "My God. Fourteen years, and it ends like this."

It was a bad sign. Even with Maxim's death, and the resulting loss of protection: the KGB didn't summon an officer this abruptly without good reason. Irina kept coming into the bedroom. The car would be here in a few hours. Lara would be ready by then, yes? Did she need any help? No? She smoothed her daughter's hair, over and over.

"Good girl," she said. "That's my good, strong girl."

Lara moved in a fugue state. Folding T-shirts and jeans, tucking socks inside of shoes. On her bedside table, the clock ticked and ticked. There was no way to get hold of Walter Smith. Not with this kind of notice. Oddly, she didn't feel a sense of panic. Panic was pointless; there was nothing she could do. How many times had she thought to herself: *What do I do? Which side do I pick*? Well, here it was. The universe was picking for her. In her heart, she had known the promise of America was too good to be true. Fate couldn't be escaped. Tomorrow she would wake up in Moscow, and soon she would look back on this Parisian spying adventure as just a lark, without so much as a souvenir to show—

And then it came, the bright bolt of panic. *The lighter*, Lara realized. She couldn't leave the lighter behind. Someone would find it, and would figure out what it was, and it would be instantly incriminating. She needed to find it—but where was it? In her purse, yes, she always kept it there. She grabbed her purse. Coins, keys, lipstick, pencil stubs, cigarettes spilled out onto the carpet. No lighter. She sprang to her feet, her heart pounding. She shook the purse again, to be sure.

But the pit in her stomach had grown too large to ignore. She knew, with certainty, that she hadn't misplaced the lighter. Which left only one possibility.

Someone had already found it.

An hour later, a black Citroën pulled up to the curb on the rue de la Faisanderie. The Orlov family lugged their suitcases downstairs and loaded them into the trunk. It was a gorgeous spring evening: cherry blossoms, nightingale song. The car drove away from the apartment, toward the airport. The family was silent during the ride. Natasha was scrawling one last message for Arkady on a postcard. Irina held a handkerchief in her lap, twisting it into knots.

Fyodor stared blankly out the window. Each of the Orlovs had their own idea about what awaited them in Moscow.

But Lara was the only one who really knew.

—~—

Lara took a step forward, her hands clasped tight. "Walter," she repeated. "I'm so sorry."

Walter Smith shook his head. "There's no need for that."

She looked down. "But the things I said last time—"

"It's okay," he said. "Really."

Her smile quivered. She blinked, but couldn't keep the tears from spilling down her cheeks. "Look at me," she said, dabbing at her eyes and laughing nervously. "I'm a mess."

Walter took a step forward, too, closing the gap between them. He touched her arm. "It's okay," he repeated. "We're going to figure this out."

My jaw was hanging open. I was completely baffled—Walter Smith? In my apartment? *What the fuck is happening right now?*—but in that moment, part of me felt an unlikely tenderness toward Lara. She looked shy, uncertain, and yet strangely strong. So much, in other words, like the portrait she had spent the last eight months painting: so much like the teenage Larissa Orlova.

"I'm sorry," Ben blurted. "But why are you— Who are you— *What is going on?*"

Walter extended his hand. "You can call me Walter," he said. "I'm sorry for the intrusion."

"The *intrusion*!" Ben said. "You were hiding in our staircase! How did you get in? How long were you in there?"

"Oh, just for a few minutes," Walter said, as if it were the most ordinary thing in the world. "I had some help from your neighbor Maurice. I waited in his apartment and came downstairs when I saw Mrs. Caine's car arrive."

"*Maurice?*" I exclaimed. "What did you do to Maurice?"

Lara turned to me. "Nothing, Sofie. Maurice is perfectly fine. In fact, he wanted to help."

It had been a long time since I'd thought about that afternoon with Tatiana Sokolov, but it suddenly came back to me: the silver-framed pictures in her living room, Tatiana standing beside Maurice. I began to open my mouth, but Ben interrupted.

"Walter? As in Walter Smith? As in the officer from the Central Intelligence Agency who ran Lara Orlova in Paris all those years ago?"

Walter smiled slightly. "I thought Sofie did an excellent job with her article."

"Wait a second." I wheeled around to look at Lara. "What you were saying before. You were *thanking* me? This doesn't make any sense."

"I'm sorry about that, Sofie." She looked genuinely pained. "I had to ask Gabi to say those things. I had to make it look real."

"Look real?" I said. "What are you talking about?"

"I was never upset with you. You did exactly what I hoped you would do. You told the story I've been too afraid to tell on my own." The bracelets on her wrists jingled as she grabbed my hand again. "This, *this* was the point of everything. I'd hoped you would be brave enough to do what was right. And you were."

"Brave enough?" I said. "I don't understand."

Beside me, Ben shook his head. "The NDA," he said. "That's why she never had you sign one." He stared at Lara. "You always wanted her to publish the story. You always wanted it to end this way."

Lara drew a deep breath. "There's a reason I needed to talk to Walter today, and I promise you, I'm going to explain everything. But I had to find him. Sofie, I needed you to tell my story. This was the only way to bring us back together."

I laughed. I felt incredulous, and also angry. I didn't understand what was happening, but one thing was clear: she'd been using me all along. "The *only way*?" I said. "You're telling me that the First Lady can't find whoever she damn well pleases? Or you know what, even forgetting that, even forgetting the power of the United States government. What about, oh, I don't know, the Internet? Or the *phone book*?"

"Can we sit down?" Lara said. "This is a long story, and I want to tell you all of it. Please, Sofie."

I looked over at Ben, who was running his hands through his hair and shaking his head. He caught my eye, exhaled heavily, and shrugged. But my hesitation only lasted a moment—because, despite my frustration, *of course* I wanted to know the truth. Lara knew my curiosity would always get the better of me.

We went into the living room. Ben and I sat on the couch. Lara sat in the leather armchair. Walter pulled out a chair from our dining table. The apparent normalcy of this—just the four of us, sitting down to chat—made it all the more bizarre. *This is so weird*, I thought. *So fucking weird.*

"I told you about the original plan," she began. "That I wanted to leave for America. But we never got that far. My father was recalled to Moscow. The KGB suspected him of treason. Him, not me. When they executed him, I knew it was my fault. My father was dead, and it was *my fault*. I might as well have pulled that trigger myself. My life changed on that day, Sofie."

She looked down at her hands, clasped so hard that her knuckles were white. She took a deep breath, then looked back up.

"I had betrayed my country," Lara said. "And betrayed my family. If I had been less of a coward, I would have admitted the truth and paid the price. But I was *terrified*, Sofie. So terrified that I couldn't even look at myself. The only thing was to pretend it never happened. To push the truth down, dark and deep. To kill off the part of myself that had killed my father. This was how I would survive, I thought. Never think about, never talk about that part of my life again. *Never*. And never make those same mistakes again.

"When I left Moscow, I started over. People knew nothing about my past. Maybe it had worked. Maybe I would never have to face the old Lara. But then, when I came to New York, Walter found me."

She looked at him. "The things I said to you . . ." Her voice faltered.

"They were perfectly true," Walter said. "Go on. Please."

Lara took another deep breath. "It was September 1999. I'd been in New York for almost a year. One afternoon, I stepped out onto the sidewalk, and there he was. Clear as daylight. As if he'd been waiting for me for the last eleven years. But I didn't want anything to do with that. I *couldn't*. I told him to never come near me again."

There was a beat of silence. I ventured: "And was that the last time—"

"No," Walter said. "I wasn't good at taking the hint."

Lara continued: "He tried a second time, the next year. And then he tried a third time. I was leaving Saks. It was two weeks before my wedding. I'd just had the final fitting for my dress. There he was again, waiting on the sidewalk. That last time, something snapped. I wasn't just scared, you see. I was *angry*. Walter and the CIA, they were also the reason my father was dead. My father, an innocent man, but what did they care?" She shook her head. "I lost my temper. It was so bad that the tabloids picked it up. Page Six. 'Henry Caine's Bridezilla.' They assumed I was screaming at a Saks employee."

"And *that* was the last time I saw her," Walter added.

She turned to me. "Do you see, Sofie? I thought I could leave it behind. Pretend that foolish girl had never existed. I was marrying Henry. My mother and sister were moving to New York. Everything was going to be okay. That day, Walter promised he would never contact me again. *Good*, I thought. I wanted to burn every last bridge, forever."

She paused for a moment and coughed. "I'm sorry," she said. "My throat is a bit dry. Could I trouble you for a glass of water?"

"I'll get it," Ben said, standing up. He returned, and after she took a long drink, she set the glass aside. "Thank you," she said. "I'm afraid this isn't easy to talk about."

"You're doing fine," Walter said, giving her a slight smile. Just like the old days, I imagined. Nudging his agent forward. Lending her his courage. *Keep going*.

"In my new life," she said, "I thought I had what I needed. Henry is flawed, but that was the bargain. The modeling work was drying up, my visa was expiring. I could marry him, or I could return to Russia. Henry was my way of starting over. Providing for my family.

"I was a different person, you see. Nothing connected me to the old Lara. I was no longer the girl Sasha had fallen in love with. No longer the daughter my father confided in. No longer the ally Walter trusted. No longer brave, in any way. Instead, this was the real me: the coward. I deserved to know that. Every day, I would wake up and look at this life—a life that only continued because of my deceit—and I would remember what a coward I was."

There was a long silence. Lara stared down at the carpet, shifting in her seat. She opened her mouth, then closed it. She did this over and over. The words wouldn't come.

"But something changed," Walter prompted.

"Something changed," she echoed. Another pause, and she nodded. "A few years ago—this was a few years after Henry was elected—something changed. It was the strangest thing." She smiled a sad smile. "That day, it was almost like he walked back through the door. I could feel him standing beside me. And he didn't leave. The weeks went by, but he was still there. I say 'he,' but it was more than one person. Often it was Sasha. Sometimes it was my father. Sometimes it was even you, Walter."

Walter glanced down at the carpet and blinked.

"That day, something changed." Her words strengthened as she continued. "My eyes, which I'd kept shut for so long, were finally opening. And I felt sick to my stomach. I was appalled with myself, and with the choices I had made, and I felt so sad. But that sickness, that sadness was also—how strange to say it—it was also a gift. Because that was what brought him back to me. I felt, somehow, that I was no longer alone. It took me a long time to trust that feeling, and to realize what I had to do. Longer than it ought have. But this is why I'm here today."

She took a deep breath. "It happened in Dresden. Do you remember that meeting?"

Dresden. The word sent an eerie shiver down my spine. Where had

I heard this before? And then I remembered Eli's tossed-off remark on election night, the year before. *I've got this guy at Langley, he's convinced there's something weird about that Dresden meeting.*

"Dresden," I said, the details coming back. "Where President Caine met with Gruzdev and didn't let any of his aides into the room. Not even an interpreter for our side. Just him, and Gruzdev, and a Kremlin interpreter."

"Yes," she said. "Except that he *did* have an interpreter in the room."

Walter shook his head. "The fourth man."

Lara smiled weakly at him.

"Fourth man?" I interrupted. "What are you talking about?"

Walter turned to me and Ben. "Ever since that Dresden meeting, there's been a theory in intelligence circles. We've always seen that meeting as the Rosetta stone. Whatever arrangement exists between Caine and Gruzdev, it was established in that room. Neither leader, nor the Kremlin interpreter, is going to tell us what the arrangement is. Except for a persistent rumor. That there was, in fact, a fourth person in that meeting."

My eyebrows shot up. "You?" I said to Lara.

"Henry doesn't trust his translators," she said. "But he trusts me. He likes that I have no political agenda. *I love how you Russians are*, he'll say. *No hang-ups. You get how the world really works*. And how convenient that we speak the same language. So he brought me into the room.

"My husband and Gruzdev got along very well. They look at the world in the same way. They began to . . . arrange certain things. That's when I felt it happen." She closed her eyes for a moment. "I could suddenly sense Sasha standing over my shoulder. Watching me. Waiting to see what I would do.

"*So you're back*, I thought. *But then tell me why you're back. Tell me what you want me to do!* But this ghost refused to speak. He just kept watching. We left Dresden, and still, I didn't understand what I was meant to do. But then—do you know when it began to change, Sofie? A few months after Dresden, during that tour in Europe. Our last night in Paris. Gabi said a reporter was asking questions about my father's job."

She smiled at me. "The answer became clearer to me. It would take another two years for me to find the courage. But I began to understand. That foolish girl—she was still in there. I never managed to leave her. There were still traces of her in this world. And it was the strangest thing. When I allowed myself to look at her again, I realized that I no longer hated her. I actually, in a way, *admired* her. And she knew. She knew the time had come to stop this."

She paused for a moment. "To stop what?" I prompted.

"To stop standing by and pretending not to care," Lara continued. "And to stop my husband. I could no longer do nothing. Could no longer *convince* myself that doing nothing was the only option available."

I shook my head. "But I still . . . I still don't understand. I'm sorry, but why am I here? What does this have to do with *me*? With the biography?"

"When I realized what I had to do," Lara said, "I also realized how difficult it would be."

"Difficult?" I asked. "How?"

"I had to find a way to hide the truth in plain sight," she said. "And it was you, Sofie. You were the perfect cover story."

CHAPTER FIFTEEN

I laughed in disbelief. "A *cover story*?" I said. "What are you talking about?"

"What I witnessed in Dresden," she continued. "I had to tell someone, but the right someone. This part is difficult. You understand that I can't simply call up the CIA. Henry is paranoid. He knows everyone I meet with, everyone I talk to, inside and outside the White House. We're surrounded by his loyalists. He's gotten rid of anyone who *isn't* loyal." Lara shook her head: "Walter was the only person I could trust. He could take what I heard in Dresden and do something about it. But how could I find him? I didn't know if he was still alive, or still working at the CIA, or even his real name. And God knows he wasn't going to come to me. I had to show him that I had changed my mind, to prove to him that I was on his side again. I had to hope that Walter was out there, watching. And that, finally, he would see my signal."

"Your signal?" I said, confused.

"It's not the rue Cler," Walter chimed in. "But it did the trick."

It took me several moments to remember the pictures in the *Daily Mail.* The ice-cream cone. The purple sweater. The Birkin bag over her left arm. In broad daylight, during that Sunday outing with her daughters, Lara Caine had activated their old code.

"Oh God," I said. "You've *got* to be kidding me."

I glanced over at Ben, who had been silent for a while. He shook his head slightly. He was staring into the middle distance, lost in thought, gnawing at a fingernail.

"It *worked*, Sofie," Lara said. "Your story, and my signal, they worked. Walter called my office the next day. He told my assistant that he was an old friend from Paris. We only spoke for a minute or two, but it was enough to figure out a meeting point. Which brings us to today."

"But this is crazy," I said, my head swiveling back and forth between them. "This whole elaborate ruse? And it was just for . . . this? There *had* to be a simpler way for you to find him."

"Maybe there was," Lara said. "I spent months—years—trying to come up with the perfect plan. But every plan came with risks. There were risks to this approach, too. But they never really worried me. Do you know why?"

Her gaze, so trusting and pure, bothered me. I didn't like what it implied. *Stop it*, I thought. *Stop treating me like your friend.*

"Because I was finally telling the truth," she continued. "And even if the plan didn't work, I would have gained something along the way. And you listened to me, Sofie. You gave me the chance to tell the truth."

She made it sound so simple. No: it wasn't simple at all. "But you *weren't* telling the truth," I insisted. "Isn't that what you're saying? That, actually, none of this was what it appeared to be?"

"Sofie," Walter interrupted. "You're a journalist. Have you never painted yourself in a certain light, or left out certain things, to get a source to trust you? You know what it means, to work in service of something bigger. There are different levels of truth."

I turned to Walter, feeling a surge of frustration. "And what about you?" I asked. "You watched her husband get elected. You watched everything that came after. What were you waiting for? You . . . you . . . you could have *done* something. You could have called her! None of this had to happen!"

"I had to take her at her word," he said calmly. "Lara had made it abundantly clear that she never wanted to see me again. She had chosen Henry. I had to believe that. Even with her husband in the White House. *Especially* with her husband in the White House."

"Especially?" I said. "Why especially?"

"Because," Ben said, finally speaking. "What we're talking about is treason."

•

The room fell silent. I started to open my mouth, but Ben jerked his head at me in warning. *Let me handle this.* He was staring at Lara and Walter.

Then, in a hard voice that sent a chill down my spine, he said, "I don't know if Sofie and I should be here for the rest of this conversation."

"I understand," Lara said. "You don't have to be a part of this."

"Just to be clear what you mean by 'this,'" Ben said, his nostrils flaring. "Just to be a *little* more precise. You have some kind of incriminating information about your husband. You're planning to share that information with the CIA. The CIA is then going to use that information against President Caine, as a form of blackmail to force him out of office. Do I have that right?"

The atmosphere had suddenly tautened. "Yes," she said.

"The CIA taking active measures against a sitting American president," Ben said. "You realize how that sounds. You realize what that *is*. It's a coup, Mrs. Caine."

"Yes," she repeated, with a steady gaze.

"But it might not work," Ben pressed. "And then?"

"And then I'll go to prison, I expect."

His mouth set into a grim line. "But it's more than just your personal martyrdom. You said it yourself. Your husband is paranoid. This would be confirming his worst paranoia. That the intelligence community really *is* against him. That the deep state is real. He'd defund the CIA in a heartbeat. He'd strip it and sell it for parts. Think about the damage to the country."

"Think about the damage now," Walter interrupted. "Is this the country you want?"

Ben bristled. "Of course not, but—"

"I don't think we have time for *buts*." Walter's tone had grown cooler, matching the atmosphere. "This may be the only option left. Besides, Caine doesn't need an excuse to defund the CIA. He would have done it already if he had the votes."

"I understand your concerns," Lara said to Ben, glancing at her watch. "But we don't have much longer. I need to tell Walter the details about Dresden."

"Sofie?" Ben kept his eyes on Lara. "Do you want to stay for this?"

The sudden intensity was making me dizzy. These unreal words: *treason, coup*. "I have no idea," I said. "You're the lawyer."

"No." Ben shook his head. "It's not about legality. This is about the principle."

"What principle?" I said.

"Do you want to be a part of this?" He took my hand. "You have to decide. You're the one who brought us all here."

"But it wasn't my idea!" I cried, yanking my hand away in reflex.

"Sofie," Lara interjected. "Listen to me. I could have asked anyone to write my biography. Do you know why I picked you?"

A long beat of silence. My heart was thumping. Finally, I shook my head.

"Because," she continued, "I could tell that you were strong enough. I knew that, if everything in the plan worked, I would someday put the person in an impossible situation. Like this, right here. You have to pick a side. It isn't easy. But I knew you could survive that."

"*No*," I insisted. "How can I trust anything you say? You manipulated me. You used my own curiosity against me."

"You call it curiosity," she said. "I call it bravery."

"Bravery!" I laughed harshly, but she kept gazing at me.

"Yes," she said quietly. "Bravery."

I looked down at the carpet, blood pounding in my ears. I could feel Lara's eyes on me. *This is just another trick*, I thought. *She's being nice to you, she's manipulating you again, because she needs you to stay, because she needs you to go along with it, because—*

Because why?

At that moment, if I stood up and walked out of the room, and never spoke to Lara again, would her plans change? She had done what she needed to do; the next phase would begin, regardless of whether I stayed or left. It hit me like a bolt: she no longer needed me.

So then why was she saying these things to me?

I lifted my head. Lara sat a few feet away, surrounded by the materials of my life. The water glass ringed with her lipstick. The armchair, with its faded leather, which I'd inherited after my mother died. Sometimes you look at a person, and they look at you, and you see it like the clearest water flowing over a riverbed. So quick and invisible that it almost looks like nothing. Only the ripples, the moments of uncertainty, reveal it for what it is.

Consider everything that happened. How could she possibly care about me?

But then again: How could she possibly not?

•

For a moment, I closed my eyes. There would be time, later, for everything rushing through my chest. Right now, there was only one decision to make. I turned toward Ben.

I didn't need to do anything else, she'd said. But I wanted to.

"You're really fine with it?" I said. "If we see this through?"

"What's the expression?" He squeezed my hand. "In for a penny, in for a pound?"

Walter cleared his throat. "Ben, those risks you pointed out: those are very real."

"I'm a lawyer, Mr. Smith," Ben replied. "It's my job to imagine the risks. It doesn't mean that the risks aren't worth it."

"Well," Lara said, sitting up straight, looking at her watch again. "I think the time has come. Let me tell you about Dresden."

•

It happened on a July day, three years before.

The president and First Lady stood in the courtyard of the

Zwinger palace, gazing at the intricate facade. "It is one of Dresden's most beloved jewels," said the German official. "The building was nearly destroyed in 1945. The Soviets rebuilt it soon after."

"It's beautiful," Lara said, smiling politely.

The Caines approached the entrance, trailed by an entourage of ministers and diplomats. On a normal summer day, the palace would be bustling with tourists, there to gawk at the art collection and the famous glockenspiel. That day, it was the backdrop to a more sedate occasion. The Germans, who were hosting the summit, were determined to make it a success. Recent decades of European peace and prosperity had served their country well; one couldn't blame them for wanting to keep it that way. In a large marble-floored hall inside, the German chancellor stood behind a lectern, welcoming the American and Russian delegations. This was indeed a historic moment, the chancellor said: the first-ever meeting between President Caine and President Gruzdev.

The two men stepped forward and shook hands. Flashbulbs popped and camera shutters whirred. A few minutes later, the presidents and their delegations were led to a nearby room, taking their seats on opposing sides of a long table. The Germans had put a great deal of thought into staging the room. There were silver trays of coffee service and strudel; paper cards listing each person's name; and at the end of the room, two flags hanging side by side, American stripes and Russian tricolor.

In the meantime, Lara was being shown the wing of the palace that housed the Old Masters Gallery. She spent a few minutes admiring each painting before moving on. She nodded thoughtfully whenever the German official interjected with another bit of historical trivia.

("But I wasn't paying much attention," Lara said. "It had already been a difficult day. Henry was in a bad mood. On the plane to Germany, his advisers kept warning him to be careful. 'Don't get too friendly with Gruzdev. Don't get too close.' Well. You can imagine how much he disliked *that*.")

The official ushered Lara onward. She felt distracted and jet-lagged, and already looking forward to the conclusion of this long day. But as they entered the next room, a painting on the far wall caught her eye. Newly attentive, Lara approached the canvas. "Ah," the official said. "Yes, this one is beautiful. You are a fan of Vermeer, perhaps?"

Girl Reading a Letter at an Open Window, the placard said. Lara squinted, admiring the details. The texture of the silk drapes and woven carpet; the faint reflection of the girl in the glass; the tension in her hands. Such an ordinary moment. She wondered, as she always did with Vermeer: What drew him to it? Out of every story he might have told: Why this story?

Lara had once—once, a long time ago—known what that impulse felt like. Why paint this painting? Why sketch this scene? Well: Why do *anything*? Because you are alive. Because this feels right. Because it is enough to have the impulse; you don't always need to understand the reason for the impulse.

After a few hours, the delegations broke for lunch. Lara joined her husband at their table, sitting between him and President Gruzdev.

("What was that like?" I interrupted. "Meeting Gruzdev for the first time?"

Lara blinked at me, summoning herself back to the present. "Gruzdev," she said slowly. "He was quite soft-spoken. He said very little during the meal. But he wore a small smile. Not a friendly smile. A smile as if he knew something.")

The meal was long and leisurely. Beside her, Lara felt Henry jiggling his knee. Near the end, as the waiters appeared with coffee and petit fours, he abruptly stood up.

The German official materialized out of nowhere, prepared to escort away the First Lady as the president resumed his work. "Mrs. Caine," the official said smoothly. "Perhaps it would interest you to have a tour of the porcelain collection?"

But Henry took Lara by the elbow. "She can't. I need to speak with my wife in private."

The president walked quickly, leading Lara away from the table. "We need a room," he snapped at a nearby German aide.

The aide hurried them to an office down the hallway.

"Sit down," Henry said to Lara, pointing at a small table. "Stay here. I'll be back."

He closed the door to the office. Ten minutes passed. Fifteen minutes, then thirty. An hour later, the door finally opened. Three men walked in.

("Ah," Walter interrupted. "That explains it."

"Explains what?" I said.

"People in Dresden saw those three men leaving the talks together. Caine, Gruzdev, the Kremlin translator. That's why we assumed we could never find out what happened among them, in private. No one realized Lara was already waiting in the room."

"Well, *someone* must have realized," I said. "What about that aide?"

"There were rumors," Walter replied. "But they were dismissed. No one really believed that Lara Caine was"—his gaze shifted, resting on her for a second—"that she was important enough to be at the center of this.")

The Kremlin translator locked the door behind them. "Perfect," Henry said, clapping his hands. "Look at this. Nice and easy."

Gruzdev nodded. "A clever idea, Mr. President."

"His English isn't so good," Henry said to Lara. "He tells me I can trust his translator, but look. It's better this way. We each bring our own person. Perfect, right? I always knew your Russian would come in handy, baby."

The three men sat down at the table. Lara felt a sudden chill. At lunch, the chattering crowd had blunted Gruzdev's menacing air. Here, in this small room, his proximity set her on edge. She wanted to leave, but she couldn't. Henry wouldn't let her. He needed her. He couldn't trust any of the translators in the American delegation to keep this private.

Gruzdev gazed at her with his cruel little smile. In Russian, he said, "I was telling your husband that he has chosen well. Russian women are the most beautiful in the world."

Goose bumps prickled across her arms. *Calm down*, she told herself.

Gruzdev turned toward Henry, continuing to speak in Russian. His translator said, "Forgive the haste, but we only have so much time. May we speak candidly, President Caine?"

Henry glanced at Lara. She nodded, verifying the translation. Henry leaned back in his chair and laid his palms flat on the table. "Fire away," he said.

(Lara shook her head. "It's funny," she said. "People have so many elaborate conspiracies about Henry. But the truth is very simple. Maybe that's why it worked. No one wanted to believe it could be this simple.")

Here was the problem, Gruzdev said. Russia was planning a new gas pipeline to connect the country to Europe by way of the Baltic Sea. It was called Nord Stream 2. President Caine knew all about this, of course. And President Caine knew how important it was to build a pipeline of the absolute best quality. Nord Stream 2 was critical to Russian interests. Gruzdev was concerned about picking the right contractor. One had to know, one had to *trust*, one's partner in the project.

"Of course," Gruzdev said, via his translator. "It's a sizable project. Several bids have been submitted already. These companies are desperate for the chance to build Nord Stream 2. But there is one company we haven't heard from."

He knows, Lara thought, her heart pounding. *Of course he knows*. Henry Caine had always claimed to have nothing to do with the family business. The ongoing work of Caine Oil, the operation and construction of offshore platforms and undersea pipelines, he'd handed that over to his consiglieres from the moment he arrived in the Oval Office. Everything was perfectly legal. He never involved himself with the business. He wouldn't *dream* of crossing that line.

Gruzdev folded his hands atop the table with an air of perfect composure. That was the scariest thing about him. So calm, so certain. How could he know this would work? But in the end, it was simple. Gruzdev knew it would work because when he looked across the table, he saw a man just like himself.

"It's only unfortunate," Gruzdev said, brow mock-furrowed,

"that your political position takes your company out of the running."

Instantly, Henry leaned forward, like he'd just smelled a steak sizzling on a grill. "*Well*," he said, with a big grin. "Let's not get ahead of ourselves, Nicky. Can I call you Nicky? Well, you're right. My company would do a beautiful job. What would we be talking, anyway? Exactly how big is the scope?"

("Gruzdev must have known this, too," Lara said. "That this was Henry's deepest insecurity. Money. Always money. Henry was always well-off, of course, thanks to his parents. But he could never quite *win*. What he wanted was complete superiority. To be rich in a way that would set him apart. To be richer than every other person in his life.")

Gruzdev stated the number. It was enough money to buy an island, or a soccer team; enough money to vault Henry high into that glorious level of the stratosphere.

"Well." Henry chuckled. "You know what, Nicky? Normally I would say I'm too busy to get involved with a thing like this. You know, I'm running a country, I've got a lot going on. But you're right, Nicky, you're absolutely right. If you're going to build a pipeline, it needs to be the *best* pipeline. And ours would be truly beautiful. You know what? For a friend like you, I would be willing to do that."

Lara stared at her husband. She knew where this conversation was going, but part of her was surprised at how fast it happened. Another part of her wasn't. It was always going to come down to this. Henry gave her an impatient glance. She swallowed, then translated his response.

Gruzdev nodded, a curt dip of his head. He said, "I'm glad to hear this. Of course, we must be fair. Other companies have submitted their bids. These bids are compelling. I would need to know—"

Before the translator had even finished, Caine interrupted: "Sure. So what is it? What do you want for it?"

("Good God," Ben said, shaking his head.

"It was *that* easy?" I asked.)

"I want fairness," Gruzdev said, with that same chilly smile. "That's all I ask. The Cold War has been over for a long time. But America makes it very hard for us. America insists on beating her chest in our backyard, and she forces us to respond. You see, Henry, your country's behavior only serves to create more aggression. More tension, and more pain for everyone. What I am asking for is more room to breathe."

Caine didn't miss a beat. "Meaning what?" he said. "Brass tacks, Nicky."

("Why did I stay?" Lara interrupted herself. "I could have walked out, then and there. But I told myself: What difference would that have made? Henry would have simply relied on the Kremlin translator. My leaving wouldn't stop what was going to happen.")

"For instance," Gruzdev said. "Remove those American troops from the Baltics. Remove the Aegis missile systems from Romania and Poland. Here is the thing, Henry: Do your voters in America worry about this part of the world? Eastern Europe, which is very far from you, but happens to be my backyard? No? Then why all this fuss? NATO was made for a different era. You spend a fortune to prop it up. Think of the money you'll save by doing this."

("I felt helpless," she said. "Here it is, I thought. This is what the bargain comes down to. This is your destiny, Lara. You will be a part of this, this tragedy. And there is nothing you can do about it. Because you *chose* this.")

Caine and Gruzdev leaned across the table as they hashed out specifics: timelines, deliverables, assurances. Laughing and smiling like men who know the world belongs to them. There, in that small office in the back hallway of the palace, Lara felt a familiar numbness creeping in. She welcomed the numbness. It was her most reliable companion. Translate without listening. Talk without thinking. *Distract yourself*, she thought. She surveyed the room. The office belonged to a museum administrator. BETTINA, the name plate in the hallway had read. A desk, a computer, a lamp. A framed family snapshot, a calendar hanging on the wall. Lara felt a strange pang of sympathy cut through her numbness. Bettina's ignorance of what happened in this room wouldn't change the fact of it happening. The sneakers tucked under her desk. Poor Bettina. What had she done to deserve this? The pang persisted. It was an unpleasant sensation. Look at this brutal greed. This embrace of evil. Bettina didn't deserve this. No—more than that—the *world* didn't deserve this. Lara squirmed in her chair, but the pang wouldn't go away. In fact, it was growing.

And that's when it happened.

"Like a sudden change in temperature," Lara said. "I actually looked to see if there was a draft from the window. It was like a knowledge that someone was *watching* me. A presence, of some kind, waiting to see what I would do. Do? Do? What a ludicrous idea. I can only do this, can only do what I've *always* done. But this presence wouldn't listen to such reasoning. From that day onward, it refused to leave. Bothering me constantly. Like a ghost. Or like a . . . like a . . ."

"Like a conscience," I suggested.

"Yes," she said. "Like that."

After that, the four of us were quiet for a while. Performing mental calculations. Thinking back over the past several years. Inexplicable events suddenly made explicable. Disparate points of behavior, clicking together into a pattern. A pattern that Lara Caine was now, finally, ready to expose.

But how on earth was this going to work?

"Lara," I said. "You said he was giddy about the deal. Euphoric. How can you use this as leverage against him if he doesn't think he's done anything wrong?"

"But he does," she replied. "I know my husband. He can't resist bragging. Can you imagine how much he'd love to brag about this? How he faced down Nikolai Gruzdev, and made the deal of the century? The fact that he has kept his mouth shut—it shows that he understands. He knows exactly how dangerous it would be if this leaked."

Ben suddenly sat up straight. "If it leaked," he repeated. "But isn't that an easier way to handle this? Mrs. Caine, why resort to blackmail? Just give the story to the media. Let them run with it. Let that do the work for you. The public outrage would be enormous."

"Yes," Lara said. "It would."

Ben looked confused. "And?"

"I considered that option," she said. "But has it ever worked? When the public gets outraged, Henry gets defensive. He only fights harder. He would never give in. He refuses to look weak. And so the outrage might defeat him, but it might not. And if it doesn't, then where are we?" She shook her head. "It needs to happen quietly. So that he can seem to leave on his own terms. He'll come up with some excuse, I'm sure. Lying is easy for him."

The implication finally hit me. "Wait a second," I said. "So everything you just told us—no one will ever know about the deal he struck in Dresden? That he was willing to sell out his country for a few billion dollars?"

For a long time, Lara looked at me, not saying anything. What words could bridge this gulf, suddenly opening between us? She was asking me to take the final leap, which was the biggest one yet. The country ought to understand exactly why he was leaving. America deserved that catharsis; that truth. *Will you believe me?* her gaze said. *When I tell you that this is the way it has to be?*

Walter cleared his throat. We had played our part. The next chapter was beginning. The professionals were taking over. "The best operations," he said, "are always invisible."

CHAPTER SIXTEEN

Croatia, eight months after that day.

The lobby of the Hotel Danica was thronged. Older American tourists, maps in hand and cameras around their necks, dressed in lightweight jackets and sensible sneakers. A group of beautiful Spanish men, sprawled across a pair of couches, laughing off last night's hangover. A Chinese family with shrink-wrapped suitcases, checking in at the front desk. In this crowd, a lone American woman wouldn't attract any notice. Still, it was habit. I took the elevator to the seventh floor, walked along the hallway to the stairwell, and jogged down two flights of stairs—just in case.

I knocked on room 507. A moment later, the door opened. Walter Smith looked older and grayer than last time. "Come in," he said. "Any problems getting here?"

"I wouldn't have come if there were," I said.

He gestured us toward a pair of chairs near the open window, looking out over the glimmering sea. The hotel room had seen better days: pilled polyester bedspread, faded wallpaper, chemical cleaner and traces of cigarette smoke. "But the view is spectacular, isn't it?" Walter said, as if reading my mind. "Would you like anything? Coffee?"

"I'm fine, thanks."

Walter turned back toward the open window. Older, grayer, but as calm as ever. When he spoke, he seemed to be addressing himself more than me: "Greta speaks highly of you."

"Really?" I raised an eyebrow. "Most of the time I feel like I'm letting her down."

"She tends to keep things close to the vest."

Maybe it was the placid expression on his face, or his way of letting silence comfortably fill the room, but I felt the itch to unburden myself. I said, "But it's never been clear whether I'm actually helping. Most of the time I feel like I'm just a kid, playing some silly game."

He smiled gently. "Would it help if I told you that I could relate to that feeling?"

"Sure." I grimaced. "Tell me whatever you want."

"I mean it," he said. "It's a question I often ask myself. Is what we're doing helping? Is it hurting? Are we playing a silly game? Would the world be better off if we just left it alone, and did nothing? And I'm never able to find a satisfying answer."

"That's bleak," I said. "Then why do anything at all?"

"The same reason as you. What did you say to Greta, back in January? That you couldn't just stand on the sidelines?" Walter tilted his head. "I understand how hard it is, Sofie. Never knowing whether you're doing the right thing. But that's part of this work. And in this case, I can assure you, you *did* help. Your reports have been useful."

I shook my head. "I think you're just being nice."

"I'm not *that* nice," he said. "See, we never know which detail is going to matter. That crucial piece of intelligence could come from anywhere. It's not always from the most experienced or most highly placed agent. So we collect everything. We keep sifting, and sifting, and sometimes, if we're lucky, we find a bit of gold. And your reports showed us something crucial."

"How?"

"Three weeks ago." He turned back to the window, squinted into the sunlight. "You noticed that something changed. Describe those changes for me."

"You mean with the Russians parked down the block?" I rewound through my memory. "Okay. Early April. Three weeks ago. The black Mercedes used to leave when Ben and I turned out the light for the night. Not anymore. Since three weeks ago, the car has been there twenty-four/seven. They take shifts. Six men total, as far as I've seen, with two in the car at a time. When I leave the apartment, one of them follows me on foot. The other stays in the car."

"And if Ben leaves the apartment?"

"Ben hasn't noticed anyone following him." A prickle on my neck. "But I think he doesn't always know what to look for."

"And what else?" Walter asked.

"Strange things with my phone," I said. "When I turn it on, the screen flashes white for two or three seconds. And our mail is clearly being opened. I assumed this was happening all along, since we first arrived. But now it's more brazen."

"And what can you infer from this?" he prompted. "Who gives these men their orders?"

"Someone back in Moscow." I paused, thinking. "Which means something happened in Moscow, something to make them more suspicious of us. Which means"—it finally clicked. My eyes widened. A small smile spread across Walter's face.

"Let's back up," he said. "You deserve to hear the whole thing."

•

After that August day in our apartment, Walter said, he had to come up with a plan. He went back to Langley, and considered the angles. No one could know Lara's role in this. That was the most crucial thing. He had failed to protect her once; he wasn't going to fail a second time. Walter had a few highly placed agents inside the Kremlin. In the months that followed the August conversation, he dramatically increased his contact with those agents. Meetings at security conferences in Vienna and Helsinki and Prague. Dead drops on quiet Moscow streets. Generous transfers to Swiss bank accounts. This last gave brief pause to each of the agents, because they knew their intelligence wasn't worth *quite* this much, but these men were just the right combination of greedy and pragmatic, which was exactly why Walter had chosen them in the first place.

When the record was sufficiently juiced, Walter finally went to the CIA director with the Dresden intelligence. It was easy to attribute it to his productive Russian moles.

"This was almost two months ago," Walter said. "The director understood the implication of the intelligence. We can't allow a foreign power to have this leverage over the president of the United States. The director went to see Caine, just the two of them, in the Oval Office. At first, Caine played dumb. He didn't realize he was doing anything wrong, it was just two men being frank about the world, so on and so forth. But like Lara said, he gets how bad it is. He agreed to drop the deal—that was the most immediate problem to address—but we didn't know when that call to Gruzdev was going to happen. Caine wasn't exactly going to pick up the phone in the Oval Office and do it, then and there. We needed a way to verify that he actually made that call."

I was trying to put the pieces together. "And my report did that?"

"You've attracted Moscow's suspicion from the beginning," he said. "They never believed that Sofie Morse was simply a writer who wrote a story about Lara Caine. They assume you're working for the agency, in some capacity. And that you were all along."

"But how can they . . ."

"There's precedent for it," he said simply. "The agency has always had close relationships with certain journalists. Moscow identified both you and Lara as operatives. That's why they've been watching you. But they weren't treating you, Sofie Morse, as a particularly big threat. Until three weeks ago. And there's one obvious reason for that change."

Walter waited for me catch up. "Because," I said slowly. "Caine must have finally called Gruzdev to back out of the deal."

He nodded. "Gruzdev isn't stupid," he said. "He knows that Caine would only do this if outside pressure were being applied, which would require someone spilling the truth. There were only two other people, besides them, who knew about that deal. One of them is the Kremlin translator. The other one is Lara, who has now publicly spoken about working for the agency. Gruzdev assumes Lara is behind this. Which means, to Moscow, Sofie Morse becomes much more suspicious."

My heart began to pound. "So he can see the whole thing," I said. "Gruzdev must know everything. He must know that Lara was sending up a flare with that story. And that you—"

"Not necessarily," Walter interrupted. "He probably can't connect every dot. But that doesn't matter. Right now he's reached the correct conclusion, which is that Lara Caine is behind the leak. We need to alter that conclusion."

I felt like a naive idiot. The Russians down the block. It had been right in front of me for the past three weeks. "I just thought they were . . ." I trailed off. What *had* I thought? How had I explained the change to myself? I hadn't, I suppose; I had simply accepted it. I shook my head.

"But this is *bad*," I said. "If Gruzdev knows it was me. We should leave. Go back to the States."

"You're no safer at home than you are here," he said. "Henry Caine may be reaching the same conclusions as Gruzdev. If he suspects his wife is behind this, he'll suspect you, too. And if he refuses to leave, and stays in power, he'll want to punish you—both of you—for this. Or the Russian government may wish to pursue charges against you and Lara. Most American presidents wouldn't extradite their citizens to the Russian government. But Henry Caine just might do that."

"So you're saying we're screwed." I laughed, panicked and involuntary. "Whether we stay or go, we're screwed."

"We need to alter the conclusion," Walter repeated. "Over the last few months, we've taken steps to plant another narrative. We need Gruzdev to believe that our intelligence came from another source. You remember those sources I mentioned, inside the Kremlin. They're good at starting rumors. Such as rumors about a translator who has grown unhappy with his standing. Unhappy, and sloppy, and talkative."

"But will that . . . can that really work?"

"We only need to plant a seed of doubt in Gruzdev's mind," he said. "Maybe it was Lara. Maybe it was the translator. He can never really know. But it will be easier for him to punish the translator—and remember, he's the kind of man who enjoys inflicting punishment—so that's what will likely happen."

"Wait a second," I said. "When you say 'punish,' what does that mean?"

He blinked at me. He knew that I knew the answer.

"Jesus, Walter!" I cried. "An innocent man is going to be *killed* for this! And this doesn't bother you? You don't care about that?"

"Of course I care," he said quietly. "It's an awful thing. A tragedy. But that doesn't mean, in this situation, it's the wrong thing to do. It's my job to look at it, and not recoil from it, and call it what it is. Everything has a cost."

I wondered how many times Walter had this conversation with other people; or how many times he had this conversation with himself, in the silence of his own heart. What he was saying was so brutal, so *hard*. But he also, I could tell, believed what he was saying.

I shook my head. "Even if you convince Gruzdev," I said. "What about Caine? How will you convince *him* that it wasn't Lara—wasn't me?"

Through our whole conversation, Walter had looked perfectly calm, if a little tired. But at that moment, he flinched. Something passed through his eyes, like a cloud dimming the sun. "That part," he said. "Is up to Lara. She has to give the performance of a lifetime."

He turned toward the window. I looked away, too, down at my lap. Whatever the expression on Walter's face was, it felt too personal to witness.

After a minute, he cleared his throat. "She understands him better than anyone," he said. "She knows exactly how he thinks. When the director went to see Caine two months ago, he made it very clear. He told the president that he would have to resign, because even the *former* existence of the Dresden deal gives Gruzdev leverage for blackmail. But Lara has to get us across the finish line. To protect herself, she has to make her husband believe that she's as loyal as she's ever been, and absolutely incapable of betrayal. And she has to persuade him to resign."

"Persuade him how?"

"She has an idea," Walter said. "It's clever. Simple. I'm not in the habit of making predictions. But I feel confident that this could work."

I swallowed. "Which means—"

"Which means," he said, "America will probably have a new president by next month."

He paused, tilting his head, absorbing those words. Then he sat forward, placed his hands against the arms of his chair, and pushed himself to standing. "You sure you wouldn't like a cup?" he said, switching on the Mr. Coffee machine on the bureau. "The jet lag gets to me more than it used to."

I shook my head. While he tended to the machine, I sat and stared out the window. The sheer white curtains lifted in the breeze, billowing into the room. This hotel was built in the 1960s, when Croatia was part of Yugoslavia, when the landscape was shaped by Tito and Communism rather than tourism and capitalism. Was this really how it happened? The grand global order reduced to the most human of emotions. Greed. Shame. Fear. Two men, driven by material appetites and old humiliations, gambling with the lives of millions.

Sadness washed over me. I ought to have been relieved—happy—*elated* that Henry Caine was going to be gone. But I kept wondering. Was this the best way for change to have come about? Deep in the shadows, hidden behind a facade of untruths? Or did it not matter, if in the end we were getting what we wanted?

I'd been silent for several minutes. Walter sank back into the armchair with his cup of coffee. He said, "It's quite a thing, isn't it?"

"How do you do it?" I said, turning to him. "How do you keep doing it?"

He blinked. "How much did Lara tell you about my time in Vietnam?"

"Only that it led you to this work. You didn't want to stay in the army, and give your life to a proxy war. You wanted to get closer to the heart of the matter."

He nodded slowly. "I wanted to get to the place where I could stare the problem right in the eye. You can't defeat a thing without knowing what a thing is. I wanted to know what evil looked like. What evil *is*. I wanted that clarity. And do you know what I realized?"

I shook my head. "What?"

"That evil changes shape every day. Fixed definitions aren't useful. The world spins too fast for that. Your ally today can be your enemy tomorrow. Vice versa, too. Notions of good and evil are too simple for the world we actually live in."

I turned to the window again, feeling like I might cry. *But it matters*, I thought. *How it happens matter. It* has *to matter.*

He sighed. "I know, Sofie," he said. "I've become a cynical old man. My younger self would be so disappointed. Sometimes I wonder if it would have been better to die in that proxy war."

There was a long pause. I didn't know what to say.

"But I didn't," he continued. "This is the course my life has taken. I'm old enough to know that these chances don't come around often. You take them when you can. And maybe you get it wrong, but you have to try."

—∞—

The plane took off in darkness. They sat two by two, Fyodor and Irina on one side of the aisle, Natasha and Lara on the other. Natasha promptly fell asleep, head tipped back and mouth hanging open. She was never one to preoccupy herself with unknowns. So they were going back to Russia—so what? Life was random; things happened.

The stewardess came down the aisle, dressed in her perky Aeroflot uniform. Irina ordered a glass of wine. Her hand shook as she reached for the cup. She took a long sip, and then placed the cup down, her movement a bit steadier. From across the aisle, she smiled tightly at Lara. "Try to get some sleep, sweetheart," she said. "You'll feel better once you've slept."

Lara obediently closed her eyes. A few minutes later, she squinted them open, and looked over at her father. For hours now, Fyodor's gaze had been blank and unblinking, fixed like a compass. The scenery before him changed, the car window became a plane window, the streets of Paris became the dark altitude of Europe, but Fyodor just kept staring. Maybe he was absorbing these last fleeting views: the moon high in the sky, the clouds drifting past, the sparkle of a distant city. Or maybe he was wondering how this could have happened.

He's scared, Lara realized. She swallowed, her throat hardened. *I've never seen him scared.*

When the plane touched down in Moscow, the passengers immediately sprang to their feet, shoving and jostling to get to the front of the plane. Several broke into loud argument, despite the stewardess's pleas for them to remain seated. Irina began rising, but Fyodor placed a hand on her arm.

"Sit, please, Ira," he said. "You too, girls. Let's wait for everyone else to leave."

When the plane had emptied, Fyodor took Irina's hand. He gazed across the aisle at his daughters.

"I don't want you to be frightened," he said. "Whatever happens next, don't fear for me. I'll be fine. I promise you, my darlings, I'll be fine."

For the first time in her life, Lara watched her mother burst into tears.

"Papa?" Natasha asked, her voice trembling. "Why are you saying this?"

"I love you," he said, squeezing Irina's hand even harder. "I love you very much. Nothing could ever change that."

Irina was hunched forward, her shoulders shaking, one hand pressed over her eyes. She couldn't bear to look at any of them.

But Fyodor could bear it. He had to bear it. He knew it was the end, and the end was when it mattered most.

"I need you . . . ," he began, but then he coughed, and cleared his throat. His tone grew firmer. Now he was gazing at Lara alone. "I need you to be strong. Take care of one another. We are a family. Do you hear me? A family must always stick together."

The stewardesses passed through the cabin, folding blankets and collecting trash. They looked askance at the lingering foursome. Fyodor smiled apologetically at them. "Excuse us. We'll be going now," he said.

Fyodor waited until they had gathered their things—Natasha stuffing her Walkman into her backpack, Irina tightening the belt on her coat—and gestured for the women to go before him. When they stepped onto the jet bridge, the Moscow air was bitingly cold. Irina walked first, followed by Natasha, then Lara, then Fyodor. Their steps were slow and deliberate, like they were approaching the edge of a gangplank.

Lara could sense her father behind her. She could hear him breathing as he took each step. She tried to memorize the sound.

The jet bridge ended. For a moment, at the threshold, the four Orlovs paused. It was just past 1:00 a.m., and the airport was nearly empty. Flickering fluorescent lights overhead. An old babushka with bandaged legs, running a dirty mop over the linoleum floor. Lines of empty chairs, tufts of white stuffing emerging from the cracked leather. Irina took a step forward, turning to survey the space. She looked back at Fyodor, and for the briefest moment, hope appeared on her face.

"Fedya?" she said softly. "Could it be . . . ?"

But Irina wasn't able to finish her sentence. At that moment, two men appeared from around the corner. Two men in dark coats, striding with purpose, their eyes locked on Fyodor Maximovich Orlov.

◆

Outside the airport, two black Volgas idled at the curb.

"Where are you taking him?" Irina cried, when Fyodor disappeared into the back seat of the first car. From the second car, another officer emerged. He told the women to come with him. Irina whipped around: "Well, then, where are you taking *us*?"

"I am taking you home, Comrade Orlova," the officer said.

The drive from the airport felt interminable. Irina sat between her daughters in the back seat, holding their hands, trying to reassure them, and to reassure herself.

"We're almost there," Irina said, as the car drove west down Kutuzovsky Prospekt. "You'll see, darlings. It's a wonderful home. Once we get home, everything will be okay. See, there it is. Number Twenty-Six. Wait!" She leaned forward. "Comrade, you passed it!"

The officer was silent, staring straight ahead.

Five minutes later, he exited onto a smaller road. After a series of turns, the car stopped in front of a squat building. It was ugly and crumbling, and the sidewalk outside was heaped with trash. "You get out here," he said flatly, nodding out the window at their new home.

◆

Irina was frantic to find out what was happening to her husband. When every question made through official channels was met with obfuscation, she turned to unofficial channels. She called all of their old friends in Moscow—high-ranking party officials, members of the nomenklatura—but her calls went unanswered. The old friends felt justified in this. How long had it been since they last laid eyes on Fyodor and Irina? The old friends were well-trained in editing the past; in remembering only what was useful to remember. Above all, one had to survive. This was 1988, not 1974. They knew where their bread got buttered.

Finally, after three agonizing months of silence, one of their old friends answered the call. He said he would come by for a visit. He didn't know much, but he would tell Irina what he knew.

Lara watched her mother dress in her smartest outfit, apply lipstick and perfume, check her reflection before answering the knock on the door. The material comforts of Paris were already like a different lifetime. But Irina, with everything she could muster, was going to maintain her dignity, even in this decrepit apartment.

Irina opened the door. The visitor removed his hat as he came inside. Boris Andreevich Sokolov was a tall man, with the same friendly and bearish quality as Fyodor. In fact, when they were younger, the two men were often taken as brothers. But this was a long time ago, he explained to the girls, as Irina poured tea for all of them. Decades ago. Back when they were schoolboys.

Irina said proudly: "Boris Andreevich is your father's oldest, dearest friend."

"I was smart to befriend Fedya." When he smiled, the lines around his eyes crinkled. "He was much stronger than me. Better in a fight than I was. True, Fedya is a kind and gentle man, too. But let us think of him that first way, Irina Mikhailovna. As a fighter."

The smile on her face froze. "Please," she said hoarsely. "Tell me."

It turned out that Boris Andreevich had a useful friend in the KGB's counterintelligence division. This friend told him that Fyodor was being held in a basement cell in Lubyanka. An investigation was ongoing. The KGB suspected him of passing secrets to the Americans while he was stationed in Paris.

"The *Americans*!" Irina cried. "But this is ludicrous!"

Lara felt her heart pounding. She stared at the floor, terrified of what her expression might reveal if she looked up. A horrifying moment, that when fear crystallizes into knowledge. Yes, the worst possibility had come to pass. Yes, this was her fault. *Yes, Lara, you did this. You.* She noticed a hole in the toe of her stockings. In Paris, it would be a simple matter of stopping at Le BHV to purchase a new pair. Not anymore! Her thoughts became manic and strange. How careless and silly one could be in Paris! Here in Moscow, she would have to make these stockings last for a very long time.

"But where is the proof?" Irina said, her voice pitched with fury. "He would *never* do such a thing. What gives them the right to make such an accusation?"

"The KGB has a mole inside the CIA, in America," Boris Andreevich said. "The mole alerted them to it. The CIA has come into possession of certain top secret Soviet documents. And apparently those documents could only have come from someone in Fedya's division. The trail points directly to him."

Irina stood up, pacing the tiny living room. "But—that cannot be—it just *cannot* be—it isn't—"

"Irina Mikhailovna, you must have faith. You must *all* have faith." He raised his voice bravely. The pit in Lara's stomach deepened. "If they were certain of Fedya's guilt, this would be over by now. The investigation is still ongoing. This means they haven't found anything definite. There is hope yet."

◆

Hope. Yes: surely Walter would do *something*. Surely he wouldn't abandon them to this fate.

Lara couldn't let herself panic. She had to take action. She'd gotten them into this mess; she had to get them out of it. *Think, Lara, think.* Step one: Walter needed to locate her. Once he knew where she was, they could establish a way of communicating. How could she get a signal to him?

There was the American embassy in Moscow. Maybe she ought to walk past it, and hope that someone was watching. The old signal from Paris, the ice-cream cone and purple sweater: Would it work here? She found excuses to visit the Arbat District, where the embassy was located. She walked past the imposing structure, back and forth, day after day. But there was the problem of the black Volgas, parked permanently across the street from the American embassy. The KGB kept an eye on everyone who came and went from the building. Surely they knew who she was. She, the daughter of the suspected traitor. If Lara even hesitated, if her gaze in that direction was even a millisecond too lingering, they would certainly find that suspicious.

Her father was still alive. Which meant that the Bic lighter, back in Paris: maybe they *hadn't* found it, after all. Maybe she'd simply misplaced it. Could it just be a coincidence? Yes, it must be a coincidence. It *needs* to be a coincidence. And if that were the case, she couldn't give them any reason to think that the Orlov family was compromised. Trying to contact Walter wasn't worth the risk. Not while her father's life hung in the balance.

◆

It dragged on for longer than any of them expected.

Certain forces worked in Fyodor's favor. The Soviet Union was changing. Glasnost was thawing the frozen tundra of repression. The KGB had grown sensitive to the old accusations of Stalinist show trials. It irritated them, the perception that they were less than fair to the accused. Fyodor was of a high enough rank for them to tread carefully. Evidence was required. The investigation continued.

Once, Irina was permitted to visit Fyodor at Lubyanka. She returned to the apartment looking broken and exhausted. "Excuse me, my darlings," she said, shutting herself in the bedroom. Although she no longer allowed herself to cry in front of her daughters, they could hear it through the closed door, the heart-splitting sound of their mother's wails.

1988 ended. 1989 began.

Once, the Orlovs had possessed enough privilege to insulate themselves from the poverty and violence of Moscow. Now they lived as everyone lived. Now they saw the world as it really was. In the public toilets on Tretyakovsky Proyezd, there was a thriving black market. Lara always volunteered to get what her mother needed.

"I'll go out, I don't mind," she would say, buttoning her coat before Irina could object. Lara had a stronger stomach for the haggling and arguing, not to mention the stench of those toilets. Doing something, even the most unpleasant thing, was better than sitting in that tiny apartment, thinking constantly of her guilt, powerless in the face of the anguish she had created.

After she was finished at Tretyakovsky Proyezd, her walk back to the Metro took her past Lubyanka, the headquarters of the KGB. Lara would often stop in her tracks and stare at the vast yellow building for fifteen minutes, or thirty minutes, or an hour. Her father was somewhere inside. And she was the cause of it. She was the reason her mother was growing frail with grief. She was the reason her sister woke up crying from nightmares. The decisions she had made. Her foolishness—her blind love for Sasha—her childish desire for revenge—her fucking *ego*—this was why all of them were here.

She could walk into that building, right now, and confess everything to the KGB. It was her fault. She deserved to die. Not her father. *Isn't life beautiful?* he used to say, pointing to the most ordinary things. A lonely cloud in the sky; a dried leaf skittering along the sidewalk. Fyodor deserved to hold his wife in his arms. He deserved to live and to become a happy old man.

Sometimes she got within a few feet of the door. Sometimes the security guard asked: "Do you have an appointment, comrade?" Sometimes she almost blurted it out, right then and there. *Take me. Not him.* Why couldn't she do it? Why couldn't she just tell the truth?

I need you to be strong—that was the last thing her father had said to her. Backing away from the security guard, shaking her head, walking to the Metro on trembling legs, clutching her ill-gotten parcels close to her chest, trying to slow her racing pulse, she could only feel like a failure. None of this was strength. This was cowardice, plain and simple.

◆

And then, late one night in February 1989, there was a knock on the door.

"Boris Andreevich," Irina said, tightening the belt on her dressing gown. "What a surprise. Please, come in."

He removed his hat and took a seat. Irina offered to make tea, but he shook his head. For a moment, she froze. Then she took a deep breath, and sat on the couch, gesturing for Lara and Natasha to join her. She took their hands, gripping them hard.

Lara's heart pounded in self-accusation. Thump-*thump*, thump-*thump*. *You waited too long*, it said. Struggling to break free of her weak, frightened flesh. Too-*late*. Too-*late*.

When Boris Andreevich lifted his head, tears brimmed in his eyes.

Mama! the voice inside her cried out, as she felt the tight pressure of her hand in her mother's hand. *Mama, Mamochka! Forgive me. Forgive me.*

"He had grown very weak," Boris Andreevich said, the words raw with emotion. "His body couldn't hold out any longer. They are saying it was pneumonia. Fedya died this morning."

CHAPTER SEVENTEEN

When I returned to the apartment from the Hotel Danica, I said to Ben, "Let's go for a walk. I have to tell you something."

After telling him what Walter said, I guess I was expecting Ben to share my relief. True, there were a few hurdles left to navigate, but the plan was actually *working*. "It's great news, isn't it?" I said, glancing at him as we walked through Marjan Park.

Ben nodded, but he didn't meet my eye. "Yeah," he said. "It is."

"God," I said, flinging my arms wide. "What a day. Hey, look! Let's stop at the ice-cream stand. Get a chocolate cone to celebrate?"

"Actually," he said. "I'm kind of wiped out. Mind if we just go home?"

The strained silence lasted the rest of that day. And the next, and the next. He was resistant to my attempts at distraction. It began to grate. After a few days of this, I pleaded for him to come to the café with me—it was a beautiful day, too beautiful to stay inside—and finally, he relented.

The Adriatic that morning was a tropical blue, and the outdoor tables were packed. "Mr. Ben!" Mirko exclaimed. Ben, a long-suffering Knicks fan, was Mirko's favorite person to talk basketball with. "You're here! You're never here! Why the long face, my friend? You missed me, didn't you?"

But after Mirko brought us our coffee, the silence returned.

"Are you mad at me?" I asked.

Ben shook his head, stirring his coffee.

"Okay," I said. "But if you aren't mad, then what is it? Ben, just tell me."

He kept stirring. "I feel stupid," he said quietly.

"Stupid why?"

"Because it took me this long to understand that this whole thing was real. I don't mean just the getting-rid-of-Caine part. I mean everything that comes with it."

After several years of marriage, I thought I'd seen every possible version of Ben, every mood and every expression. We argued, like every couple, but I always *understood* those arguments. So much of my sense of security depended on this known-ness. But when he finally looked up at me—soft eyes, silent and beseeching—my stomach plummeted in confusion.

Last year, as the plane took off from New York, I'd said to him: *You don't have to do this*. He didn't have to pay the price for what I'd done. He didn't have to sacrifice his career, his city, his family, his friends. But as the plane reached altitude, Ben shook his head, held my hand, and said: *I'm not leaving you*. In that moment, and many moments that followed, I thought he was so much braver than me. Ben. Steady, and calm, and unafraid.

"I'm so sorry," I blurted, and suddenly knew how true that was. I was sorry for everything. For my foolish decisions. For the naivete, and the arrogance, and the danger I'd put us in. "God, Ben, I should have said it sooner. This is my fault. This whole crazy situation. I made these mistakes, and now you—"

"You shouldn't be sorry," he interrupted. "It was the right thing to do."

"But I never realized . . ." I faltered, losing my words.

He smiled slightly. "It's fine. You can say it."

I shook my head. *I never realized you were scared, too*. The noisy, crowded café. The two of us, sitting in silence, our coffees untouched. Why was this so hard to talk about? I looked down at the table, my eyes stinging. I felt so sad, and I didn't know why.

No, not true. I *did* know why. I always thought Ben was the strong one. But if both of us were scared, where did that leave us? How did we fix this? What were we meant to do?

Later, as we walked home and rounded the corner to our block, my gaze flicked automatically to the black Mercedes. Ben took my hand. A kind of hysterical laughter bubbled in my chest. *These men want to kill us! Great! And you* chose *this, Sofie!* But even with the black car, even with the pulse quickening in my throat, I found myself recalling, with a sudden strange calmness, what Vicky had said, so many years ago. *The things I love exist* here.

I felt, for the first time, that I might understand those words. Even though the fear remains: look at what exists right here. Right here, right now. The warmth of the sunshine, the breeze from the sparkling sea. And more than anything, the feeling of Ben's hand in mine.

•

The week before, as I was getting ready to leave room 507 in the Hotel Danica, Walter Smith said, "Oh, Sofie, there's one more thing."

He opened his leather briefcase and pulled out a small digital recorder, just like the one I'd always used during my interviews with Lara Caine. He said: "This is from her."

"What is it?" I asked. "I mean, what's on here?"

"I don't know," he said. "She said it was personal."

For several days, I left the recorder sitting on the kitchen counter in our apartment in Split, a shiny silver totem from another part of my life. The thought of hearing her voice again—of allowing myself to listen to her again—of stepping into that murk again—something inside me clenched up. I wasn't ready. Morning after morning, I wasn't ready. But several days went by, and one morning the apartment was particularly quiet, and the air through the open window felt like summer, and I thought: *Okay.*

I sat at the kitchen table and plugged my headphones into the recorder. There were a few moments of empty silence. Then scratching and rustling, like fabric against the microphone. Then the sound of a throat being cleared. Then, suddenly, her voice inside my head.

Hi, Sofie. She sounded hesitant. *I hope this is going to work. I asked my assistant to buy the same version you always used. Apparently this model is very good, it can hold up to 250 hours. I think that should be more than enough.*

A pause. Footsteps crossing the room. *There,* she said. *I just had to close the door. I feel a little silly, to be honest. It was always so easy, talking to you. But now I'm just talking into this . . . thing. I'm trying to imagine you here, sitting across from me. I'm in the residence right now, in the kitchen. I'll have to pretend that you're on the other side of the table, drinking tea with me. It was easier to talk about these things when you were asking the questions. Now, I guess I'll try to do both. I'll imagine you asking your questions, and then I'll answer them.*

Well, I bet your first question is, what am I doing? She laughed. *I always thought the story would end where it ended. If you're listening to this, that means you've seen our friend, and he's told you what's happening.* Her voice lowered a notch. *Can you believe it? It's strange. I thought I'd be relieved to get this far—of course, I* am *relieved. But I never thought I'd actually miss it. I mean, miss what you and I were doing. But the talking has been good for me. It's made me feel so much better.*

So maybe I'm just doing this for myself. But I think about you, too, Sofie. I think about you constantly. I wonder how you are doing. Do you miss New York? I would. I imagine you miss your sister, too. (Here, I had to pause the recording for a long time.) *I suppose I feel guilty at the idea of your talent going unused. I'd always hoped you would keep writing, even while you're away. But recently I realized: How can I wish for this if I haven't told you the rest of the story?*

I don't know if you care anymore. Maybe you've already stopped listening, and now I'm just talking to no one. She laughed again. *Oh well. I'll give this a try. I'm going to keep telling you what happened. Let's see.* The sound of pages rustling, Lara flipping through her meticulous datebook. *Okay. The last time we talked was in July, up in Connecticut. I told you about operation FOLIANT, and how I wanted to go to America for university. Of course, that didn't quite work out.*

So, after that, the next time I saw Walter was in May 1987. He'd come up with a plan. Every year, the CIA had a quota of green cards. . . .

•

That August day, when that strange cast of characters descended on our little apartment on East Seventy-First Street—Lara Caine, Walter Smith, and later, Maurice Adler—it was like an elaborately laid table had just been swept to the floor; a violent shattering of everything I had assumed to be true. The shards took weeks and months to sort through. Each one cut sharp and painful.

The pain that lasted longest was my anger with myself. What had happened to my skepticism? To my objectivity? Meals in the White House; afternoons in the family kitchen; sun-flecked intimacies in the Connecticut countryside. I'd gotten so sucked in that I'd actually been *writing* her story. I devoted so many hours and days to the vivid re-creation of her old life, even though I knew—I knew!—it was a bad idea. The only reason I didn't delete the files from my computer entirely was because that felt like too great an admittance of my stupidity.

But after listening to the first few hours of Lara's recording, I found myself navigating back to those old files, the ones I thought I could never bear to look at again. For the first time in over eight months, I opened them. Here, at this borrowed kitchen table in this borrowed city, I stared at the screen for a while. The last words I'd typed when I had no idea of my true purpose in this story, another year, another lifetime—

And yet the cursor blinked patiently, as if no time had passed at all.

I didn't know whether there was a point to it, or whether these words would ever find a reader. *So maybe I'm just doing this for myself*, Lara had said. She had to finish what she had started. And maybe I did, too.

—∾—

"Pneumonia! A likely story. Fedya had never been sick a day in his life. Pneumonia! You know what this really means, don't you? It means a bullet in the back of his head. *Bang.* Just like that."

For years afterward, whether with friends or colleagues or complete strangers, this was how Irina began almost every conversation. She didn't believe the KGB's story for one second. Fyodor, she knew, was *executed* by the KGB. In a strange way, this fact made her happy. Pneumonia was proof of her husband's innocence. The KGB never had enough evidence to convict him properly. If he had been truly guilty, they would have had no qualms in saying they executed him.

"Lara?" Natasha whispered, about a month after their father died. "Are you awake?"

Lara rolled over, facing her sister in their narrow bed. "Yes."

"Do you believe what Mama says?"

Lara paused, straining to detect sound through the paper-thin wall. The girls shared the bedroom, and Irina slept on the couch. Their mother was probably asleep by now—she tended to collapse around 10:00 p.m., having spent all day on her feet, mopping floors at a hospital—but even so, Lara pulled the blanket above their heads before speaking further. They couldn't allow Irina to hear them questioning her version of the story.

"I don't know," Lara said quietly, in the muffled darkness. "Do you?"

"I want to." Natasha paused. "I'm worried about her."

"She'll be okay. It will just take time."

"But how do you *know* that?" Natasha said, her voice cracking.

Lara didn't know. That was the truth. But what was the point in letting Natasha get carried away? After Fyodor died, Lara located a surprising hardness within herself. It was over. The crime she had committed was now irreversible. She saw things clearly; more clearly than ever before.

In the past, when making a decision, she had weighed the consequences, teased apart the threads, considered every step. What a fool she had been! What a waste of time. To imagine that she, one minuscule person, could understand the ripple effect of any given decision; that she could make some kind of difference. Most of the time (no, she corrected herself: *all the time*) the decision didn't matter. Now, when she was presented with a difficult question, she simply decided.

Besides, their lives contained enough uncertainty without her adding to it. Each new day brought with it the same relentless questions. What would they eat? How would they endure? Lara queued for hours every day, playing the endless waiting game that was life in the Soviet Union, lining up for whatever lone item the store carried that week. The family had long since sold their Paris possessions on the black market, converting fine jewelry and Pierre Cardin dresses and Walkmen into rubles, which they used to purchase sugar and butter and meat. Lara learned to clutch those items close as she carried them home, climbing the reeking staircase in their apartment building. Once, a shabby-looking man loitering on the stairs had attempted to wrench the bags away from her. But he was a drunk (glassy gaze, foul breath, a black mouth of missing teeth), and she held on tight and kicked him in the crotch. He doubled over, howling in pain. She felt a flinch of guilt—wasn't he just as skinny and hungry as they were?—but then it passed. These things belonged to her. Not him.

During the hours she spent in the bread lines, her mind often wandered to Walter Smith. What was he doing at that moment? Wearing clean clothes, eating good food, sleeping on a comfortable bed? Did he ever even think about her? How impossible to imagine that right now, in the spring of 1989, Lara could have been finishing her first year at university in America.

Except that it was always going to end like this, she told herself. *I was never going to get away with it. Never. Walter must have seen that, too. But I was useful to him.*

She did her best to keep them afloat, but she couldn't do everything. Without Fyodor, the family was lopsided. The three women bickered and argued. Who was there to make them laugh? To sing along to the Bee Gees and Beatles? To sweep Irina into a spontaneous foxtrot? *He was joyful to the very end,* Boris Andreevich had said. *The guards said he was kind and generous, even during his final days.*

Lara thought of those last moments on the airplane, when her father told her to be strong. He wasn't just speaking of bread and milk and butter. A person needs more than that to live. A person needs laughter, and lightness, and joy. But she couldn't do it. He had asked too much.

He had asked her to live when all she could do was survive.

◆

With the money from the last of her treasured Western clothing, Natasha bought a television set on the black market. The seed of political engagement that had always been present within her began to blossom after Fyodor died. Natasha watched TV constantly, chain-smoking on the couch. One day in June 1989, when Lara returned from yet another queue, Natasha waved her over.

"Lara, look!" she said. "Come see what's happening."

That year, for the first time, the Congress of Soviets was televising their sessions. Two weeks of live and uncensored broadcast. The Communist Party still retained control of the congress, but after competitive elections earlier that year, Soviet citizens finally could see the opposition at work, speaking their minds and shouting their dissent. Natasha stared at the screen, riveted.

Lara joined Natasha on the couch as the congress voted to end debate. But General Secretary Gorbachev indicated that there was one more speaker, to whom he would offer five minutes. The man ascended to the podium. His head, bald on the top, was haloed with white hair. His large glasses kept slipping down his nose.

"Who is he?" Lara asked.

"Andrei Sakharov," Natasha said, with reverence.

Sakharov, Lara thought, as he launched into his impassioned speech. *Why do I know that name?*

Sakharov shouted and gestured about the failure of the congress to achieve any meaningful change. There were urgent problems facing the country—and what was being done about them? Why was so much power allowed to remain in the hands of the oppressors? When his five minutes expired, Gorbachev pressed the buzzer to cut him off. Sakharov showed no inclination to stop. "Time's up," Gorbachev declared. "Don't you respect the congress?"

There were riotous shouts in the hall. "I respect humanity!" Sakharov cried. "I have a mandate that goes beyond the limits of this congress!"

The memory suddenly came back to her: 1985. Her last summer with Sasha. A late night in the café on rue Saint-Bernard, across the street from *The Spark* offices. Sasha talking excitedly: that summer Andrei Sakharov, the heroic nuclear-physicist-turned-dissident, had embarked on a hunger strike. His wife needed surgery in America, but the Soviets wouldn't let her leave. Her internationally famous husband would starve himself until the government ceased their cruelty against his wife.

He's a romantic, Sasha said. *You see, he wouldn't just die for his country. He'd die for love, too.*

And you would do the same for me? Lara said teasingly.

Without question, he replied.

(The words in her memory were as unreal as those spoken by actors on a stage.)

I guess you're a romantic and I'm not, she said.

No, Lara, he said. *You only pretend that.*

Sakharov was shouting back at Gorbachev. This man, a prisoner of exile until a few years ago, was now fearlessly berating the leader of the Soviet Union. He raised his voice and waved his arms with a hectic energy.

You can't shut me up! his gestures said. *You can turn off my microphone, you can kick me out of this room, but you can't stop me! Just try! Just try!*

Tears fell down Natasha's cheeks. "Papa would have loved this," she said.

Lara felt disturbed by the wetness in her eyes, too. She blinked, not wanting her sister to see. It would do them no good if Lara fell apart.

◆

Natasha seemed to have the healthiest relationship with her grief. At the kitchen table, while they ate their thin soup and stale bread, she would often bring him up. *What would Papa think of this?* Her voice thickening with tearful emotion. *What would Papa say about that?* Like Lara and Irina, she felt bursts of anger, but more than anything, she was simply sad. Losing her father had set her adrift, like a cork bobbing on a vast ocean.

But with no direction, perhaps it was easier for her to feel where the tide was turning. To the surprise of Lara and Irina, Natasha's grief gave way to a sustained hope. She soon fell into synch with the rest of young Moscow, and their unfolding political revolution. Those light-blue magazines that everyone on the Metro seemed to be reading: one day Natasha arrived home clutching a copy. "You must read this, Larochka," she said, pressing it into her sister's hands. "It's called *Novy Mir*. Have you heard of this man, this George Orwell?"

The newly free press exploded. In 1990, Natasha found a job at one of the newspapers, writing scathing criticisms of the government. Her byline was right there, in black ink: Natalya Fyodorovna Orlova. Lara thought about the pseudonyms, the coded phone calls, the smuggled copies, the many precautions Sasha had taken; and yet the words in *The Spark* weren't nearly as provocative as the ones being boldly printed today. If Lara had told Sasha that this was what Moscow would look like in a few short years—would he have believed it?

"Come with me," Natasha always urged, before she left for that day's meeting or protest. "Lara, you can't just sit here! You're missing out on history!"

But Lara always shook her head. History? She knew what happened when an individual concerned herself too much with history.

The pendulum swung wildly. Action caused reaction. The Berlin Wall came down. Gorbachev received the Nobel Peace Prize—but then his approval rating plummeted. 1990 turned to 1991. The Baltic countries moved toward independence—but then Soviet forces squashed the uprising, killing protesters in Lithuania. Historical archives were unlocked. Stores ran out of bread. The country was freer than ever, and poorer than ever, and they wondered whether they had gotten it all wrong. Seventy-four years of Soviet rule began to look like a mistake.

Natasha made signs for the protests. One of them read: WORKERS OF THE WORLD FORGIVE US.

In August 1991, there was a reactionary coup against Gorbachev. The military hard-liners failed to get rid of him, but that didn't matter. Soon enough, he left on his own accord. He signed a few pieces of paper. His office was emptied. As the year ended, the flag flying atop the Kremlin changed from the Soviet hammer-and-sickle to the Russian tricolor.

A glacier cleaving down the middle with one great crack; and then the ice slipping noiselessly into the ocean, like it was never there.

◆

In those years, one of Irina's few comforts were the regular visits of Boris Andreevich. He sometimes brought along his beautiful young wife, Tatiana Ivanovna. While Boris and Irina talked about the old days, it fell to Lara to entertain Tatiana.

Lara didn't know what to make of her. Tatiana was out of place in their crummy apartment. She wore tight dresses and fur jackets and red lipstick, just like a mob wife, which she was, in a way. Boris Andreevich was fast becoming one of the wealthiest men in Moscow. He had gotten wind of a new technology (something called *cellular*, Tatiana explained), and was bringing it to the newly capitalistic Russia. A gold rush was happening, and the Sokolovs were right at the heart of it.

Tatiana liked to fuss over the girls, in the way that wealthy people always like to fuss over their inferior friends. "Much too skinny," she said. "You girls need a good square meal. I tell Borya that we must have you over for dinner. But it's too painful for your mother, I think. Too many memories. Well, Lara, perhaps you can come by yourself sometime?"

The Sokolovs lived at 26 Kutuzovsky Prospekt, the same building where the Orlovs had lived in the 1970s, before they moved to Paris. These days Lara was rarely curious about anything, but for some reason, her curiosity about that era persisted: that unremembered life, the parts of herself that she couldn't recall. Toddling through the spacious apartment; playing in the verdant courtyard; greeting her father at the end of the day. The curiosity was enough for her to finally accept the invitation. One afternoon in 1992, she knocked on the Sokolovs' door.

"I'm so glad you came." Tatiana kissed Lara, then stepped back, assessing her frankly. "Too skinny, yes. But you have grown into a gorgeous young woman, Lara."

Lara followed Tatiana into the apartment. If she was looking for a glimpse into her family's past, she wouldn't find it here. The Sokolov apartment was decorated in a starkly modern style: white carpeting, glass coffee tables, sleek metal furniture. Tatiana admitted that she'd spent a small fortune importing these items from France and Germany and Britain. But she'd seen it in a magazine, and she simply *had* to have it.

"Are your boys at home?" Lara had rehearsed her questions ahead of time, fearing that her social graces had rusted from neglect.

"They're still in school. I hope you can meet them another time." Tatiana smiled as she poured their tea. "Oh, they're terrible, such tyrants, but they're also wonderful little gentlemen. But can I confess something, Lara? In my heart, I always wished for daughters. Alas, it wasn't meant to be. Well, enough of that." Her voice shifted into a serious tone. "I want to speak to you about something important."

Lara froze. "Oh," she squeezed out.

Her heart pounded in sudden, irrational terror. The world had long since moved on from Fyodor's death. But the fear still shadowed her. Could this be it, the awful moment? Boris Andreevich had visited with Fyodor several times in his final days. Perhaps Fyodor had suspected Lara's role in the situation. Perhaps he had confided this to his friend.

Tatiana's grave expression. Furrowed brow, pursed lips. She stared intently at Lara, as if she could peer inside her mind. Lara would spend the rest of her life dreading that look.

"Your mother is struggling," Tatiana said. "She puts on a brave front, but Borya and I are concerned. She shouldn't have to spend her life mopping floors at that miserable hospital. But when Borya managed to get her that other job . . . well, you know what happened."

What happened was Irina got herself fired after three weeks. This was a few years earlier. Boris Andreevich had arranged for Irina to work as a secretary at a bank, which was relatively pleasant and lucrative work. But at her new job, Irina continued to harp on about Fyodor's death. This irritated her boss, who had plenty of friends in the KGB, and didn't enjoy her criticism. When he fired her, she said indignantly: "I never liked him, anyway! A coward. I'd rather mop floors than look at his repulsive face!" In the meantime, Boris discreetly arranged for Lara to fill her mother's vacancy. Lara had been working at the bank for the last two years.

"And your sister isn't able to hold a steady job, either. Oh, she is so wonderfully *passionate.* I admire this about Natasha. But she is also a little bit . . . green. Yes? Always the idealist. I fear that Natasha doesn't quite understand. And so we come to you, Lara."

Lara swallowed. "I'm very grateful for what—"

But Tatiana waved a hand. "I mean that you're the *practical* one in the family. This is a new world. There are ways for a smart person to make money. You are the one who will have to take care of your mother and sister. *You.* And you are a strong young woman. There are ways for you to succeed, Lara."

Gradually, as she listened to Tatiana, the fear loosened its grip on her heart. Tatiana was saying much the same thing that Fyodor had said on the airplane, three years earlier. But unlike her father, Tatiana was here, she was *alive*, she wasn't going anywhere. Despite her frivolous trappings, she understood how the world worked. *I'm here*, her gaze said, *to help you.*

"Have you heard of a man called Zaitsev?" Tatiana asked.

"No," Lara said. "Who is he?"

"We will go see him. Tomorrow. And, Lara, darling—wear something nice."

◆

The next day, Tatiana and Lara arrived at a building on Prospekt Mira. Tatiana confidently led the way through a series of rooms bustling with women at work, each of whom greeted Tatiana with deferential affection.

"Everyone *has* to be kind to me," she whispered. "I've spent an unholy amount of money here."

In the back room, Tatiana found the woman she was in search of. Olga was tall and thin, wearing a simple black dress, her gray hair swept into a chignon. In response to Tatiana's question, Olga shook her head. "I'm afraid Slava is traveling this week. But never mind." She turned her gaze to Lara. "Is this the girl you were telling me about?"

Tatiana nudged Lara forward. "Olga Andreevna, please meet Larissa Fyodorovna."

"Yes," Olga said, as she shook Lara's hand. "Yes, I can see what you mean."

"I'm so glad." Tatiana beamed, a wide lipsticked smile. "Should I bring her back when Slava has returned? Surely he'll want to meet her."

Lara shifted uncertainly as Olga stared at her. Eyes flicking up and down, raking across her body, as if conducting a series of measurements. (Later, Lara would realize that this was precisely what Olga was doing.) "Do you know, Tatiana Ivanovna," Olga murmured. "I don't think that will be necessary."

"Oh." Tatiana seemed to wilt. "But—"

"What I mean," Olga continued, "is there is no need to wait for Slava's return. She is perfect. He will love her. I'd rather we get started right away."

◆

Two weeks later, Lara walked in her first fashion show.

Slava Zaitsev was the most successful designer in Russia; the only Soviet designer who had managed to attract attention on the other side of the Iron Curtain during the Cold War. In Moscow, his runway shows were a staple of the city's social scene. These weren't like the stately fashion shows of Paris or New York or Milan. These were a spectacle of noise and excess, a welcome distraction for Muscovites. The designer himself emceed the shows, introducing his models: willowy women from Kiev and Minsk, from Tbilisi and Tashkent. There were mirrored runways, deafening music, flashing lights. High hems, high heels, long legs. The Zaitsev girls walked the runways three times a week in a large auditorium. Tickets sold out far in advance. At a time when Russian reality remained grim, the audience was desperate for this: beauty for beauty's sake.

On the day of her first show, Lara stood backstage, waiting. The rigid clothing and teased hair felt like a carapace, layered over her real self. A glimpse in the mirror sparked unwelcome questions.

What would my father think of this? She touched her hair, stiff with hair spray. *What would Sasha think?*

"Try it for a little while," Tatiana had said. "And, darling, if you hate it, you can do something else." But that wasn't how Lara worked. Already, she knew, this would be her path. When she made a decision, there was no turning back.

Hands pressed against her shoulders. A voice whispered, "Walk! Walk! It's your turn!"

Blinding spotlights. Loud music. She couldn't see the people in the audience. The models had been told to leave their expressions blank. It wasn't their job to convey emotion. They strutted down the runway in order to express another person's vision. Certain girls struggled with this, with achieving that perfect blankness.

Not Lara. As she put one stilettoed foot before the other, she found that it came effortlessly. What did she think? What did she feel? Nothing. Nothing at all.

Loud applause at the end of the show. Slava was pleased with her, Olga said. She was a natural. Would she come back next week? Yes, of course. And the next, and the next.

With the opening of Russia to the West, Slava Zaitsev was having a moment. Lara rose from her station like a prima ballerina plucked from the corps. Zaitsev selected her to wear his most exquisite creations, and to close out every show. Life, which had once crept by with such aching slowness, was suddenly speeding up. This was how it happened, she realized. This was how the past got left behind.

◆

Soon, Moscow began to feel small.

"Of course you must go." Irina squeezed Lara's hands. "Go, darling, go!"

She moved to Milan, where the competition was stiffer. It demanded greater canniness. In 1993, she hired an agent to help her secure bookings. At the age of twenty-three, Lara felt ancient compared to the teenagers around her. Backstage, the models sat before bright mirrors while makeup artists tended to their long lashes and exquisite cheekbones. Most of the teenage girls were gawky as newborn foals, mumbling and glancing away, still learning to navigate their beauty. Lara had a maturity that these younger girls lacked. She tried to use this to her advantage. Some designers preferred that seasoning.

She shared an apartment with several other models. She booked runway shows, catalog shoots, the occasional TV commercial. She took what money she needed to live, and sent the rest back to Irina and Natasha in Moscow, who depended on Lara's income to remain fed and clothed.

When work brought her to Paris, as it inevitably did, she kept the trips as brief as possible. Airport, car, hotel, photo shoot, airport. At night she watched TV and ordered room service and drew the curtains against the lights of the Eiffel Tower. The city was dangerous, filled with land mines. She didn't know what those old memories might do to her. She didn't want to find out.

"We should talk about America," her agent said. A late spring night in Milan, sitting outside, at a café facing the Duomo. The cathedral glowed pale in the darkness, as pretty and delicate as a shell. "That's the future, babe. It's not here. It's not Paris. You move to New York and I *guarantee*"—he snapped his fingers—"you'll have more work than you can handle. So how about it? Have you ever thought about America? I'm telling you, Lara, this is the thing."

It made her think of Sasha, but only for a second. He never made it there, after all. America was the part of the story that hadn't yet been written.

She landed at John F. Kennedy airport on October 8, 1998. It was twelve years, nine months, and fourteen days after Sasha died. Nine years, seven months, and twenty-nine days after Fyodor died. Her heart kept track even when her mind moved forward. How strange, she thought, as she walked off the jet bridge: everyone in the airport was *smiling*. In that moment, she couldn't help thinking of them. Sasha and Fyodor had both been so curious about this country. They would have loved this. This moment, right here, arriving in a new world. The immigration officer flipped through her red-and-gold passport, filled with entries and exits from her years crisscrossing Europe. Finally he found a blank page, and brought the stamp down with a satisfying *thunk*. He handed it back to her and said, "Welcome to America, ma'am."

The radio in the taxi was filled with reports about Congress planning to impeach the president. "Excuse me," she said, leaning toward the driver. She was determined to improve her English, to expand her limited vocabulary. "What does this word mean? This *impeach*?"

A few years earlier, the Sokolovs had been forced to leave Russia for reasons that Boris didn't like to discuss. When Lara arrived in New York, they insisted that she live with them in their Fifth Avenue apartment. Lara worked hard. She rarely drank, and never did drugs, and never missed a call time, and kept sending money back to Moscow. Though Boris and Tatiana loved her like a daughter, she was always careful to be the perfect guest. Polite, quiet, unobjectionable.

On rare occasions, Boris gazed at her and said: "It's such a comfort, my dear. When you're with us, it's like part of Fedya is with us, too."

But for the most part, he didn't speak of the past. None of them did.

As Lara approached thirty, the jobs began slowing down. Just the way it goes, her agent said. They're tired of you. Nothing personal. She fired him and hired a new agent. For a little while, things improved. But Lara could see that her window was closing. New York was hard. It demanded more than Europe did—and yet she loved it. It fascinated her in a way no other place ever had. She wanted to stay. But how? She needed more money to bring over her mother and sister. She needed a green card, too. The expiration date on her visa was fast approaching.

As the old millennium turned to the new, another model invited her to a swanky New Year's Eve party at Windows on the World, high atop the World Trade Center. The view was spectacular: the harbor spread out like black velvet, moonlight dancing on the water. Lara was gazing out the window, sipping a glass of champagne, when he approached.

"You're way too beautiful to be standing alone." He extended his hand. "I'm Henry."

◆

Other boyfriends in New York had come and gone. For those men she was merely filling a role, passing the time, serving as an exotic distraction. Henry was different. Henry was a man who knew what he wanted, and what he wanted was *her*. He proved his love with a towering pile of expensive gifts. A diamond bracelet from Cartier; a mink stole from Bergdorf. She needed them, he said. She *deserved* them. She was the most beautiful woman he'd ever known.

"He *is* persistent, isn't he?" Tatiana said, raising an eyebrow.

The doorman had just brought up a bouquet of red roses, the third from Henry that week. Lara blushed. A romance with a famous Manhattan playboy didn't feel like something Larissa Fyodorovna Orlova would do. But perhaps that was exactly the point. And Henry was charming, in his own crude fashion. He asked nothing of her except that she exist. *Don't ever change, baby,* he said. *You're perfect just like this.*

And he was certain about her. Very few people could offer such certainty.

Several months into the relationship, she introduced him to the Sokolovs. "They are like my parents," she explained.

Henry was awed by Boris Andreevich. "The real deal," Henry kept saying. "Baby, that man is the *real deal.*" In his mind, Lara's association with these vaguely scary Russian oligarchs was a plus rather than a minus.

It was only a matter of time, she knew, before he asked. Late one winter night, Lara and Tatiana sat in the living room, chatting and drinking tea. Lara was only half-present, distracted by the thoughts circling in her head. Distraction, indecision; these were old and alien feelings. She never had problems making decisions. So why, at this moment, why couldn't she simply decide?

The fire was dying. Lara knelt down and added another log. She had been with the Sokolovs for nearly three years. She couldn't stay forever. She stared at the wood for a while, waiting for the flames to revive. "Am I making a terrible mistake?" she blurted.

Tatiana patted the seat beside her. "Come here."

You are the one who will have to take care of your mother and sister, Tatiana once said. *I need you to be strong,* Fyodor once said. And what did strength look like?

She would never love Henry the way she loved Sasha. *No, Lara, be honest with yourself.* She would never love Henry, period.

But she loved her sister. She loved her mother. She missed them terribly. It had been seven years since she'd seen them. Back in Moscow they got by, thanks to the money Lara sent, but only just.

Enough for food and rent, but not enough for new winter jackets. Enough to survive in the moment, but not enough for the future. If she turned down Henry, and watched her modeling career wither, and moved back to Moscow, what would she be proving? She'd followed her heart once before. Look where that had gotten her. *No, Lara, be honest with yourself*—where it had gotten all of them. *You must be practical. You already know the answer.*

But her soul rebelled against this calculation.

"Larochka, sweetheart." Tatiana took her hand. "It's not for me to say what is or isn't a mistake. There are many people you have to consider right now."

"Please," Lara said hoarsely. "Just tell me what to do."

Tatiana shook her head. "Darling, I can't make this decision for you."

There was a long silence. The flames cast dancing shadows across the walls. "He'll take care of you," Tatiana said quietly. "There are worse things than that."

—∞—

A few weeks later, in the middle of the night in early May, my phone rang.

"*Sofie!*" Jenna exclaimed. "Are you awake?"

"Huh?" I said groggily.

"Something big is happening. Go turn on a TV. Go!"

I kept Jenna on speaker while I hurried into the living room and turned on my laptop. The CNN stream was buffering when Ben padded out, pajamaed and blinking.

"What time is it?" he said. "What's going on?"

The video snapped into focus. The television cameras were trained on a lectern, placed at the entrance to the stately East Room. The red carpet, the white paneling, the mahogany door, the glittering chandeliers. The presidential seal on the podium. My stomach dropped. This couldn't be it. Could it?

Ben stood behind me, hands gripping my shoulders. Through the speakerphone, I heard Jenna shushing the twins. Back in DC it was past their bedtime, but she would let them stay up. My mind raced, scrambling to fill the ticking seconds as the cameras filmed the empty room. Wouldn't I have heard something? Received some kind of advance notice from Walter?

Or maybe Walter was just as in the dark as we were. Maybe he too was hunched before a laptop in some far-flung corner of the world, watching this unfold. Waiting to see if the screaming meteorite of history was about to arrive.

She knows exactly how he thinks, he'd said. *She has an idea.*

At the far end of the East Room, the door swung open.

On the day of the wedding, she and Boris Andreevich stood in the church vestibule. "Your father would be so proud of you, Larissa," he said. "Look at the life you have made for yourself."

A Fifth Avenue church, crammed with Manhattan's boldest names. A reception to follow at the Metropolitan Museum of Art. A newly purchased penthouse. An adjoining apartment for Irina and Natasha. A lavish monthly allowance. A green card. A new start for all of them.

She no longer fooled herself into thinking this was love. She had known love, and this wasn't it. The memory of it would have to be enough.

Inside the church, the organ thundered with Handel.

"Almost time," Boris said, squeezing her hand.

Lara smiled weakly at him. Would her father be proud of her right now? Proud of what waited upon that altar? Was this what he had imagined? She wasn't so sure. She glanced down and smoothed the skirt of her wedding dress. It was a gorgeous creation, but she had come to dislike it. She couldn't look at the dress without thinking of the day she had picked it up from Saks, and Walter Smith waiting on the sidewalk outside, and the ugly scene that ensued. The past was always threatening to drag her back down. She wouldn't let it win.

In the years to come, she tried so hard to wrestle free. Throwing herself into endless distractions. Decorating their new apartment. Hunting for the right country house. Renovating it to perfection. Chairing committees. Planning fundraisers. Trying to get pregnant. Failing to get pregnant. Succeeding, at last, after years of agony. Raising her girls. Refusing help. Sticking by her husband. Agreeing with him. Supporting him. Turning a blind eye. *Who am I to judge?* she thought. *I, who have done far worse things?* Keeping her mouth shut. Smiling for the camera. Losing herself in the swirl. Letting herself go blank.

You put your family first, she told herself. But those words left her hollow and cold.

She knew that she deserved this loneliness.

Crowded Manhattan sidewalks. Noisy restaurants. Glassy airport terminals. Years passing. Campaign rallies. Cheering crowds. Speeding motorcades. Thousands of faces—but never his. She found herself thinking about Walter more than she would have liked. A stubborn splinter that she couldn't dig free. *But he stopped looking for me*, she thought. *He finally realized the old Lara is dead.*

And he must be right.

He *must* be right.

The music ended. Silence filled the vestibule. Lara drew a deep breath, taking in the scent of lilies and candle wax. Boris Andreevich offered his elbow to her. He patted her trembling arm. As the church doors opened, he whispered, "It's going to be okay, darling."

—∞—

The president strode toward the podium. As he straightened his tie and unfolded a piece of paper, he glanced over his shoulder to make sure she was still there. Lara stood behind her husband, dressed in a somber black sheath. When she nodded at him, it seemed to give him strength. He turned around and squinted down at the paper.

Henry Caine looked sweaty and puffy, like he hadn't slept for several days. He glanced at the paper again, and opened his mouth, and was just about to speak when he crumpled up his notes and shoved them in his pocket. My heart skipped a beat.

"I have an announcement to make," President Caine said. "I had this whole speech, but I'm just going to say it. I'm just going to say it, okay? We've had an incredible run, folks. We've made this country better than ever. And that's why I've decided to step down."

There was a ripple of reaction among the press. Caine glanced back at Lara. She gazed at him steadily, and he turned to the podium again. "My wife, actually, pointed it out. She said, 'Henry, look, you're an original kind of guy. What kind of president do you want to be? You've gotten this country into the best shape ever.' And I thought, *Wow, Lara, she's right*. She's not just a pretty face, folks." He chuckled. "This country is in perfect condition. Literally perfect. I gave you a great economy, great jobs. I got rid of the wars. No more wars! It's beautiful, isn't it? I realized there's nothing left for me to do. So now it's time to give someone else a turn."

I felt dizzy and light-headed, and that I might possibly be dreaming.

"This man," Ben whispered, "is *fucking insane*."

He glanced back at Lara again. "Actually, you want to know the truth?" he said. "I'm doing it for her. You all have given her a hell of a time, especially with those awful lies about her past. She's sacrificed a lot, and *I've* sacrificed a lot. I've sacrificed more than any president in the history of this country. But I'm a family man, always been a family man. It just isn't fair to her. You can't say these vicious things about her anymore." He glared at the assembled press. "*Some* of you are okay, but the liars out there, they say whatever they want, and—"

As he began to ramble, slipping into a version of his stump speech, Lara gave a small cough. Caine shook his head, awakening from his digression, and said: "Right. So, anyway. At noon tomorrow, I'm resigning the presidency. God bless you all. Good night."

"Mr. President! MR. PRESIDENT!"

Caine turned around, ignoring the deafening chorus of shouted questions and camera shutters. He and the First Lady walked hand in hand, back through the East Room, creating a perfect picture of unity. Husband and wife, together forever. But I'd been staring at Lara the whole time he spoke, searching for a reaction. And just before she took her husband's hand, I could have sworn I saw it, a blink-and-miss-it moment on the face of America's mysterious ice queen: the tiniest, satisfied smile.

CHAPTER EIGHTEEN

In the months following his East Room address, feverish speculation swirled: Exactly *why* did President Caine step down? The press attempted one last act of vivisection before the corpse of the Caine presidency went cold, but none of the answers were satisfying.

No one actually believed that he was doing this for Lara. Henry Caine, sacrificing his hold on power for the sake of his wife? In the vacuum left by this laughable explanation, conspiracy theories blossomed. He had cancer. He had dementia. He had been lobotomized, or hypnotized, by the vice president. No, he was puppeteering the vice president, who was now the new president. Actually, he was going to stage a comeback and run for president *again* in the next cycle. None of the speculation involved the CIA.

On that silver recorder, she talked about their relationship. *I never loved Henry*, she said. *But I didn't feel that I was tricking him, because he never truly loved me. I'm not sure he's really capable of loving another person.*

What he *did* love was the sight of his own reflection. Through the decades of their marriage, Lara kept the truest parts of herself buried. He never saw who she really was. Instead, he saw a blank, shiny, impenetrable surface: a surface that formed a perfect mirror. Lara understood this. She understood that he had mistaken his egoism for love. And when the critical moment arrived, she knew that if she could pull this off—if the mirror remained smooth and flawless—he would convince himself that it was really *his* idea to step down.

And what about the betrayal? What about the leaking of the Dresden deal: Was it Lara, or was it the translator? But Lara had never given him cause to think that her devotion could waver. When Henry Caine looked at his wife, he only saw his own reflection. And there was no way that his own reflection could betray him. His mind didn't extend to such complexities.

Right after the resignation, Vicky Wethers emailed me. Did I know anything? Was I hearing anything from my East Wing sources? She missed me. We needed to get lunch. We had *so much* to talk about. Most important: When was I coming home?

•

Maurice and I continued to speak on the phone occasionally, but he preferred writing letters. It was the easiest way for him to express what he was thinking. He'd had an email address at Hunter, but he abandoned it when he retired. Life was simpler without it.

A long letter arrived, a few weeks after the resignation. In light blue ink, the stamp said LENOX HILL STATION. The seal on the envelope was loose. Maurice was careful to always write in code.

> *You know how I love when my old students come to visit. Yesterday, one of my oldest and dearest students came to see me. She brought along my favorite things—black tea with thyme, a jar of sea buckthorn jam—so thoughtful of her. We sat in the living room for several hours, talking and talking about the past.*
>
> *She never had time to visit me before. She had quite a demanding job, you see. But she recently left that job, and now she has more time on her hands. Sonechka, you remember what it's like when you leave a job, don't you? Especially one that you've been doing for many years. There is this overwhelming sense of possibility—of newness—of*

the unknown. Scary, yes; but wonderful, too. She seemed stronger, braver than she had been before. I believe that this change will lead to other good changes in her life.

What else can I tell you, my dear? Sadly, the strawberries have been uncooperative this summer. They refuse to ripen. Maybe the plants miss you! You know, if I happen to drop something in the early morning hours (I shattered one of my favorite plates last week while having breakfast—a shame), I think: Maurice, you clumsy old idiot! You're going to wake Sofie and Ben! The guilt lasts for a minute or two. And then I remember. It seems I've never quite gotten used to the emptiness downstairs.

•

She was never his student, of course. Sasha was.

In the final moments, that day in our apartment, Lara glanced at her watch and said, "You should probably go, Walter."

Walter stood up and tugged his jacket straight. As he approached the door to the staircase, the question came hurtling back to me. "Wait a second," I said. "You never explained. How did you get into Maurice's apartment, anyway? What did you say to him?"

Walter paused, hand on the doorknob. "I didn't have to say anything."

"Sofie," Lara interjected. "Do you remember what I told you, about the day of Sasha's funeral? That rainy day in December? The people who came to see him buried?"

"Sure," I said. "His classmates were there, and his old—"

My mouth hung open, dumbstruck. I blinked at her. "And his old professor," Lara continued. "I'm sorry. There was so much I wanted to tell you."

Maurice: the man with the trench coat and tidy mustache. The philosophy professor with whom Sasha was so besotted. When Lara moved to New York in 1998, she bumped into Maurice at a cocktail party thrown by a friend of the Sokolovs. They each remembered the other—how could they forget?—and after that, they stayed in touch. She treasured their friendship. He was the rare person who understood her sadness without her needing to explain it. In later years, he encouraged her to tell her story. *You could write about it, you know. It might be good for you*, he said. *No, I'm not a writer*, she replied. *Then tell the story to someone else*, he said. *But who?* she said. *Who can I trust? It's so delicate.*

And then, toward the end of her husband's first term, when it became clear that Henry Caine's reelection was inevitable, when the prospect of another four years became too much, Maurice sent her a note. Entirely innocuous, in case anyone else happened to read it: *I know you've been considering a biography, and you've wondered who the writer should be. Well, I've had an idea. I know a young journalist named Sofie Morse.*

Sofie Morse? she thought. Where did she know that name? And then she remembered that trip to Paris in the first term, and my question about her father. The last of her doubts were finally swept aside. Dresden was the most urgent reason for telling her story: she had to try and stop what she had the power to stop. But at the same time, her motivation was simpler.

She was ready to tell the truth.

At the very end of our time together, I heard footsteps descending the stairs. Maurice appeared in the doorway. He smiled at Lara. "My dear," he said. "You look a hundred pounds lighter."

She returned his smile. "Don't you see, Sofie?" she said. "It was too perfect to be a coincidence. The trip to Paris. Maurice giving me your name. It was a sign."

Maurice Adler, standing at the bottom of the stairwell. His pleated khakis, his gray mustache, his Turnbull & Asser shirt. The retired professor. The quiet upstairs neighbor. When Lara hesitated, he nudged her forward. When I faltered, he urged me onward. The man on the sidelines, helping history to unfold.

Too perfect to be a coincidence. Later it occurred to me: Lara had never fully explained how Sasha came to know Walter Smith. What brought the agent and the officer together in the first place? Or rather: Who?

•

A few days after the resignation, Greta signaled to me from across the café. In the bathroom, she locked the door and ran the faucet. I was still absorbing the delightful fact that Henry Caine was gone—actually gone!—but Greta wore the same serious expression as ever.

"A message from our friend," she said. "He trusts that you'll keep up the good work until he next comes back to town."

"Oh," I said. "Well—when is that?"

"Not for a while. Autumn, perhaps."

It was May, at this point. The entire summer lay ahead of us. Autumn felt like a distant dream. That afternoon, when Ben got home from the grocery store, I said, "Let's go for a walk."

We found a bench at the neighborhood playground, where the shrieks and shouts would muffle our conversation from the watcher who lingered a dozen yards away.

"This fall," I said, as we sat down. "That's the soonest we'll be able to leave."

Ben looked puzzled. "But if it's over, why can't we leave now?"

"The cover story," I said. "If we leave right now, the Russians will put two and two together. They'll know I had something to do with Caine's resignation. We need to wait a while. Make it look like we're here because we want to be here. It's not just us. If they suspect us, that puts Lara in danger, too."

For a while, we sat in silence, gazing at the playground. There was a merry-go-round that dissolved into a colorful blur. Two little girls (sisters, they looked like) took turns pushing the other, stumbling and laughing. I missed Jenna. I missed Sam, and Derek, and Luke, and Maurice, and Vicky. But the feeling had grown softer and mellower over time. I often found myself talking to them in my head. *You'll wait for me, won't you? You'll still be there?*

After a while, he said: "Well, summer's going to go fast."

I turned to him, surprised by the optimism.

Ben shrugged, smiled a little. "And don't you feel like we're just getting the hang of this?"

•

The extraordinary had become ordinary. This unfamiliar city had become something like a home. Ben was right. Summer passed in a blink.

One day in September, I was having breakfast at the café. Mirko brought out a plate, cupping his hand around it in a strange fashion, wearing a bizarre smile. When he set it down, I saw what he had been protecting: a flickering candle, stuck into a slice of walnut cake. Written on the edge of the plate in chocolate drizzle were the words *HAPPY BIRTHDAY*.

"Mirko," I said, laughing. "It's not my birthday."

"Yes, I know!" he said. "But I didn't know what else to say. You have been coming here for exactly a year now. Is that not a birthday? What do you call it, then?"

"An anniversary, I guess. Well—thank you. This is so nice."

"You should blow it out," he urged. "And make a wish!"

I closed my eyes and thought for a moment. Then I leaned forward and blew out the candle. Mirko applauded. Only after taking a large bite of the walnut cake did I notice the napkin tucked beneath the plate.

•

"Why the napkin?" I asked, sitting with Walter in room 507, a few hours later.

"It's better that Greta doesn't know we're meeting," he said. "When you leave, she needs to think you were acting with, let's say, a little disobedience. Getting out over your skis."

"When we leave?"

"Surely you noticed the Mercedes is no longer parked on your block."

Two weeks ago, the Russians had disappeared. No more ominous black car outside our apartment. No more thuggish men following us on foot. I'd reported these facts to Greta, who relayed them to Walter, but I didn't allow myself to extrapolate what it meant for us.

I'd long ago learned that whatever I saw, whatever I noticed, it was only one piece of the larger puzzle.

"It worked," he said quietly. "Gruzdev is convinced that his translator betrayed him. Our sources in the Kremlin confirm that. There is no doubt that Gruzdev pins the blame on him."

I felt nauseous. Both of us understood what *no doubt* meant. Our freedom came with an ugly price. There were no trumpets, no glory to this moment. Merely the silent dissolve of danger. The empty parking spot down our block. The ability to walk anonymously through the narrow streets.

"So that's it," I said. "It's really over."

"Indeed," he said, with the slightest hint of irony. "And you never have to see me again."

•

"Do we need to rush, though?" Ben asked, as we began to face reality. Packing up our possessions, buying plane tickets, saying our goodbyes. Mirko gave me a bone-crushing hug and promised to look me up when he eventually made it to New York. I had to turn my head so he couldn't see me getting teary.

"I feel like we need to mark the occasion," Ben said. "Celebrate somehow, before we go home."

On our way west, we stopped in Paris. We'd been there separately, but never together. It was time to remedy that. We checked into a small hotel in the Seventh Arrondissement. We spent evenings down by the Seine. We bought ice-cream cones from Berthillon, chocolate running down our wrists. We sat outside at a bistro in the Marais, sharing a bottle of wine.

"This was a good idea," I said.

Ben smiled. "I've been known to have them," he said.

It was surreal to wander through those streets, the rue de la Faisanderie and the rue Saint-Bernard, the places I had spent so much time imagining. To look up at those windows, and to realize: *She was here. She was real. That girl was a living, breathing person.*

That August day, as she was heading for our front door, I called out: "Lara, wait!" One last question. After all, I might never see her again. "What about your mother? And your sister? What did they say when the story came out?"

"I don't know," she said quietly. "They went to Connecticut on the day the story appeared. We haven't spoken since."

"You haven't talked for two weeks?"

She shook her head. "My mother always believed my father was innocent," she said. "I imagine part of her is relieved to know that she was right. And the other part of her . . . well."

What was this worth to her? Was it worth risking her most precious relationships? Was it worth resurrecting her oldest fears? Was it worth wading into the darkness, uncertain of what lay on the other side? During those days in Paris, it circled in my head, the question that remained hardest to answer. *Why did you do it, Lara? Help me understand.*

Ben and I had just finished our last leisurely lunch: a sunny table, a platter of oysters, a chilled bottle of Sancerre. Our flight to New York was the next morning. "I think I'm going to take a walk," I said. "Just need to sort through some things. Is that okay?"

He nodded. "Of course. I'll see you back at the hotel."

I walked for a while, and eventually wandered over to the Luxembourg Gardens. Mint-green metal chairs scattered across the gravel. Colorful sails gliding across the boat pond. Music drifting from the nearby carousel. This was where Lara used to sit, waiting for Walter Smith. A teenage girl, bouncing her knees to stay warm. Full of hope and heartache and fury. And something else, too.

Full of love.

So many afternoons with Sasha in these very same chairs. Lara with her sketchbook, Sasha with his galleys. Looking up, every now and then, to smile at each other. And then a year later, two years later, she sat here with Walter, finishing the work that Sasha never got to finish. Her love of Sasha had spurred her to take that leap, and it kept her going, and it kept her going—until the moment when everything collapsed. The spectacular, violent, terrifying crash. The crash that sent her into hiding for decades.

So why did you do it, Lara? Why risk it again?

That August day in our apartment. The day I kept returning to, trying to make sense of everything. Lara described how the ghost entered the room during the Dresden meeting. *Often it was Sasha. Sometimes it was my father.* But this puzzled me. Why would the ghost be her father? How could she think that Fyodor wanted her to take this step? Fyodor didn't know about that part of her. Fyodor was the person she had betrayed.

Unless—sitting there in the Luxembourg Gardens, it hit me like an electric shock, a sudden flash of clarity—unless Fyodor knew exactly what Lara was doing.

The late nights in the living room on the rue de la Faisanderie. The papers scattered across the carpet. The constant references to his work. The casual inclusion of important details. Feeding his daughter's interest. Refusing to vilify the other side. Fyodor was a smart man. He knew the protocol. What if none of that was an accident?

What if Fyodor had seen the same thing in Lara that Sasha had seen?

What if he wanted her to discover what she was capable of?

The midnight click of the hidden camera. The dead drops in the dusty art store. The chalk signals on the lamppost. The trusting biographer. The carefully engineered reveal. The game that was so much bigger than her. How could she know that she was doing the right thing? But of course she couldn't know that. She could never know that. She could only keep going.

I don't know what good this will do. I don't always know what the point is. But I will trust that your love was telling me the truth. I will let the boundaries blur. I will confuse your life for mine. I will make mistake after mistake. I will keep going. "You call it curiosity," she once said to me. "I call it bravery."

Because you have uncovered something in me, and I cannot live with myself if I do not try.

ACKNOWLEDGMENTS

My biggest thanks go to my agent, Allison Hunter, and my editor, Carina Guiterman, both of whom have been with me from the very beginning. I'm so grateful that these two brilliant women decided to take a risk on me. Actually, "grateful" doesn't quite cut it. The truth is that my career wouldn't exist without them.

Thank you to so many others at Simon & Schuster who have made this book into what it is: Marysue Rucci, Lashanda Anakwah, Maggie Gladstone, Bri Scharfenberg, Elizabeth Breeden, Evan Gaffney, Carly Loman, Morgan Hart, Erica Ferguson, Andrea Monagle, and Linda Sawicki. I'm lucky to be in their wise, supportive, and talented hands.

In the fall of 2019, as I was finishing an early draft of this book, I was able to spend an afternoon at the Central Intelligence Agency, where Randy Burkett and Ursula Wilder answered my questions and shed fascinating light on the world of espionage. I'm deeply grateful for their generosity, insights, and expertise. Thank you to Randy and Ursula, and to Sara Lichterman for graciously hosting me that afternoon.

Around that time, I also spent a week traveling through Russia, filling in some of the final gaps in the research and idea-gathering for this story. Both of those experiences—my afternoon at Langley and my week in Russia—were invaluable to the writing of this novel. And both of those experiences, in a way, felt like a culmination: getting a glimpse of the realities I'd spent such a long time reading about. From 2018 through 2019, I'd spent the better part of a year immersed in research, letting myself fall down the rabbit hole, too fascinated to stop. I read a lot of books. A *lot* of books. There's no substitute for real-world experience, for talking with the people who have actually experienced the thing itself, but in writing this novel, I was both grateful for, and astonished by, how much my understanding of the world was challenged and expanded by these books. Histories, biographies, memoirs, essays, novels (too many to list here!): some of them with direct relevance to the subject matter, some with only a tangential connection, but all of them invaluable. When I first got the seed of the idea for this book, I wasn't expecting it to lead me in these directions, but I'm so glad it did. Writing this novel gave me the chance to let my mind roam free in a new way.

Which leads me to the New York Society Library. Thank you to the Society Library for the dozens (and dozens and dozens!) of books that helped shape my thinking around this novel. Thank you to Carolyn Waters and to all of the people who make the Society Library what it is. It's the most beautiful home-away-from-home that a writer could dream up.

It's a funny thing, to be writing these acknowledgments in the year 2021. This book was mostly written before the COVID-19 pandemic began, but the long process of revising and ushering it into the world took place against that backdrop. I think it will take me a while to understand the changes wrought by this era, but here's what I know right now: it was a lonely time, but family and friends, readers and strangers, made it much less lonely. Even the smallest conversations and interactions were a thing to be treasured. A text, a phone call, an email, a wave, a walk through the park, a sense of a smile behind a mask: I'm grateful for all of it. There are so many people whose presence in my life I regard as a mystifying source of grace. This is always true, but never more than in 2020 and 2021.

Thank you to my family and family-in-law, my deepest anchors, the people who taught me how to love: Kate Barber and Ed Pitoniak; Nellie Pitoniak and Ned Lindau; Richard Bartholomew and the late Julia Moore Converse; Alex, Amy, Daniel, and Mallory Converse; Denis Converse and Julie Tambe, and the newest addition to this list, Izabella Converse.

Thank you to those near and far who kept me afloat, in ways big and small: Angela Le and Jay Overbye, Caitlin Rempel, Cal Leveen and Stephanie Urban, Chelsea Macdonald, Clarissa Lintner and Jordan Brown, Danielle and Ryan Williams, David Katzman and Natalie Kotkin, Elaine Sullivan, Emily Fu, Emma Brodie, Emma Ledbetter and Mark Iscoe, Erica Gonzalez, Jonathan Darman and James Lawler, Kesley Tiffey, Kevin Irby, Lily Brooks-Dalton, Lita Tandon and Jim Ligtenberg, Liz Miller and Dan Lee and the entire Miller family, Marta Hodgkins-Sumner, Mia Kanak, Michela Adair, Molly Lorincz and Ed Slater, Natalie Gibralter, Ruth Kim, Sabrina Hartsfield, Samo Gale, Tom and Tara Ginakakis, Windsor Jones, and more.

A special thank you to two people for their invaluable help: my friend Sol Black, and my professor-turned-friend Vladimir Alexandrov.

Thank you to Andrew Bartholomew, my first reader, my cornerstone, and the infinite love of my life.

Finally, though her name appears above, and also at the beginning of this book, I want to end by thanking Angela Le one more time. She taught me the meaning of wisdom, and, in doing so, also taught me what it means to be brave. This book is for her.

ABOUT THE AUTHOR

ANNA PITONIAK is the author of *The Futures*, *Necessary People*, and *Our American Friend*. She worked for many years in book publishing, most recently as Senior Editor at Random House. She grew up in Whistler, British Columbia, and now lives in New York City and East Hampton.

OUR AMERICAN FRIEND

Anna Pitoniak

This reading group guide for Our American Friend *includes an introduction, discussion questions, ideas for enhancing your book club, and a Q&A with author Anna Pitoniak. The suggested questions are intended to help your reading group find new and interesting angles and topics for your discussion. We hope that these ideas will enrich your conversation and increase your enjoyment of the book.*

INTRODUCTION

Tired of covering the grating dysfunction of Washington and the increasingly outrageous antics of President Henry Caine, White House correspondent Sofie Morse quits her job and plans to leave politics behind. But when she gets a call from the office of First Lady Lara Caine, asking Sofie to come in for a private meeting, her curiosity is piqued. Sofie, like the rest of the world, knows little about Lara—only that she was born in Soviet Russia, raised in Paris, and worked as a model before moving to America and marrying the notoriously brash future president.

When Lara asks Sofie to write her official biography, and to finally fill in the gaps of her history, Sofie's curiosity gets the better of her. She begins to spend more and more time in the White House, slowly developing a bond with Lara—and eventually a deep and surprising friendship with her.

Even more surprising to Sofie is the fact that Lara is entirely candid about her mysterious past. The First Lady doesn't hesitate to speak about her beloved father's work as an undercover KGB officer in Paris—and how he wasn't the only person in her family working undercover during the Cold War.

As Lara's story unfolds, Sofie can't help but wonder why Lara is rehashing such sensitive information. Why to her? And why now? Suddenly Sofie is in the middle of a game of cat and mouse that could have explosive ramifications.

For fans of *The Secrets We Kept* and *American Wife*, *Our American Friend* is a propulsive Cold War–era spy thriller crossed with a fictional biography of a First Lady. Spanning from the 1970s to the present day, traveling from Moscow and Paris to Washington and New York, Anna Pitoniak's novel is a gripping page-turner—and a devastating love story—about power and complicity and how sometimes, the fate of the world is in the hands of the people you'd never expect.

TOPICS & QUESTIONS FOR DISCUSSION

1. Consider the epigraph from Arthur Koestler (page ix). How does this passage set the tone of the novel? Who do you think is the "one" referenced in the quote? How is reading similar to thinking "through other people's minds"?

2. In the opening chapter Sofie encounters Greta, who tells her to fend off a snooping journalist by feeding her a story, saying "She's just looking for a good story. . . . Isn't this the nature of your work?" (page 8). What do you consider the nature of Sofie's work? How did Sofie's perception of her work, or her purpose, change during the course of the novel?

3. "Lara Caine had made it impossible for the public to get to know her. Like the rest of America, I'd assumed things about her without really *knowing* anything about her" (page 10). Does Lara Caine remind you of any real individuals in the celebrity or political sphere? Do you think the American public deserves to know the life stories of the people in the White House? Are public figures obligated to share details of their personal lives and histories?

4. At its heart, *Our American Friend* centers on an unexpected relationship between two women. Would you call the connection between Sofie and Lara a friendship? What are the moments when their relationship seems to change? How do you define a friendship?

5. Following Henry Caine's second election win, Maurice and Sofie discuss the variable differences between knowing a fact, articulating a fact, and actually understanding a fact. Have you ever had a moment in your life where you've struggled to put something you know into words? Are there other examples in the novel where this consideration for knowing versus articulating versus understanding could be applied?

6. Early in the novel Sofie thinks to herself: "Some moments in history arrive quietly. In graduate school, we talked about the hidden turning points, which are only revealed with plenty of retrospect. Who could imagine the ripple effects of these contingencies—the heir born with hemophilia; the Austrian boy rejected from art school; the invisible mutation of a spike protein structure? But other moments in history arrive like a screaming meteorite. You can't help but know that you're living through something" (page 12). Have there been times in your life where you felt you were witnessing something of historical importance? Can you compare which instances felt obvious, and which arrived "quietly"?

7. Consider the novel's structure. How did the multiple timelines and story-within-a-story contribute to your reading experience? Did you have a favorite perspective or period in Sofie or Lara's stories?

8. The novel shares many ingredients with classic spy stories and Cold War novels from writers like John Le Carré, Graham Greene, and Alan Furst. Many of these stories center on male

protagonists and male spies. How is female voice and agency incorporated into *Our American Friend*?

9. Loyalty and trust are two themes that go hand in hand throughout the novel. Consider these themes in regards to Lara's relationship with her family, especially her father. How do Lara's loyalties evolve alongside her trust? Who and what is Sofie loyal to throughout the novel? Is there a difference between being loyal to an individual versus loyal to an ideology or state?

10. Describing Sasha's point of view in 1980s Paris, Lara observes: "In a world full of murky unknowns, Sasha believed in certain incontrovertible facts. The KGB was always watching, women always wanted children, and so on. He could never quite let go of those bedrock assumptions" (page 143). What other "bedrock assumptions" are at play in the novel? What certainties do these characters cling to? And how do these certainties impact their decision making, for better or for worse?

11. *Our American Friend* is partially set in the 1980s, a period of open hostility between the United States and the Soviet Union (and their respective allies). How familiar were you with this period of history before reading the novel? Did you learn anything new? Did it challenge your opinion of the period or its ideologies?

12. Lara had specific reasons for choosing to tell her story through a biography rather than her own memoir. Putting yourself in her shoes: Would you prefer to write your own memoir or share your life with a biographer? If you could write the biography of someone—a celebrity, a historical figure, or even someone in your own life—who would it be and why?

13. Consider Lara's age when she first met, fell in love with, and then lost Sasha. How do you think her actions would be different if she were older, or at a different point in her life? Discuss the arc of Lara's motivations throughout the novel. What were the dramatic turning points which affected her actions?

14. Maxim, Lara's grandfather, refers to her family's life in Paris as "living with contradiction," in that they "must hold two ideas in [their] head at the same time . . . *love*—as real as it feels—is not *reality*, and it will never alter reality" (page 115). Are there other examples in the novel of characters living with contradiction? Do you believe Maxim's statement that love is not reality? What are the instances where this is statement is illustrated, or challenged?

15. When Ben and Sofie decide to go live in Croatia, they are both making sacrifices that have immediate and long-term consequences. How would you feel if you needed to pick up and move your life to a totally new or foreign location? If you could choose one person to share that experience with, who would it be?

ENHANCE YOUR BOOK CLUB

1. Find a recipe for the traditional Russian snack Irina makes Natasha and Lara as children, sirniki, or cheese pancakes, and share with the group. Try a variety of savory and sweet toppings like jam, sour cream, cheese, or fresh fruit!

2. If you're interested in experiencing more spy drama set during the Cold War, consider watching the films *Tinker Tailor Soldier Spy* or *Bridge of Spies*, or the TV shows *The Americans* or *The Company*.

3. Virtually visit Paris! Head to www.360cities.net and search for the Luxembourg Gardens, or use Google Maps to follow Sasha's journey (found on page 140) from the offices of *The Spark* to the Île de la Cité and use street view to see the Notre-Dame cathedral.

4. Check out one of Anna Pitoniak's previous novels, *Necessary People* or *The Futures*. Learn more about both and author updates at www.annapitoniak.com.

A CONVERSATION WITH ANNA PITONIAK

Q: ***Congratulations on publishing*** **Our American Friend*****! Can you tell us about the inspiration for the novel? Did you have any specific questions motivating your writing?***

A: Thank you! The story evolved over time, but the first seed for this book was planted back in the spring of 2016 when I read a profile of Melania Trump. One detail really stuck with me: she grew up in Yugoslavia, in a Communist country where most people had very little money, but her family was well-off. Her father had a comfortable job, and he was a member of the Communist party.

I kept wondering what this would be like, to grow up with one culture and ideology, and eventually occupy the pinnacle of power in a very *different* kind of culture and ideology. What would that be like? Did her values change? Did her loyalties change? Had something *happened* to cause these changes?

I knew that I didn't want to write about the real First Lady. I wanted to let my characters emerge from the imagination. So Lara Caine has a few things in common with the real First Lady, but she is also very much her own person.

Q: ***What kind of research did you do while writing? Were you very familiar with the Cold War era or spycraft before working on*** **Our American Friend?**

A: I was already curious about the Cold War and spycraft, which is probably what spurred me to write this story! But as I began the first draft, I realized how much I *didn't* know. So I threw myself into research. I wanted to know the details of what it was like to be alive at that time, in 1980s Moscow and Paris, and what it was like to work as a spy for both Russia and for America. Most of my research came from reading, from dozens of books—biographies and memoirs and other nonfiction. But the coolest part of my research involved a visit the CIA headquarters down in Langley, and a week-long trip to Russia. Those in-person experiences were hugely helpful.

Q: ***Do you think you could have made a good spy? Did you have any favorite spycraft details that stuck out to you?***
A: I don't know! Some of my novelist skills might have come in handy. Making up a cover story or identity might not be *that* different from writing a scene in the novel. But it takes so much courage to be a spy, to actually put your physical self on the line, to risk that danger. That isn't easy. Spies have to be cool under pressure, and able to think on their feet. If they get trapped in a lie, they have to talk their way out of that trap.

I loved learning the details of how spies communicate with one another. They have to assume they're being watched, which means everything happens in code. A spy might walk out of her house wearing a particular piece of clothing, or carrying a particular kind of bag, and that might communicate a very specific and urgent message to her handler. I loved that idea of secret messages hiding in plain sight.

Q: ***It's difficult to categorize* Our American Friend *into one genre! Was it hard to pull elements of historical fiction, spy novels, political thrillers, and romance together? Did you always know what the structure of the novel would be?***
A: I didn't set out to write a specific genre; my only goal was to tell the story of Lara and Sofie in a way that was exciting, vivid, and moving. It turned out that this meant pulling from all those different

categories! I tried to let it unfold as organically as possible. At the beginning of the writing process, I played around with a few approaches, but quickly realized that, in order to tell the story I wanted to tell, I needed a two-part structure: the present-day story of Sofie uncovering the mystery, and then the biography of Lara, which takes us into the origins of that mystery.

Q: ***At its heart,* Our American Friend *is the story of two women from wildly different backgrounds who must trust each other. How do you see the relationship between Sofie and Lara? Was one character more enjoyable to write?***

A: Their relationship definitely evolves over time. Lara is a cold and private woman married to a cruel and greedy man. At the beginning, Sofie is wary of her. But as they spend more time together, Sofie sees that Lara is more conflicted and complicated than she might appear, and that there's a story behind this conflict. She starts to unravel the threads of Lara's pain. Do they wind up being *friends*? I've never been sure about that word. I think their relationship is both deeper and more fraught than a friendship.

I loved writing both women, for very different reasons. They both wound up surprising me.

Q: **Our American Friend** ***explores questions of complicity, loyalty, and objectivity; as an author you must have found yourself wondering how you would react when put in either Sofie or Lara's positions. Did you come to any conclusions? Did your position change during the course of your writing?***

A: I wondered it all the time! Writing about Sofie's journey was, actually, my way of asking myself some of those questions. Does a person like Lara Caine deserve my empathy or attention? Does telling her story imply that I "approve" of her story? Am I creating harm in the world by asking people to understand her? These are slippery questions. Even by the end of the book, I didn't feel that I had found any answers. But I think the act of *asking* those questions is still important, even if we can't be sure.

Q: *Did you have a favorite scene or section in the novel which came to you most easily? Was there a part that was more difficult to write than others?*

A: I loved writing the scenes between Sofie and her sister, Jenna. They were looser, more restful, and less pressurized. In so much of the story, a character is forced to wonder: *Is this person trying to hurt me? Is this person trying to manipulate me?* But Sofie and Jenna love each other so much. Even when they disagree, the love is there. The trust is there.

The opposite also holds true: the hardest scenes to write were those in which trust is questioned. When everything feels uncertain and a character has to make an important high-stakes decision. Those scenes were very stop and start, and took a *lot* of revision.

Q: *Did you always know you wanted to be a writer? How did the experience of writing* Our American Friend *compare to your previous novels?*

A: I've always loved reading. Books have kept me company for my entire life! When I was a little kid, like eight or nine, I dreamed of being a writer. And then, interestingly, for a long time I thought I couldn't be a writer. That maybe I wasn't talented or special enough. It took many years for that old confidence to come back to me—but eventually it did!

With all of my novels, I've done a huge amount of rewriting. It's not until I'm finished with the first draft that I actually understand what the story is about. At that point, the draft is a mess! I have to throw it out and rebuild it from scratch. In the second draft, thankfully, things are a little easier. They move a little quicker. I finally know what I'm trying to say.

Q: *What do you hope readers will take away from finishing* Our American Friend*?*

A: I hope *Our American Friend* gives you a good dose of escapism. I hope it whisks you away to another world and lets you forget about the stresses of your own life for a little while! But, at the same time,

I also hope that this book raises certain questions. That it makes you wonder what you might do if you were in Sofie or Lara's shoes. A morally provocative page-turner: that's always my goal.

Q: *Do you have any advice for aspiring novelists?*

A: My best advice is to read. To read everything! To expose yourself to writers and ideas from all different backgrounds, cultures, and genres. To read books that push your boundaries, that disrupt your understanding of the world, and that raise uncomfortable questions. To be a good writer, you first have to be a good reader and a good thinker. The learning never ends. Only when you are challenging yourself are you growing.

Turn the page for a preview of
Anna Pitoniak's new novel

THE HELSINKI AFFAIR

Coming in Fall 2023

CHAPTER ONE

It wasn't exactly the sensible thing to do, standing outside in the hot noon sun in July in Rome. Semonov paced back and forth, mopping his brow, his handkerchief long since soaked with sweat. No, this wasn't sensible. He ought to have done as the Romans did, escaping the heat by stopping at Giolitti for a cone of gelato, or napping in a shuttered bedroom, or fleeing the city altogether for the breezy hills of Umbria. But Konstantin Nikolaievich Semonov was not standing here, pleading to be admitted to the American Embassy, insisting that he had urgent information to share, because he was an entirely sensible person.

In his air-conditioned booth, the soldier hung up the phone. "You need to make an appointment. No one can see you today," he said.

"Sir!" Semonov exclaimed, leaning toward the pinprick holes in the glass. "You are a Marine. I am speaking to you as a fellow military man. I am an officer in my nation's army. My nation which is *Russia*." A needless emphasis, as ten minutes earlier, he had slid his passport under the bulletproof glass barrier to identify himself. "You must understand. I have information that matters *today*. Not tomorrow, not next week."

In fairness to the soldier, Semonov was a hard man to take seriously. His shirt buttons strained to contain his plump stomach. His pockets jingled with loose change. Behind his round glasses, his eyes were wide and guileless. But when the Marine hesitated for a moment, Semonov's instinct, which was well-honed, told him to seize his opening.

"I am from Moscow." Semonov lowered his voice. "I am here in Rome on holiday with my wife. It would not be possible for me to communicate this information while in Moscow. The nature of my work means that I am closely watched. Do you understand? The nature of my work has also exposed me to certain *information* that I believe your officials will value."

"Even if that's true," the Marine said. "You still need to make an appointment."

The Marine was no more than twenty-four or twenty-five years old. Crew cut, clean shave, trim as a sharpened pencil, a good soldier, a rule-follower. To grant exceptions to the rules—to take pity, for instance, on a sweaty stranger with a thick accent—required the seasoning of age, which he didn't have. And so Semonov realized, with some reluctance, he would have to resort to blunter tactics.

Semonov stood up straight. A change passed over his features, like a shadow passing over the sun. Staring at the Marine, he said: "My information concerns Robert Vogel."

The tiniest flinch in the young man's brow as he registered the name.

"Senator Vogel's flight is due to land in Cairo in one hour," he continued calmly. "His life is in danger."

As postings went, Rome was one of the sleepiest. It had its perks, of course. The glamorous garden parties at the Villa Taverna, where the American ambassador plied his guests with crystal flutes of prosecco. The wine-soaked weekends in the hill towns of Tuscany. The simple ability to walk home from the embassy without an armed escort. But Amanda Cole would have gladly given up any of those perks for the chance to do her job.

Her *real* job. The job she had trained for. Back in Washington, when she received news of this posting, her boss in the Directorate of

Operations only shook his head, both sympathetic to and bemused by her obvious disappointment. "Enjoy it," he'd said. "Try to make some memories, Cole. You'll be glad to have them when you get to the next Third World bunker."

Italian-style lunch breaks were another perk of the posting. On any given day, between the hours of noon and 3 p.m., most of her colleagues were nowhere to be found. They went home to eat and take a midday siesta, or they enjoyed a leisurely meal at one of the city's finer restaurants, entertaining a source on the government's dime. They had learned to take the work for what it was. If they were bored, at least they were bored in comfort.

On that hot July afternoon in Rome, Amanda Cole was halfway through her two-year posting as deputy station chief for the Central Intelligence Agency. She was forty years old—though everyone said she looked much younger—which meant that she'd been in this line of work for almost seventeen years. It was the only career she'd ever had, if you didn't count her stints as bartender and dishwasher and au pair. After graduating high school, she'd had no interest in college. Beyond that, her sense of her future was painfully unclear, so she decided to travel the world, paying her way with a series of short-lived jobs. It wasn't until she eventually came home and started at the agency that she learned to channel her restless curiosity to more productive ends. To succeed in the clandestine service required an appetite for the world's chaos. Travel had whetted that appetite.

Her success, over time, had made her more disciplined. Amanda knew how to play the game. From the moment her flight landed at Fiumicino, not a single word of complaint had passed her lips. She nodded, smiled, acted the team player. And yet she wasn't *exactly* one of the gang. The ambassador's dinner parties, for instance. They tended to run late, but Amanda always left early. After she had departed, when her colleagues were deep into the Montepulciano, they sometimes speculated. Was she running something off-the-books? Was she trying to set an example? In any case, they agreed, among themselves, that there was something obnoxious about her workaholism.

Regardless of her reasoning, the fact was that Amanda was the only person there, in Rome station, to answer the phone on that hot July day, and to tell the young Marine *not* to admit this strange Russian man to the building. This was a problem for their embassies around the world. All kinds of people liked to bang on the gates and demand an audience. Ninety nine percent of the time, they were utter kooks.

After hanging up, Amanda stared at her computer screen, trying to regain her concentration. She was in the midst of approving a spreadsheet of expense reports, which (no one ever warned you of this) comprised a significant portion of her work as deputy station chief.

The phone rang again. She picked it up and said, irritably: "You know, sergeant, if you want to talk to me so badly, you can just ask me on a date."

"He says he knows something about Senator Vogel," the Marine said. "He has all the details about his trip to Egypt."

"Bob Vogel?" Amanda sat up slightly. "What else did he say?"

"He said . . ." The soldier hesitated. Amanda could imagine the young man's gaze flicking back to the visitor, wondering if repeating the words would make him sound like an idiot. "He said Senator Vogel's life is in danger."

She could have laughed at the melodrama. But when she glanced around, taking in the deserted station, the dull windowless chamber with its beige walls and gray carpet, with its long fig leaf plant yellowing in the corner, she found herself thinking: *anything is better than these spreadsheets.*

"Fine," she sighed. "Send him up."

At least the conference room had a window, and made for a change of scenery. Amanda slid a bottle of water across the table. Konstantin Nikolaievich Semonov took it gratefully and gulped it down. Amanda raised an eyebrow and said: "Would you like another?"

"Please," he said. "It is very hot today."

Despite the air-conditioning, Amanda noticed beads of sweat kept gathering on Semonov's brow. She noted, too, the wedding ring on his right hand, and the meticulous care with which his shirt had been patched and mended, and the gold watch on his wrist. She folded her hands atop the table. "So," she began. "Mr. Semonov. I understand you have some information you'd like to share with us?"

"I apologize. My English isn't very good," he said.

"It sounds quite good to me. But if you'd rather continue in Russian, we'll have to wait until one of my colleagues returns, because I don't—"

"No," he interrupted. "I am your guest, of course we will speak English. But I say this because I must have misunderstood. You work on economic affairs for the U.S. State Department?"

"That's right. I'm an attaché in the economic section."

"But my information does not concern economic affairs."

"Well." She smiled brightly. "It's July in Italy, Mr. Semonov. The embassy is a little bare-bones at the moment."

"I see." After a long pause, he said: "So you are Amanda Clarkson. Amanda Clarkson, the economic attaché."

He was staring right at her. She could perceive, beneath his sweaty brow, a deeper calm. Something inside her twinged to attention. The detached part of her brain carefully registered it as another data point.

"That's me!" she chirped.

"Very well." Slowly, he nodded to himself. "Very well, Amanda Clarkson. Even if you are the economic attaché, I hope you can help me. I come to you today with information concerning Mr. Robert Vogel. He is a senator in your country, from the state of New York. A powerful man, I understand. An aging man, too. I have read reports that his health has been declining recently."

Another twinge. "Yes," she said. "I've heard that, too."

"He is part of a delegation en route to Cairo. Yesterday evening, the delegation boarded a plane in Washington. In less than an hour, that plane is due to land. A military convoy of the Egyptian government will escort the Americans from the airport to the Four Seasons, where they are staying. Tonight, at six o'clock, the convoy will escort the Americans to the Heliopolis Palace, where they will be dining as guests of the president."

He could have googled this, though, she told herself. *It would only take a few minutes.*

"The military convoy will accompany the American delegation for the duration of their three-day visit." Semonov spoke with bureaucratic precision. "The Egyptian president is determined that their safety be absolute. He does not want his guests exposed to unstable elements. There will be one exception, though. Tomorrow morning, the delegation will be participating in a review of the Egyptian military. This is the primary purpose of the trip to Cairo. For the American visitors to assess the strength of their ally."

She kept smiling, even as her pulse accelerated. Sure. Nothing unusual about this. Nothing weird about a Russian man walking in with detailed knowledge of the Senate Foreign Intelligence Committee's movements.

"During this review the Americans will, of course, be surrounded by the military," Semonov continued. "It will be the safest place in all of Egypt. Therefore, there is no need for the convoy. The Americans will be free to move about, speaking to various generals, examining the artillery, interacting with soldiers. The review will begin at eleven a.m. At that hour, the temperature is typically thirty-seven or thirty-eight degrees centigrade. They will be assembled outdoors. There will be very little shade. The president has ordered that the review last no more than one hour. He is aware that several of his guests are older, and may struggle in the heat. Unfortunately, his precaution will not be enough. Just before noon, Senator Robert Vogel will suffer a heat-induced stroke. He will be taken to the nearby hospital where he will be pronounced dead."

She swallowed. There was no mistaking this internal quiver. But now, right now, it was important not to spook him. "Okay." *Piano, piano,* as a Roman might say. "Okay. Mr. Semonov. Let me begin with an obvious question. How can you know about a stroke before it happens?"

"I can't. But there are certain chemicals that produce symptoms in the human body, which appear very similar to those of a stroke. So similar that there is no reason to question the initial conclusion. Especially when the deceased is eighty-one years old, and in frail health."

"I'm sorry, Mr. Semonov. What you're describing sounds like an assassination."

"Yes, it is."

"And how could you know about this assassination before it happens?"

"Because I work with the men who will carry out the assassination."

"And where is that?"

He squeezed the water bottle, the thin plastic crackling in his hands. "You don't believe me, do you?"

"It's not a question of—"

"Then I should leave. I shouldn't be here!"

He began to stand, but Amanda placed a hand on his arm to stop him. "Mr. Semonov," she said. "I *want* to believe you. I want to take this seriously. But in order to do that, I'm going to need more information." She paused. "You work with the men who will carry out the assassination. Where do you work?"

The tension in his forehead was visible. "I work for the General Staff of the Armed Forces of the Russian Federation."

"And which division, specifically?"

"The Main Directorate," he whispered. "The GRU."

"Jesus Christ," he said. "Cole, are you drunk?"

Osmond Brown stood behind his desk, hands planted on his hips, narrowing his eyes at Amanda Cole, who had followed him into his office as he returned from lunch. Amanda Cole, who was more than thirty years his junior. Amanda Cole, who worked for *him*, but who never seemed to remember that goddamn fact.

Amanda closed the door behind her and gestured for him to sit down. There was something especially impertinent about this coming from *her*, what with her slight stature and the childish freckles across her nose. He almost snapped at her (this was *his* goddamn office, *he* would decide whether to sit down), but then he shut his mouth, and sank to his chair. Over the past year, Osmond had discovered that it was difficult to raise his voice at Amanda. She never flinched, no matter how much he yelled, and this was strangely deflating.

"He's telling the truth," she said.

"And how on God's green earth can you know a thing like that?"

"Because he's scared. He's terrified. It's not the kind of thing you can fake."

"Did you ever stop to consider," Osmond said, in his Mississippi drawl, which often grew exaggerated after a glass or two of wine, "that maybe the man is so goddamn *terrified* because he's being dangled as bait to the Americans?"

"They would never pick a man like him for a dangle."

"Oh yes. My apologies, Ms. Cole. I seem to have forgotten you're a mind reader, too."

"If the Russians were trying to sell us on an agent," she continued, ignoring Osmond's sarcasm as she always did, "they'd pick someone who looks the part. Someone with an obvious motive. Greed, preferably. Greed is always the most convincing."

Osmond scowled. "Let me guess. Now you're going to tell me that your new friend doesn't have a greedy bone in his body."

She held up her wrist. "His watch. He's wearing a Tag Heuer. So he's well-off, he's comfortable, but his shirt is mended in least half a dozen places. He clearly doesn't care about money. Not enough to make for a convincing dangle. The Russians only pick people who *look* the part. Semonov doesn't, and he's terrified. That fear is the information we're working with. And in less than twenty-four hours, there's going to be—"

"Whoa," he interrupted. "Whoa! Hold it right there. You're acting like we have to *do* something about this."

"Well, yeah. Of course we have to."

"Says who, Cole?"

"Says the evidence, *sir*."

Across the expanse of his desk, Osmond regarded her. Despite his best intentions, he had allowed himself a glass—okay, two glasses—of Vermentino with lunch. How could he resist, when it paired so beautifully with the sweet summer cantaloupe? But now he was tired, and he had a headache, and this whole thing sounded like a boondoggle, and Amanda was possibly the stubbornest person he had ever met. Dealing with this woman was one of the more exhausting parts of the job. And yet, he knew her kryptonite. Amanda Cole did, despite appearances, possess an essential kernel of respect for the Ways Things Were Done. She would push back, but she wasn't one to disobey a direct order. At the end of the day, he saw it as his task to remind her of her fealty.

Well, clearly she was all worked up about this. Why not indulge her a few moments longer, before he lowered the boom? So he settled back into his chair, folded his hands on his stomach, and said: "Okay, Cole. Let's talk this one through. Let's say we decide to believe this guy, this what's-his-name—"

"His name is Semonov," she interrupted. "Konstantin Semonov."

"Sure. Okay. Let's say we decide to believe this Semonov, and decide that the threat to Bob Vogel is real, and decide to act on it. We'd need to get word to Senator Vogel about what's happening, and tell him to skip the review. How do we do that?"

"Verbally. Send someone to tell him. One of our people in Cairo."

"But when? Where? How? Every minute of the delegation's schedule is accounted for. They have some downtime at the Four Seasons, but you can't just have one of our people waltz in. Everyone in that hotel, from the maids to the managers to the goddamn window-washers, *every* person in that hotel is on someone else's payroll. That hotel is wired six ways to Sunday. So if we send one of our people to deliver the message verbally, what happens when that person arrives at the Four Seasons, and beelines straight for Senator Vogel? Hmm?"

The furrow of her brow softened slightly. *I'm a good teacher*, Osmond thought. *No one ever wants to admit it, but I've got a knack for this part.*

"You think they want to blow our network in Cairo," she said.

"Bingo."

Amanda nodded. Osmond was pleased. See, at the end of the day, he just wanted these kids (and yes, they were kids, he was older than most of their fathers) to be a little more *careful*. Not to get themselves *killed* for no good reason.

But instead of thanking him, she said: "I don't buy it."

He sighed. "And why is that?"

"He's telling the truth. I'm *certain* he is. And don't just say he's their useful idiot, that his bosses at the GRU gave him this line to swallow and counted on him feeling guilty and running to the Americans. He's smart. He'd see through it. He saw through my cover in about three seconds flat."

"Look, Amanda, I get it. You're bored out of your mind." He tapped a finger against his temple. "Nothing happens in Rome. This isn't where the action is. And they know that, too. They're trying to use that boredom against you."

"You're really suggesting we do nothing about this?"

"I'm not suggesting. I'm *telling*."

She shook her head, but her eyes went glassy. She tended to do this, to retreat into cool detachment when she was overruled, to suddenly go quiet. Osmond respected her for fighting as hard as she did, but he also respected her for knowing when to surrender.

"We're the soft underbelly," he explained, feeling that pleasant flood of paternal benevolence which was, quite frankly, the only aspect of the job that still made him feel good. "Our networks in the Middle East are airtight. It wouldn't work to target them directly. So the Russians try to take the back door. They plant a seed in Rome and hope the tendril reaches Cairo. All they need to do is keep an eye on Senator Vogel for the next twenty-four hours. If we send someone to meet Vogel at his hotel, bingo: they've just identified the Cairo network. It's clever, isn't it? So the best response, or actually the *only* response, is to do nothing. You see?"

But that was the point, Amanda thought. The scheme Osmond had just outlined was too clever by half. It wasn't how the GRU worked. The many moving parts, the subtle contingencies: it lacked their signature bluntness.

Amanda left his office and walked through the bullpen, back toward the door that led to rest of the embassy. One of her colleagues called after her ("Hey, Cole, that guy in the conference room one of yours? The fat guy with glasses? James Gandolfini past his prime?"), but she didn't hear him.

She buzzed through the unmarked door, walked down a hallway, up a flight of stairs, down another hallway. Through the glassed-in walls of the conference room, she saw what her colleagues would have seen as they returned from lunch. Semonov, pacing back and forth, like a goldfish desperate to escape the confines of his fishbowl.

Amanda had been trying to figure out what to say, how to explain this failure of hers, but as soon as he turned and looked at her, he seemed to know. As she closed the door, Semonov shook his head. She felt a strange gratitude for his perception. It was a terrible feeling, having to deliver this kind of bad news, having to shatter another person's desperate hope. Semonov had just spared her that feeling.

He silently dropped his head into hands. She sat beside him, touched him on the elbow. "I'm sorry," she said. "I'm really, really sorry. I did everything I could."

He was saying something, but his voice was muffled by his hands.

"Mr. Semonov?" she said. "I can't understand you."

When he lifted his head, tears were spilling from his eyes. "My mother died last year," he said. "It was a spring day. The lilacs were in bloom."

"Oh," she said. "I'm, um . . . I'm sorry to hear that."

"Just before she died, she called me to her side, and she said: Kostya, you have a soft heart. You must be careful. The world suffers when there are too many soft hearts. She was right! I've been a fool." He shook his head. "A fool of the worst kind. I knew that this day would come. And what did I think? That I could stop it? Look at what I have done!"

Amanda slid a box of tissues across the table. Semonov looked at her with watery gratitude and blew his nose with a comedic honk.

Your menagerie, her best friend Georgia once called it. *Your strange little petting zoo.*

Bartenders in seedy dives, hostesses in swanky clubs. Taxi drivers with photographic memories. Hairdressers with a knack for gossip. Restaurant owners with private back rooms. Chambermaids and bellboys and window-washers at five-star hotels. They liked making the extra money on the side, and they liked how seriously she took them. They liked to feel that occasional brush with danger. Together they comprised her strange little petting zoo. It was part of the job, collecting people like this, although Amanda tended to hang on to the assets even when they had ceased offering any obvious utility.

Look at what I have done! Semonov had exclaimed. She was curious about what, exactly, he meant by that; what role he played in the Vogel story. The expense reports could wait. So Amanda patted his hand, and said: "Tell me about your mother. What was her name?"

Osmond Brown was usually the first to arrive in the station, but that Friday morning, the door to his office remained closed. Amanda stared at it, puzzled, until one of her colleagues noticed. "He's out today," the colleague said. "Frolicking with the ambassador in Capri this weekend."

"Right." She nodded. "Forgot."

She looked at the clock on the wall. 8:47 a.m. Having lain awake all night, she was almost delirious from lack of sleep. The morning stuttered by in miniscule fragments. 9:03 a.m.: writing her contact report. 9:17 a.m.: locking the bathroom door and splashing water on her face. 9:42 a.m.: making a cup of coffee. 9:45 a.m.: finishing the coffee. 9:47 a.m.: considering making another. Amanda wanted to be proven wrong. She had never wanted this so badly. There was a bar on the Via Ludovisi, one block from the embassy. At 12:01 p.m., she decided, at the precise moment when Senator Vogel and the rest of the delegation departed the military review and returned safely to the Four Seasons, she would go to that bar and reward herself for her wrongness with a shot of tequila.

11:06 a.m. They would have arrived by now. 11:31 a.m. They

would be moving among the troops, examining the artillery, talking to the generals. She turned off her computer screen so she didn't have to look at the time. She gnawed on her thumbnail. She jiggled her knee. One of her colleagues glanced over, but when he noticed the look on her face, he thought better of asking her what was wrong.

Amanda turned her screen back on. 11:57, 11:58, 11:59 a.m. Noon! Noon on the dot! She broke into a giddy smile. "I'm going to lunch!" She jumped up from her desk and reached for her bag. "If the chief calls, tell him I got drunk and went home."

"Uh," her colleague said. "Really? You really want me to—"

But he was interrupted by a sudden, high-pitched chirping. Halfway across the room, Amanda froze. Every computer in the bullpen was emitting that identical electronic chirp. *No*, she thought. *No, no, no.*

"Holy shit," the colleague said. "Holy *shit.* Cole! Did you see this?"

She felt her stomach plummeting.

"It's Bob Vogel," he said. "He's dead."

